"I see you changed your mind."

A shiver ran down my spine. Don Randall was directly behind me. I could feel the heat of his body on my back. Granted, the cocktail dress I wore bared my skin halfway to my waist, and I wasn't sure that Don wasn't standing a bit too close. I turned around, careful to make sure I put a little distance between us. I was prepared to greet him with a smile and a comment. But seeing him dressed in evening clothes, a black suit with a gleaming white shirt and black crossover tie, took my words away. He was gorgeous.

He reminded me of a movie star I'd once seen. When he appeared on the screen for the first time, I was so unprepared for his good looks that I melted down into my seat. I felt that way now, but locked my knees to keep from repeating that movie experience.

Also by Shirley Hailstock

Last Night's Kiss
On My Terms
The Secret

Published by Kensington Publishing Corp.

Some Like Them
RICH

Shirley
Hailstock

Dafina
BOOKS

Kensington Publishing Corp.
http://www.kensingtonbooks.com

DAFINA BOOKS are published by

Kensington Publishing Corp.
119 West 40th Street
New York, NY 10018

All Kensington Titles, Imprints, and Distributed Lines are available at special quantity discounts for bulk purchases for sales promotions, premiums, fund-raising, and educational or institutional use. Special book excerpts or customized printings can also be created to fit specific needs. For details, write or phone the office of the Kensington special sales manager: Kensington Publishing Corp., 119 West 40th Street, New York, NY 10018, attn: Special Sales Department, Phone: 1-800-221-2647.

Dafina and the Dafina logo Reg. U.S. Pat. & TM Off.

ISBN-13: 978-0-7582-3145-1
ISBN-10: 0-7582-3145-8

First mass market printing: March 2011

10 9 8 7 6 5 4 3 2 1

Printed in the United States of America

To Candice Poarch, who listens to me whine.
And to Donna Hill, who teaches me
even when she's just talking.

Some Like Them
RICH

Chapter 1

Life had to change. Specifically, *my life*. Never again would I let a man put me through what Emile had. It had been a year since we separated for good. Add that to the two years we were together. I gave that man three years of my life. And what did I have to show for it?

Nothing.

Nothing, except muted pain and knowledge. He taught me well. And now I was done. From now on, I was no longer looking for love. Rich was just as good. Maybe better. No, definitely better. As my best friend, Jack, that's Jacynthia Sterling, liked to say, "It's just as easy to fall in love with a rich man as a poor one." Not that she'd put practice to her words. But they are good words. Ones I intended to live by.

So *love*, the now-and-forever, dying-for-you type of love, was no longer on the menu. *Rich* is the operative word. I'm a woman of action, never sitting back and letting things happen, so when I decide to do something, I waste no time in researching the options.

You see, I'm not so impulsive that I don't think things through before starting the engine. I'd done that with Emile. At least I thought I had. He was French, born and bred. A second-generation war baby with beautiful latte skin, dark eyes that oozed chocolate, a smile that melted my heart, and an accent that charmed my clothes off. Unfortunately, he proved to be a French pastry that was more puff than substance.

Emile was the grandchild of a Parisian nurse and a U.S. soldier who'd met briefly during World War II. He'd come to America to study at Columbia University and stayed on working at the United Nations until several months ago, when he'd dumped me and returned to his native France.

One thing I would miss was our time in bed, which was most of the time. I fanned myself, using both hands, as heat flashed through me. My body still went hot when I thought of some of the things we did in bed—and other various places that will not be named or revisited.

I plunged into life, lust, and love with Emile. From the moment those beautiful eyes found mine, I thought I'd found the mother lode. I had fantasies of spending my life with him, but that is where the understanding between us ended. Even with a two-year association, great sex, and conversations that went long into the night, he was not interested in stepping up our relationship.

So we stepped it down.

He was gone. Good riddance! And now I was on to another plan. And another man. You see, I wasn't totally off the species. And I didn't want to make the next one pay for Emile's shortcomings. We all get born naked and new, without the knowledge of someone else's baggage.

So here's the plan. The Amberlina Nash Marriage Plan. That's me. Amber. It reads Amberlina on my birth certificate, but no one would dare call me that except Jack and my mother. And both of them would have to be really angry to do it.

But back to the plan: go to a place where the richest black men under fifty hung out. I really wanted one who was under forty, but in a stretch, who knows? I wasn't someone who wanted to marry a man three times my age. I didn't want to nurse him into the casket and make off with his money. I was perfectly willing to try the love thing.

Again.

I'd certainly be the best wife he ever thought he deserved. But I was not going to fall so hard that I lost my mind. My reward for playing the role was to live in luxury. Houses, clothes, cars, kids—notice they are all plural—and membership in the country club. If I was really lucky, there'd be travel, political or embassy parties. I'd also sit on charity boards and make a valid contribution to underprivileged causes. I'm not totally shallow.

But country clubs and underprivileged causes would have to wait. First I had to find the perfect husband—well, the almost perfect husband. So where are rich, black men under fifty?

Martha's Vineyard.

My face fell a few hours later as the computer screen displayed the spreadsheet I'd created. "It won't be enough," I said out loud. This plan called for enough money for me to appear rich. People with money tended to like to keep it close. It was a small group, and admittance to it was rare.

But not impossible.

I looked at the spreadsheet again. I'd tabulated the columns up, down, and across, and I knew even with the technology of a machine to do my arithmetic that I didn't have enough money. The sheet stared back at me as if accusing me of being poorer than I wanted to be. *The Amberlina Nash Marriage Plan* was in bold across the top. Along with the dates: June through August. In the next three months, I was going to find a husband.

But as I looked at the numbers that made up my bank account, I couldn't make them change to meet my needs if I was to get this venture off the ground. I needed partners. Of course I could count on Jack to help out. She didn't approve of most of my plans, but she tolerated them, saying when they blow up she'd be there to carry me to the hospital or plan my funeral, whichever came first. Jack had a good heart and was always looking for Mr. Right and finding Mr. Wrong. Well, I had a deal she couldn't refuse.

Not that I would let her.

Jack was instrumental for my campaign, the future one. She'd been there to help out in the past, like when Emile boarded the plane and flew back to some unpronounceable city in France and I went on a chocolate and Chinese food binge while crying rivers of tears for three days. But that was part of my past. I was only looking forward now.

Jack, recently joining the ranks of downsized employees (as if that term meant shedding weight), could research anything and anybody. That would be useful since I wanted to make sure the guys we spent our time on had bank accounts to afford us. So she was a given. I just had to convince her. Or more likely tell her the plan and that she was in. No discussion. No dissension. I needed her. She'd be there.

"Are you crazy?" Jack's voice was accusatory. "That's my entire life savings." Several hours later we sat in her kitchen, a high-ceilinged, muted yellow room that had been painted and repainted at least a thousand times. It overlooked Brooklyn's Prospect Park, and that was the best thing about it.

"Jack, you work for an insurance company."

"*Worked*," she corrected. "As in the past tense." Jack's voice was definitely alto, but when she was angry, upset, or nervous, it took on a shrill quality.

"All right, you *worked* for an insurance company," I conceded. "What's your life expectancy?"

Jack's eyes rolled up toward the ceiling as if she was thinking. Then she looked at me and ticked the characteristics on her fingers. "Black female, unmarried, doesn't smoke or do drugs, exercises occasionally but is still slightly overweight." She paused, staring at me, waiting for a comment.

While she was more than slightly overweight, I wisely clamped my jaws together. Jack was taller than I was and outweighed me by thirty pounds. But on her it looks good. I wouldn't say it, because even a compliment like that veiled an insult.

"My life expectancy is about seven-five to eighty years, more if I eat healthier and start a regular exercise program."

"See, you've got time to amass another life savings. Take a chance. If you're lucky, you can marry your life savings."

Jack cut her eyes at me as if I'd set her up. And, of course, I had.

"I swear, Amberlina, you come up with the most asinine schemes anybody has ever heard of. Who would think of going to a music festival to find a husband?"

"*Rich* husband," I corrected her. "Let's get our adjectives correct." I paused for effect. "It's not just a music festival. It's on Martha's Vineyard. It's a huge gathering of black people coming to hear the greatest musicians of our time. You know how black people love their music. The Vineyard is a perfect place to assure us of meeting wealthy men."

Jack stared at me as if that was not a valid explanation. She waited for me to continue. Her expression didn't change and her foot didn't move, but I could hear the toe-tapping impatience vibrate through the air.

"Jack, we're getting older. We'll be thirty in two years. Have you thought about what you want to do with your life? Do you want to stay in these rooms for your actuarial lifetime?"

Jack's chin dropped a fraction before she raised it again. "I don't have to go to a music festival to find a husband."

"No, there are plenty of men right here in Brooklyn." I spread my arms, taking in the entire New York borough.

Jack nodded as if she'd won an argument.

"And you've lived here all your life?"

"So have you." She cut her eyes at me for asking a stupid question.

Refusing to be deterred, I pressed on. "How many of those men have you met that you'd consider husband material?"

From the expression on her face, Jack seemed to be reviewing her history of male relationships. "If I considered any of them worthy, I'd have married him by now."

"Does that mean you're in?"

She stared me down for a long moment. I refused to drop my gaze. I believed in the plan. We had to do something. No man was going to come knocking on our doors and say *here I am*. We had to go find them. And this festival was a place where men gathered. The Vineyard provided sun, sand, music, moonlight, and sports men liked, with the exception of football and basketball. But there was always television to cover testosterone-reeking men, and anyway, summer put those sports on hiatus.

"What about my apartment?" Jack asked. "I can't afford to pay rent and go away for three months. Especially since I now *don't* have a job."

"Jack, give up the damn apartment," I said. "You don't like it anyway."

Jack's legs and arms went slack and she slumped back in her chair as if every muscle in her body had suddenly relaxed, including her jaws—her mouth opened as if to catch flies.

"Give it up? And what am I supposed to do when I come back? After *you* lose all my savings, I'll be both poor and homeless."

"You can find another apartment. You can move in with the man you meet. You can stay with me until you find something if nothing pans out. There will be options, Jack. Stop putting obstacles in the way and get onboard."

"All right," she sighed after a long delay. "I'm in." Her voice held none of the enthusiasm I had hoped for.

"Good. Now we need a third."

"A third?"

"Pooling our money won't be enough. We're hunting big-time, Jack. We need to be able to put on a good show, and for that we're going to need someone else. Preferably someone we won't mind spending the summer with."

"Ya think?"

The house sat across from the ocean, a hundred yards or so from the famous beach, the Inkwell. The place was a huge Victorian with a wide porch and plenty of gingerbread scrollwork.

Checking out the house was something I always did when a new tenant was due. Although I owned the property, I didn't manage it. I'd grown up in the hotel business. Customer service was in my blood. And it helped to know that the management firm I'd engaged was doing an admirable job.

It appeared I had nothing to worry about. The rooms were spotless. Everything neat and in its place. Fresh flowers adorned a center hall table. Juice and water in ample quantities covered two shelves of the refrigerator. Bathroom amenities were fragrant and in place. I was sure the women would like the look.

Finishing my inspection, I headed for my car and the short drive back to the St. Romaine, a hotel I'd managed for the better part of a year.

A limousine turned into the driveway as I slipped behind the wheel of my car. Since it sat in front of the house, I had a clear view of all activity. I waited, interested in the new tenant. There were a lot of comings and goings during the summer season.

People brought their cars, light trucks, and SUVs, but few limos boarded the ferry for the trip from the mainland. I knew there were eyes behind the neighboring windows, searching for a glimpse of the newest summer inhabitant of the island.

I'd intended to find out more about Ms. Amberlina Nash when my agent said the house had been taken for the season by one tenant. It was rare for a vacationer to stay the entire summer without having relatives on the Vineyard. My duties at the hotel had eclipsed any thought of Ms. Nash until today, when the reminder notice popped up on my electronic calendar.

The limousine door opened and one long, shapely brown leg slid to the ground. My stomach clinched. The leg ended in a red high-heeled sandal. I waited, holding my breath, not sure why. I appreciated anatomy, especially female anatomy. I wanted to know if the owner of the leg could follow through on the whole package.

My eyes followed the shape of her ankle, sliding up her calf to the secret skin behind her knee as if my hands could feel the weight and texture of her skin.

The driver reached the side of the car and took the woman's hand. Her fingernails were the exact same color as the shoes. She stepped out. She looked like trouble. Trouble for *me*.

"Damn," I said out loud, breath leaving my body as if all the air had suddenly been snatched from the earth.

This was Amberlina Nash, the woman who'd rented the only Sheldon St. Romaine property for three months, at $3,000.00 a week plus security. She was an anomaly. Most people came for a week or

two. A few for a month. With the music festival
increasing rental fees, mine included, I expected
more tenants and more turnover, but here was my
summer ticket, guaranteed.

It wasn't that I needed the money. I'd bought the
house years ago trying to prove to my father that I
was the son he'd always wanted and not some playboy spending his money as fast as he could make it.

I'd failed miserably. That is, until a year ago,
when I'd convinced him to bet on me and my ability to change his mind.

I looked back at the woman in the driveway. Ms.
Nash looked out of place. It wasn't the clothes. She
was impeccably dressed. I didn't recognize women's
designers, but she looked as if she'd stepped off the
pages of a fashion magazine wearing all the best
labels. No shorts and T-shirt for Lady Legs. She wore
a white linen dress with slits up both sides. They
stopped mid-thigh, enticing the viewer with the
promise of concealed secrets. Her hair was perfect,
dark, thick, lustrous, and piled up on her head, allowing a view of her long neck. My hands itched to
touch that hair, sink my fingers into the mass, releasing it from the pins that held it up and feeling the
softness of falling tendrils.

This was bad. I shook my head. I was on the
Vineyard with a mission. I'd been here for nearly a
year, and the task I set out to do was just shy of
completion. I couldn't afford to be distracted this
close to the finish line. But I couldn't deny the attraction I felt for the woman in white—and red. It
was a good thing I wouldn't be near this house. I
lived at the hotel. The island wasn't that large, but
with me working, and her vacationing, our paths
didn't need to cross more than once or twice. At

this moment, I was thankful that a real estate firm managed the house. She didn't even need to know I had any interest in it. And since I was undercover as Don Randall and not Sheldon St. Romaine, son of the hotel owner, she need never know anything about me.

I stared as she and two other equally good-looking sisters walked up the five steps on the side to the wide porch and disappeared inside the front door.

I remained where I was, staring after them. It had been too long, I told myself, since I'd been with a woman. They came and went at the hotel, some demanding, some seductive. But I'd kept my liaisons to a minimum and I was both careful and discreet. However, this woman had an effect on me. I followed her movements like she was a magnet and I was the opposite pole.

Even after Lady Legs was no longer in view, I thought of her, recalled her unhurried movements and how she made me feel. I wanted to go back, flip the heavy knocker on the wooden door, and review that wide smile, the long sensual legs that extended down to high red shoes, and watch the teasing slits in her dress move back and forth showing those long, shapely legs.

I started the engine, pushing my thoughts aside. I was lusting after a woman I didn't know.

And she had yet to learn my name.

"Oh my God, can you just smell the testosterone?" With both hands, Jack pushed the French doors open. They gave an expansive view of the back lawn. She took a deep breath, letting it out slowly. If I didn't know better, I'd think she was about to begin that exercise program she often speaks of but never finds the strength to follow through with.

"Wow," Jack said, turning back to the room. "Can you believe this place?" She looked around the beautifully appointed room. There were paintings on the walls of higher quality than mass-produced hotel stock. The furniture was solid and made of dark wood. The rooms were warm and inviting, filled with large windows and plenty of light. Flowers cheered every room, bringing the outdoors in and perfuming the air with their redolent sweetness. "I am so glad I decided to come. And I didn't see many women on the ferry. How many men do you think are here?"

She decided to come, I thought. Jack had a knack for inventing her own history. It wasn't a month ago that I had to practically force her to join me, and now she acted like the idea was all hers.

"Yeah," I said flatly.

"It's like a buffet of men and us ready to choose the size, the weight, and the glorious bank account," Lila said.

Lila Easton was our third. Recently on the make, she nearly jumped at my proposal. I knew she was still rebounding from her last boyfriend. She might not find a husband this summer. It was too soon anyway. But at least this atmosphere would help her release, or at least file away, her feelings for Orlando Robinson, a man unworthy of her brain or talents. Yet as a friend, I knew I could never explain that to her while she was blinded by love.

"Did you notice all the people looking at the limo as we rode by?" Lila was saying. "Not to mention the ones on the ferry. I swear I never felt more like a movie star in my life."

"Hold on to that thought," I told Lila. "For the next three months, you are a star."

The three of us had come up with new biographies. We weren't going to tell any actual lies, but we planned to evade the whole and complete truth and allow people to believe we were rich.

"I'm going to change into my suit and go to the beach," Lila said. "I've heard a hundred things about the Inkwell. Now I'm going to see it. And it's probably the place to begin looking for guys."

Her enthusiasm was a little too over the top. I knew she was acting, putting on a front for Jack and me.

Grabbing her smallest suitcase—she had five of them, all pink—Lila headed for the stairs.

"Wait for me," Jack called, turning faster than she usually did and joining Lila on her way to the bedrooms. I followed. May as well begin the plan at the beginning.

After we sorted out the bedrooms, unpacked, and donned our new bathing suits, we left for the Inkwell.

"Oh my God," Jack said for the second time that day as the three of us moved through the sandy hill and the stretch of famous beach opened up in front of us. The place was a triangle of rocky sand dwarfed by an endless ocean. It was crowded with people, families, couples, and groups of singles.

"This is it?" Lila asked, a frown marring her forehead.

"I thought it was much larger," Jack said.

"From watching that movie they made about this

place, this space should be huge," Lila went on as she scanned the small square of beach.

We all looked at it. In reality, the Inkwell was less than half the size the television screen had made it seem.

Lila smacked her lips as if she'd found something delicious to eat. "I don't care that it's smaller. It'll be easier to meet people."

"Showtime, ladies," Jack said.

"How can you tell which ones are rich?" Lila asked as we picked our way down the sloping hill to the flat sand. "I mean, this is a public beach. Anyone can come here."

"You can't tell by looking," I told her. "We'll get their names and Jack will work her magic on the computer to find the pertinent facts and *figures*."

"And I'm looking," Lila said.

Lila and Jack moved ahead of me. I looked down at my feet to keep my footing when I saw something from the corner of my eye. A car stopped a few yards down the beach. A man got out and went around to open the door for two women. The women were giddy and with a wave headed for the water. He stood back, his hand up hooding his eyes, and watched them. I watched him. He was tall, wearing a suit. It was too early to be heading for cocktails, so he had to be employed somewhere. I permitted myself a moment to admire him. He looked confident, with short dark hair and broad shoulders. He looked nothing like Emile, yet something about his stance reminded me of Emile. I shook off the thought. Emile was out of my life, and I wasn't about to let any thoughts of him cloud my mind or push them off on another man.

Not that this one was in the running. He was

obviously a working man, and while rich men worked, they probably weren't doing it in a suit on the Vineyard. Yet I'd keep my mind open.

"Amber, where are you?" Jack called.

I looked toward the place where she and Lila stood. They weren't far away and Jack hadn't shouted, yet the man I'd been looking at turned and made eye contact with me. The hand shading his eyes dropped to his side. I expected him to smile, but he didn't. He blatantly stared at me. I felt no sexual pull, more like he was assessing my body in parts as if I were a horse he was thinking of buying.

Turning my attention back to my friends, I walked toward them, but not the way I'd walk if there was no one looking. Despite my beliefs that the man was not suitable, I presented my profile, sucking my flat stomach in and thrusting my breasts out like a runway model. I joined Jack and Lila without looking back at the man. I wanted to, yearned to see if he was still staring at me, but I forced myself to keep my head high and act as if I didn't notice him at all.

The sand was dotted with people. A volleyball game was in full swing a short distance away. The water had sailboats breaking the landscape between sea and sky.

"He's still looking at you," Jack said.

"Who?" I asked.

"The man you couldn't take your eyes off."

"And I might add, it looks as if he can't take his off you either," Lila said, laughter evident in her voice.

I turned and looked before taking time to think about whether I should let him know I was aware of his presence. For a long moment he didn't move, then he raised his hand and gave me a nod and a short wave. I thought of a king waving to his subjects. Without waiting for my reaction, he opened the door to the car and got in. I felt dismissed, and it irritated me.

"Not even a name," Lila said. "He must know that he'll see you again."

"I'm sure I don't want to see him," I said, not bothering to disguise my anger.

Jack looked up the hill at the man in the car. "It's a small island," she said.

Chapter 2

I found out how small the Vineyard was the very next morning as I decided to do a little window-shopping. We'd come with a full complement of new clothes. I didn't need anything, but I wanted to become familiar with the area, find out where things were and, more importantly, check out the activities that might attract the most rich men.

My walk led me to one of the hotels, the St. Romaine at Martha's Vineyard. The lobby wasn't as vast as other hotels I'd been to, but it was inviting and comfortable, a place where guests could meet and talk, whether casually dressed or decked out for a society wedding. This morning the place was very busy with guests standing or sitting in small groups and engaged in conversation. The concierge would be able to tell me the schedule for the coming week. But as I entered the front door, I came face-to-face with the man from the car.

Impeccably dressed again, this time in a cream-colored suit that contrasted with the deep brown color of his skin, he detached himself from four gray-haired women and came straight toward me.

He was tall, well over six feet. His hair was short and neat and his suit had to be custom made. As was his winning smile. I felt it. That sounded strange. I couldn't analyze it. It's the only way I had of describing it. But all those qualities paled beside his aura of authority. I could easily see him in a military uniform, barking commands and having people jump to carry out his instructions.

But there was also a gentleness about the way he approached me. What a contradiction, I thought. What a package. I couldn't help wondering what that hard command combined with gentleness was like in bed.

"Welcome to the St. Romaine," he greeted me.

I offered my hand and he enveloped it in both of his. They were large and warm, and he held mine a moment longer than necessary. I noticed he was wearing no wedding ring. No jewelry at all. While many men sported an earring in one or both ears, his ears had never been pierced.

I wondered why I was scrutinizing him in such detail. I hadn't done that since . . . I couldn't remember when. I guess it was the formal way he greeted me. After seeing him at the beach yesterday, I expected that he would acknowledge that encounter. But it appeared he was choosing to ignore the fact we had even seen each other. Working in a hotel, he must meet scores of people on a weekly basis, but I hadn't thought I was that unmemorable.

"I'm Don Randall, the manager here. Is there something I can help you with?"

I smiled, hoping my face didn't reflect the disappointment I felt. The name plate on his breast pocket read Donald Randall, Manager.

"You're the hotel manager?"

"Don Randall." He smiled and nodded as if I didn't get his name the first time he'd said it.

My heart did a little dance in spite of the fact he'd just confirmed his unsuitability for my purposes. Even if this was a St. Romaine hotel and it was on Martha's Vineyard, Don Randall couldn't be among the wealthy men I was looking for.

"Amber Nash."

"Well, Ms. Nash, how can I help you?"

"I'm new to the Vineyard." I was careful not the say *the island*. Being from New York, *island* rolled fluidly off my tongue, but the Vineyard had its own identity. "And I was wondering what kinds of activities are available. My plan was to ask the concierge. I wouldn't want to take you away from your duties."

I didn't like the way my heart beat a little faster because he was near me. It was better to get rid of him right away. I looked over his shoulder for the concierge's desk. Unfortunately, it was hard to dismiss the broadness of those shoulders or the way his suit seemed to be made for his body. In a place where the dress was casual, he stood out, but then I would have noticed him even if he was wearing cut-offs and dressed in mud. I couldn't point out anything in particular that drew my attention. He had a charisma that pulled at me. But I wasn't interested in a hotel manager.

"Thank you for your help." I moved to go around him, but he took a step and blocked my way.

"She's got a line." He glanced back at the desk. There were five people waiting. "Come with me. As manager I'm required to be able to fill in for anyone."

"So you're willing to step in the role of concierge for me?"

"You're a guest."

"I'm not staying at this hotel. I've taken a house." I don't know why I said that. Did I want him to know that I was out of his league? Maybe I was trying to reinforce my goal to myself.

"You're a guest on the Vineyard."

"You own the whole island?"

He smiled. His teeth were white and even. I wondered if he'd had them bleached or if he used one of those over-the-counter products that promised not only white teeth but sex appeal. Whatever the reason, he had sex appeal. I smiled back and followed him past the line to where he grabbed a map of the island and several brochures. Instead of staying at the desk, he led me outside, away from the crowd. He offered me a chair on the patio. The place was virtually empty, with only a few people sitting a discreet distance away and enjoying the soft island breeze.

"Would you like something to drink? I can suggest the Orange Island. It's the hotel's specialty, made with fruit juices."

"No alcohol?"

"None." He waved at a waiter, who immediately came over. I nodded when he asked if I wanted the Orange Island.

The waiter left to get the drinks.

"Now, for the activities. What kind of person are you? Sports-minded? Intellectual? Artistic?"

He leaned comfortably back in his chair while I sat on the edge of mine.

"A little of each," I said. "But I'm interested in the sports."

"Player or spectator?"

"Player."

He glanced up at me and I wondered if he took a second meaning to the word. There was one, but not that he knew or should infer. Men liked competitions. Women liked to sit and talk.

"Well, you have several choices," he continued. "There's swimming, sailing, waterskiing, parasailing depending on the wind. On land, there's horseback riding, beach volleyball, tennis, and soccer. At night there are dances here in the hotel. Many singles attend. Sometimes there are singles beach parties."

"How do you know I'm single?"

He looked a little embarrassed. "I saw you and your two friends arrive."

I looked at him but said nothing.

"I realize that doesn't mean you're single . . ."

"I am," I stopped him. "I've rented the house for the summer. They came along for the ride."

"I see," he said.

I knew he had no clue what he saw, but this was not the time to enlighten him. There would be no time to do that.

"Would you like the hotel to book any of these for you?"

"Not now. I'll take the brochures, if you don't mind. I'd like to let my friends look at them, too."

He pushed them toward me. "They're yours to keep. All the phone numbers are on them."

The waiter returned with our drinks. The tall glass was frosted and filled with an orange concoction. I expected it to taste like sweet water, but it had a surprisingly refreshing taste, like orange juice with a kick.

"Like it?" he asked.

"It's very good," I admitted, just barely remembering not to gush over how good it really was. "Are these sports organized or do people just show up for them?"

"Both. Many people come in groups, but if you need a partner, we can help you with that. Most of the sports require advance reservations. Tennis, parasailing, horseback riding . . ." He ticked them off on his fingers. "There are also fencing lessons if you're interested in that."

"Fencing?" I was intrigued. "Who takes fencing these days?"

"The class is just forming, but it's proving to be a crowd pleaser."

It was obvious that I was interested in that one. The only time I ever saw fencing was on late-night television or during the Olympics. There it got about ten seconds of screen time before the networks cut back to one of the more popular sports. But if rich men took the less-traveled road, maybe fencing was the place to find them.

"You mentioned artistic and intellectual. What would be included there?" I asked.

"There are several museums and art galleries. One museum details the history of the Vineyard, one is a maritime museum. The art galleries showcase local artists and some of the paintings go back to the early settlers. You won't want to miss the library with its extensive collection of historical volumes, and of course, there's the music festival."

"For such a small island, there seems to be an awful lot to do."

"We try to make everyone enjoy themselves no matter what they like."

"You seem very well versed. Have you managed this hotel a long time?"

"About a year."

"You seem so comfortable. I'd have thought it was longer."

"Have you stayed in many hotels?"

I wondered if that was a pointed question. Was I not playing my role well enough? I decided to evade the answer.

"I've been in a number."

"Why didn't you choose to stay this time? The St. Romaine has an excellent reputation."

"It hasn't always had that."

He raised his eyebrows. "So you know our history, too."

"I'm not a scholar, but I have friends who have been here before. Since I was staying for the summer, they said the house was a much better choice."

He relaxed a bit.

"With three of us, we needed more room than a hotel suite could provide, not to mention our own bathrooms. It's no reflection on your hotel," I said.

"I'm glad to hear that."

"Have you been solely responsible for the turnaround?"

"I'd like to think so, but it takes an army of people to run this place."

"But only one man to manage it all."

"I have two assistants. Both female, in case your mention of the word *man* was more than the generic use."

"It wasn't." I smiled, letting him know that I really hadn't branded him as a chauvinist. "I'm afraid I have to go now. It's a good walk back to the house."

I stood up and gathered the brochures. He stood, too.

"You're walking?"

I nodded.

"If you want, I can have a car take you back."

"That won't be necessary. I'm walking for the exercise."

He looked at me, and although the glance was quick and cursory, it took in my entire frame. I knew he was determining whether or not I needed the exercise.

"I've ordered a rental car. I'll be picking it up later today," I said. "But thank you for the offer and for all the information." I glanced at the brochures in my hand.

"You're welcome. There is one more thing," he said.

I waited for him to go on.

"Tonight, here in the hotel, there's live entertainment and dancing. If you'd like to come, you could be my guest."

I weighed this for a moment. "Are you asking me for a date?"

"I suppose I am."

"Suppose? Don't you know?"

"Yes, I am."

"Thank you, but I'm afraid I'm busy tonight."

"Don't tell me. You have to wash your hair?"

I almost laughed at the absurdity of the question. I had nothing planned for the evening. The whole day stretched before me and once the car arrived, I could begin touring the Vineyard or do one of the many activities he'd outlined. But what I wasn't about to do was go out with the hotel manager.

"I will not be washing my hair."

"Well, if it doesn't work out, the offer stands."

He glanced behind him as if someone might need his attention.

"Thank you, Mr. Randall." Again I held up the brochures.

"Don, please."

"Don," I said, but didn't offer my first name. I didn't want him to feel any familiarity with me.

We shook hands again. For some reason I looked at his left hand. It was clear of a wedding band, the brown skin even over his fingers, indicating that there hadn't been a recent change in his marital status.

Why I looked, and looked twice, I don't know. He'd been coming on to me, and I wondered if I'd have a reason to refuse him outright.

The excuse I would give him was practiced and designed to brush off any man who challenged my goal, but I had the feeling this one wouldn't take no for an answer.

And I wasn't sure I wanted the word in my personal dictionary.

Chapter 3

This was a mistake, I told myself. I know I'd agreed to Amber's plan. It sounded good in my tiny apartment back in Manhattan, especially since I'd just broken up with Orlando Robinson, the latest man who couldn't see beyond my breast size. He loved my body but never made an attempt to see if I had a mind.

But now we were on the Vineyard, and all I wanted to do was get back on the ferry and return home, call Orlando and tell him we should try again. In time he would figure out I was more than big tits, long hair, and legs.

I knew that wouldn't be the case. It wasn't rational. Orlando was never going to change, but neither could I change the way I felt.

Standing up, I went to the window. I was alone in the house. Amber left early this morning and Jack went for a walk, something that was usually last on her list of things to do. "But this is a new place and I want to see the sites up close and personal," she said, when my lifting eyebrows questioned her.

Jack was stepping outside of her comfort zone. It

was time I did the same. But where would I go? Being solo wasn't my usual method of cruising. I was often with a friend, make that a man. Chance meetings happened to me all the time. Meeting men had never been my problem. They flocked to me because of my face. But I knew that looks could be a blessing and a curse.

In my job as a pharmaceutical rep, I wasn't stupid to the fact that some of the males I dealt with gave me orders because of my bra size and not because of the product's efficacy. Yet I had no issues with the efficacy. They were superior products and I stood behind them. And orders were the name of the game here.

The curse was that many men tended to see me as all looks and very little brain. They assumed I was a good lay, and that was their primary goal with me.

I'm sure that was what was on Orlando's mind when I met him. I needed a new sweater. He was in the department store looking for a present. When we reached for the same item, I apologized, but the chemistry between us was immediate. His eyes covered my entire body in a matter of seconds. I immediately saw the expression and dismissed him as another male on the make.

But when he spoke, my heart melted. He bought the sweater and I found myself having lunch with him in the store restaurant. I was completely floored a couple of days later when the sweater arrived by special messenger with a card that had his phone number on it. Of course I dialed the number and started down a well-worn path. Unfortunately, I had blinders on and couldn't see around the bends in the road. I knew there were pitfalls, but together I was sure we could avoid them. What I couldn't see was that Orlando wasn't on the same path I was walking. And the rest is history. Ancient history at this point. We went out for months, or I should say we were together for months. We didn't go out much. Mostly we spent our days and nights in bed. Who would ever think that would get old? But after a solid six months of it, I wanted to do something else.

He didn't.

Then Amber and Jack showed up. I, Lila Easton, who always threw men over, was in the third stage of grief, bargaining with myself on how to get Orlando back. I was ripe for their plan. I needed a diversion, a safe haven to keep me from wallowing in grief and calling the bastard.

And now that I was here—I straightened my shoulders—I had to do my part. No use coming all this way and spending this much money to sit around a beautifully appointed room and stare out the windows.

The car I'd rented sat in the driveway. It was a red sports car and I'd had to have it delivered by ferry. It was costing a fortune, but Amber said it was worth it. And I loved it. In the city I didn't drive a car. The congestion and the cost of parking, not to mention parking tickets, was prohibitive.

As I'd already been to the beach, I slipped behind the wheel of the BMW and headed away from the center of activity. I wasn't likely to find a date going this way, but I wanted to see more of the land than where the tourists hung out. It was the real Vineyard, the neighborhoods where the residents lived, places where no tourist shops or souvenir kiosks appeared, just ordinary people living their lives.

Driving up one street and down another, I saw homes like any other in New England. At the end of a broad street, well, broad for the Vineyard, were several official-looking buildings: post office, court house, city hall, and a museum. In Manhattan, this would be the center of town. Here it was quiet and residential—almost postcard perfect.

After parking on the street, I went into the museum. It was nothing like the Met in New York. It was probably one-tenth the size. A combination art gallery and artifact museum. I enjoyed looking at the paintings, although there was no name I recognized. The artifacts were all about the sea.

Then I found the room with photos of African Americans on the walls. There were several other people in the room. Most appeared to be tourists, from what I could hear of their conversation. Steering away from them, I went to a wall that had only a few people at it. Sepia photos of people of color adorned the frames. They showed scenes of the Vineyard, the beach, the houses, all from an era of the thirties and forties, according to the small cards pinned next to them.

I smiled at one of five bathing beauties in old-style one-piece bathing suits. They had their arms linked and a leg thrust forward in the tradition of the Rockettes. Wide smiles split their happy faces. Each had curls that the wind had played with at the moment the shot was captured. I felt somehow connected to them, as if I had once been a happy, carefree girl whose only concern was which bathing suit to wear to the beach.

"Odd, isn't it?" someone said.

I jumped at the unexpectedness of the voice so near to me.

"Excuse me," he said. "I didn't mean to startle you."

"I suppose I was concentrating on the photo," I said, covering my sudden nervousness. I hadn't expected to speak with anyone. Museums and art galleries could be solitary places, as quiet as libraries, often attracting more women patrons than men. That might be why I'd subconsciously gone inside.

However, I'd noticed him when I first came into the gallery. He was very tall and very thin. I wondered if he was an artist. He didn't look like the type I usually saw in galleries—uninterested in the artwork and looking bored, continually checking their watches as if they couldn't wait to get out of there. This man had the appearance of comfort, as if he frequented these places often.

I looked up from the photo. "Why odd?" I asked.

"We don't often see that pose by a line of African American women."

"That's true, but the Vineyard had a large African American population. I don't remember when it changed, but it must have been after the forties, according to the card." I gestured toward the miniature wall plaque.

"The community has shrunk in the last thirty years or so, but there is a substantial population still living here. Politicians, artists, writers have homes here. In the summer the population swells more with summer residents."

"You seem to know a lot about the Vineyard."

He smiled. His teeth were even and very white. I thought of the whitening products they were advertising on television these days and wondered if my teeth were as clean. He'd make a perfect model for the product.

"I'm going to be teaching art at the local high school this fall. I just moved here and thought I'd learn about the island."

A high school teacher, I thought. Low income. Even the highest-paid teacher's salary in the country was too low for my purposes. But he was a nice enough person. It wouldn't hurt to talk to him for a while.

"Have you been a teacher for long?"

"Fifteen years."

"You must like it."

"I do."

We moved on to another photo, falling in step together. It was as if our few comments had joined us. We moved together like friends instead of strangers who'd only met an instant earlier. The photo before us was of a neighborhood with many blacks relaxing on porches and wearing long, colorful gowns.

"I thought about being a teacher once," I said. "But I got over it."

We laughed. Yet for me it wasn't altogether that funny. I still thought of getting a teaching certificate and going into the classroom. It wouldn't pay as much as my job as a pharmaceutical rep, but it felt like something I wanted to do.

After a moment I noticed him looking me up and down. I'd seen that look of appraisal all my life. From the time I became aware of boys, they'd given me the sexual look. Either they were undressing me or they were trying to get next to me. And I mean get next to me in the physical sense—close enough to rub their bodies against mine. He wasn't being quite so bold and I appreciated that, but his eyes were just as interested.

"Kids are kids," he said. "Every year they try to test you, but I've been around the block a few times and I know all of the tricks."

"You must be very good."

He looked a little embarrassed and said nothing.

"Kids need a firm hand," I said.

"Do you have children?"

I shook my head. "I'm one of the ones you talked about. When I was in school I would test the teacher to see what I could get away with, although at the time I never thought of it as testing."

"Neither do they," he said.

We continued moving about the room, reading the photo notes and talking. He was easy to talk to and didn't act like the normal Lothario I was used to meeting.

By the time we'd circled the floor, I recognized the signs. Men were so transparent. He'd begun the dance, the perfect steps that would lead to him asking me out. This was the prelude to sex. I was in no mood for it. And gravely disappointed in him. I'd begun thinking there was one man who wouldn't follow the pattern. Why I'd expected to meet that one man in an art gallery on Martha's Vineyard was the real question.

Checking my watch, I looked at the art teacher. "It was good meeting you," I said. "I have to leave now. I'm meeting a friend for lunch." I knew he'd probably think that was a man. I didn't bother to correct the silent thought.

"Nice talking to you, too," he said. "By the way, my name's Jason Michaels. I hope we meet again."

"Lila Easton." I smiled, doubting that we would.

* * *

Of course I had no plans to meet anyone for lunch. In the car, the rest of the day stretched before me like an endless universe. What was I going to do now? Jack and Amber were out. I was the only one who felt footloose, with nothing to do but mope.

Jason Michaels had been pleasant, but he was forgettable. Orlando still filled my thoughts. Pulling my cell phone from my purse, I hit the Address button and Orlando's name popped up on my speed dial. I stared at it, my finger hovering over the Send button. It was so easy to make the call. And I wanted to. I wanted to push that green key and send a signal up through the heavens to be bounced back to earth and find the one man I wanted to talk to wherever he was on the planet.

But I didn't. Slowly I moved my finger and flipped the phone closed. That part of my life was over. Orlando had made it clear that he was no longer interested in me. If he wanted to resume our life together, he had to take the next step.

And if he didn't, I had to go on.

Dropping the cell phone back in my purse, I heard the rumbles of my stomach. I was hungry. This morning's breakfast wasn't as large as the previous one. My hips couldn't take a summer's diet that rich, but I needed something to eat.

I hated eating alone. Going back to the house didn't guarantee me company, but it would save me from having to enter a restaurant without a partner.

Not that I would be alone for long. That had been true my entire life. But today I wasn't in the mood for the usual banter of getting to know you, getting next to you, getting in your pants. Jack and Amber had embraced our common goal and gone off to begin the hunt. While the three of us had agreed not to move as a group, but to each act independently, I didn't think we'd go in separate directions our second day here.

I looked at the sea and sky. Thank goodness I had the foresight to order a car before leaving Manhattan. This was a small island, and if I'd waited there might not be any left. Amber was renting one today. It was the one thing she had not thought of in her perfect plan.

I drove along until I came to a small shopping area. Inside was a grocery store. I decided on a salad.

Going through the single glass door, I found the aisles about the size of those in the city. The carts were nonexistent. A few people carried canvas bags and put their food inside as they went.

Not having one, I found a wire basket that would have hung over my arm if both handles had worked. As it was, I carried it lopsided. Heading toward where I assumed the salad bar would be, I found nothing even resembling it. I turned around several times, visiting each aisle before it dawned on me there was no salad bar.

It's amazing what you come to expect when you live in New York. The larger subway stations had everything from sushi to doughnuts. Every tiny grocer had a salad bar, either pre-made or made-to-order. And how quickly I forgot that the world outside of Manhattan was different.

Produce, I thought. I could make a salad. Finding this section of the store, I discovered it well stocked. The fruit and veggies looked great. I started filling up my broken basket. It was the cantaloupe that did it. I placed the small melon on top of my lettuce, tomatoes, radishes, onions, and cucumbers, and the whole thing toppled down my arm and spilled onto the floor. Tomatoes, lettuce, cucumbers rolled away in a rainbow of streaming color.

I dropped down and started retrieving the sprinting produce.

"Here, let me help you," a voice said above my head. I looked up. He was practically at face level and holding the cantaloupe and two tomatoes.

Dark brown eyes looked into mine. I stared, unable to turn away. Inside me something jerked. Not a huge jerk, just a small one, like when the car behind you gently taps yours in a line of traffic. You look up in the mirror, then immediately forget it. Somehow his eyes said *you'll remember me*. And I knew I would. I'd just left one man whose features were already fading in the glow of the dark brown-skinned man holding my tomatoes.

"You need a better basket," he said.

"It was the only one I could find," I said, wondering why I couldn't think of anything more appropriate to say.

"You're not from the Vineyard." He made it a statement, as if he knew I didn't live here.

"No, I'm renting a house for the summer."

"And stocking up on food?"

I nodded. Letting him believe the lie was easier than explaining that I didn't want to eat alone. Retrieving the rest of the loose produce, the two of us put it back in the broken basket. He lifted it as we stood up. He placed it on top of an amphitheater display of Idaho potatoes.

"Here, why don't you take my basket. I only need a few things."

I looked at his perfect basket. Inside it lay a small jar of peanut butter, three apples, a disposable razor, and a tube of toothpaste.

"Is that all you're getting?"

He nodded. "I have a craving for apples and peanut butter."

I thought about that. The idea didn't sit well with my stomach. Apples and caramel sauce was okay, but peanut butter?

"Be careful. People will think you're pregnant."

We both laughed. I liked the sound of his voice. I was thinking of Orlando just minutes ago and now this brown-eyed stranger had pushed him aside.

"I'm serious about the basket," he said. "I'm done anyway. Just one or two more things and I'll be done."

"I can't do that. This one will be fine."

"I insist." He took the meager contents out of his basket and put them on the bags of potatoes. Then he transferred my salad fixings into the unbroken basket and handed it to me.

"Thank you," I said. "You live here, I take it?" I wanted to stay and talk to him more. It wasn't often I ran across a true gentleman. I knew I should go, pay for my salad and go back to the house, but we were on this island to meet men, and this one was just my type. Meaning he in no way reminded me of Orlando. I could only hope he was high on the other attributes the three of us had mapped out before making this journey.

"I live in DC."

"But I thought . . ." I said, looking at the food about me as if it could answer my unasked question.

"I'm here for the jazz concerts and a little R and R.

I also have an aunt here on the Vineyard. I come up a couple of times a year to make sure she's all right and to see if the house needs any repairs."

"That's wonderful." I looked at him then. Really looked. He was tall with dark skin and short hair. He had a mustache and dark eyes, piercing, probing, look-into-your-mind eyes. His voice was deep, almost radio DJ quality. And he was honorable.

"But she doesn't have any peanut butter or apples," he said.

I smiled. Conversation had come to an end. We couldn't stand there in the produce aisle forever. There were other people trying to get around of us.

"Thank you for the basket," I said, giving it a little swing. I turned to walk away.

"Have you eaten yet?" he asked.

I turned back. "What?" I hedged for time.

"Have you had lunch?"

I looked in the basket. "This is my lunch."

"Just that?"

That was all I was intending, but I found myself saying, "I haven't finished shopping yet."

"Would you like to have lunch with me?"

The question took my full attention. I didn't want to eat alone, and how could I say no when inside me a field of butterflies escaped?

"How could you tell I hate eating alone?" I replied in answer to his question, while giving him one of my brightest smiles.

"Then I suppose we should exchange names. I'm Clay Reynolds."

"Lila Easton." For the second time that day, I was introducing myself to a man.

Clay fell into step beside me and we walked about

the tiny store, picking up meat and vegetables, staples, everything a well-appointed kitchen needed. By the time we left the store, I had two bags in my arms, Clay had another two in his, and I had no idea how to cook any of it.

Chapter 4

What was going on? I could not believe my eyes as I looked out the front window. Jack in the arms of some stranger, a man who looked liked he dug ditches for a living. He wore riding boots with jeans stuffed into the tops. Mud caked the boots and most of his pants. A stable boy. She was with the stable boy. All these rich guys for the taking, and wasn't it like Jack to find the poorest of the poor?

I went to the door and swung it open just as he reached the stairs. Without a word, I stepped back, allowing him access to the room with the load he carried.

"You can put her down over there." I indicated the sofa. He gently laid her down. Jack smiled up at him like he was the cure for cancer and she was riddled with the disease.

"Thank you," she cooed, her smile as beguiling as someone with a secret she was dying to share.

"It was my pleasure." His voice was smooth, like water running over silk. I recognized the look on Jack's face. She was about to find the next Mr. Wrong.

"I'm sure she'll be fine," I said, flatly.

Jack glared at me a moment before turning back to the stable hand. "This is one of my roommates for the summer," she said. "Amber Nash, Harley Prentiss." She waved her hand between the two of us.

Harley straightened, glancing at me as if he'd forgotten I was in the room. Turning back, he looked at Jack. Using a gesture straight out of a Wesley Snipes movie, he clicked his tongue, winked, snapped the fingers on both hands, pointed his index fingers at her, and said, "Be well."

Give me a break, I groaned inwardly, rolling my eyes to the ceiling. It was time for action, and I was here to act.

Taking his arm, I moved him around. Away from Jack. "Thank you, Harley, but she can't get well until I can look at that ankle."

"Are you a doctor?" he asked.

I kept ushering him toward the entrance. "I am today," I said.

Pushing him outside, I closed the door and returned to my *invalid* friend. Crossing my arms, I stared down at her. "Jack, why are we here?"

"My ankle," she said weakly, pointing at her leg as if that's where the answer lay. I glanced at her naked feet. Wherever her boots were, Mr. Wrong hadn't brought them with the package he was carrying.

"Jack?" Moving my hands to my hips, I raised one eyebrow and leaned forward. She knew what that meant.

"I fell off the horse. He was just nice enough to bring me back. That's all."

"That's all," I nearly shouted. "Jack, the man was practically making love to you with me in the room.

And you—" I went on, cutting off the protest I could see coming. "You looked like you were itching for him to go ahead."

"I was not!"

"Could you remember why we're here? And if you forget that, remember your life savings are tied up in the deal."

Jack looked nonplussed. Then anger came to her aid. "What do you suggest? We're here now, and I thought I was doing what we planned. I went horseback riding. Didn't you say men liked sports?"

"I did. But the stable boy is not the man I had in mind."

"He's not a stable boy. And even though his clothes were dirty, you don't know that he wasn't a guest on the island, that he likes horses, might even have enough money to own a few."

I stared at her. "Does he, Jack? Is he a millionaire who likes to get his hands dirty, not to mention his face, arms, and clothes?"

She looked away, then back, almost in defiance. "We didn't get around to discussing what he does for a living. I fell off the horse and he was there to rescue me. Amber, if you could have felt the strength in those arms . . ."

She trailed off when she saw the look I leveled on her.

"If not him, what is your suggestion?"

I thought for a moment. Don Randall's invitation came to mind. I didn't want to suggest that we go, but I couldn't think of anything else to say.

"There is a dance tonight in the St. Romaine. You're bound to meet men there."

"All right," Jack acquiesced. "I'd better look for

something to wear." She got up and started to walk toward her room.

"By the way," I said, after she'd taken several painless steps. "How's the ankle?"

The ballroom was thick with people when we entered it later that night. I smiled. This was what we'd been looking for. While everyone had been clad in casual clothes or beachwear during the day, their ballroom attire could rival the gown department of any Fifth Avenue specialty shop. I could almost smell the money. Hopefully, Jack and Lila could, too. And hopefully they would get back on track to our purpose here. First Jack had shown up with a stable hand and then Lila was in all smiles for a deliveryman. She'd been to the grocery store and bought food. What was she thinking?

We weren't here to cook. Why did she assume we needed food in the kitchen? The place already had an abundance of bottled water and juices. I could understand it if she'd bought things to snack on—breakfast foods or even junk food would be acceptable—but she'd come in with meat that required a major effort in the oven. By the end of the summer it might come to us having to fix our own meals, but there was no reason to expect that would happen. I'd budgeted carefully, and barring any unforeseen circumstances, we'd barely need to enter the kitchen, let alone have it fully stocked.

And the guy she was with! Clay Reynolds, a furniture salesman. And more than that, the guy cooked us lunch. He wasn't dirty like Harley Prentiss, and the food *was* delicious, but his mastery in the kitchen and his good looks didn't count in this venture. We all knew even a good cook didn't come with gold cards.

So, unfortunately, we were taking Don Randall up on his invitation to join the party this evening. Only he didn't know it, and I hoped I could get through the night without having to eat crow.

"Let's get a drink," Lila suggested. Again she looked around the room as if her hunger was for more than the steaks she'd placed in the freezer earlier today.

I stifled the smile that came readily to my lips. At least now she was going in the right direction. Lila led us with Jack following. I hadn't taken three steps before a voice stopped me.

"I see you changed your mind."

A shiver ran down my spine. Don Randall was directly behind me. I could feel the heat of his body on my back. Granted, the cocktail dress I wore bared my skin halfway to my waist, and I wasn't sure that Don wasn't standing a bit too close. Plastering a smile on my face, I turned around, careful to make sure I put a little distance between us. I was prepared to greet him with a smile and a comment. But seeing him dressed in evening clothes, a black suit with a gleaming white shirt and black crossover tie, took my words away. He was gorgeous.

He reminded me of a movie star I'd once seen. When he appeared on the screen for the first time, I was so unprepared for his good looks that I melted down into my seat. I felt that way now, but locked my knees to keep from repeating that movie experience.

This wasn't the first time I'd met Don Randall, but it was the first time the entire package was so completely attractive. This afternoon he'd been sexy, charming, and entertaining. Tonight he was devastating. My body acted like it knew his.

Or wanted to know it.

"Good evening, Don," I said. "When I mentioned your invitation to my friends, they were eager to accept."

"And that left you with no choice?" He raised his eyebrows mockingly.

"Absolutely none."

"I'd say I win, in that case. Would you like to dance?"

He extended his arm toward the dance floor. At that moment the live band began to play "The Greatest Love of All." The tempo was slow and the song was long. I knew being in his arms would be another test, but I prided myself on being up for the challenge.

I lost the contest the moment he turned me into that rock-hard chest of his and put a hand on my naked skin. His arms held me tightly against him. The music conspired in my head and I forced my eyes to remain open, refusing to let them close, knowing if they did I would sink into that pleasant place that seemed to find me each time I met a man who would leave me heartbroken and lonely.

And I hated to think it, but Don Randall had heartbreak written on those finely shaped and very kissable lips that were a mere inch from my own.

He hummed in my ear. I felt his voice rumble against my stomach. The sensation was warming, more than warm, titillating, erotic even, but I fought it, stumbling over his feet in the process.

"Excuse me," I said.

He leaned back and I smelled his clean breath. He said nothing, but the look of need in his eyes could fill volumes at the New York City Library. His hand ran slowly up my back. The sigh that escaped my throat told him what he was doing to me. Averting my eyes, I leaned against him again. His chin rested on my temple. I felt the change in his jaw and knew he was smiling. I was his conquest and he was getting over.

By the time the music ended, I was wet not only with perspiration but with sexual desire. I wanted this man. And sooner or later I knew I would have him, but only for an appetizer. He was not the main course.

Don didn't immediately release me as the last note died. He did something totally unexpected. Even I never saw this coming.

"Thank you for the dance," he whispered in my ear, his lips so close they kissed my skin, sending tendrils of electrical sensation through me. Then as his head moved back from mine and I turned to acknowledge his comment, his mouth brushed across mine. The actual touching was barely an instant long, but it was deliberate, designed to let me know that what I'd put into the dance had been communicated to him. He knew my feelings and he wanted me to know that he knew.

His hands skimmed down my arms to my fingers, and after a charged moment he let go. I needed a drink.

And a shower.

Not even thinking of what happened to Lila and Amber, I headed for the bar. Water would probably be the best thing to drink, but after that dance I needed tequila. A full bottle and a fresh lemon would be the order of the day, but since that would be foolhardy and I wasn't going to let it happen, I settled for a tequila sunrise.

An hour later I had done little except follow Don's movements around the room. Jack was having a great time with the son of a man who owned his own investment company. I approved of second-generation money. The sons didn't have problems with spending money, lavishing it on the women they loved. Love hadn't happened yet, but in time it could. I remembered Jack's statement: it was just as easy to fall in love with a rich man as a poor one.

Don Randall's image jumped into my mind. I'd admonished both Lila and Jack about their choices in men, yet I'd done the same thing with Don. It wouldn't take much to get me into his arms, not to mention his bed, yet he hadn't come near me since my initial entrance.

But I'd kept tabs on him.

Frustrated with what I was doing, I knew it was time to go. I found Lila first. The tall, sexy brunette was working her magic with a man easily twice her age. She excused herself when she saw me coming.

"How's it going?" I asked.

"Great," she said. "He's a banker from Illinois, newly divorced, and probably looking for someone to replace the older model."

"Be careful, he's probably got grown children who won't take kindly to you."

"He does." She took a moment to glance at him and give him a sexy finger wave. "One of them, a daughter, is here. I haven't met her yet. How are things with you? I saw you and that guy from the beach practically stuck to each other."

Lila's comment caused a flush of blood and heat

to infuse my body. Don came to mind and the flesh-and-blood man crossed my field of vision. He was dancing with a woman about my age and she was looking at him as if he was chocolate candy. My teeth clamped down and I felt an instant dislike for her.

"He's the hotel manager, not husband material."

Jack joined them at that moment.

"I am having a *gre-at* time," she said, stretching the word into two syllables. She raised the glass of champagne in her hand and sipped the bubbly wine. "Coming here was the best idea. I am so glad you suggested it."

"I can see you're feeling no pain," I said. "Just be sure to keep your head on straight."

"I'm not and I will," she said. "I met Gerard, and he likes *big* women." She took a moment to do a little shake with her shoulders and hips before looking over her shoulder. "That's him over there at the bar, getting me another drink."

I looked to the place she indicated. Gerard couldn't be more than an inch talker than Jack if he was that. He looked like a football player, thick neck and arms.

"What does he do?" I asked.

"You'll approve." She smiled. "His father owns Niagara Investments and he's one of the chief investors."

"Good choice," I said.

"So what's up with you?" Jack asked, draining the last of the liquid in her fluted glass.

"I'm going to go back to the house."

"What?" Lila said, looking surprised. "With all the men here, you're going to pack it in and desert?"

"I'm not in the mood."

"You were before we came," Lila said. "Just what did that guy say to you?"

"It's not him," I protested, knowing she was right. Don Randall had spoiled my evening. All he'd done was dance with me. And whisper in my ear.

"Hey, this was your plan. Don't change the rules in the middle of the game."

"Don't worry, Lila," I said. "I'm seeing this through to the end."

"Well, I have a ride back," Jack informed us, still smiling at the man near the bar. "You don't have to worry about me."

"Me either," Lila said. "Take the car."

"Thanks, guys. You can tell me all about it in the morning." Picking my way through the crowd, I headed for the door. Moments before I got there, Don Randall stepped in front of me. I wondered if he'd been following my movements as I had been following his.

"You're not leaving?" he asked.

"That was my plan," I answered, stepping around him and continuing toward the exit.

"The night is still young." He fell into step with me.

"There will be other nights," I countered.

"I suppose you have to get back to whatever was going to keep you busy tonight?"

I stopped halfway to the door. The ballroom could be reached through its own entrance and was across from the parking lot where I'd left the car. There was no one in the long anteroom. The suggestion Don gave me was an easy answer and I latched onto it. "Yes, I do."

"I know assumptions are dangerous, but I think you'll be finished by midnight. Meet me here." He pressed an electronic key in my hand. "Guest house.

Take the path behind the tennis courts. It's the only one there."

When I looked up his back was disappearing through the ballroom door. I took a step toward him and stopped. More emotions than I could name raced through me. Anger was the most prevalent. No way was I going to his guest house. What nerve! Who did he think I was? I know some rich women were known for their bedroom antics. But why would he assume I was one of them? My photo had never been splashed on YouTube or supermarket tabloids.

Swinging around, I stamped through the ballroom door. Every line of my body charged with rage. By the time I got back to the rental house, my anger level was high enough for steam to expel from all my orifices. I wasn't some bimbo looking for a summer fling. I had serious business on my mind, and if I'd once entertained the thought that he could possibly fit into the picture, I didn't now.

I would not be there. I simply would not go, I told myself. He could wait all night for all I cared. It would serve him right for making the assumption that I would fall for something this theatrical. I mean, slipping keys into women's hands? That went out in the decadent eighties. Of course, I was born in the eighties, so no one had ever handed me a key to his hotel room. Not even the rough or semi-rough men of Brooklyn had done a thing like that.

As I turned the plastic rectangle over in my hand, it felt warm. Probably because I was so hot with anger at the suggestion it represented. But there seemed to be something else about it, too. I looked at the clock on the mantel in the living room. It was just shy of eleven o'clock. I knew what I would do. I'd teach him a lesson. I would go. Right now. I'd leave the key. No note. I'd leave it in the middle of the bed. He could wonder what it would have been like to have sex with me. And I hoped the thought kept him awake all night.

My breath came in short gasps as I approached the door to the guest house. I had to hold on to the courage that wanted to desert me. I trumped it up and kept walking, my eye on the goal. I'd come this far, and the party was still going on in the ballroom. Don was likely still there. Hadn't he said it was his job to take care of his guests? What he wanted to do with me went beyond the bounds of his profession.

The guest house set alone in a crop of woods that made me think of either *Little Red Riding Hood* or *Hansel and Gretel.* In either case, I could be devoured. Better to do what I came to do and escape back to the safety of my own guest house.

I pulled the plastic key from my bag and stepped onto the porch. Before inserting it, I listened for any sign that he might be inside. Silence greeted me except for the chirping of crickets, the arresting sound of the ocean in the distance, and the breeze moving the tree branches. The distant sound of music from the ballroom didn't reach the secluded building.

The latch released with a click the moment I pushed the key into the specially fitted door lock. The door was pulled inward. Don Randall materialized before me.

"You're early." He smiled, opening the door wider and giving me a full view of him. He wore only a pair of boxer shorts.

My eyes grew large and bright like stars. My

breath came in short gasps. I tried to speak only
to find my voice had abandoned me. I was so surprised to see him, I could say nothing.

"I only came to return your key." I held it out to
him. He reached for it, but his hand wrapped
around my wrist and he pulled me over the threshold. The door closed, the compressed-air mechanism forcing it shut, the way all hotel room doors
closed. The click was as loud as a cell block lock-
ing for the night.

"That's not why you came," he said.

Chapter 5

Touching her told me what I already knew. She was hot. Like a beautiful fire, red and gold as it burned, drawing its prey closer to the flame until it was engulfed, unable to escape without serious burns. I knew better, knew I should move away. I should never have invited her here. The next three months were crucial to the deal I'd struck with my father. I had to stay on point, stay focused on my goal. But I was finding it hard, maybe even impossible to turn from her. She was here and I wasn't letting her leave.

"I wasn't sure you'd take me up on my offer," I said, but I knew it wasn't true. I would have bet good money she wouldn't show. I'd given her my key, something I'd only done for my sister or when I came to the platonic rescue of a friend. I'd never given it to a woman I'd only seen a few days earlier. Amber was no platonic friend. Tonight I had nothing like that in mind. And Amber Nash knew it.

She had class. A lot of it. But I'd seen two sides of her personality. She'd been straightforward and businesslike this afternoon when she asked about the Vineyard's activities. On the dance floor, she'd been warm and exciting. She held herself as unapproachable, quick to brush off anyone she didn't think was worth her time. But anyone looking at the luscious way she moved would know where there was heat, there was fire. And where Amber moved, she burned a trail.

"I'm glad you came," I said.

She looked up at me. "I gave my actions serious thought."

"I'd be disappointed if you'd decided against this." I couldn't tell her how much it meant to me that she'd opened the door.

"Would you?"

"Extremely," I said, pulling her into my arms. She came without resistance, still wearing the satin gown she'd had on at the party. I slipped my arms around her waist. I liked the feel of the fabric; like water it skimmed her body, covering, clinging, enfolding. Often cool to the touch, beneath it was a warm, hot, vibrant woman.

And I wanted her.

My mouth settled on hers, hard, hungry, insistent. I wanted to devour her. I *was* devouring her. I wrapped myself around her, drawing her to me, pulling her inward as if I needed her to be part of my makeup, part of me, inside the same skin, sharing the same heartbeat. My blood was her blood.

She met me with a force I'd never known. My tongue dipped deeply into her mouth, plunging, mating, dancing, fighting, dominating. Sounds smacked as our heads moved, shifted, our lips sought the others. My arms welded her to me. She was soft, like cotton candy, a pure confection that could evaporate on touch, but she remained solid in my arms.

I needed her now, wanted her in my bed. A need so strong I thought I'd burst washed through me. The bedroom was a world away, almost at the other end of the bungalow. I didn't know if I could make it, didn't know if the force that both pulled us together and kept us in individual bodies would allow me to get that far. I found the zipper at the base of her dress where the back plunged into a tantalizing V. Slowly I pulled it down. Opening it was like peeling back the door to a furnace; inch by inch, heat radiated from her skin. As I separated the teeth, I could feel the steam of her desire against my fingers. I touched the widening space. Her skin was sizzling. My body grew harder. I didn't think it could do that. Then Amber melted in my arms.

Pulling her closer, I went to heaven in the fantasies that skated through my mind just by her being there. I pushed the dress down. Starting with the area right above her breasts, slowly I ran my hands over her, feeling her accelerated heartbeat, hearing the hitch in her throat when my fingers encountered puckered nipples, stopping at her waist and riding the curve of her hips until the dress slipped away and fell in a heap at her high-heeled feet.

Her hands reached the waistband of my shorts. Thumbs reached just inside them and circled, like a branding iron, around my waist and back. Reflexively my hands tightened on her. I squeezed her as sensations went through me. Her hands came together at my stomach. With her palms against my skin, she moved them up and down. Starting at the top, she slid her fingers into my waistband. Fire flashed, torrid and explosive. Blood gushed from every point in my body, centering in my groin. I grew even harder, erect, and full of need. Using her hands like weapons of sexual destruction, she set my skin ablaze.

She kissed my chest, her tongue licking like dragon fire, burning me, teasing me. Every molecule of my body tightened, stiffened, hardened, in want of mating with her. Long fingernails scored my penis, seeking, traveling, working their way up and down, surrounding its head and teasing the hard ridge until every arousal point in my body was shouting and bending her backward, escalating the fever pitch of my need. Still she kept her hands on me, moving them up to the top of my shorts.

"Amber," I groaned. I couldn't stand it much longer. I was going to explode in her hands if she didn't stop.

"What is it?" she asked, her voice darker and deeper than I'd heard it before. I had the feeling she was trying to control it. "Want me to stop?"

I couldn't answer. Her fingers met my shorts and conquered the barrier. Freeing me and imprisoning me at the same time, her hands were a practiced instrument, caressing me, teasing my penis as she placed her skin to mine. I groaned, the strength in my legs threatening to give out. I forced my knees to support me.

The hook on her bra was low, almost at her waist. I released it. It fell away. I took the weight of her breasts in my hands. In a frenzy, I undressed her, our mouths staying together as if glued. Our hands washed over each other as if contact was as necessary as air. I pushed her against the wall, pinning her there, burying my tongue in her throat and imprinting her with my form.

I could stand it no longer. I grabbed my shirt from the sofa and pulled a condom from its pocket. Quickly I sheathed myself. Amber was back in my arms the moment I finished. I lifted her. Her legs went around my waist, her red heels digging into my legs. I forced her against the wall and drove into her. Her back arched, holding on to me. I filled her, rooted myself inside her. The sound that came from her throat was a language all her own, but it was music to me. I drove harder, banging her as pictures danced and jumped. Feeling the softness of her flesh as my hands contracted and released in the same rhythm as I plunged and released inside her, I couldn't get enough. I needed more and more of her.

She clung to me, holding on as I rode her, rode hard and fast, harder and faster, so fast I thought I'd break through the wall. But it felt good. She felt good. I was lost to stop, to do anything but continue this exquisite torture. To say I was out of control was like saying I could lasso the moon. Unable and unwilling to stop, I felt I was going to die here. The two of us could be nothing more than a rapid fireball that ignited and consumed us. Yet the prospect of it did nothing to quell my energy. If anything I pumped faster, filling and releasing, lost in a zone so sexually charged that I was sure an explosion was imminent.

I felt her scream. I had never shouted before. I thought it was Amber shouting, but the voice when it registered in my ears was mine. I was calling her name, calling the Lord, thanking the heavens for the one flash of light so blindingly pure and carnal that I prayed it would come more than once in a lifetime.

Sweat poured from us. I collapsed against her, my slick, liquid body holding her up with strength that was nearly expired. I was weak from my arms to my knees. Her feet slid to the floor, but we remained joined in the most intimate way. Gasping and gulping air, I knew I was in trouble.

Amber Nash may try the ice princess persona. She might present that face to the world at large, but to me she was the soul of fire, hot, blistering, consuming, electrifying, passionately torrid.

She brought out the beast in me. One I wasn't sure would ever be able to go back in.

"I need a drink," I gasped. My voice was raw and my body throbbed with the aftermath of an experience I could compare to nothing previous. Sensation rioted through me like a rocket defying the bonds of gravity. I wasn't sure I could stand on my own if Don disconnected from me. My body was full, my need satisfied. Yet I was hot enough to spontaneously combust and thirsty enough to drink the Atlantic dry.

Don took a step back, taking me with him. My legs slid down the length of his and touched the floor. I was still wearing my heels. The rest of my clothes were scattered about the room.

Taking my hand, he said, "Come on."

As we went toward the kitchen, I saw his shirt lying along the back of a chair. Grabbing it, I slipped my arms through the sleeves. Don hadn't bothered with his shorts, comfortable in his nakedness. He had a beautiful body.

The room was dark. He turned on a soft light over the sink. It provided weak illumination and filtered delicately through the room, turning table and chairs into definable three-dimensional objects.

I stared at him as he moved, totally comfortable in his suit of brown skin. He was more powerful out of his clothes, fully aroused and at ease with me watching him. I hadn't grown up in a house where people walked around undressed. Sometimes one of my sisters might show up for breakfast in a bathrobe, but we were generally fully dressed and presentable before we appeared. I liked this feeling of freedom. This was his domain. He had the right to move through the space in whatever form of dress—or undress—he pleased.

He opened the refrigerator to get us something cold to drink. "Glasses are over there," he said, indicating the cabinet behind me.

I stared at him a moment before turning. His chest was defined, flat stomach, long legs. His coloring was even from what I could see in the dim light after the refrigerator door closed. I got the glasses and approached him. I hadn't buttoned his shirt. Don's eyes stared at the gap of skin peeking out between the white columns of cloth. Deliberately I walked slower, letting him look at me. I felt sexy, totally female, and I liked having him look. The shirt slipped and gapped as I moved and Don's eyes followed the fabric's movement. I'd never felt this way before, sexy, wanton, and ready to repeat the scene we'd finished only moments ago.

"I like the shoes," he said.

I didn't look down, although the urge to do so was sharp. The tone of his voice caused my nipples to point. It wasn't my shoes that his eyes were on, but the triangle of skin from my neck to my breasts. He knew how to get to the point without words.

After only a few minutes, my body was growing hot again. I wanted him again. I wanted him to run his hands over the fabric, pushing it from my body and smoothing his hands over my burning flesh. Evidence of our previous engagement had my legs sticking together. Yet heat and color ran like a river under my skin.

"I'm never going to think of that shirt again without seeing you wearing it," he said. I knew he understood what I was doing, what my body was saying.

I set the glasses on the table and he poured. We drank, each looking at the other. I couldn't believe I wanted him again. I felt the tightening of internal muscles, the wet flowing sensation that signaled arousal. And I could see the evidence clearly on Don. He'd removed the condom, but his erection was still straight and hard. Both our glasses thudded on the table at the same time.

I reached for him. My hand traced his chest, outlining it as if I were a sculptor taking in all the angles, every valley and nuance of change, every shadow, every rock-hard surface. My fingers skimmed his nipples. I both saw and felt the intake of air that signaled an ageless need.

I leaned forward, kissed his neck. His skin was as hot as mine. His heart drummed against my tongue as I licked the pulse in his neck. His fingers closed like viper grips around my arms. I knew it was to support himself and I smiled as I worked my way down his chest. My mouth opened and I sucked his nipples. He shuddered. I felt it run through him, knew the tighter squeeze of his hands on my arms.

I pushed him into a chair and straddled him. I kissed his neck, his cheek, and his mouth. It was hot, wet, hungry. I matched him, sitting up, controlling the kiss, my tongue deep in his mouth, his hands spiraling small circles under the shirt. Fire ignited trails wherever he touched me, over my back and stomach and up to my breasts. I moaned when his thumbs padded across my nipples. My breasts were heavy, areolas distended and pointing. His hand went into the pocket of the shirt. I felt his fingers on my breasts. My nipples crested into small pebbles. His eyes met mine and held. For an instant or an eternity, we spoke only with our eyes.

Then he pulled a second condom out. As he cracked the foil packaging, I took it from his fingers and slowly covered him with it. My eyes never left his face as I sheathed him in the second skin.

His body jerked at my touch. I felt his hardness grow stronger. Something inside me tightened. Lifting my hips, I anchored myself over him.

Don pushed the shirt from my shoulders and kissed me. Sensation erupted throughout me, like some powerful light beam that shot through my system, telegraphing erotic signals with his touch.

I reached down, between our legs, and took him in my hands. Slowly I sat, moving a centimeter at a time, swaying my hips to the music in my head. I held my breath as the pleasure of him moving upward and inward filled me. His head fell forward, against my shoulder. His arms circled my waist and drew me more fully on his lap, more securely over him.

I heard the huge breath he took in, knew he was

covering an emotion so strong it could reduce him to weakness. I started the rhythm. Pacing it, bracing, arresting, then increasing, building speed until I was riding him wildly like a horse racing the wind. Don grabbed my waist, working with me as I rocked back and forth on the heels of my shoes. He moved me up and down to a rhythm in our heads. Control snapped. To my ears it was like a gunshot.

I no longer cared about anything except continuing the feelings, the pleasure, the sensation that Don was giving me. It took over my entire body. I had no mind, only passion, only nerves that were high-energy fibers wanting to be stroked, and each stroke brought on more need, more want, more pleasure. I wanted it, needed it, would allow nothing to stop it. I rode with him, thinking of nothing except the rapture that spread through me. More and more, faster, harder we rode each other, bucking like a new bronco that neither of us wanted to tame, to destroy that wildness that was its nature.

Don's hands raked over my skin. His fingertips squeezed my breasts tightly. My head fell back as I felt both pain and pleasure. I had never felt anything like this. And I loved it. I didn't care if he knew. I wanted him to know.

I could hardly stand it. Don's palms made wide circles on my breasts as he thrust inside me. I sat on his thighs, my legs spread and hanging on either side of his. Curling my legs around his, like braided dough I sat while his rock-hard penis jackhammered into me. Calling his name was like saying hallelujah. "Yes!" I whispered, then shouted, "Yes!" Again and again, I repeated it, each time in rhythm with his thrusts. I wanted more. I wanted him like I've never wanted a man.

Don made love like no one else. I couldn't remain reserved with him, couldn't hold on to any decorum. I let go. With Don it was to the rafters, let the games begin, shout, stomp, make some noise, let the church say amen.

A-men.

Chapter 6

There wasn't much that could be called a lonely beach on the Vineyard. With the influx of tourists in the last ten years, the beaches were full unless it was extremely early in the morning. Even darkness didn't afford the sand and surf a rest. Bonfires and beach parties competed with the Vineyard's nightlife of cafés, concerts, and house parties. Morning was the part of the day that I liked—later than daybreak, but before most of the sun worshipers were up. It was my practice to jog along the beach every morning, but I'd only added this stretch of sand to my routine since Amber had come to the island. The hotel was equipped with a weight room, two swimming pools, and an aerobics theater, but I preferred the beach. I liked the sand under my feet, the salt air on my face and my body. I liked the smell of the ocean and the sound of the gulls overhead as they cawed and dipped their beaks in the clean water for breakfast.

And after our encounter . . . Encounter? I couldn't call it that. Searching my mind, I tried to find the word to describe what had happened between

Amber and me. It took a few seconds, but I knew there was none. Nothing could describe what had happened between us. It was an experience like no other. And it defied both definition and description.

There was a verse I'd read long ago, one I couldn't quote. It had something to do with the creation of fire. That was as close as I could come to describing the phenomenal sensation that had taken us as close to heaven on earth as God ever intended.

And then I saw her.

I nearly stumbled, my ankle turning in the soft grains underfoot. Amber Nash sat on a beach chair ahead of me, her long legs extended in the warm sand. A lone figure amid the white sand, dark water, and golden horizon. Her one-piece swimming suit was in her signature red. I hadn't seen her here before, although I ran this way in the hope of finding her peering through a window or having coffee on the porch.

It had been two days and two nights since she was with me, and I hadn't heard a word from her. Sure enough of myself not to think I hadn't satisfied her, I wondered if I'd done or said something to keep her away.

I had been busy at the hotel. Groups were checking in and out all the time, and the past two days had demanded an unusual amount of personal attention on my part for guests who thought their needs were the most important in the world. Luckily they had all been satisfied. Yet I missed seeing the brown-skinned woman in the red shoes. I was quite fond of those shoes. I expected to see Amber or her two friends dancing or playing one of the many outdoor sports the Vineyard provided to the cast of summer thunder that burst onto the island for three months every year. But she'd been absent, at least from my view. She'd imprinted herself on my mind *and* body, which even now hardened in anticipation of a repeat performance.

It was a feeling I liked; just looking at her aroused me. Some men looked in magazines, others watched late-night adult movies, and still others had anatomically correct plastic toys. Me, I preferred the real deal.

And it got no realer than Amberlina Nash. I knew that from firsthand experience.

She hadn't seen me yet, sensed my presence. I slowed to a walk. She had her head down. As I got closer, I could see she was writing something. Journals, trip diaries, and postcards were common for the Vineyard's guests, but Amber's concentration denoted something more than what I expected of a tourist. I wondered if she was trying to put our experience into words.

"Good morning," I said as I reached her. She turned with a jerk as if my voice surprised her. Her face quickly transformed from concern to a smile and then to something else. "I see you're an early riser," I said.

"You, too."

She looked me up and down, sweeping her eyes from my head to my toes. I wanted to turn, find a position that didn't so clearly show her how much she affected me. I dropped to my knees and sat back on my legs.

"This is my favorite time of the day," I said, unable to think of anything else. I waited a moment before speaking. "I missed seeing you." My voice was low and soft with just the right amount of sexual persuasion in it.

"Don," she began. "I know we spent the night together." She paused. I knew what was coming. It was evident in her tone when she said my name. My heart constricted and my throat tightened. Why? I wondered.

"It was phenomenal," she went on, yet her face showed no animation and I could hear the caution in her voice.

"But," I supplied.

"But I want to be up front with you. I don't think we should continue to see each other."

I hesitated a moment, incapable of speech. Scenes like this were played out on silver screens in darkened theaters. Not in real life. The night we'd spent together was more than phenomenal, it was indescribable. How could she turn away from such an all-consuming, fire-producing, life-changing experience? It was totally incomprehensible.

My shoulders dropped. If that's the way she felt, I couldn't make her change her mind. All I could do was get away from the situation with as much dignity as my legs would allow.

"All right," I said, finding my voice and amazed that it was even. I felt as if she'd punched me squarely in the stomach. Our night together was beyond comprehension. "Before I go, I deserve to know why. What is it about me you don't like?"

"Nothing," she said.

"Nothing?" My voice was so low, I could hardly hear it myself. I looked at the ground a moment before bringing my gaze back at Amber. The light was growing stronger and I saw the brightness highlighting her eyes. They were a soft brown, but I knew they could turn a deep, dark, rich chocolate when she was naked and in the throes of rapture.

She was shaking her head.

"Then why the hell . . ."

"I'm looking for someone," she interrupted.

"Someone like a man?" I nearly choked on the word.

"So to speak."

"Someone like a husband?"

"So to speak," she repeated.

"What does that mean? Are you saying you're *married*?"

"No."

I got it. "You're not married, but you're looking for a husband?"

Again she nodded.

"Is it a particular husband you're searching for or will any husband do?" I was angry and not quite understanding why. I had no intention of pursuing this woman. Sure, I was attracted to her. What red-blooded male over sixteen wouldn't be? She was beautiful, but I'd seen plenty of beautiful women. To be so flatly denied future encounters like the previous one was an unexpected blow.

Many women had walked through my life. When the association proved too restricting, I'd been the one ending it before it became a relationship. None of those women could hold a sexual candle to the knowledge, power, and command of the act Amberlina Nash had shown me.

Heat flashed through me with the power of an island-producing eruption.

"I am very particular about who will do," she said. "And it has to be someone with a net worth greater than a hotel manager earns."

Her words were like bullets. Money. She was a gold digger. I hadn't seen it in her character. It was the last thing I expected.

"I see," I said, not really seeing at all. Standing up, my body no longer in any danger of telegraphing its need to join with hers, I straightened my shoulders, showing her the pride I felt in what I did. "I am the manager."

I *was* the manager, but my father owned the property. Just as I owned the gingerbread-laden, double-porch Victorian Amber rented. I'd studied architecture in college, but found my interest lay in the hotel business. Not the giant well-run hotels—I excelled in the small sick establishments where I could root out the issues, fix them, and bring the glory back to where it was when the building was planned.

I couldn't tell her that, and if she was shallow enough to want to marry for money, I wanted nothing to do with her. There were plenty of other women in the world. Why should I waste my time on her? Then I remembered the fire analogy. I saw us naked, drenched in the sweet smell of sex, our bodies rolling around on sheets as behavior so basic and so earthy took us to the edge of time.

"I apologize if the other night led you to believe—"

I raised my hand, stopping her. A replay of that night had already formed in my head. I didn't want a play-by-play from her or for her to put any tarnish on the images in my mind. And I didn't want to hear any apologies. That night had been one of the few times in my life I could say something mind-shattering had happened. And if I had to go to my grave never experiencing it again, I wanted to keep the memory of it untarnished.

"Why don't we just agree to disagree?" she asked.

I heard the dismissive element of her tone. It was time for me to go. Unlike her, I had a schedule to maintain. "Enjoy yourself," I said, then remembering my place as she had given it to me, I continued. "If you have a free moment, drop by the hotel. The food is excellent and many of the hotel's extras are available to the public."

"That's good to know," she said, neither smiling nor frowning.

I nodded and continued my jog. The air was warm and warming by the minute, but I felt a slight chill from the cold fire she'd turned on me. The sand no longer felt good under my feet. My legs were as heavy as tree trunks, and I felt as if I was jogging through molasses. I wanted to run, sprint, shoot around the island like a rocket, getting as far away from Amber Nash as the eighty-seven square miles of the Vineyard would allow.

But I didn't. I maintained my leisurely pace. She could have been watching me. I was sure she was. I could feel her eyes keeping cadence with the pounding of my feet. But I refused to glance over my shoulder and confirm it.

Another time, I might have taken her words as a challenge, pursued her, forced her to prove her words, shown her that I could make her change her mind. But I knew the risks. I had an agenda of my own and she didn't fit into it. At this point in the summer, I needed to keep my eye on the prize.

And as much as my body ached for Amber Nash, as much as I felt like grabbing her and kissing her into submission, *she* was not the prize.

* * *

I followed Don's movements as he jogged away
from me. My fingers gripped the tablet in my trem-
bling hands with a G-force to rival astronauts in
training. Don made me tremble. He scared me. I
couldn't believe the night we had together actually
happened. But I knew it did. Not only did I act
like someone I didn't know, but the reward of our
joining was undeniable.

Yet he wasn't the one. I wasn't here for him.

What a waste, I thought. He was exactly what I
was looking for. Well, almost. He had a great body.
I knew the feel of it, the touch of his hard muscles,
the way I could make him weak and wanting. Our
time in his bed defied words. He'd found a part
of me previously unknown and unleashed. And
like a devil, he'd turned the key in the lock and it
bounded free. Who was that woman sitting on his
lap, making love as if the world's end was only seconds away?

I shook away the thoughts. In no way was a hotel
manager in the running for my affections. Dragging my eyes away from his figure, I went to my writing. The Vineyard seemed to have a strange effect
on me. It wasn't just Don and our incredible night
together. In the back of my mind I'd told myself
someday I would write a novel. I liked the idea of
having written a novel, but not the actual act of
writing one word at a time. I wrote greeting cards.
I thought in short phrases, rhymes, sentiments, not
in lengthy passages that required story arcs and
character development. Yet the moment I found
this quiet beach, the urge to write felt like it was
what I was supposed to do. Today I came with a pen

and a notebook. Five pages were already filled before Don Randall interrupted me.

I looked down the beach. He was still jogging, but he'd turned and was heading back toward me. A twinge of excitement pinged inside me. I wondered if there was a way we could be friends. Quickly I rejected the idea. I could not be friends with a man who turned my body to molten lava. He loomed larger as he came closer and closer. I wanted to turn back to my notebook, but I found myself staring at him, watching as his feet punched into the sand. Time seemed to slow down and I followed the flexing and relaxing of his leg muscles as he raised and lowered them in the regular cadence of the jog. I couldn't help my thoughts from turning back to the way I'd ridden him in the kitchen chair, the way his arm muscles had held me, his hands skimming over my skin and squeezing at the right time. The way his body fit so well with mine as if the two of us had been molded from the same piece of clay.

I shook my head, forcing myself to brush thoughts of him aside. I tried to go back to my writing, but my concentration was blown. I felt like a fraud, a female heel who'd treated a man as if he was little more than a fly. We'd spent the most incredible night of my life together and I'd banished it as if it was no more than an annoyance, while what it had been was a live-wire attached directly to my erogenous zones. And I wanted it again. I wanted it for life. This is what all the love novels talked about. I'd read my share of them, but I never believed that kind of lovemaking was possible. If it was, there would be no need to write it in novels. So it must be something that was unique, a plane of

existence that was unknown to most people. Don
and I had found it, created it, shared it. But it was
one night in a lifetime of nights, I told myself. I
wasn't going to let it sway me from my goal.

I told myself I would smile at him as he went by,
but I would not invite him to engage in any further
conversation. I didn't write anything before looking up again to gauge his progress. He wasn't there.
Sitting forward in the chair, I whipped my head
about in all directions. I checked the water. I stood
up, hooding my eyes with my hand, scanning every
bit of land, but I was alone. Nothing stretched
before me but sand and sea. Disappointment the
size of the island wedged inside me.

It was just as well, I told myself. He's not in the
league I was interested in anyway. But he'd de-
stroyed my writing time.

And my morning.

Possibly my life.

Collecting my beach chair and writing book, I returned to the house. Jack and Lila had stumbled
out of bed in search of coffee when I walked in the
kitchen.

"Well, look who finally found her way home,"
Lila said, her eyes opening wide when she saw me.

"What are you talking about? I haven't been any
farther than the beach for the last two days."

"You haven't been here. You came in, sometime
in the early morning hours yesterday. Then you
changed clothes and left before breakfast. What did
that guy do to you?"

"What guy?" I asked.

"The one you spent the two nights with," Jack
joined in, each word dripping with sarcasm.

"You think I spent the night with Don Randall?" I protested.

"Let's analyze the situation." Jack took a seat and a sip of her coffee before speaking. She faced me fully. On her fingers she ticked off her terms. "First you dance with the guy looking like the stars are hung in his eyes. Then you leave a perfectly good party early for no apparent reason. When we get back here, there is no you and no sign that you've even been here. Then you sneak in the house, still wearing your cocktail dress, just before sunrise. I'd say all the evidence points to spending the night or nights with the hotel manager." Her smile was of the Cheshire cat variety.

I knew they were teasing me, but I didn't like being on that side of the banter.

Protesting to Jack and Lila would do no good. No one believed me. Not even me. I spent most of the first night in Don's arms, but I returned to the house before daybreak. Both Lila and Jack were asleep. At least I thought they were. I didn't check their bedrooms, but I saw Jack's purse on the kitchen counter when I went to get a bottle of water and the shoes Lila had been wearing were lying next to the front door as if she'd stepped across the threshold and out of them at the same time.

I knew Jack and Lila would question me about Don, so I got away from the house before they were up and about. I kept my distance, but this morning I'd encountered Don on the beach.

"I guess you were here before the sun was fully up in the sky," Lila said.

I can't say. I'm a heavy sleeper.

Unlike Jack, I thought, who'd wake up at any noise, strange or familiar.

"I told you guys, he's not in the league where I'm casting my net."

"I don't think *he* knows that."

"He knows," I whispered, but neither one of them heard me.

Chapter 7

"Well, let me tell you about my date." Lila smiled, taking the attention from me and doing her usual "it's all about me" routine. I was happy to relinquish the floor and have the subject changed.

"Can you do it over breakfast?" Jack asked. "I'm hungry. And I hear the food at the hotel is good." Jack cast her eyes at me. I refused to react, at least on the outside. "Why don't we go there and eat?" Jack continued.

The last place I wanted to go was the hotel. "Count me out," I said.

"We'd have to get dressed," Lila said at the same time.

"That would be a must," Jack answered as sarcastically as she could.

"Who told you the food was good?" I asked.

"The manager," Jack answered, looking at me as if she was playing Cupid.

"Then he could be lying. About the food, I mean," Lila interjected. "Why don't we just have coffee here?"

Not a morning person, Lila didn't really wake up

until noon. But after that she could hang with the best of them.

"We could eat some of that food you bought," I said. Lila smirked and childishly stuck her tongue out at me.

"You can, but we need to be seen," Jack said, including me in the grouping when the last place I wanted to be seen was the St. Romaine.

"You can't believe anyone is up at this hour." Lila squinted. "What time is it anyway?"

"Lila, stop complaining." Jack grabbed her hand and pasted a cup of coffee in it. The house was fully equipped if we wanted to use the kitchen, but I saw no reason for that unless we were entertaining. Jack didn't cook often. She ate out a lot, and that accounted for her weight. I'd been taught to cook by my mother and grandmother. Lila could boil eggs and make a sandwich, and that was the extent of her kitchen skills. She'd explained that the food seemed to appear in her basket after Clay exchanged the broken one with her.

"All right." Lila finally agreed. "I guess it's all right since you say the food is good, and if Amber didn't spend the night with the manager, there's no reason to stay away. I'll go get dressed."

This was a mistake, I told myself as I slipped into cotton pants and a long shirt. I did not want to go to the St. Romaine, but I'd trapped myself by insisting that Don and I had not slept together. And that he wasn't in the running for my affections or my plan.

So again the three of us were off to the one place on the Vineyard I was loath to visit.

"What are your plans for today?" Jack asked Lila after we were seated at a table near the wall in the hotel restaurant. The waiter had served her a full plate of hotcakes, dripping with butter and maple syrup and bacon on the side. It smelled wonderful. I was envious of her as the waiter set a bowl of fresh fruit in front of me. I didn't think I'd be able to eat. I was still nervous about being in a place where Don Randall was likely to appear without notice. At any moment he could come through the door. And while I'd seen him on the beach, I felt there was unfinished anguish to be assuaged before we could meet without enmity being as solid as a rock between us.

"I'm meeting Hank and we're going antiquing."

"Hank?" I asked.

"Antiquing?" Jack said.

"What happened to the banker?"

She frowned. "Richard? I'm not up to dealing with his family. The daughter is a bitch."

"So where did you meet Hank?" I asked. "And what is he—"

"Worth?" Lila finished. She smiled. "Millions," she whispered, leaning into the table conspiratorially. "He's the latest winner of the mega lottery."

"Wow!" Jack said. "Aren't you the lucky one."

"Amber, you're awfully quiet. What are you doing today?"

I had no real plans, but felt I needed to do something. This scheme was mine and I needed to get into it. "I thought I'd try parasailing."

"That's a good idea, but it could be dangerous," Lila said.

"I have an idea," Jack said. "Why don't you fall in the water and act like you're drowning. You can get one of those lifeguards to rush out and help you."

"Jack, I swim like a fish and a lifeguard is not exactly on my radar."

"Oh, yeah," she said, defeated.

"Hello, ladies."

I tensed at the voice. It was Don. When we'd entered the dining room, I'd deliberately angled for the seat next to a large plant and away from any view of the entrance. The subterfuge, however, was not strong enough to conceal me from him. I knew this would happen if we came to the hotel. I expected to see him—at a distance. I didn't think, after this morning on the beach, that he would even speak to me, but apparently he wanted to shame me in front of my friends. My fingers curled under the table as I braced myself for his revelations.

I'd slept with this guy, made fantastic love with him, but I didn't know him.

"Hello," Lila said, her smile as chipper and innocent as a child's.

"Are you enjoying yourselves?" Don asked. I heard the poison laced in his voice. It wasn't just an innocuous question, although Jack and Lila probably didn't notice. But then they hadn't sat on his lap and abandoned the world in his arms.

"We are," Jack answered for all of them.

"And you, Ms. Nash? Has the Vineyard provided you with what you wish?"

I heard the double entendre in his question. My two friends stared at me as though they were waiting for the answer, too. Both obviously noticed the formality of his address.

"I haven't been here that long," I hedged. "I'm sure the summer will be an interesting one."

"There is a large group checking in tomorrow.

I'm sure you'll be interested in meeting some of them."

There was a slight emphasis on the last word. By *them* he meant men.

"Maybe," I said, coldly. Then I turned and looked at him, speaking quietly so only he could hear me. "I am capable of making my own way. You needn't bother with me again." I turned back to my fruit bowl.

"Good morning, ladies," he said as a good-bye. "Let me know if there is anything I can help you with."

I breathed a sigh of relief when he walked away.

"What a charming guy," Lila said.

"That's only one side of him," I said. Both of them looked at me, but I didn't explain.

At loose ends, I decided to see if I could find someone to play tennis with. If not, I'd use the ball machine. Pick-up tennis wasn't a usual occurrence, but I needed something to pound. I was a sports-minded person. I'd gone through college on a diving scholarship, keeping up the swimming instead of joining a gym. I played tennis two mornings a week with another freelance writer who worked for the same greeting card firm I did.

Entering the clubhouse, I went to the service desk and asked the desk clerk if there was anyone looking for a game or just wanted to hit some balls.

"I'll hit with you."

For the second time that day, I tensed over the voice. Stepping away from the desk and out of earshot of the kid who looked like he spent his days on the court and his nights on the beach, I said, "Don't you have to work sometime?"

"Yes, but I'm free for the next hour or so." Taking my arm, he led me to the door. "I have a reserved court."

"Don't you have a partner?"

"Normally I play with a doctor friend of mine, but she had an emergency call."

Just my luck, I thought. But the word *she* caught my attention. I hadn't thought of there being a *she* in his life. That was stupid, I told myself. The man was gorgeous. Of course there was a she. There were probably a lot of shes. And if he made love to them, the way . . . I stopped myself from completing that thought. The memory of it was mine and mine alone. I wouldn't let the knowledge of other women intrude on what I considered mine.

Taking my racket out of its case and opening a can of balls, I didn't wait or ask if he wanted to play or just hit. I wanted to pound, and it was good Don was on the other side of the net. I wouldn't have to imagine him there.

I served the first ball. Don smashed it back to me. It went by so fast, I hardly saw it and had no time to react to it.

"Love-fifteen," he called. I heard his message. We were playing a game. If that was the pace he wanted to set, I was up for it. The next ball had all my power in it. Surprise showed on his face as it hit the ground fully within bounds, but out of his range to pack it back to my side of the net.

"Fifteen-all," I called.

We traded back and forth. I ran and hit, trying to kill the ball with my racket. Don did the same. Sweat poured off me. My hair had fallen down and wet tendrils smacked me as I rammed the ball across the net. I'd reached a zone, but each time my eyes connected with Don's, my anger was renewed and I hit the ball even harder. I wondered which one of us would give out first. I was determined it wasn't going to be me.

We kept it up for longer than an hour. "Game and set," I shouted.

Don's skin was shiny as he stared across the net. He pulled a ball from his pocket and got in position to serve it. Neither one of us looked as if we were going to end the competition. A crowd gathered and was watching us. Applause erupted after each point, regardless which one of us won it. I ignored them and their applause. I wasn't playing for their approval or satisfaction. I was trying to pound Don into the earth.

As one of my balls hit the court and skidded out of Don's range, Jack walked out on the court, standing on the middle line at the net and looking back and forth at me and then Don.

The cessation of movement had me breathing hard. I leaned over, my hands on my knees as I sucked oxygen into my lungs. My body was hot, my sweat glands unable to keep up with the anger infusing my system. Chugging air as if it was liquid, I finally stood up and walked toward Jack.

"I don't know what you two think you're doing," she said before I could speak. "But this is not the way."

"I'm not doing anything," I said, taking a breath between each word.

Jack left her position and walked to within earshot of me. "Amberlina Nash, this is Jack." She placed her hand on her breast as if she needed to identify herself. "I've seen you play before, and I've never seen this much intensity. If that is what this man does to you, then you two need to talk, not try to beat each other to death."

Don came up at that moment.

"I'm afraid I'm going to have to leave now. I have to shower before going to work. Nice game. We'll have to do it again sometime." With that he walked away. I checked to see if he had the strength to walk normally or if his body had taken the same beating as mine. There was no indication that anything more than a simple game of tennis had occurred.

His cordial good-bye did nothing to appease my temper. We weren't friends, as indicated by the short war we'd waged. I knew it was a battle, one that had been interrupted by Jack's appearance. Despite the logic of her words, I knew the war would continue.

The crowd realized the drama was over and with whispered conversations they left, returning to their previous positions. I knew we'd be the topic of speculation and gossip for the rest of the day.

Jack held a bottle of water toward me. I took it and drank the contents in one long swig before gathering my things from the side of the court.

We returned to the house together. I had driven to the tennis club, but Jack drove back.

"I don't think I'll be able to walk again," I said as she parked in the driveway.

"Then let me get you another water. You must be totally dehydrated by now." Jack went to the kitchen as I hobbled into the living room. She joined me, carrying three bottles of water. Two of them she handed to me. I drank one and opened the second bottle, taking a long drink.

"Talk to me, Amber. This behavior is out of character for you."

I would have loved to talk to Jack about this, but I didn't know what was happening. "Jack, nothing was really going on. We started hitting balls and then things got competitive. You know how I am with a challenge. I couldn't let him think he could have the upper hand."

"Are you sure that was all that was going on? You looked as if you would die before you gave up."

I defended myself. "So did he."

"So did he," she conceded. "This is why I believe you two should have a talk."

"Not a good idea." I took another drink to buy myself some time. "I met him on the beach this morning."

"You did. You didn't mention it when you came in."

"You and Lila were so intent on where I'd spent the night, I didn't want to give you additional fuel. But you were right. I did spend the night with him." I stopped, taking another drink. "He assumed we'd started something."

"And he wanted to continue it?"

I nodded. "I told him I didn't want to see him again."

"And he took that as a challenge?"

"I didn't think so. I mean, I knew he was angry, but he seemed to accept it and go about his business."

"No man does that," Jack said. "You should know that."

"It was a one-night stand," I said, trying to convince myself more than Jack. "It's not like we had a relationship."

"Then he comes over at breakfast," Jack said. "Don't think all that formality masked the tension between the two of you. I don't think this plan of yours is working out for you."

"We've only been here a few days," I said, but I knew Jack was right. It wasn't working for me. "Things will get better," I answered. "I can steer clear of Don Randall."

"That might be the best thing."

It was the only thing, I thought. The man was driving me mad.

Chapter 8

This was not Brooklyn. I didn't have to pinch myself to know that. If this had been Brooklyn, I wouldn't be so self-conscious. I looked good. Both Amber and I knew clothes and we knew brands. I had been fitted by some of the best women in Saks Fifth Avenue. My clothes fit perfectly for a woman of my size. I just wasn't used to being stared at so openly. I couldn't tell if the looks were admiration or plain stares.

I smiled, as Amber had told me to do when this happened. I'd frowned at her, skeptical that anything would come of this summer. But she was so positive. That's how Amber was when she came up with these ideas. God knows what married life would be for her. Would she ever stop thinking of schemes to achieve something?

And would this one work for me?

I hoped so. I wasn't tall and thin like Amber or beautiful and willowy like Lila. I was the fat one, the one that didn't have a hope of snagging a guy in a bar if I was with either of them. But they were my friends and here, on the Vineyard, we would not be a trio. We were individuals who could inhabit the same space, but not be required to spend all our time together.

I'd wanted to plan something I could do with Amber to keep her mind off her encounter with Don Randall. I suppose I wanted to protect her in my own way. However, she'd seen through my plan and gone out on her own.

And this is how I found myself alone, walking along the beach. Well, not in the sand. I was walking along the road. The beach was on my left. Half a dozen men looked at me. I wasn't wearing a bathing suit. I had no intention of going in the water and I was self-conscious of how much skin I had to show. So I wore one of the new outfits— shorts that didn't ride up in the front, looking like an ill-fitting overblouse and creating a wedgie in the back. I topped them with a scoop-neck shirt and a short-sleeved jacket. According to the woman in the plus-size department, it was elegant and understated. The impact would be irresistible, she'd said.

I was beginning to think she might be right.

I was no longer in a residential area. The houses gave way to shops and tourists. People moved in and out of the stores. I window-shopped, stopping to check out the sea-related jewelry in one store, the summer outfits in another.

I opened the door of one. It had shot glasses with *Martha's Vineyard* written on them under a standard picture of the beach, collectible spoons, back scratchers, decorative plates, pillows, and T-shirts. I bypassed them all, going straight for the revolving stand of postcards.

I selected six or seven with pictures of Martha's

Vineyard by day and by night, photos of the Inkwell, making it look larger than it was. There were the houses on the Bluff, which I found irresistible and bought several of, along with some stamps.

Near the front door was a mailbox and behind the shop were several umbrella tables. I went out and looked for an empty place to sit and write out the cards. All the tables were filled. Most had a family or a couple sitting there. One had a solitary man who was also writing on postcards. I started to turn around and head back to the house to write the cards, but taking a deep breath, I decided to approach him. I only wanted to share his table, not give birth to his children. And this was an opportunity to step outside my comfort zone.

"Excuse me," I said as I reached the table. "Is it all right if I write my cards here?"

He smiled and nodded, extending his hand in friendship.

"Thank you." Sitting down, I put the small bag with the cards and stamps on the table. I searched for a pen in my purse. I was sure I had one, but I couldn't find it. I kept searching, sure it was there.

"Here, use mine. I have another one." My eyes went from the pen in his hand, angled toward me, to the man holding it. He had nice brown eyes and a sweet smile. He looked like he could have played football in college, but his fingers were rough when I took the pen and they brushed mine. I wondered what he did. Would he make the cut according to Amber's criteria? He smiled at me, and I returned it.

"Thanks again," I said.

Pulling the cards out, I looked at one, thinking about who to send it to and what to say.

"That's a lot of cards. You must have a lot of friends missing you. Do you always send that many when you travel?"

I looked up again, surprised that he was speaking to me. I'd sat down to share the table, not to pick him up or have him pick me up. The thought, however, sent shivers down my spine.

"I don't travel much, but I liked these. I'll probably take some of them home with me."

"To remind you of your vacation?"

I nodded, suddenly remembering that I was supposed to be a socialite and admitting that I didn't travel much was a blunder.

"Everyone collects something—Lladrós, pearls, art, diamonds. I collect postcards."

"And friends, I assume." He pointed toward the cards.

I smiled. "You can never have too many of those."

"All guys, I'm sure."

I recognized a come-on when I heard it. "There is no special man at the moment." That I got right, fully in character now. I checked him for interest, wanting to see if he was coming on to me, hoping that he was, but unable to read anything in his expression.

"I travel a lot and I like postcards, too."

I wasn't writing or even thinking of anything to write. I was interested in talking to him.

"I always try to think of something funny to put on the card."

"Something more than 'wish you were here'?"

He laughed. "Actually, I've never written that."

"It is something a woman likes to hear when

she's a long distance from her man." I was fishing, wanting to know if he was sending a card to a special woman.

"Like you, I'm between women at the moment."

I laughed and he flashed me an even white-toothed grin.

"So tell me some of the funny things you write."

He got up then and moved around to sit next to me. He wore khaki shorts and a sky blue golf shirt. His legs seemed to be as strong as the shoulders I'd admired earlier. Instantly, I went hot. I hoped my shower that morning could contend with the furnace that flared up inside me.

"You have to look at the picture first." He showed me a card. The picture was of the Inkwell. On the top, in a recognizable script, were the words *Martha's Vineyard*. I had one just like it. I knew on the back in a tiny font was printed *The Inkwell*.

"I'm sending this one to my mother. I thought about the sand and that glass is made from it. Then I thought about all the times I broke something in the house. And this is what I wrote."

He turned the card over and let me read it. "Mom, someone dropped an inkwell and it shattered to smithereens. I didn't do it. Love, Shane."

I laughed and my arm brushed his. I moved aside. "So you're Shane?"

"Shane Massey."

"Jacynthia Sterling." I offered my hand. "My friends call me Jack." He took my hand and shook it briefly. Again, I noticed the roughness of his fingers, but strangely his palm was callous free.

"Jack? That's a rather masculine name for one so obviously female."

I dropped my head so he wouldn't see me blush.

The words were standard. Flattery. I'd heard them before. I'm sure every woman in America over the age of fifteen has heard them. But nevertheless, they had the ability to make me go mushy inside.

"What's on the other card?" I asked, hiding the way I felt. And I was dying to see if he was sending it to a woman.

"This one is to my best friend. We went to high school together."

"Where was that?"

"Johnson City, Tennessee. Ever heard of it?"

I shook my head. "Sorry."

"It's in east Tennessee."

"I'm afraid I know nothing about Tennessee."

"Where are you from?"

"New York."

"Oh," he said.

"What does that mean?" I looked at him, offended, defensiveness rising in me like a soldier ready for battle. He'd said it as if there was something wrong with New York.

"Being from New York is like being from Texas. You believe there are no other state except New York . . . or Texas, if you're Texan."

I smiled proudly and relaxed. "There aren't." I picked up the card and looked at the address. The name was Jim Chancellor in Nashville. "Jim lives in Nashville?"

He nodded. "We both do."

"So tell me the story of this card." The photo was of the princess houses on the Bluff.

When he turned it and held it up for me to read, it said, "Little Red Riding Hood slept here, but not with George."

I laughed, thinking it was strictly male humor. I

understood that the George mention was George Washington, who seemed to have slept everywhere in the Northeast according to numerous plaques that were fixed to historical and would-be historical sites.

"How about this?" I picked up one of my own and looked at the picture. It was of the shopping area at night. The lights colored it brightly. "It's a strange world here. Night falls in color."

He smiled and leaned a little closer to me. I felt the heat of his body and smelled the pleasant mixture of male cleanness and raw sexuality.

I lost interest in the postcards. I wanted to know more about him.

"So what are you doing on the Vineyard?"

"I'm in the band."

"Band?"

"Yeah, part of the music festival going on this week."

I nodded.

"Well, I'm in the band, playing with Mike Adams."

I was impressed. Mike Adams was a sensation with a clarinet. He'd won more than one Grammy for his recordings. And I owned a couple of his CDs.

"Have you been with him long?"

"A couple of years."

"What instrument do you play?"

"Keyboards, trumpet, guitar, a little sax." He shook his hands, indicating he was shaky on the sax.

"How did you learn all those instruments? I took piano for three years and can't play anything except one Christmas carol."

He grinned, showing me his even white teeth again.

"My mother said I had an aptitude for music. I wanted to play baseball some of the times she made me practice, but eventually I came to enjoy it." He paused a moment. "It impressed the girls."

I smiled, knowing I'd been one of those girls who was fascinated by a guy in the band in my high school.

"Anyway, after taking piano lessons for several years, I went to New Orleans on spring break and in one of the clubs I met a guy playing guitar. He was so good. I wanted to learn what he did. The next day I went back to the club. It was closed, but I knocked on the door until someone opened it and I asked where I could find him. They wouldn't tell me anything except his name. I went from club to club asking about him. Eventually, I found where he lived and I went there and asked him to teach me the guitar."

"And he did?"

"Not at first. He threw me out."

I sucked a laugh back, wondering how anyone could throw out a guy with shoulders and legs as strong as this guy's.

"But I was so impressed with his ability that I kept after him until he realized the only way to get rid of me was to teach me. Every free moment I got, summers, holidays, breaks, I'd go back to New Orleans and work with him."

"Do you play guitar in the band?"

He shook his head. "Mike needed a keyboard player when I joined him."

"You make me wish I'd spent more time learning that piano instead of fighting my mother to let me quit."

"You can always pick it up again," Shane said.

"That's true," I agreed. Talking to him had inspired me. Not to return to piano lessons, but that I could do whatever I wanted to do. That if there was something I wanted, I should go after it. This was Amber's approach to the world. It's what had brought us to the Vineyard.

Shane checked his watch. I knew he was about to leave and I was sorry for that. I enjoyed talking to him and wouldn't have minded spending the rest of the day sitting right there.

"I have a rehearsal," he said. "But if you'd like to see the concert, I could leave a couple of tickets for you."

"I'd like that."

"Jacynthia Sterling, right?"

"Right," I said, impressed that he remembered my name—both first and last.

He stood up. "They'll be there tonight."

Flashing me another of his great smiles, he left. I watched him walking away. He stopped a moment to drop his postcards in the mailbox. *What a great guy,* I thought. *I'd like to know him better.* But he wasn't the reason I was on the island. Yet I followed his walk, analyzed the way he moved, transferring his weight from leg to leg like a confident lion.

I looked a little longer before the sound came out of me. I growled.

The Howard University crowd registered in throngs. The noise level rose to the double ceiling. Often it was punctuated by squeals of reunion. A steady rush of guests ready for the annual pilgrimage of sun and music kept the registration desk busy for hours. By noon tomorrow the hotel would be full to capacity with the Bison Music Festival tour group. Howard University alumni came every year, but this year due to the music festival the organizers had gone out with a special promotion and increased the number of guests by a third.

Their coming meant extra work and even more personal attention on my part, but I looked forward to them coming. Most were the older alumni, but there were a good number of people who'd graduated in the past ten years and were working the corporate ladder. They dropped money like discarded candy wrappers. The gift shops, restaurants, and concierge services would likely break previous sales records.

I appreciated that. It meant the summer would end on a banner financial note. My father would be more than pleased. I would win my bet. And maybe Amber could find her millionaire among the guests. I frowned at the thought.

Getting up from my desk, I observed the lobby through the glass wall and door of my office. I shoved Amber to the back of my mind. I'd been looking over the accounts, but the moment her image flooded my mind all else failed. Yesterday had been a disaster. I was still kicking myself for acting like an ass. Everyone on the Vineyard had heard about the tennis game. Some had suggested I enter the annual tournament. Others thought I was showing off and getting put in my place by a woman. I couldn't say her sex had nothing to do with it. It was because of her sex that I was an ass, that I'd tried to force her to change her course or purpose for being on the island with the force of a tennis racket. And the more I knew I was beating my head against a rock wall, the harder I hit the ball.

Amber didn't retreat. She gave as good as she got—better than she got.

What those people watching us didn't know was that the two of us weren't battling over a game, but something completely different. Our fight, at least mine, was over feelings. I understood that now. The long hours of the night had made it clear to me. She'd gotten to me. The short time we'd known each other didn't matter. But her rejection based on her perception that I wasn't rich enough pissed me off. I could have told her, but I'd made the deal with my father when I took on this project to be totally anonymous. If people knew I was really Sheldon St. Romaine, they would treat me as the owner's son and I wouldn't be able to turn the place around. And if money was all she wanted from me, I didn't want her.

I dropped the pen in my hand and left the office. This was a new chapter in my life, I thought. I'd never wanted a woman before, not like this. I'd wanted many women, had plenty of them. They followed me around. I could choose the size, the weight, the color, and with a crook of my finger, have a partner for the night. In the light of day, we went our own ways. No strings, no need, and no regrets. So why did her comment to end anything between us make me so angry?

I walked into the hotel reception area. The place was standing room only. Every day I surveyed the property, making sure everything was in order. I didn't call it an inspection, but I checked to make sure things were functioning properly.

It was just after ten o'clock. The last of the breakfast stragglers were leaving the room and the lunchtime crowd was a couple of hours away. Still, I needed to pick my way through the throngs of guests.

My first stop was always the fitness room. I would check in with my friend Jeff, the hotel's personal trainer, and spend a few minutes talking about last night's sporting event. It didn't matter which one. Jeff loved all things sports.

When I entered the room, there was no talking at all. Everyone in the place was staring outside. Jeff stood at a table on which he usually folded towels, but his hands were still. His attention was focused on the windows that looked out on the pool.

Unlike most hotels, especially resort hotels, the St. Romaine's outdoor pool was Olympic size. At the time the hotel was built in the 1940s, swimming champion turned actress Esther Williams was burning up the box office with her films, all of which had long sequences of her swimming or doing water dances. The architects and owners thought they would capitalize on this by building a pool that could entice people into thinking they could swim the way she did.

It worked and drew people to the hotel, the pool being as popular as the Inkwell. That was until times changed, the world became more mobile, the enticement of Europe took families and their money to European or African capitals.

Lately, there was a renewed interest in staying home, seeing America, and driving to vacation destinations. I made sure the Vineyard, specifically the hotel, was one of those locations. And it looked as if my technique was working. However, as I followed the line of Jeff's gaze, I saw what everyone was looking at. It wasn't a thing, but a person. A woman.

Amber Nash.

Jeff was mesmerized, as was every other male staring at her. I did a double take when I saw her standing on the high diving board.

"How long has she been coming here?" I asked without acknowledging that Jeff was even in the room.

Jeff glanced at me. "This is her third morning."

"Is she any good?" I asked.

He spoke without look at me. "Watch."

Amber stood concentrating. For a moment she seemed to block out the world and pull whatever senses she needed together. In one fluid motion she raised her arms and sprang off the diving board. Her long body went up in the air. With lightning speed, she twisted, somersaulted, turned, defying all the physics I'd ever learned, then headed arms first into the water. Her body cut a clean hole in the liquid, barely making a splash.

"Da-mn," I said, holding on to the word as if it was two syllables. It was out of my mouth before I realized I'd said it.

"That's right," Jeff acknowledged.

"She is good."

Seconds after she'd entered the water, she surfaced, snapped the water from her face, and pushed off in long strokes for the side of the pool.

There were a few people sitting around the edge of the water on the hotel's pink and white deck chairs, but Amber had the full pool to herself.

"Feel like applauding?" Jeff asked me.

I nodded.

"The first time she came, she only swam laps," Jeff said. "About a hundred of them."

"A hundred laps?" I frowned. I remembered her running for every ball I shot over the net and not even looking like she was winded.

Jeff nodded. "Then yesterday the diving began on the low board. Today all the stops came out. There are only a few people out there. They applauded several times. Then I think she rendered them silent. Each time she dives, she does something different. I think she awes them and they can't do anything but watch with open-mouthed stares."

"Where'd she learn that?"

"Don't know. I haven't gotten to talk to her. She finishes up just before the real crowd comes in. Then she's gone."

I didn't say anything. The door swung open and in came a guest. I smiled and walked through the door leading to the outside pool deck.

Amber came out of the water. A boy about ten years old ran over to her. "Can you teach me to do that?" he asked, obviously in awe of her.

"Joel, don't bother the lady," a man who must be his father said. The kid and the man looked too much alike not to have the same genes.

"It takes time to learn to do that," Amber said. She glanced up and saw me. For a moment our eyes locked and that invisible connection linked us before she turned back to the boy. "Can you swim?" she asked.

He nodded enthusiastically.

"Can you swim laps?"

He nodded again, but this time not so confidently.

"Would you swim one with me?" Amber looked up at the boy's dad. The man nodded once.

"Sure," the boy said with a big smile. He headed toward the deep end of the pool.

"Careful," she warned. "We have to do it together."

In a moment they were in the water and swimming toward the shallow end. Amber pulled back, matching the child's excited strokes, while hers were smooth and controlled.

As soon as they reached the edge, the boy was out of the water and headed again for the deep end.

"Joel, not so fast," his father warned. Then the man turned to Amber. "Casey Edwards," he said. "This is my son Joel."

"Amber Nash." The two adults shook hands.

"He liked watching you. He swims well, but has never dived. Don't let him monopolize your time."

"I'll just give him a few pointers." She smiled her white-toothed smile, which I would know if it was on a page among hundreds with a caption asking you to identify the one that belonged to Amber Nash.

"If the excitement keeps up, you might have to give him lessons when you get home," Amber said.

"I'd be glad to," Casey said. "Joel hasn't shown much interest in anything since his mom died. But he liked you from the beginning."

Inwardly I groaned. I could see it. Casey Edwards was flirting, cruising, whatever you call it, he was doing it. And he'd started with the king of lines, going right to the top of the deck with a dead wife story. Who could resist that, a cute kid who'd lost his mother and didn't respond to anything except her? The story took me back to college when we'd make bets on how fast we could get a girl into bed. Casey Edwards had perfected the technique. He'd extract an invitation to dinner with Amber before lunch was served and have her in bed before morning.

I gritted my teeth.

What could I do? I was the manager. Casey Edwards was a guest. Technically, so was Amber. I'd invited her here, giving her permission to use the various facilities. My position was to see to their needs, not engage in those needs, however much I might want to.

Amber and Joel sat on the side of the pool. She spoke softly to him, demonstrating her lesson with her arms and hands. I looked around. Everything was in order. There was nothing more for me to do except leave them to their devices.

And I didn't like any of the devices that came to mind.

Chapter 9

I'd just finished blow-drying my hair when I heard the front door open and close. Leaving the upstairs bathroom, I went to the top of the stairs. Jack looked up at me.

"Jack, glad you're here. Would you curl my hair?" It was something she and I had done for each other since we began experimenting with our own styles.

She came up the steps. "Let me put these down and change my shirt."

I followed her into her bedroom where she dropped two small bags.

"Where'd you go?" I asked as she removed her suit jacket and found a T-shirt.

"One of the tourist traps in town. I bought some postcards and a couple of souvenirs."

Jack had her back to me, but I could tell from the tone in her voice that there was more to it than a simple shopping trip.

"Did you meet anyone?" I asked as innocently as I could muster.

Jack turned and faced me. "I'm not Lila. As much as I wish I had her charisma, I don't meet a man every time I leave the house." Her words were harsh, but her delivery of them softened their impact.

"So you did meet someone?" I smiled, making the question more a statement than anything else.

Jack dropped her eyes. Then looked at me straight on. "Not exactly. Where's your curling iron?"

"In the bathroom." I left, got it, and returned in a moment. It was already hot since I thought I'd have to do the curling myself.

Jack had a chair turned around facing the windows, away from the mirror in the room.

"Sit down," she said, tapping the back of the chair with a comb she held in her hand.

I sat in the chair. "How inexactly was it?"

Jack sighed as if resigned to tell me the details. She pulled the comb through my hair and sectioned off an area before lifting the hot curler from its base. "Outside the souvenir shop were tables where people could sit and write out their cards. I sat with a nice young man and wrote mine out."

"Nice young man?" I asked. "Does that mean someone in his teens or someone in your age bracket?"

"He was a member of the band. Mike Adam's band."

"Band, huh," I said, dismissively. Guys in the band rarely made enough money to sustain themselves and they were always out of town. You couldn't trust them. Too many groupie females flaunting themselves and trying to get into bed with them. And of course, the guys fell for it every time.

"You don't have to say it like that," Jack said. "I shared his table. I didn't make a date with him."

"You didn't?" I was sure she'd make a date with someone good looking, but well out of the range we'd established.

"No, I didn't," Jack said. Her words were distinct, spoken as if to a child. She also pulled my hair a little harder than I thought necessary, but I said nothing about it. "He did say he'd leave me tickets to the concert, but it's not likely I'll see him again."

"No backstage pass?"

"Amberlina, I know the reason we're here. I'm not taking up with a member of the band."

I could tell I was irritating Jack. For several minutes I said nothing. Jack worked in silence. After all the years of practice, she was a wizard with a curling iron. I heard the metal-clicking rhythm as she twirled hair between the heated tongs. I knew when she finished, I'd be able to turn Don Randall's head.

"Ugh." I coughed. Why did I think of him? It was Casey Edwards's head I needed to turn.

"Did I burn you?" Jack asked. I heard the concern in her voice.

"No, I swallowed wrong." It wasn't totally a lie. I had done it as a result of the thought that had gone through my head.

"Who did you meet today?" Jack asked.

"A widower with a small son. He's from Atlanta and is an executive vice president for Coca-Cola."

"I'm impressed," she said. Jack didn't ask if I wanted her to check him out. We researched everyone. So far they were who they said they were. Unlike us, I thought.

I shook my head, trying to dislodge the thought that we were pretending.

"Don't do that," Jack said sharply. "I nearly burned you."

"Sorry." There was nothing really wrong with what we were doing. Women had done this for ages. And these men were looking for women, too. Otherwise they wouldn't approach us.

"Where you going tonight?" Jack asked.

Glad for anything to divert my thinking, I was happy to talk about Casey and his little boy. "Dinner."

"Just dinner?"

"*Just* dinner," I said, repeating her words. I knew she was thinking about my night with Don Randall. I supposed I would never live that down.

And why should I? He was a good lay. Better than good. He was fantastic. Nothing like him had ever happened to me before.

I felt my legs begin to stick together and my breasts begin to point against my Wonderbra. I started to shake my head again, but remembered Jack's warning. Why couldn't I get that man out of my head? I had to. I didn't need any further thoughts of Don Randall. From now on, he was someone in the past. A door closed, never to be opened again. I had a mission, a job to do, and only one short summer to complete it.

If I could just keep Don Randall from encroaching on my thoughts.

The lights dimmed as someone offstage played a kettle drum. The audience settled, quiet descending over the room as the sound announced the beginning of the concert. My heart beat with the tempo of that drum. The first concert I'd ever attended was in Madison Square Garden. I was thirteen and screaming at every movement of the group on stage. At nearly thirty, the feeling was the same. I no longer screamed, but the excitement flowing through me was the same. I was at a Mike Adams concert. It didn't matter that there were hundreds of other people there or that my date was Lila.

The opening act was a comedian-singer named James Windsor. I'd heard of him, but never seen him perform. He was funny and had a good voice. I'm sure he'd be a headliner someday. He prepared the audience and we were ready for the main performance.

During the intermission I'd hoped to see Shane setting up, but the thick curtain that closed after James Windsor left the stage obscured any view of what was happening behind it. When it opened to the rolling drumbeat again, Mike Adams was sitting on a bar stool in the center. And Shane Massey sat at a massive piano directly behind him. A voice off-stage introduced Mike Adams, and the audience applauded and shouted their appreciation.

"Is that him?" Lila whispered as if the two of us had a conspiracy in progress.

I nodded. "That's him."

"I can see why you'd want to take him home."

"Oh, I'm not taking him home," I whispered back. "We only had a few minutes together."

"But he gave you tickets to the concert. You must have made some impression."

Mike Adams began to play. And Shane's hands moved across the keys. I watched every movement he made, my eyes riveted to his hands. His fingers danced across the black and white keys. There were times his eyes closed, the music affecting him as if it had entered his soul and taken root there. On slower songs, he caressed the notes. I could feel them. I felt him touching the piano, making music with the combination of sounds, lightly pressing the black and whites. And then I felt his hands on my body. I had become part of the song, been transported from my seat to the bench next to him. His fingers played me.

I was a Mike Adams fan. I thought I'd be enthralled with him, but Shane had my full attention the entire time he was on the stage. The band continued to play as the audience filed out of the rows humming the last song. When Mike Adams finished his encore and left the stage, I remained in my seat. Lila didn't prompt me to leave. I don't know how long we sat there—at least as long as it took for Shane to play his last note and collect his music.

"Let's go backstage," Lila whispered when we stood and filed out of the row.

"We can't go back there," I told her.

"Why?"

"We don't have passes."

"Oh, Shane will get us in."

Shane had left the stage. It was an empty cavern, although the patrons were milling around, talking to each other as they moved up the aisles toward the exits.

"You don't even know him," I told Lila.

"But you do, and you want to see him."

"I never said that."

"You don't have to. I saw you watching him."

I turned to fully face Lila, my hand automatically going to my hip. "I met the man once, Lila."

"But he gave you tickets, good seats."

We were in the eighth row, center. Perfect seat, just where the floor in the theater crested upward. It gave an unobstructed view of the stage.

"He was just being nice."

Lila gave me a look that said no man is ever just being nice. Grabbing my arm, she pulled me against the flow of traffic and toward the stage.

The night had been long. Very long. I didn't get to bed until two, and it wasn't because I was having a good time. Casey was a nice guy and he had a beautiful son, but the one person I wanted nothing to do with was an invisible stranger at the dinner table with Casey and me. I didn't seem to be able to let go of the memory of Don Randall.

And it pissed me off.

Why was he invading my thoughts when I was with the kind of man I was looking for? And why was I here at the beach?

Casey had seen me back to the house and I'd gone straight to bed, where I'd spent the night turning over and over and listening to the distant surf.

I found my place on the sand earlier than usual and sat down to write and wait for Don to come and talk for a bit before he continued his morning run. Despite my telling him he had no place in my life, it had become routine for him to stop and talk to me for a few moments. I secretly looked forward to seeing him. He taunted me and disapproved of my intentions, yet I could be myself with him.

And the fact that he was only slightly dressed made it all the more appealing to watch him.

The first morning after our discussion on the beach had been awkward. Don was ridiculing and sarcastic. I knew he had a right to his feelings, so I let him vent them. I took the abuse—to a point. I ignored most of his comments and only answered the ones I felt like answering. By morning my anger had dissipated, until we now talked like civilized adults. He'd taken an interest in my book, but I hadn't come to the point of sharing the story yet.

Settling in my chair, I pulled my book out and began to write. The pages were filling up and I found myself lost in the story I was creating, so much so that I didn't even hear Don until he plopped down in the sand next to me.

"How was your date?" he asked, without even saying good morning.

"How did you know I had a date?"

"I didn't really. Not until now, but I didn't think you could resist after I heard Mr. Edwards talking about his son and his wife."

"His wife is dead."

"I heard that part, too. So how was it? Are you the one to help him get over his grief?"

"This is the kind of conversation I have with my *girl*friends."

"You can think of me as a girlfriend if you like. After all, I know your secret. Isn't that what girl-friends are for?"

"They are. And if you notice, I brought a couple with me for support such as this."

"But I'm truly interested. So was it good or not?"

"It was good." I nodded.

"I see," he said.

His tone told me he was reading things into my answer and while he might be right, I objected to it.

"It was fine," I said. "Casey is a very interesting man." And did he know it, I thought. All through dinner he told me about his job, his research, his accomplishments, his awards. It was all I could do to get my food down. And then he suggested the lounge. Martha's Vineyard was a dry island, so it surprised me to learn that Casey had brought his own beverage for our evening.

We sat and drank and he talked the night away. Occasionally we'd dance. Then he'd tell me about his son. I did enjoy listening to stories about Joel. Finally, my yawn caught on and he took me back to the house.

"Is there another date planned?"

Don's voice snapped me back to the beach.

"We haven't set one."

"Oh."

There was that tone again.

"Why don't you have lunch with me?" Don delivered the invitation with the same amount of innuendo he would use if he'd said, "Have sex with me."

"I'm busy," I said automatically, not giving myself a moment to think about it. If I did, my answer might be different.

"I have a proposition for you."

I raised my eyebrows and looked at him over the top of my sunglasses.

"It's not that kind of proposition," he said. "Although if you're agreeable, I could make it that one. We *were* incredible together."

"I am not agreeable," I said, but I couldn't stop the infusion of heat that flashed through me or the memory of the two of us entwined like tree limbs together on crumpled sheets. His smile said more than his words. Images winked through my mind at the speed of light, but not fast enough to keep my body from remembering how well the two of us fit together or how unbelievable we had been in each other's arms.

"Just checking," he said.

"What is the proposition?" Curiosity got the better of me.

"I thought I'd help you with your problem."

"I have a problem?"

"Of a kind," he answered.

I swiveled around in the chair, putting my feet in the sand and looking him straight in the eye. "Wanna tell me what it is?"

"You wanna find a rich husband."

"And . . ." I said, wondering where he was going with this.

"I happen to be in a position to know the right men. With my help, you won't have to spend time triaging the lot only to find out someone doesn't meet your particular requirements."

He made it sound cold and calculated, but I refused to allow his swagger to infiltrate a well-organized plan.

"You're willing to give me the skinny on your guests?"

"Absolutely not," he said. "That would be morally wrong, not to mention illegal."

"Then what do you plan to do?"

"I'll point you in the direction of the men with the most money. I won't tell you how much they have, only that they're in your bracket. Anything else is up to you."

"And what do you get in return for this help?"

"You go to the End of the Summer Dance with me."

I'd heard of the End of the Summer Dance. It was traditional for the Vineyard and signaled the return of the summer residents to the mainland. The island would close up for the coming winter. Tourists would return to their lives and relinquish the sand and surf to the permanent residents of the Vineyard.

"A dance?" I questioned, raising my eyebrows. "A single dance? You're willing to send me off to look for another man for the price of a dance?"

He nodded. It sounded absurd. I wondered what ulterior motive he was hiding. This behavior was counter to that of any man I'd ever met.

"The end of the summer is a couple of months away. By then I could be engaged to one of the men you point out."

"I'll take that chance."

I scrutinized his eyes for any sign of humor. I had the feeling he was making fun of me, but I saw nothing. I can't say there was sincerity in his gaze. It was unreadable.

I really didn't need his proposal. Jack could find out anything we needed to know. She'd done fine so far. But . . . I thought, if Don could give us direction, we wouldn't have to weed through everyone.

"I tell you what," Don said while I was still trying to make sense of his proposition.

"What?" I asked.

"Robert Yancey checked in today. He headed a pharmaceutical venture capital firm three years ago. They got FDA approval for a breakthrough drug and since then his company is rolling in money. They had a buyout bid from of the major pharma houses, but turned it down. Last January the company went public and their stock has been the hottest thing on Wall Street."

"Ummm," was all I said.

"He loves tennis. I could arrange a game for you, but I suggest you let him win."

"Oh," I said. "He's one of those."

"Those?"

"Men who can't stand it when a woman is better at something than they are, especially sports." I looked him directly in the eye. Both of us knew we were thinking of our do-or-die tennis game. "As if they have the right to be bigger, stronger, and better. It's a game of skill, not necessarily strength."

"I know," he said. "Do we have a deal?"

I thought about it, not answering immediately. Something about this struck me as bad. I felt as if I was intentionally putting myself in harm's way.

"This is just a dance?" I questioned.

He nodded.

"Three hours of my time?"

"Four, actually. The dance is from nine to one." He flashed a smile.

"Nothing strange about this dance? I mean, you're not going to get me in the middle of the floor and announce that I'm looking for a husband or some other situation where you can embarrass me?"

He raised three fingers in the Boy Scout salute. "This is strictly on the up and up."

I shook my head. "There's something you're not telling me." But I found myself offering him a handshake to seal the deal and hoping I wasn't sealing my fate.

Don took my hand, but he didn't shake it. He used it against me, pulling me off balance. My chair tipped and I fell forward into his arms, which were waiting to catch me. Immediately he buried one hand in my hair and pressed his mouth to mine. For a moment I thought of resisting, but my brain lost contact with my body the millisecond his lips met mine, and the thought was gone.

His hands dug into my hair as he held my mouth to his. The position was awkward. The chair had pitched over with me, its arm digging into my side. As that was the side that also lay against Don, there was. nothing I could do about it. Grains of sand scratched my belly, but the sensation of Don's mouth working magic against mine blocked out any discomfort. I moved my free arm, running my hand up his jaw to his ear and hairline.

Don shifted, his arm going under mine and making me more comfortable. Then suddenly I was free. With lightning speed, he broke contact and righted the chair with me still in it. He smiled at my surprise as he stepped back.

"See you at lunch. Right after your diving lesson."

He ran off down the beach, leaving behind a confused and frustrated me. I grabbed a handful of sand and threw it at him, but the wind forced it back and tiny granules as sharp as glass bit at my face.

Chapter 10

It felt good to be pursued again. After meeting Clay Reynolds in the grocery store, I never expected to see him again. But he'd called me several times, inviting me out. I'd refused, every time.

Until now.

Going parasailing with him was the least I could do. And it was something adventurous. I wasn't very adventurous by nature. I often chose the safe road, ordering the same thing in restaurants, eating the exact same lunch every day, shopping in the same store, buying the same styles. But on the Vineyard, I was different, free. Amber's idea of enhancing our biographies also meant I could change my life. At least for now I could have some fun.

"Are you ready, Lila?" Clay shouted over the wind.

I nodded, adjusting the harness. "This is very tight," I said.

"It has to be," the trainer said. "It's a safety feature and we're all about safety here." He smiled reassuringly.

A band was strapped under my breast circling my body. Another went through my legs and connected to the first one. Over my shoulders were other bands made of some super-strong material. Together they forced me to stand erect, giving me perfect posture.

"Just relax and let the wind do all the work," the trainer instructed me again.

I checked my snaps and buckles as I glanced at Clay. He was no longer in his harness, since he'd gone first and I'd watched him soaring in the sky. It was now my turn to sail into space. My harness was attached to the giant sail that was to be my guide to the heavens.

"Ready?" Clay shouted again.

"As ready as I'm going to be." I smiled tentatively. My heart was pounding. I could feel it in my ears and my head. I was scared, but I was going to do this. I'd spent my life being safe, staying on the straight and narrow road, not making waves. I know now that I wanted more than that. And I wouldn't get it by always being safe.

I signaled to the boat driver that I was ready. Clay and the trainer stepped back and the boat took off. Moments later I was airborne, as if my weight was half what it was and what I worked at keeping it. The wind embraced me, lifting my feet from the water, invisible hands pulling me above the earth and all that tethered me to it.

I was free.

The air pulled at my hair, pushed against my breasts and my body with equal force. I held on as tight as I could while the world below me surrendered.

It was exhilarating, like nothing I'd ever felt before. I looked down on the island. Houses, cars, and people were reduced to doll size. I don't know how long I stayed in this new world, but it wasn't long enough. When the boat dropped me into the water and Clay's strong arms lifted me back on the dock, I wanted to do it again.

"It was wonderful," I said, breathless and excited. "I want to do it again. It's like flying on the wind. You can't imagine how great it is."

"Lila, take a breath," Clay said. The smile on his face was huge. His white teeth gleamed, a perfect picture framed by lips that I wanted to kiss. "I knew you would love it."

Without thinking I threw my arms around his neck. "I did," I said.

No one had ever taken me parasailing before. No one had even suggested anything out of the ordinary: dinner, movie, renting DVDs. Clay was different. He thought beyond the ordinary. No box forced him inside. He was as free as the air that let him float to earth.

Moments later, as I tried to pull back from the embrace, Clay's arms tightened around me. It felt good being held. I hadn't been really held by a man in a long time. I could smell the dried water on his skin. It was mingled with another smell all its own. Clay's unique smell. I liked it, to the point that I wanted to open my mouth and taste his skin, feel the warmth of his naked body against my tongue.

I swallowed, forcing myself to keep from acting on my thoughts. I hadn't known Clay very long and wouldn't get to know him any better. He was everything I was looking for in a man. Everything except the money, I thought.

There were other qualities I needed other than money. It was ironic that I wouldn't get to know any of the values Clay held. Our one date was all there was and all there would be.

"Let's get dressed and have something to eat?" he suggested.

The trainer was already unhooking me from the harness. I looked at the people waiting for the chance I'd just had to sail above the water.

"Lunch sounds wonderful." I smiled, knowing that second to flying again, I wanted to spend more time with Clay.

"What would you like to eat?"

It had been a while since anyone asked me. They thought because of my looks, my head carried no brain. The fact that I'd been top salesperson for the last three years made no difference. To them it was an invisible act. People ordered from me because I had great tits and ass. Some of them did, I admitted that. But all procurement officers, formulary directors, and material management professionals weren't male. The fact that a lot of the purchasing agents I dealt with were heterosexual females was immaterial to a man who naturally figured my presentations involved a big smile and a double-D cup.

"Seafood, of course."

"How about the hotel restaurant. I've eaten there a couple of times and the food was good."

"You mean the St. Romaine?"

He nodded. "It's not far. We could walk." He looked at my bare feet. My shoes were flats and I would have no problem walking, but I frowned at the thought.

Going to the St. Romaine meant my chances of running into Amber increased fourfold. So far my day with Clay was going great. I didn't want to spoil it by having Amber cut her eyes in my direction.

"We don't have to go there. We can go anywhere you like. I'd just like to spend some time with you."

My heart warmed. I smiled, unable to stop myself. I'd heard that line before. Most times I rolled my eyes and walked away. It was code for "I want to feel your breasts and go to bed with you." From Clay I didn't have that impression.

Maybe I didn't want it. *Surely*, I didn't want it.

"I noticed a small restaurant on the other side of the island. It's near that grocery store where we met."

His mouth turned up in a memory-smile. I could read his thoughts since they were as clear as my own. We both remembered the tomatoes and cantaloupes rolling around the floor in the store.

"You know the way, you drive," he said fifteen minutes later when we were standing beside his car. He flipped the keys toward me. Instinctively I caught them.

"You want *me* to drive?" The surprise in my voice was unmistakable.

"Sure. You couldn't have gotten to that store without a car. So I assume you drive."

"I do, but . . ."

"But?" he questioned.

"But cars are generally an extension of—" I stopped. Who was being the chauvinist now?

He completed my sentence. "Male sexuality."

Biting my lower lip, I nodded.

"I don't really like to drive," he said. "You'll be doing us a favor."

I smiled broadly. "I love to drive," I said.

"See, we're compatible."

With a laugh we got in the car and headed toward

the place of our first encounter and the restaurant along the opposite shore.

The restaurant had both inside and outside seating. We chose the outside and were seated at the edge of the railing looking at the ocean. A soft breeze blew over us. Clay laughed when I ordered a salad.

"That's not all you're going to eat?" he said. "Not after that ride on the parasail?"

I remembered my vow to take chances. "That's to start," I lied. Scanning the menu, I chose a lobster tail with drawn butter, a baked potato loaded with sour cream, and broccoli spears. It was partially healthy, I rationalized. At least the salad was.

And I ate it all. I'd never felt so satisfied in my life. We lingered over coffee and dessert until the place was empty of all patrons except us. Clay kept me laughing with stories of his childhood and escapes from his aunt.

"How about a walk?" he asked when we finally relinquished our luncheon seats.

"Along the beach?" I suggested.

He nodded.

We stepped from the restaurant directly onto the sand. I grabbed his arm. His muscles clenched under my hand. Bending down, I took off my shoes. He wore sandals and he removed them, too. Then as natural as sunshine, we linked arms and began walking.

"It's so beautiful here," I said. "I'm glad Amber talked me into coming."

"Amber, that's your friend? The one with the disapproving eyes?"

I looked up at him. "She's really a wonderful person when you get to know her. You saw her on a bad day." I lied so easily. I didn't usually lie, didn't have to, but this was a summer of deception and I knew that from the beginning. Even though I wanted to be totally honest with Clay, I had to maintain the story we'd agreed on. Telling one person we were not who we appeared to be could lead to disaster for us all. And while I might leave the Vineyard exactly as I'd come, there was no reason to think that Jack and Amber wouldn't find what they were looking for.

"It's your turn now," Clay said.

"My turn for what?" I asked.

"At lunch I told you all about me. Now it's your turn to tell me your story."

I looked down at our feet as we walked. I thought about what to tell him, what to say.

"There isn't that much," I began the partial truth–partial lie we'd rehearsed. "My father owns a pharmaceutical company. I work there."

"There's more to you than what you do and what your father owns."

In truth, my father was a vice president of a company that manufactured flooring supplies: wood, tiles, stone, gluing products, and carpeting. He made a modest middle-class income. We never wanted for anything. His job afforded his four children things like dance lessons, football camp, and the universities of our choice. But we were far from rich.

"So, tell me about Lila." Clay squeezed my arm, bringing me closer to him. It was the perfect gesture, but more than that, his words were like shining beacons to my psyche. Most men's next question would've been what pharmaceutical company did my father own. Dollar signs immediately appearing in their eyes.

But Clay had broken the mold on that. More for me than my job, than my fictitious parent. He really wanted to know about me and not look at or Braille my outer frame with hands that couldn't find a place to rest.

"Do you have any sisters or brothers?"

"Three," I answered. "Two brothers, both older. One sister, younger."

"Are you a close family?"

"Yes." I smiled, thinking of the last Thanksgiving we'd all been together, plenty of food, laughter, and love. "When we were kids, we hated each other, but we grew closer as we got older and started our own lives."

"Families are generally like that. Do they all work in the pharmaceutical business?"

I shook my head. "I'm the only one who followed my father. One of my brothers works on Wall Street. We call him the financial wizard. He always liked managing money. Now he does it for the family. The other brother owns a bank and my sister lives in Italy and manages an art gallery."

"Wow! I'm amazed you even spoke to me."

"Not speaking would be rude," I said, grinning. "Especially when we were chasing tomatoes."

The truth was I did have three siblings. And my brother did work on Wall Street, but he was no wizard. He was a trader and good at what he did, but he wasn't rich. My second brother was a vice president of a small bank in Chicago. He didn't own it, and everyone in a bank was a vice president.

My sister was an art student in Italy. And our father had never set foot in a pharmaceutical company.

Clay and I continued walking, but I steered the subject away from personal issues. After a while we stopped talking altogether. We walked along the edge of the water. Our feet were wet, but our hearts were linked. My hands had moved from holding his arm to circling his waist. Like lovers, we followed the sun. Finally it was time to turn around and return to the car.

I thought of it as relinquishing the fantasy and returning to the real world. But for another hour or so I could stay in the perfect world that had surrounded me the moment Clay had appeared at my door to take me out for the day.

"Where are we going to have dinner?" Clay asked.

"Dinner? We just had lunch." I put my hands on my stomach. "I'm not sure I'll ever be able to eat again."

"You will."

"Can we go somewhere and relax? Or would you like to rent bicycles or roller skates, maybe a flying saucer for a trip to the moon?"

"You're laughing at me?"

"I am, but it's been really fun. I've never been asked to do some of the things you suggested. Parasailing was wonderful. I'm glad we did it."

We'd stopped walking and were looking out at the water. It seemed to go on forever, at least until it met the sky. I sat down in the sand. Clay joined me. The sun had me squinting. It turned the ocean surface into a shimmering dance of jewels.

"It's so beautiful here," I said.

He looked at the water, his eyes sweeping the

limitless ocean and the uncluttered beach area. His eyes came back to me. "It surely is."

His arm went around my back. I leaned into him, my head resting on his shoulder. I inched closer to him until even air couldn't pass between us. We sat like that watching the gulls, the sky, and the water for longer than I'd ever been with a man who didn't try to make a move under those circumstances. The difference with Clay was I wanted him to make a move. I yearned for it, but he only held me.

We stayed at the beach talking and exchanging stories until dinnertime. Then we had dinner in the same little seaside restaurant. We ate inside, in a quiet little corner. And we danced afterward. Clay was a wonderful dancer, and being held in his arms was like heaven.

By the time I slipped my key in the door of the house, the day had died and slivers of sunlight streaking the eastern sky announced the beginning of another one.

"Today was perfect," I told him.

"Almost perfect," he said. His eyes bored into mine. I watched as he leaned into me, his mouth aiming for mine. When our lips met, the heavens must have had everything in alignment.

"Now it's perfect," he said.

I exhaled, then smiled.

Clay touched my chin. "You have a beautiful smile," he said.

I knew it was flattery. Yet it didn't keep me from giving him an even bigger smile and another laugh.

I felt wonderful. My heart was singing. Nothing could spoil how perfect this day had been.

"So tell me, you haven't thought of that other guy once today, have you?"

Except that, I thought. Orlando immediately came to mind. I hadn't thought of him all day, but I said, "What other guy?" I hoped Clay's reply wouldn't have anything to do with Orlando. He didn't know him, didn't know anything about him.

"The one who put the hurt in your eyes."

My smile froze as solid as the two miles of ice in Antarctica. I dropped my eyes. I wanted to turn away, put some space between us, but I stood my ground. "You know Orlando?" I hadn't said a thing about Orlando and I knew Jack and Amber wouldn't tell him. He didn't even know them.

"Is he the man who broke your heart?"

A million things went through my mind as to how I could respond to that, but none seemed as adequate as the truth.

"Was I that obvious?"

"You hide it well," he said. "But I've been there and I know the signs."

"You had a man break your heart?"

He laughed, stepping back and folding his arms across his chest. "It was a woman. About five years ago."

"How did you get over her?"

"Time, good friends, and traveling helped."

"How long did it take?"

"I don't know." He shrugged.

I'm sure I looked confused. I was confused.

"It doesn't happened from one day to the next. Just one day the hurt is a little less and finally it's gone. It does help if you have someone to guide you through it."

I looked skeptical. This sounded like he'd led

me straight to a pick-up line. "And I suppose you're applying for the job?"

"Not exactly." He voice was serious. I stood up straighter as if his words had strings that pulled me up.

"So you decided to be my savior?" I said as if he hadn't spoken.

"No!"

"You decided I needed someone to help me through the crisis, through my *bereavement*? And you appointed yourself."

"No, that's not how it was at all."

"Well, I don't need your sympathy. Thanks for a perfect day."

I turned the key in the lock so hard it should have broken off. But the door opened. I went inside and turned to slam it closed. At the last minute I remembered Jack and Amber were sleeping and softly closed and locked it.

In my room, I flopped on the bed and cried. How could he spoil such a wonderful day? I thought he was really interested in me, when all the time he was practicing drugstore psychology. But what really made me angry was it worked.

I hadn't thought of Orlando since the telephone rang and Clay's voice was at the other end.

Chapter 11

Joel was progressing well. He'd graduated from the side of the pool to the low diving board. The child and I were a lot alike. Joel wanted something and he was willing to work hard to get it. In his case, however, it was innocent and healthy.

In my case . . .

I couldn't finish the thought. I didn't know want to think about it. Don had planted the seed in my mind that I was cold and calculating. I was doing nothing more than anyone who went to an online dating service would do. I was typing in my qualifications and reading the messages that came my way. It was the same. Instead of a computer scanning the entries, Don was doing it for me. He was my dating service.

Or my pimp. Except that I only had to share one four-hour dance with him at the end of the summer.

I checked my watch. It was nearly noon. Time for me to meet Don for lunch. I slammed the locker closed in the ladies' dressing room and hoisted my gym bag over my shoulder. Moments later I dropped it in the car and returned to the hotel as if I'd just arrived.

Don met me at the dining room entrance. His ready smile, the one he used for guests, was in place.

"Hello," he said, as if we hadn't met on the beach that morning, as if he hadn't pinned me to the sand and kissed me wildly. Taking my elbow, he led me to a table near the windows. A man stood up as we approached it.

This had to be the man Don had mentioned this morning. I wasn't ready to meet him and Don probably knew that. I needed more time to figure out why Don had kissed me this morning. After telling me he was willing to join me in my plan, he ruined it by having my heart, body, and mind remember the feel of him, the taste of his mouth on mine. It wasn't a memory, something nebulous and without form, but a physical touching, holding, reacquaintance with a part of my makeup. Was he using it as a method of throwing me off guard? Of saying one thing while he did the opposite?

I stood up a little taller and squared my shoulders. Like Don, I smiled as we reached the table.

"Bob, meet Amber Nash," Don said.

"Mr. Yancey, Don has told me you like tennis."

"Bob, please. And I adore tennis," he replied. We all sat down, Don maneuvering me to sit next to Bob Yancey. "He tells me you're quite awesome on the court, too."

The waiter came over and took our drink order. I wondered if Don was planning to leave me alone with Bob, but he ordered a glass of iced tea and I took that as a signal that lunch would be for three.

I relaxed a bit knowing he would be there. At least he was someone I knew. I hadn't been on a blind date in forever, and I didn't much relish breaking the ice with someone I had not chosen to spend time with.

But as the waiter approached with our tray of drinks and took our food order, Don excused himself under the pretext of having things that needed his attention. He took his glass of iced tea and smiled at us as he walked away.

I searched for something to talk about when I turned back to Bob. I could ask about his business, but he might decide to tell me. I'd made that mistake with Casey, so I thought I'd go with something I liked. But Bob got there before me.

"When did you begin playing tennis?" he asked. "Don tells me you creamed him on the court the other day."

I smiled, taking a moment to think about my answer. "I started in grade school. My father was very sports minded and my sister and I tried everything. I love tennis, but I was on the diving team in college. For strength training, I used to play tennis. It helped with breathing and stamina."

"You must be good. I've played with Don before, and he can be formidable."

"I didn't exactly cream him. The game was interrupted by his job. He had to return to the hotel before we could finish."

"But you would have?"

"It ain't over till it's over," I hedged, falling back on the cliché. I knew the match could go either way. I could suddenly lose my edge or Don could find his. There was no telling until the game was finally done. But I felt I would have beat him if Jack hadn't interrupted the spectacle.

"Don said he scheduled some time for us to-morrow. Are you willing?"

"Of course," I answered. Then I challenged him. "Don also tells me I should let you win."

He sat back at that, his eyes opening a little wider than they had before, but not enough to feign surprise.

"Does that mean you're a sore loser or that winning is everything?" I asked.

"I like to think that I can win what I go after, but if I lose, I can take it."

I wasn't sure he meant he could take it from a woman.

Our food arrived and talk of tennis was dropped.

"Are you here for the music festival?" I asked between bites of my salad.

"That's one of the reasons. I come every year if work permits."

I kept myself from rolling my eyes. I didn't want him to go into a tirade on his job.

"How about you? Is this your first time on the Vineyard?"

I was so surprised I had to cover myself by taking a drink. Few men ever wanted to talk about what I did. They were too much into themselves. Bob might be the exception. I decided not to judge him and see where this went. Although I did remember to stay in character.

"I usually go to Europe, but this summer my two friends talked me into coming here. They're into jazz."

"And you're not?"

"I like the music, but I'm not as much into it as they are."

"So you're not planning to go to the concerts."

"Oh, I am. I wouldn't come this far and not go to the event of the summer."

"This far? Where are you from?"

"New York." I intentionally left out Brooklyn, although I was supposed to say Manhattan. And I left that out, too.

"I'm from New Jersey."

"A lot of pharmaceutical companies are in New Jersey."

"That's why I located mine there. Although I'm not in the corridor."

"Corridor?"

"There's a section of the state where the majority of them are concentrated. You can practically step from one company to the next along the same road. Mine is located farther south in a county with a lower tax base."

"I see." I wondered if this meant he was not only rich, but frugal, too. Well, wasn't that how the rich got rich? By being frugal?

"I learned the business by working for the big ones, but once I was downsized, I decided it was time to branch out on my own."

"That must have taken a lot of capital."

"There are investors out there. You must know, the rich only want to be richer."

I nodded without saying anything.

"When I explained my proposal and the product I was developing, the money came."

"I've invested in a few things, mostly stocks and bonds, but never in pharmaceuticals." That was true, but not on the order that I led him to believe.

"You should have your investment firm look into it. When you get a winner, it's very lucrative."

"I'll remember that," I said.

As the meal went on, I relaxed, laughed at his jokes, and enjoyed myself. When he asked me to have dinner with him, I readily accepted. Don had been right, I decided.

I did like Bob.

I skipped down the stairs at the sound of the doorbell ringing. Jack or Amber must have forgotten a key. Pulling the door inward, I was surprised to find the FedEx man standing on the porch.

"Package for Ms. Lila Easton," he said, pronouncing my name as Lilly instead of Lila.

"I'm Lila Easton."

He thrust an electronic signature notebook in front of me.

"Sign here?"

I signed in the desired space with the leadless pencil he handed me. No image appeared in the space but on an LED panel above the writing area.

He smiled and handed me a box. I thanked him and he walked back toward the truck parked at the curb.

Looking at the address slip, I wondered who it was from. I wasn't expecting anything. My parents knew where I was, but it wasn't my birthday or a holiday. The office wouldn't send anything here either.

Lifting the box closer and squinting at the light script, I deciphered Clay's name. The package was from Clay. I dropped it on the table in the kitchen. I hadn't taken his phone calls since our perfect day.

I suppose this was his way of contacting me, forcing me to communicate.

Well, he was wrong.

He had no right to assume that I needed a baby-sitter. That I needed someone to guide me through the process of getting over Orlando. It was a private matter. He had no right to invade my life, to assume that he knew what I needed better than I did.

I left the package unopened on the kitchen counter and returned to my bedroom. I was going out. I'd been in the house too long. This was what I did when Orlando left me. Other than work, I secluded myself in my apartment, eating chocolates and ice cream. It changed nothing. I was going to go out and find someone. Someone unlike Clay. Unlike Orlando. Someone who didn't think he could or needed to make me over.

When I dressed and returned to the kitchen, the package was still there. It called to me. I wanted to know what was inside. It was a small box—too large to be jewelry, but too small to be anything significant. Yet I wanted to know what was inside.

"Shit," I said. "Open the damn thing."

Grabbing the box, I ripped the tape from the seams, cutting through the address label with Clay's name on it. Pulling back the flaps and removing the packing material, I found a small wooden rocking chair. It was doll-size, intricately carved, and the back had my name painted in a scroll design.

My breath caught at the loving detail that had gone into the work. Unexpectedly, tears came to my eyes. I blinked them away, catching sight of a piece of paper with writing on it.

Please forgive me, was all it said, each word underlined for emphasis. It was signed *Clay*, in a strong and sure handwriting.

I picked up the chair again, caressing it as if it were fragile and more precious than gold.

As I left the house, I heard someone call my name. I knew instantly it was Clay. Turning in the direction of his voice, I saw him standing near the edge of the driveway looking at me. He wore khaki shorts and a green T-shirt. Over his left breast was a pocket with faded words I couldn't read.

"It's beautiful," I said as he approached me. "I've never seen anything as beautiful. Thank you."

"It was my pleasure."

"You carved it?"

He nodded.

"It's a treasure." I hesitated a moment. "I'm sorry for the way I acted," I continued.

"I am, too. I should never have tried to give you advice on something I have very little experience doing."

"It was kind of you to think to help me. I should be grateful for that."

"Friends again?" he questioned.

"Friends," I said, seeing his shoulders drop in relief.

He came forward then and embraced me, kissing my cheek. I felt as if I'd been parted from him for a lifetime instead of a few days. His body was warm and his smell sent a thrill through me.

His hands followed my arms down to my hands and he held them, taking a step back. "What would you like to do today? How about going on that trip to the moon you mentioned?"

I held my laughter and played along. "I don't have the proper clothes for space travel."

"Then how about a plain ol' swim? For that you don't have to dress at all."

Blood poured from where he touched my fingers to my face, heating my ears at the sexual insinuation evident in his tone. A mental picture of his body, naked and erect, flashed in my mind. I blinked to dislodge it, but it wouldn't leave, giving me something to carry around for this and the next lifetimes.

"I'd better get my suit," I said. "Come on." I rushed inside and up to my room. Clay came inside, but waited downstairs. The distance between us helped me to keep my thoughts from continuing on the track they were headed. Quickly I changed clothes, returning in five minutes with everything I'd need for a day at the beach.

As I ran down the stairs, Jack came in.

"Hi, Jack," I said. I wondered if Amber was anywhere near. Quickly I introduced her to Clay. Then, like a teenager hiding something from my parents, I ushered him out the door and into the car.

Clay drove to the beach where we'd sat like lovers a few days earlier. It was great to be back with him again. I liked him, liked him a lot. I felt I could be natural with him. He didn't ask probing questions, so I didn't have to lie about my background.

There was a moment when I thought he could see through the veil. That he didn't believe my father owned a pharmaceutical company. But when he brought up Orlando, I felt if he didn't believe me, he'd have said something.

Clay spread a blanket on the sand along with a picnic basket he brought from the backseat of the car. I sat on it and looked at him.

"When did you have that made?" I ask, indicating the basket.

"I didn't have it made. I made it. Well, most of it."

"Who made the other part?"

"My aunt. Right after she told me to go and take you swimming."

"Your aunt?" I was clearly surprised. "You told your aunt about me?"

"I'm her favorite nephew and she could see I was unhappy."

I felt a little guilty for making him unhappy. I understood how he felt. I'd been miserable during the days I hadn't seen him.

"How about we swim first?" he suggested.

"Sure." I grabbed at the offer, needing to pass the moment.

Together we pulled off our clothes. I prayed he was kidding about not needing a suit. I also sent up a prayer that if Clay was wearing one, it wasn't a Speedo. The gods were with me.

My attire was a one-piece hot pink, high-thigh-cut suit I'd bought at Saks before we came here. We ran toward the water, rushing into it only to find the surf shocking and cold. Yet it felt good compared to my warm skin. In minutes I was swimming across the surface, keeping a well-fixed distance between myself and the black Adonis nearby.

Clay's sure and strong strokes reached out toward me, but I was a good swimmer and we found ourselves racing. There were no boundaries in the ocean. He pursued and I eluded him. He finally caught up with me.

"You're a strong swimmer."

"I love swimming and do it regularly," I told him,

both of us treading water. I felt a thrill that he acknowledged my ability.

"Well, this exercise has made me hungry. Wanna race me back?"

Instead of answering him, I took off, giving myself a two-stroke lead over him. I wasn't sure I could win. I was tired from the previous race and Clay was right on my heels. As I kicked, I sometimes slapped his hands with my feet. The knowledge threw me off. I'd forget to breathe and be disciplined with a mouthful of water.

As we neared the shoreline and the area where we'd left our blanket and clothes, I stood up and walked, the surf curling around my ankles. Sand coated my legs as I headed for the blanket. Just as I reached it, I could feel Clay behind me. I turned to see how far back he was, figuring he'd let me win the race and that he was admiring my backside as I strolled across the warm sand.

He was about six feet away, far enough for me to watch him, see his body from head to toe. He didn't look like a guy who made furniture, more like someone who did bodybuilding. His arms and shoulders were massive. I could almost feel them holding me, although he wasn't touching me.

And I suddenly wanted to be touched.

As he neared me, I raised my arms. Clay walked into them and I hugged him close. Angling my mouth, I sought his, yearned for the feel of it. His mouth came down on mine as if he had a right to it. I didn't struggle. I'd wanted him to kiss me since the day he took me parasailing, since the moment I saw him over the tomatoes in the grocery store.

His mouth was soft at first, unhurried. His lips skated over mine, almost asking for permission or giving me the time and space to stop this before it went any further. Stopping was the last thing on my mind. I moved a little closer to him, my hands taking a slow trip over his wet torso and connecting behind him. He wrapped me securely against him, his mouth taking charge, deepening the kiss, sweeping his tongue in my mouth as if I were the picnic lunch.

Clay feasted on me. And I had no objection.

"It's a good thing we're on the beach," he said after a moment so long I didn't think I could continue standing.

"Why?" I asked breathlessly.

"If we weren't I'd rip your clothes off and take you right here."

"You wouldn't need to rip them."

Chapter 12

I could not believe my good luck. Bob was perfect. So far.

Not that I was looking for fault in him, but other than being rich, he was considerate, charming, and funny. And he was straight. At least I thought so.

We had yet to play tennis. That would come in the morning, but after dinner and dancing tonight, he made sure I was home in time to get enough sleep for our early-morning tennis game.

"Are you an early riser?" I asked as we left the hotel.

"I'm usually at work by six," he said.

"Which is why we have a court time at seven?" I asked.

"We can make it later if that's too early," he offered.

"The time is fine," I conceded. He was also considerate of my sleeping habits and energy level for an early-morning game. As I was also an early riser, the time was not an issue.

He'd kissed me on the cheek and immediately stepped out of range. With a soft good night, he went down the steps and got into his car. I opened the door, and as he turned around and passed the house, his hand came out of the window and he waved good night.

I sniffed as I closed the front door. Something was cooking and it smelled delicious. I walked into the kitchen. The room was in disarray. Practically every pot and pan from the vast storehouse of utensils sat upright or turned over on the counter, sink, and center island.

Laughter came from the dining room. I walked to the door. Lila jumped up from a man's lap where she'd been sitting, about to feed him something from the spoon in her hand. Both spoon and food plopped to the floor. The man stood up.

"Amber, you're home early," Lila said, her voice a little shaky.

And obviously too soon, I thought.

"This is . . . this is Clay." Lila's hand kind of waved at her side, as if she was trying to hide him. As tall as he was, hiding him was a useless exercise.

I stepped farther into the room and walked over to Clay. He was a tall man with dark skin and short hair. He had a mustache and dark eyes and his arm was surrounding Lila.

"Amber Nash," I said since my friend had forgotten her manners with my appearance.

"Clay Reynolds."

We shook hands. "It's nice to meet you again." In Lila's state she'd forgotten that Clay had arrived previously with four bags of groceries. He'd cooked lunch that day, and tonight he apparently had cooked dinner.

I wanted to go to bed, but suddenly I felt like a third wheel. Lila and Clay obviously had their evening planned, and it was awkward for all of us if I was in the house. So in that moment I knew I had to leave.

"We decided to go for a swim. I just came in to change," I said. I addressed my comments to Lila. "I'll only be a moment."

Again I turned to Clay. "The food smells good. Since I know Lila is a disaster in the kitchen, you must be the reason for the delicious food."

"Thank you," Clay said. "She did help." His voice was deep, almost radio DJ quality. He had shoulders and arms to go with it. If I had to give him characteristics, cooking would not be one of them. But he was exactly the kind of man that attracted Lila.

"Good night," I said. As I turned to leave, I noticed the dropped spoon and bent down and retrieve it. Turning back, I extended it to Lila. "I believe this is yours."

I stepped through the door I'd entered only a few minutes earlier. Where was I going to go? I couldn't drive around the island in the dark. Besides, that would only take a little time. And I had the feeling Lila and Clay would be in the house a little longer than the drive I had in mind.

Don came to mind, his image filling my consciousness. I didn't know many people on the Vineyard, at least not well enough to show up on their doorstep uninvited. That left the beach as my only option. I'd changed into jeans and a sweatshirt. The beach was a little chilly at this hour. The Inkwell was deserted. There was a concert going on and it had obviously taken many of the beachcombers from their nightly party.

I sat in my car for a few minutes and then thought it crazy to forsake my bed for Lila and her date. Starting the engine, I turned the car toward the hotel. I could return to the lounge, sit at the bar until it was *safe* to go home. The problem was I wasn't a drinker. I had an occasional glass of wine and loved margaritas, but I wasn't about to get wasted waiting for her. And I was driving.

In the parking lot, I got out of the car and walked into the lobby of the St. Romaine.

"I'm sorry, Ms. Nash, but we have no vacant rooms," the night clerk said to me moments later.

"Nothing?" I asked.

"Because of the festival, we're booked to capacity."

"Could you do me a favor and call one of the other hotels—"

"They're booked, too," the desk clerk said, interrupting me. "We tried earlier to send some guests there who'd come in for the day and wanted to stay overnight. All the places we tried were full."

I knew I wasn't going to get any more out of her. I smiled and thanked her, then left. I supposed my car would have to do. I headed to the parking lot. As I stepped on the blacktop, I stopped and stared the car for a long moment. Glancing over my shoulder, I looked in the direction of Don's bungalow. Immediately I rejected the idea of going there. My heels clicked on the ground as I continued toward the car. Somewhere between getting to the driver's door and actually opening it, my feet seemed to have a mind of their own. They carried me through the hedges and past the tennis court. Without even thinking, I was standing in front of Don's guest house door.

This was insane, I told myself.

Then I range the bell.

Don answered almost immediately. Deja vu at the last time I was there flew through my mind.

"This is a surprise," he said. Crossing his ankles, he rested his shoulder against the doorjamb in a totally relaxed stance.

"I need a bed for the night," I said.

"You're in luck," he said. "I happen to have one."

"I'm not inviting myself into your bed," I said.

"I'm sure you know there is a hotel just around the path." He leaned out and looked in the direction of the main building. "Their business is to rent rooms."

"I thought of that. And both of us know the hotel has no vacancies."

"We're not the only hotel on the Vineyard." Don crossed his arms and stared at me. I couldn't help noticing the muscular definition in his arms. Or remembering how they felt when they were wrapped around me.

"All the hotels are booked, as you well know."

"Did you try Mr. Edwards's room?" Then he snapped his fingers as if remembering something. "Oh yeah, he's got his son in there. What about Bob's room? I'm sure he'd be willing to share his bed with you."

"Thanks," I muttered. "I should have known better." I wanted to kick myself for letting my feet walk me here.

Turning around, I started back for the parking lot. I'd sleep in the car before suffering through this abuse.

"Wait a minute." Don caught my arm and pulled me around. He was wearing a huge smile. "I was only joking with you."

"It's a bed I want, nothing else." I emphasized what I wanted by the tone of my voice.

Despite my voice, Don's voice was low and sexy. "Liar."

"I didn't really mean I wanted to sleep here. I thought you might be able to pull a string and find me a room. I can afford to pay for it."

I watched his eyes change, as if I'd hit him with something.

"The hotel is full." He spread his hands in defeat.

"Don't they keep a room or two for emergency VIP guests?"

"You mean like the president showing up unannounced and needing a room for the night."

I nodded. "Something like that. Although I doubt the president can show up unannounced. Or that he'll need only one room."

"No." He shook his head. "May I ask why it is you're without lodgings? You have a rented house for the summer."

I turned away, taking a few steps, then turning back to face him. "Lila has a guest. I assume he's there for the night."

"She has her own room, right?"

"Sure she does, but I felt a little uncomfortable."

"Where's your third?"

"Jack? She had a date and wasn't there when I left." I didn't think Jack would be coming back before daybreak. And since she wasn't a morning person, daybreak for her occurred somewhere near noon.

"So it was the hotel or the beach?" Don asked.

"I tried the beach. It was deserted."

"And I'm the last bed on the Vineyard?"

As usual when I was in Don's company I could

drop all pretense. I did and nodded. "I'm not asking for anything more."

At that moment, I knew there would be more. It was unfair to Don, when we both knew that I was looking for assets beyond his reach. "Thanks, Don. It won't be necessary. Lila will have to get by with me in the house." I walked to him and gave his arm a squeeze. "You're a strange man. I've never met anyone like you. Thanks for being my friend."

The comment was more for me than him. I had to keep telling myself he was a friend and not a lover.

I turned and left. I wouldn't impose on Don. I liked him. Too much, I knew. In fact, I could easily fall in love with him.

I'd taken a few steps across the tennis court, taking a shortcut to my car when I heard Don call my name.

Jogging to me, he said, "You're not leaving." Taking my arm, he led me back to the guest house.

"Don, you're wrong. I didn't come here to spend the night." Well, actually I had, but I no longer wanted that.

"Why did you come here?"

"I'm not really sure. It's just that with you . . . when I'm around you . . ."

He finished my sentence. "You can be you?"

"True," I said as we reached the guest house. He'd propped the door open. Inside he kicked the small wooden triangle aside and closed it.

"Guest room or my room?"

Incinerator-level heat shot through me, burning my throat and robbing me of the ability to speak. Don stepped forward, saving me from having to reply to his question. His arms reached out and I fell like a magnet into them. He held me, lightly at first. Slowly the pressure increased as he pulled me closer. I felt a long sigh as our bodies talked to each other. His hands moved over me, familiarizing themselves with my curves, remembering that we had stood like this before. Our bodies had known each other before.

Describing the feeling that raced through me as Don's hands closed around my waist was not possible. It was like finding safety after a long night of danger. His hands caressed my back, enfolding me to him as if I were the most precious gift on earth.

I wanted to please him, wanted to give him the same awesome feeling he was giving me. Slipping my hands under his shirt, I felt the moistness of his skin. As I moved my hands across his flanks, I felt as if they were dipped in warm, dark chocolate.

His stomach was flat and hard and he shuddered as my thumbs brushed across it and up to his nipples. Hard hands gripped my arms as if Don needed something solid to hold on to.

After holding me still for a long moment, he pushed me back for the second it took to rip his shirt over his head and throw it toward a corner. Then I was back in his arms. His mouth sank into my neck with a wet kiss that had me shivering with heated delight. I lifted my head, giving him greater access.

"That feels so good," I crooned, barely recognizing the depth of my own voice.

"Woman, you drive me crazy." Each one of Don's words was punctuated with a kiss that traveled up my neck to my ears, then across my eyes and down to the corners of my mouth.

The anticipation had me panting. I moved my

head, seeking his mouth. Both of his hands threaded through my hair and he angled my mouth to his in a kiss that burned through everything I'd ever thought a kiss could be. Life as I knew it changed. I sagged against him. His body accepted my weight and his arms moved to hold me tight.

At the same time, his mouth worked like a narcotic elixir on mine. His erection grew, pressing into my legs, which opened to accommodate him. I moaned, moving even closer to him, seeking the heat of his body, feeling his naked skin under my hands.

Suddenly I wanted my skin next to his. I wanted to feel the energy, the electricity of our bodies devoid of impediments, pressing together like matching spoons. I reached for the bottom of my shirt. Don's hand covered mine and pulled it over my head. His fingers crisscrossed my back until he'd covered my skin from waist to shoulders and down the length of my arms.

He took a moment to stare at me as the shirt pooled at my feet. My jeans and shoes joined the shirt. I wore only a bra, panties. I felt no embarrassment, no nakedness.

"I do love red," Don said, taking in the color of my silk bra and panties. He took my hands and spread them their full length, appraising me from tip to toe. I was suddenly proud of my hours of swimming laps.

Pulling me with him, he went to the bedroom. There was no question of which one. I turned into his arms the moment the door closed. My mouth quivered, itching to reconnect with his. Our kiss was wet and urgent. Want and need were evident in the pressure each of us applied to the other. Our tongues danced and mated. Pushing against him, I got closer, pulling myself up until one of my legs left the floor and wrapped around one of his.

I heard a low, guttural sound in his throat. My hands went to the belt at his waist. Loosening it, I unzipped his pants, taking a moment to press my hand against his erection. His body was hot and hard. Weakness flowed over me at the thought of him inside me. But the anticipation of it drove me on.

Dropping his pants, I grabbed his legs and squeezed them, drawing them into me. Surprise registered on his face. I slipped my fingers in the waistband of his briefs and pushed them down, exposing him to me. Magnificent, I thought. Don Randall had a beautiful body, and my hands loved touching him. I smoothed my palms over his features, moving slowly, taking time to give attention to each attractive square of skin.

Walking backward until my legs came up against the bed, I sat down. Don kneeled before me. His arms slipped around my waist. Nimbly his fingers unhooked my bra. "You know, the first time I saw you, you were wearing red shoes."

"Really?"

"Really," he repeated. "You were getting out of the limousine." He kissed my breasts, teasing my nipples, which puckered as if asking for more attention. "I was sitting in my car in front of the place you rent." Fingers slipped around the elastic top of my silk panties. I wondered what he was doing at the house, but his hands dipped inside my panties and found the one spot on my body that eliminated all thoughts of conversation and shot a narcotic of Love Potion No. 9 through me.

His hands massaged my sweet spot. My eyes closed and my head lolled loosely back on my neck. Slowly he slipped the red fabric off my body, down my legs, and over my feet.

My arms went around his neck. I felt good knowing that he'd taken the time to stare at me. I pulled him closer. His tongue laved my nipple, his mouth sucked. Clamping my teeth down on my lower lip, I held my breath as pleasure rioted through me. I didn't want it to stop. I wanted more of it. My stomach clenched and I felt a sexual need so strong it couldn't be controlled.

I pushed Don off balance and he sprawled backward onto the floor. As his arms went around me, I went with him, straddling his body and feeling the strength of his legs against mine as I teased him by moving my smooth ones over his hair-roughened ones. His mouth sought mine. At the same time, my hands closed around his penis and I guided it into the essence of my body.

Both of us sighed at the pleasure of invasion. My inner muscles grabbed Don and held him as I lowered myself over the length of him. The sound he made couldn't be described. It was a mixture of pleasure and pain. I recognized it because I knew the sound. I could reproduce it, and did when his body thrust upward into mine. A yo-yo of emotions rocketed through me. A momentary weakness had me leaning forward. Don leaned up and ran his fingers across my breasts. His mouth brushed my cleavage.

"Come on, baby, ride me. Ride me hard," he said.

I did. Planting my hands on the floor by his arms and sliding my legs up tightly against his, I set a dizzying pace. Don's moans were music in the electrically charged room. His hands on my hips mimicked the rhythm and had me panting at the sensations that flowed in and out of me. Heat surrounded me with the intensity of the sun. Sweat poured off us both.

Tension mounted in me as my heartbeat soared. I didn't think it was possible to move any faster, to have pleasure wash over me in waves of sensation. But Don's body stroked deeper and deeper into me with each rapid thrust. I felt the build. Held it off. I wanted to prolong the rapture, keep this feeling going until I couldn't stand it any longer—and then take it one step further.

But I couldn't. My body bucked and snapped as Don's thrusts became harder and harder. I heard him groaning, uttering incoherent sounds. I knew he was close to climax. I could feel it in the rising tension of his body. Suddenly something inside me burst. I didn't see stars or rainbows, just a blinding flash of light that seemed to hold an entire life in the short space of time it took to erupt, but all the pleasure of the universe sparked through my body in that one single instant.

I collapsed onto Don. My breathing was heavy and ragged as I sucked long drafts of air into my lungs. Don did the same thing. His arms lay on my back, heavy, and kept me in place. Not that I could move if I'd wanted to. My muscles were so lethargic they refused to obey mental commands.

"Are you all right?" Don asked.

I would have laughed if my body would have let me. As it was, I could only grunt, say nothing, do nothing except take in open-mouth breaths. I wasn't all right. I didn't think I would ever be all right again. This was a new experience. Never had anything like this happened before, not even with the man I was still intimately connected to. I wondered if it would always be this way. Would he surprise me again and again with the depth of lovemaking that had just occurred? Would I be more wanton with any other man? Would what I felt, what I'd done, ever happen with anyone else?

"Amber?" Don called my name. I could hear concern in his voice. I lifted my head and looked in his eyes. "Are you all right?" he asked again.

I shook my head.

Don smiled and cradled me in his arms.

Chapter 13

Don was gone when I woke up. He probably needed to be on duty for the breakfast crowd, or maybe new groups were checking in and out. I slipped out of bed. It was six o'clock and I had an hour to get back to the house, shower, change clothes, and meet Bob for our tennis game. Today's game wasn't going to be my best. After last night's sexual gymnastics, I needed time to rebound. Sleeping until late morning sounded refreshing, but standing up someone on my A-list was both rude and foolish.

Neither Lila nor Jack were around to see me creep in the front door and head straight for my bedroom. And neither one of them saw me slip out of the door and drive back to the tennis court. I parked the car and got out just in time to see Bob walk onto the court.

My body still pulsated from my night with Don. I was in no way ready for a tennis game. I wanted to go to the beach, laze in the sun, and dream about how good I felt. I wanted to indulge in the fantasy, relive the night in my mind and let the arousing effect it had on my body pretend it was real.

"Ready?" Bob shouted to me as I grabbed my racket from the back seat and started toward him.

I smiled and waved in return. I wasn't ready. And this was apparent three sets later when he creamed me 6-1.

"Nice game," he said, meeting me at the net for the traditional handshake. We walked to the side of the court to collect our belongings.

"You'll have to give me a rematch." I refused to tell him that I wasn't at my best. It would sound like an excuse.

"I'd love to. But we'll have to do it back in Jersey."

"Jersey?"

"I'm afraid I have to leave later this morning."

"Has something happened?" Don had told me Bob was staying for a week.

"Something good. It's business. A major deal with a big pharma company."

I could see the excitement in every line of his body.

"It's something I've dreamed about, but never thought would happen." He stopped and looked at the sky, giving a big laugh as a thank-you to the heavens. "We approached them with an idea for a joint venture. And I got word yesterday that they want to talk."

"Congratulations." I gave him my best smile and tried to look as excited as he felt. "When do you leave?"

"I'm taking the ferry at noon."

"Can you wait that long? You look like you could fly under your own power."

He laughed. "I have time for breakfast. Would you like to join me?"

I was starving. I hadn't had anything to eat since dinner last night. But going into the dining room or even eating outside meant Don would invariably come by, and I wasn't ready to face him just yet.

"I not very hungry," I lied. "I'll get something back at the house after I shower." I paused a moment. "I'm sure you have some last-minute packing to do and you'll want to prepare for your meeting."

"I made some notes and thought of a few other things to put in a presentation."

I smiled. I was truly happy for him.

"Well, it was great meeting you," he said. He leaned forward and kissed me on the cheek just as he done last night. His skin was warm, but nothing fissured through me at his touch the way lightning struck when Don came near me.

"I would like to see you again. New York and New Jersey aren't that far apart," Bob said.

"I agree. I'd like to see you again, too."

He handed me a card. It was his business card and identified him as the CEO of a biotech firm. On the back, in a strong scrawl, he'd written his home and cell phone numbers.

I opened my purse and pulled out my own card. It was cream colored and contained only my name and phone number. I'd had them printed a few days before we left just for situations like this one. Bob took the card. He seemed at a loss for what to say or do next.

I read his dilemma of excitement for a new challenge and confusion at leaving another one. "It's all right," I said. "You should hurry. You don't want to miss the ferry."

I watched him leave. His day was going well. I knew from the way he'd played tennis that he liked winning. The lightness of his step gave away his expectancy about the upcoming deal. Already I was a memory, replaced by a new hunt, a new hunger that was inherent in his being. Beating me at tennis was another victory he could add to the roll of good fortune that seemed to be coming his way.

I was happy for him. I wanted more time to learn about him. Maybe he was the one. He certainly had the assets. And now he had my phone number, but who knew if he'd use it.

I looked at the card I was holding. Telephone lines and rotating satellites worked both ways. And I knew how to dial a phone.

Bob had no sooner disappeared through the trees than Don came walking over. I wondered if he'd been waiting in the bushes for the moment Bob left. Slipping the business card in the pocket of my shorts, I turned to face Don.

"How'd it go?" he asked.

"Weren't you watching?" He always seemed to be underfoot, and frankly I was a little miffed at the moment. I didn't need him showing up as a reminder of what had happened last night. Or to gloat over my lost prospect. It was daylight now and things were different.

"Of course I wasn't watching. I just saw Bob bounding up the stairs. I guess that means you didn't beat him."

"He beat me solidly," I confessed. I started walking to the parking lot. Don's appearance jangled my nerves, and I needed to do something other than stand in front of him and remember the strength of his naked body plunging into mine.

"Beat you or did you let him win?"

"I never let anyone win intentionally. You should know that." As soon as the words left my mouth I realized the double meaning they could have.

"Did it have anything to do with . . ."

"He's leaving." I said it quickly, refusing to let Don complete the sentence. I didn't want to have him saying anything about last night. My feelings were as jumbled as Christmas tree lights after a summer in storage.

"Leaving?" The surprised look on Don's face told me he didn't know about Bob's good news.

"A lucrative business deal seems to be falling into place. He has to go back."

"Well, that should be good news for you. You're looking for a man with money. Bob's your man. He's got both potential and a fortune. And with your looks, you two could go to the top."

"Stop it." I stared at him, withering him with my look. "I hate it when you try to make me feel guilty."

"I'm not trying to do that. I'm pointing out the parts of your plan you don't want to confront. It's not my fault you don't like what you see."

"What do you see, Don?"

"I see a beautiful woman, selling herself to the man with the highest bank account."

"I'm not selling myself to anyone." I threw my racket through the car window and onto the backseat. Then I looked up at Don. "Would it be more palatable to you if I went to a computer and pulled up a dating service window? I could fill in all the pertinent information: eye color, weight, educational background, values, what I want out of life . . ."

"Net worth?" he supplied.

"Net worth," I continued. "Then I'd qualify to pull the dance cards of the men with the most potential and fortune."

He stood mutely.

"What I'm doing is no different. Instead of using a computer, I'm using a music festival, a tennis court, a huge house, and all the money I have in the world." I stared at him for a long moment. "It isn't me who doesn't like what I'm doing. It's you."

"You're right. You're damn right," he told me. "I don't like it. You can try to whitewash it if you want, but it sneaky, deliberate, and downright immoral."

"And you have a better plan."

He took a step forward. I wanted to move back, but forced myself to remain in place. Tension radiated between us like burning jet fuel. After a long moment, Don dropped his shoulders and stepped back. He shook his head, the gesture clearly defeatist.

"No, I don't have a better plan. But I wish to hell I did."

What in the hell was I doing? What was I thinking? Why did this woman have the ability to turn me into a sixteen-year-old, hormone-ridden kid who couldn't control his erections? I had responsibilities to the hotel guests, a meeting to prepare for, presentations to complete. Yet every moment of the day and night was filled with thoughts of Amber Nash.

I'd made sure I was around the tennis court

when she and Bob finished their game. I wanted to see her. When I'd left her sleeping this morning, I knew I wanted her there when I got back. I wanted to come in at the end of the day and find her.

But she was looking for someone else.

Hearing that Bob was leaving the Vineyard, cutting his vacation short for a business deal was a welcome relief in my eyes. One less competitor, I thought. Yet I wasn't a competitor. I wasn't on Amber's radar. So why was I beating my head against a brick wall?

I nearly fell over when I saw her standing on my doorstep last night. She really only needed a place to sleep, but I needed more than that. I needed her, and I wasn't about to forgo an opportunity to see if we could repeat our first mating.

The answer was no.

The repeat was an experience that had grown up, graduated, not by a notch but by a Grand Canyon leap. Being with her was like winning the world lottery.

But I wasn't going to be with her.

Amber pulled out of the parking lot, leaving a layer of rubber behind. It was my fault, but I didn't care. I was angry and I hated myself for it. She had not pretended with me. She told me what she wanted. I'm the fool who took it as a challenge, who thought I could change her mind. But she was on a track and nothing I did had derailed her.

I couldn't say what was wrong with me. She was beautiful, but not the most beautiful woman I'd ever met. She had brains and went after what she wanted. These were qualities that I admired, but didn't often see in the women I dated.

What ticked the hell out of me was the way we

were together. The fire and the explosions that occurred when we joined, even the sparks that flew between us when we were both in the same room, I wanted no man to know about except me. I wanted this woman like I'd never wanted anyone else.

But she didn't want me. And that pissed the hell out of me.

I made a point of not slamming the door as I came into the house. I wanted to rip the wood from the hinges. Why did I let Don Randall do this to me? And why was he always somewhere just behind me?

"Is that you, Amber?" I heard Jack call my name from the kitchen. I could hear Lila, too. I didn't expect them to be awake yet. Following the sound, I joined them.

The coffee was fresh and I poured myself a cup and leaned against the counter while I took a sip.

"Been out all night?" Lila asked, her lip turning up in a gesture of innocent knowing.

"Don't start with me," I told her. "I'm in no mood. And where I've been is your fault."

"My fault?" She feigned surprise. "What did I do?"

I glanced at the table where she was sitting. It was the same seat she'd occupied last night when I walked in on her. Except this time, it was her ass that was in the chair instead of a half-naked man's. At that moment I stopped. I could see myself about to say or do something foolish. My anger wasn't with Lila. "I'm sorry, Lila. It isn't your fault."

"What isn't her fault?" Jack asked. She swung her glance from me to Lila and back again.

"Nothing," I said and put my cup on the counter.

I walked toward the door, thinking of going to my room and sleeping. Lord knows I didn't get a good night's sleep last night. And I could kick myself this morning for what I actually did. What I told myself I would never do again.

"Amberlina." Jack knew the one word that would stop me in my tennis shoes. "What is going on?"

I turned back, making an effort to dampen the anger that flared bright red in my mind.

"Nothing is going on," I said. "I'm a little tired. I lost at tennis this morning."

"To that dreamy hotel manager?" Lila purred, her voice both teasing and approving. She scooted her bottom around in the chair and wiggled her shoulders, doing her version of the sexual dance.

I clamped my teeth together. "I didn't play against Don." That wasn't true. I'd been doing nothing except playing against Don since I stepped on this island.

"So, who did you play?"

"It doesn't matter. He's leaving this morning anyway."

"Who?"

"Why?"

Lila and Jack spoke at the same time.

"His name is Bob Yancey. He owns a biotech in New Jersey."

"Mmm, close to home," Jack said. "Owns his own company. Sounds like he fits the bill, or at least he's on the right side of the street."

I frowned. Bob had seemed perfect. Why was I second-guessing him now? "It's business that's taking him back to New Jersey. It comes first in his life. I know it always will. If I was to call him . . ." I reached in my pocket and pulled out the card he'd

given me, waving it slightly in the air. "I know I'd
never be the one. Business would always come
before me. It's not something I can't live with. It
might be a good thing. I haven't totally crossed him
off the list. In fact, he's heading it at the moment.
But I'm keeping my options open in case he's not
the man I'm looking for."

"Who are you looking for? That hotel guy seems
pretty hot to me," Lila said.

"Let's leave him out of this."

"I've always felt that type of comment meant you
think of no one else except the one you want to
leave out." Lila emphasized the last two words, giving
each one of them a full measure of time. "So come
on, tell us what's got you so agitated."

"That's who or whom?" Jack filled in. "I could
never remember the difference. But both of them
relate to a man."

"So sit down and spill it."

I hesitated a while, taking a moment to look
from one to the other, but the two women in this
room were my best friends. I walked back to my seat
and sat down. I told them the story. Everything that
had happened since we stepped out of the limousine and entered this house.

When I finished, there was silence. Jack and Lila
stared at me as if there was more, an ending I was
withholding.

"And you're not crazy about this guy?" Jack
broke the silence.

"He's not the reason I came here."

"Fuck the reason," Lila said. "He's the one."

"No, he's not," I moaned. "And I don't think he
wants to see me." I remembered our argument this
morning. Don was so angry.

"Then go see *him*," Jack said.

"Go see him," I mimicked. "I'm not going to see him. I don't care if I ever see him again."

Jack and Lila gave each other a knowing look.

"I don't," I stated as boldly as if I'd stamped my foot.

The Inkwell pitched out to sea in a triangular shape. Most people expected it to stretch around in the horseshoe arc that suggested its name. I sat in my beach chair writing. Well, I was thinking of writing. Usually this was what I did in the early morning while I waited for Don to come by on his daily jog. Usually he would stop, hunker down in the sand, and spend a few minutes with me. But he'd been missing for the past few days.

The first day I thought he was sulking. Childish behavior for a grown man, but no one liked to have their ego trampled on, no matter what age. The second and third days I chalked up to anger. Now I was wondering if something had happened to him. While I was at the hotel, refusing to change my routine even if he changed his, there wasn't a sign of him. He didn't appear while I went through my dives or when I swam laps. My daily lesson to Joel went unattended by anyone except the boy's father.

No one mentioned Don to me either, and there was no idle conversation that I overheard where his name came up. He'd disappeared as surely as a ghost could dematerialize.

Now I thought Don was avoiding me. Why? What did I do? I wasn't the one who gave him my key and invited him to my bed. I didn't ask him to get involved with me. This was all his idea. I was open with my plan. He was the one who jumped in with the suggestion of helping. So I harbored no guilt over the way he felt.

Turning back to my notebook, I read the page I had written and poised my pen to write another sentence. Nothing came. Looking out on the ocean, I listened to the lapping of waves, the caw of the gulls overhead, and the soft whisper of the breeze. And in the back of my mind, I listened for the pounding feet of a jogger heading my way.

It was a sound that did not come.

Giving up, I packed my things early and returned to the house. There was still a full day's activities I had planned. I wouldn't have to think of Don Randall unless I wanted to. And right now he was the last thing on my mind.

The fact that there was nothing else blocking him was a minor point.

Being a woman born and bred in Brooklyn, the closest to a horse I'd come, prior to stepping on this island, was seeing the mounted police in the Central Park. But of the new experiences I collected day after day, I found that I liked horses and I liked riding.

Amber spent her mornings by the ocean; I spent mine on horseback. Today I arrived a few minutes early and was doing some window-shopping at the stable gift shop when a shadow hulked over me.

I felt him before I saw him.

Whipping around, fear catching me and forcing my heart rate up several points, I saw Shane.

"Well, if it isn't the postcard lady. Jacynthia, right?"

"Shane," I said, relieved it was him and not some stranger bent on an early-morning attack in an up-scale gift shop. "Good memory."

The smile on my face, after the fear wore off, must have been as bright as the sun. For a moment my heart tugged. I hadn't expected to see him again. I wasn't sure if he was still on the Vineyard. The concert was a week ago. Yet it was a pleasure and a relief to see him.

"I thought you'd have left the Vineyard by now," I said.

"I'm here for a while," he said. "Glad to see you're still here, too."

I nodded. "I'm here for the summer." I wanted him to keep talking, wanted him to stay around. I couldn't ever remembering feeling like I wanted someone to be there for me.

"How did you like the show? I saw you in the audience."

"It was great. We tried to get backstage to thank you, but security stopped us before we could get near the entrance. Without a pass there was no going."

He nodded. "Everyplace is more careful these days."

I understood. My heart was still drumming at seeing him again. For a moment I wondered what Amber would think if she saw me talking to a member of the band. But then I pushed thoughts of her aside. I liked Shane, and what could it hurt to spend some time with him? It wasn't like we were walking down the aisle.

"I didn't have any passes with me when I met you or I'd have given you a couple."

"That's all right. It was very kind of you to give me the tickets. I was a total stranger."

"What are you doing here?" he asked.

"Killing time. I'm going riding in a few minutes."

"You like horses."

I nodded, not bothering to tell him I hadn't known of this love for the noble beasts until I set foot on this island.

"What a coincidence. I'm going riding, too."

"I don't ride that well," I told him. I wouldn't want him to think I was an expert rider and then see me bouncing around like a rubber ball in the saddle.

"Neither do I. I've been a few times over the years. And since I'm going to have some time off, I thought I'd check out some of the attractions."

"When you travel, don't you get to see places?"

He was shaking his head before I finished the question.

"The airport, hotel, and concert hall is usually it."

"That's a bummer."

"I've been around the world and seen very little of it. We usually go from one job to another. With setup, rehearsals, and breakdown, there is little time for sightseeing."

"But the Vineyard is different?"

"Mike is taking a vacation, so we have some time to ourselves."

"And you decided to spend yours on a horse?"

"And with you," he said, his tone low and sexy.

I couldn't help but smile back. He offered his arm in an exaggerated gesture and I took it. The warmth of him was as tantalizing as sugar cookies.

"What do you do?" Shane asked as we walked toward the stables.

"I own a consulting firm," I lied. Well, it wasn't a total lie. I'd thought about consulting, and since I lost my job I'd taken a few contract positions that lasted either a few weeks or a few months. If I stretched the definition of consulting, I suppose it was partially true.

"What kind of consulting?"

"Mainly computer systems. I go into companies and train their employees on how to access information. Sometimes from the Internet, sometimes from proprietary programs. You'd be surprised at the number of people who still don't understand how to use the technology sitting on their desks."

"Sounds very technical. Do you have a large clientele?"

I shook my head. "It's small and select." I added the last to make it appear that I was financially sound.

Luckily we reached the stable at that moment and I was saved from any further lies.

"Do you have a certain path that you follow?" Shane asked when we were in the saddle.

"I try to go a different route each time," I said.

"Lead on." He gestured with one hand.

I turned the horse, pulling on the reins so it went left and headed toward the woods. We walked along side by side for a while. I was racking my brain trying to think of something clever to say. Of course, nothing came to mind. Even the mundane eluded me.

"So how long is the vacation Mike Adams is taking?" I asked, feeling a need to break the silence stretching between us.

"The rest of the summer."

"Two months?"

"Maybe longer. He's going to write some new songs and he won't be touring."

"Are you staying here that long?"

"I'm thinking about it."

Shane's words made my heart act a little funny. He was going to be trouble for me. I liked him, and that wasn't good. I was here to find a rich husband, not a member of the band. I could hear Amber's voice in my head.

"Can you afford to take that much time off?" I asked seriously.

He laughed. "I won't starve, if that's what you're asking." Then he got serious. "We plan for downtime."

"That's good." Most people didn't understand how to budget from one paycheck to the next. They were often overextended with credit cards maxed to the limit.

"And now that I don't have to work and I'm staying on the Vineyard, would you like to have dinner with me tonight?"

I thought my heart was going to jump out of my chest. I had no plans for the evening. I liked this big man. He was tender and kind, and he had the nicest eyes and a winning smile.

The morning sailed by because Shane shared it with me. As on that first morning we met, he regaled me with stories. I laughed at some of the mishaps that had beset the band in places like Auckland, New Zealand, and Malaysia. I could have stayed with him all the way to dinner and through it, but he had some business to take care of. We parted at the door to the house. He kissed me on the cheek and confirmed our dinner date.

I walked in the house feeling lighter than air. Shane's lips were soft against my skin. I could feel his hands, large and strong, steadying me. Emotion welled up inside me from the whisper of my ears to my painted toenails.

Chapter 14

"I'm going to be gone for the weekend," Jack announced just as I brought the sandwich to my mouth. I stopped before biting into it. We were on the beach, at the Inkwell. The three of us had just finished a game of volleyball and we were all famished and thirsty.

We rarely saw each other for any length of time. We passed each other coming and going or we saw each other over morning coffee in the kitchen, but we hadn't had a girls' night out since our first night here. Lila had suggested we meet here for a few hours of girl talk.

And Jack greeted us with her declaration.

"What?" Lila asked. "Where? With whom?"

"Why?" I asked. "Where are you going? This is the first I've heard of you leaving." I glanced at Lila, then back at Jack.

She'd been to the stables this morning. She went there every day, even suggested that Lila and I join her. She'd talked so much about horseback riding that I felt obliged to try it before leaving the Vineyard. I wasn't sure I even liked horses, let alone wanted to sit precariously atop one of the beasts. It was enough for me to see some dead general immortalized in bronze along a highway or sitting in a park where only the pigeons noticed him.

But Jack seemed enamored of them. And the exercise was paying off. She'd lost a few pounds.

"It happened last night. I was out with Shane and he was telling me he knows Jordan West. He says Jordan was his best friend in high school and that the two of them are still tight." She crossed her index and middle finger to demonstrate. "I called his bluff, and right then and there he whips out his cell phone and calls the dude."

"Shane?"

"Shane. He's someone I met recently."

Her voice sounded a little strange, but I let it go. I knew who Shane was. He was a member of Mike Adams's band.

"It was the night I went to the music festival."

"I thought you went with . . ." I was lost for a name. It seemed there had been so many men who had come into Jack's life in the past few weeks, I was losing track.

"I went with Lila," Jack said. "And I came back with her, too, but that's where I saw Shane."

"Saw him?"

"It was the second time. I met him in a tiny shop. Well, outside of it. We were both writing postcards. I shared his table."

I remember her relaying the story the day she did my hair. She'd left out a few details and I knew it.

"Jack, do you feel comfortable enough to go away with him? How do you know it was really Jordan West?" I heard a loud sound behind me and checked the volleyball game. Obviously someone had made the winning shot. "I mean, anyone can be impersonated over a phone."

"Right, which is why I'm going away for the weekend. Jordan West is in Vermont doing a concert this weekend. He invited us up to see the show."

"Jack, are you serious? I mean, you don't really know this guy." I was concerned about her going away with a virtual stranger. Would she be safe? "He seems like a nice guy and he has a winning job, but that's no indication that he's not a pervert or worse."

"He's not a pervert," Jack said. She shifted on the blanket, turning to stare directly at me. "I understand your concern, Amber." She swung her glance between me and Lila. "I like Shane, but I don't blindly trust him. I've already told him that the first sign of a lie on his part and I'm gone. If Jordan West himself does not meet us at the airport when the plane lands, I go no further."

"You promise?" I asked.

Jack's stare turned dark. She raised herself up on her knees and put her hands on her hips. "Amber, I'm from Brooklyn."

The test of my resolve with Don came the very next morning when I drove Jack to the ferry that would take her and Shane back to the mainland and then to her trip to see Jordan West.

The last person I expected to see was Don. He hadn't been on the beach this morning or any morning since my tennis game with Bob. Don walked off the ferry dressed to kill. Most people came off wearing jeans or casual clothes. He had on a gray suit that must have cost him a month's pay. He looked like a Southern preacher. His eyes met mine. For a second, I looked back, then I turned to Jack.

"There he is," Jack said. "Now's your chance."

I wanted to glanced at Don, but forced myself to remain with my back to him. It would be easy to walk over, especially since every fiber within me was telling me to go and apologize. I wanted to go, but I wouldn't. Turning away, I walked with Jack to meet Shane.

He wasn't tall and thin, the kind of man Jack usually went for. Shane Massey ran counter to form. He was tall and built, muscle-hard and looking more like a bodybuilder than a guy who played piano. He shook my hand and smiled. He had incredible eyes. They were light, amber colored, and contrasted with his dark skin. His handshake was firm, confident. He was likable, but I was still wary of Jack going away with him.

"I left the paper with where we'll be staying on the kitchen counter," Jack said. "We'll be back on Monday."

I hugged her. "Have a good time," I said, then whispered, "Call me if there's any sign of trouble."

I shook hands with Shane again and watched as they stepped from land to sea. I waited until the ferry left, then returned to the car. I thought of Don, seeing him dressed in his suit and looking every inch the *GQ* man. As I approached the parking area and looked at my car, I stopped in my tracks. Don casually leaned against the fender, his ankles and arms both crossed. He wore a smile that could melt granite.

We stared at each other without saying anything. Then I started walking again.

"Good morning, Don," I said when I was within earshot, not slowing my stride by a single step. I got into the car and started the engine. He stepped away, turning to face me. I didn't wait to hear what he had to say. Putting the car in gear, I drove away. I didn't bother to look back. He had avoided me for a week. Just because I happened to run into him was no reason to change his tactics.

Or mine.

Don was out of my life. He shouldn't have been there in the first place. But he'd chosen the path. For a week I'd expected to find him jogging toward me. He'd avoided me. His getting over his tantrum was no reason for me to play mother and open my arms, welcoming him back into my life. He had no place in my life or my future.

But it appeared Don wouldn't be so easily shrugged off. The phone was ringing when I got back to the house and opened the front door. Some mental telepathy told me it was Don.

It rang five times before I lifted the receiver. "Hello."

"Good morning. I hope I didn't wake you?" I was confused by the voice, ready to hear Don's deep-throated baritone. "This is Casey Edwards."

I sat down, my legs suddenly weak from the absence of adrenaline that had me pumped up to rebuke Don Randall.

"I know it's short notice, but Joel and I are going on a picnic and Joel suggested we ask you along. I'd like you to come, too. Are you game?"

I smiled. "It sounds like a plan," I said.

"Good. I'll pick you up at noon."

"I'll be ready."

I hung the phone up. A picnic was nice. It would

give me something to do to keep my mind off Don. And if he happened to see me out with Casey, good!

Casey drove past the Inkwell and went to a different beach. I felt a sigh of relief when we passed the much-lauded beach that was well-known to African American visitors and very well populated as a hunting ground for every single man and woman on the Vineyard.

He'd had the hotel pack a picnic basket. While Joel and I spread a blanket on the sand, Casey unpacked the car.

"I wanna go swimming," Joel announced as sand chairs were unfolded and coolers set within arm's reach. He looked at his father.

"Sure." Casey grabbed his hand. "Join us?" he asked me. The three of us ran toward the water. The surf caught us cold. Both Joel and I recoiled and took several steps back before venturing farther into the water. After a while we were playing and swimming and laughing as if we'd known each other for years. Anyone watching us might have thought we were a family, that Joel was my son and Casey my husband.

Casey was affectionate, catching me around the waist now and then and dousing me in the water. He did nothing overt. Maybe because Joel was there, maybe because of our public position, or maybe it wasn't his nature. But I felt somehow, something was missing.

Maybe it was me. My attitude.

Don had made me angry, and for the last few days I'd wondered all manner of things about him.

Then seeing him today, healthy and looking good enough to eat, set me on edge. And it shouldn't.

I got out of the water, breathing hard, but with a smile on my face. Joel ran by me. "I want some chicken," he said.

Casey came up behind me. He slipped his arm around my waist and rested it on my right hip. I smiled at him as if I enjoyed the contact. I should have. I liked Casey, but there was no electricity in his touch. Today he hadn't talked about himself. In fact, he hadn't once mentioned his business. I knew he worked for Coca-Cola in their business development department and lived in Atlanta.

"I have two tickets for the festival tonight," he said. "I was hoping you'd go with me."

"What about Joel?"

"The hotel has a child-care service. I hired a very nice lady to watch him while we're enjoying ourselves." His hand squeezed my hip slightly. "What about it? Are you free?"

"I'd love to go."

"It starts at eight. I could pick you up at six and we could have dinner before going."

"That sounds good."

We sat down on the blanket. Joel had already opened the basket and pulled out a container. He was biting into a drumstick, chewing with gusto only known by children.

"Not so fast, Joel. You don't want to get sick," his father said.

"This is really good," Joel said. "I talked to the chef at the hotel and he's the best in the world."

"Really," I said, accepting a covered dish that Casey passed me.

"He's lived all over the world and cooked for some of the best restaurants."

"How did he come to be at the St. Romaine on Martha's Vineyard?" I asked, appearing overly interested in his story.

"Mr. Randall hired him."

There he was again. Don. I couldn't get away from him.

"Don's a really nice guy," Casey said. "He's allowed Joel to have more freedom at the hotel than most managers would."

"Have you known Don long?" I asked, keeping my voice even.

"We met my first day here, but he's the architect who's turned that hotel around."

I stabbed a small amount of the macaroni salad with my fork. "What do you mean?"

"It's a St. Romaine, and if you've been in any of the other hotels, you'd know this was little more than a third-class facility a year ago. Probably the bottom of the chain. Then Don took over, and it's a first-class place now. Getting a room there gets harder every day."

How well I knew that, I thought, remembering trying to get a place to sleep and the consequences when there was no room in the inn.

"A year doesn't sound like enough time."

"Sounds impossible." Casey laughed. "But Don put his heart and soul, not to mention his muscles, into the job. And it's paying off."

"I suppose the St. Romaines are glad they found such a good manager in him."

"They should be. He's back this morning, but he spent last week reporting to them."

"Reporting?" My ears picked up. Don had been away all week?

"They had their annual meeting last week and Don was invited to report on the hotel's progress," Casey said.

"Did he . . . did he say how it went?"

"I didn't get to speak for long. We only saw him as Joel and I were leaving the hotel. His face and body language gave nothing away. He always looks and acts the same."

I knew differently. Don was multifaceted. He was different each time I'd seen him. There were personality traits that were unreadable and those that screamed at you. He hated what I was doing, yet he'd agreed to help me. He made love to me like the world was about to end, yet he'd disappeared without a word, leaving me wondering.

"Can we go back in the water now?" Joel asked after finishing his meal. His question interrupted my thoughts, and I was glad of the diversion. I wanted Don out of my head, and talking about him wouldn't accomplish that. I didn't need him as an invisible specter intruding on my day.

"I think we should wait a while to let our food settle," I told him. I didn't remember if they had changed that one-hour rule about swimming after eating, but it couldn't hurt to wait a while.

Joel looked a little sad.

"I have an idea."

He looked up at me, his eyes hopeful.

"Why don't we build a sand castle?"

His face fell.

"I saw that look. But you've never built a sand castle with me. So if you're not up for the challenge . . ."

I turned away, picked up a small bucket, and

walked toward the wet sand. Casey followed me. And a moment later Joel joined us.

We spent the afternoon building the castle, swimming, and eating. Joel dominated the day, asking questions and telling his disjointed stories.

And I didn't have another thought about Don.

Entering the house after dinner with Casey was quite different from the way I'd entered it a week ago. Lila was there—alone this time. She was watching an old movie on the big-screen television in the huge parlor. The house had to be built in the early part of the twentieth century. The living room was called the parlor then. On the coffee table was the small replica of a rocking chair with her name painted on it. She hadn't mentioned where it came from, but I had a pretty good idea.

"How was it?" Lila asked, muting the sound on the television.

"The concert was fantastic." I slipped onto the sofa at the opposite end, where Lila had her feet curled up under her and covered by a long robe.

"And Casey, how was he?"

"We spent the whole day together."

Lila stared at me and waited.

"He's a nice guy," I said. "He's got a great son."

"But . . ." she dangled.

"No but," I said.

"Then what's wrong? You aren't dancing on air."

"I don't often do that."

"Well, I have a reason for you to dance."

I stared at her, waiting. She folded her arms and smiled Mona Lisa style, letting the tension between us build.

"What?" I finally asked.

"He called." Lila's voice was low, so low I hardly heard her. Everything inside me spasmed. *He* could only be one person.

"Who is *he*?" I asked, needing confirmation.

"Don Randall, gorgeous hotel manager."

"What did he want?" I tried to sound bored, uninterested, yet my heart thudded at the knowledge that he'd been seeking me out.

"He left a number. Said you should call whenever you got in." Lila lowered her voice in a sotto voce whisper. "No matter what time."

"I am not calling him. The man hasn't spoken to me in a week, didn't even bother to tell me he was leaving the Vineyard. And now he wants me to call. Well, he can wait until . . . until the sun rises in the west."

"Well, I see he has your pantyhose in a knot," Lila said.

"No, he doesn't."

"When you decide he does, his number is on the counter in the kitchen."

I glanced in that direction, but didn't move. "What are you doing here anyway?" I asked. "What happened to Clay?"

"He had to go back to work."

"Work? What does he do?"

Lila looked a little uncomfortable. She swallowed before saying anything. "Now, Amber, I know why we came here. Clay isn't rich, at least not in the traditional sense of the word."

"Traditional sense." I stared at her. "You mean like with traditional money, dead presidents and all. That sort of thing?"

She nodded. "He's in furniture."

"Sales or manufacturing?"

"Custom. He makes it himself."

"From scratch?"

Lila nodded again. "Please don't be angry with me. I know he's not a doctor or lawyer. But he talks to me. Listens to me. He's got rough hands. And I can't help it, Amber, I want them all over me. My heart thuds when he walks in the room."

All her life Lila had been judged by other people. They thought they knew her, but they didn't. No one knew who she really was. She was beautiful, everyone said so, but when Lila looked in the mirror she didn't see a beautiful woman. She saw a warm human being. Others saw a beauty queen. A sex goddess. Some even saw a woman of easy virtue.

Some of that was true. Lila had perpetrated that image, too. It was what men wanted, and she thought it was a way of getting what she wanted, too. But she'd found out through the hard knocks that she never got what she wanted.

Men saw the package. The flawless skin and long legs, the shape of her face. The way the light struck her features. Of course, she enhanced the image with the right makeup and the right clothes, but she also had a mind, and few men had ever seen past her measurements. Most couldn't tell you what color her eyes were, but they all probably knew her bra size.

And because they knew that statistic, they thought she was very well experienced. They were wrong. The truth was, she'd only had three physical relationships in her life. Who would believe some-one who had tits the size of hers and legs that stretched the length of the Brooklyn Bridge had only slept with three men?

Consequently, it was the first thing they tried to do. She was either a challenge or a prize to the men she met. Bedding her was like sleeping with Dolly Parton. They all wanted to see and touch what was under the layers of clothing, find out what no other man—or at least only a handful—knew.

Yet Lila had no intention of being the conquest or the notch on someone's bedpost. That's why my idea had seemed so plausible. Come here to this idyllic island and find a rich husband. But Lila wanted more than mere money in her future. She wanted a man who looked at her and saw through the exterior to the heart and brain that lurked beneath the designer clothes.

Lila Easton had grown up in Brooklyn. She thought the shortest way to a man's heart was across the Brooklyn Bridge.

I was glad she'd found someone she liked, someone who liked her for being Lila Easton and not some pinup girl or a pick-up in a singles bar.

"I'm glad, Lila," I whispered earnestly. "Following your heart is sometimes the right thing to do."

She smiled. "Thanks, Amber. Have you changed your mind? Rich is nice, but it's not any good if you don't love the guy."

"Love. I'm not in love."

"Aren't you? Think about how you're acting whenever Don is around. And when he's not. Maybe you're more in love than you think."

Chapter 15

Vermont was full of trees. It was so green. I'd never seen so many trees in my life. True to his word, Jordan West met us at the airport and rode back to the hotel with us. Shane had been telling the truth. They knew each other. Shane introduced me and the two of them started catching up. They didn't leave me out, each one taking time to turn and explain the stories to me.

The drive was short. I was in awe of Jordan. I couldn't believe I was sitting in a limousine with a man who collected Grammys like most of us collect pennies.

The hotel Clay checked us into was small but elegantly appointed with a fireplace in the room and a four-poster bed. Outside my window was a huge mountain of trees. If this was winter, the place would have been overloaded with snow bunnies. As it was, the place was packed with musicians, none of whom seemed interested in the trees.

Despite my pretense, I hadn't traveled much outside of the concrete jungle, and seeing all the foliage was like visiting an alien world.

Jordan West had an entire floor for his huge entourage. Shane and I had rooms on a different floor, but we'd been invited up for drinks after the concert. The performance had been a sellout and the suite was packed when we got there. Three security guards checked our I.D. and passes before we even got to the door.

The last song he'd sung was still humming in my ears. I couldn't believe I was on my way to party with him. Jordan West had become a household word five years ago. His name was known worldwide. He'd collected so many Grammy Awards he needed a tractor-trailer to cart them away.

"Shane! Shane Massey!" a woman shouted as we crossed the threshold. Weaving through the crowd, she pushed her way through, her smile whiter than bleached sheets, her dress as tight as a second skin, hair falling down her back and her arms outstretched and aiming directly at Shane. She skipped past a couple in front of her in her quest to reach Shane. Launching herself at him, she planted a wet kiss directly on his mouth.

I stood in place like virgin wood still on the tree. Shane pulled back after the kiss, stepping out of her path.

"Ella, I didn't know you would be here," he said a bit tightly. Then he turned to me. "This is Jacynthia Sterling. She's with me."

I liked the way he said that. It was a virtual dismissal. I also liked that he put his arm around my waist and pulled me into him as if I belonged there. I understood it was a message for Ella, whoever she was, and whoever she'd been to Shane in the past. I was with him now and *she* was not.

Amazing how my jealous fangs came out at the

thought of another woman clinging to the man
I was with. Shane and I hadn't known each other
long, but he was here with me.

"Jack, meet Ella Francis. She's a songwriter and
producer."

I nodded instead of offering her my hand. Her
nod was equally distant. Shane said she was a songwriter. It wasn't lost on me that he gave no distinc-
tion as to who I was. He also gave no indication
of what the two of them had been to each other in
the past.

And they had a past. That much was obvious.

Ella looked me up and down. I was everything
she wasn't. She was tall and thin. I was shorter, and
even though I'd lost a few pounds in the past weeks,
I was still obviously heavier. She had long, bouncy
hair and I was unsure what mine looked like now
that the concert was over and the crushing crowd
and heat were getting to it.

There was one thing we had in common. Even
though Ella's silver lamé gown was tighter than it
should be, my purple silk dress was equally impec-
cable. Amber had seen to that. I silently thanked
her for forcing me to buy a new wardrobe.

Our dislike of each other was unmistakable. It
was as if the two of us were huge cats circling the
same piece of meat.

"Shane." Jordan appeared at that moment. The
tension of the moment dispersed with his appearance. The two men shook hands, at least they went
through the ritual of hug, shake, grip, punch fists,
and fly-away hands. It was something I'd seen a
thousand times, on the streets, at meetings, wherever men met, but this time I was as mesmerized by

the practice as I'd been at the airport when they'd gone through the same reunion.

"Jack," Jordan said to me when he and Shane completed their meeting exercise. He took my hand in both his. His smile was bewitching. I still found it alien that I was actually in the same room with him and he was holding my hand. "I didn't get to tell you in the limo, but Shane has told me a lot about you." I looked at Shane, surprised that he'd taken the time to tell this superstar about me.

"I hope it was good," I said over the clog in my throat and the knocking of my heart.

"It was."

I glanced at Shane, wondering what he had said. The two of us hadn't known each other long enough for him to have a lot to say about me. He had to have told him his impression. I hoped that was good because I was truly enamored of this man.

"The concert was more than I expected," I told Jordan. I wished I'd practiced something to say other than repeating words that every groupie had said to him since he burst on the music scene. But I hadn't thought it was real. Shane said he knew him. I thought it was just talk to impress me when he said we could go to Vermont and I'd called his bluff. It now appeared the joke was on me.

"Shane and I have known each other since kindergarten, although he prefers to play in that ragtag band for Mike Adams." Jordan laughed and glanced at Shane.

"It pays the bills," Shane said, spreading his hands in defeat.

I noticed that Ella had moved around and was

holding on to Shane's arm. It took everything I had not to reach over and snatch her hand away.

Jordan was called away by the many people vying for his attention. "Hang around," he said, swinging his gaze from Shane to me. "We'll talk later."

Shane nodded and pulled free of Ella. The action made me feel good, and I boldly leaned over him and spoke directly to her. "You know, Ella, it's very bad taste to hang on to someone who obviously doesn't want you around."

With that I slipped my arm through Shane's and guided him away, but not before I saw the color rise under her skin and anger take hold of her body. Knowing it took a few seconds to find the most venomous comeback to fling after an insult, I made sure we were out of earshot.

"How about we get a drink?" Shane suggested.

I nodded and we headed that way. There was a line and we joined it. "Wanna tell me who she is?" I asked.

He glanced over his shoulder at the place where we'd left a flabbergasted Ella. I followed his look, but the woman was gone. Secretly, I hoped it was my comment that sent her somewhere crying and licking her wounds.

"We used to have a thing," he said. "It's been over for years."

"I don't think she knows it," I told him.

"Don't worry about her. She won't be a problem."

I said nothing. We reached the bar. I knew it was too early in our relationship, if we were to have a relationship, for me to get clingy and feel I had a right to ask questions.

Yet keeping quiet was killing me.

* * *

When I kicked the covers aside in the early morning, it was still dark. I hadn't slept more than an hour all night. I told myself the beach was calling, that my writing needed nourishment, but even for me it was too early to go there. And then there was Don. Would he come today? Would he jog past me without stopping as I had done to him at the ferry?

Why had he called? If he'd had anything to say to me, he could have done it before he left for his meeting or called sometime during the week.

Pushing my feet into slippers, I went downstairs. Don's phone number lay on the counter where Lila had left it. I picked up the note and read the numbers. What would he think if I called him now? He said anytime. It was four o'clock. Would he already be overseeing something at the hotel or would he be asleep in his huge bed, his strong legs curled around the sheets?

Dropping the paper back on the counter, I found a bag of microwave popcorn and popped it. Then taking an overflowing bowl and a can of diet soda, I went into the parlor. Lila had been watching a movie earlier. I turned the television on and spent several minutes flipping through all the stations, only to find nothing that caught my attention.

Tossing the remote control aside, I ate several kernels of popcorn and reached for my soda. The can sat next to the phone and the numbers on the note in the kitchen jumped into my mind. I lifted the received and stared at it.

Then I dialed.

As the phone rang, I gripped the receiver tighter

than normal. Don answered on the first ring, as if he'd been sitting next to it, waiting for it to ring.

"Well, it took you long enough," he said instead of hello.

"You said to call anytime."

"And you picked four o'clock in the morning?"

"It was convenient."

"You couldn't sleep."

"I sleep fine," I lied.

"Then what were you doing that kept you busy until this hour?"

I hesitated, trying to think of a lie to tell him, but decided the silence spoke for me. "Lila said you wanted me to call. Is there something you wanted to talk about?"

"I'd rather speak to you in person."

"Sorry, this is the best you get."

"What are you doing?"

"Right now, this minute?"

"Right now, this minute," he repeated.

"I'm sitting on the sofa."

"Which room?"

"The television room." I didn't know what else to call it and I didn't see the significance of it anyway.

"And what are you wearing?"

I sat up straight. "Phone sex? You wanted me to call you for phone sex?"

"You have to admit it could be pretty exciting," Don said.

"Not to mention safe."

"Too safe," Don said. "I'd rather my sex be actual instead of virtual. We could meet on the beach or you could come here."

"And why would I do that? You avoided me for a week."

"With good reason."

"And what reason was that?"

"Bob Yancey, Casey Edwards, and others."

He made it sound as if I was doing the island, when in fact the only person I'd slept with was him.

"Don't you want to include yourself on that list?"

"No, I don't fit the standards you've set."

"Then why are you bothering to avoid me?"

"I wasn't avoiding you. I was off the island."

"I heard."

"You did."

"People talk, I listen, inquiring minds and all that."

"I see. Does this mean you're interested?"

"It does not."

"You're very quick to say that."

"I'm very decisive."

"It's a character flaw."

I laughed. Don was trying to bait me, but I was not going to let that happen.

"What would life be like if we didn't have flaws? They make us human. Give us something to strive to correct."

"You want to correct your flaws?"

"Not mine. I was thinking of yours," I said.

"And what are mine?"

"Are you sure you want to ask that question?"

There was hesitation on the other end of the line. "I'm not afraid of the answer," he said.

"Maybe you should be."

"I'm interested. What do you think my flaws are?"

"You're persistent. Maybe a little pushy."

"Those sound like attributes to me."

I rolled my eyes. He would. I had faults, but he

had attributes. He also wanted to have his way and he liked challenges.

"Is there anything else you wanted to talk about or was it only the sound of my voice you needed to hear?"

"You do have a nice voice," he said.

Goose bumps as large as pimples grew on my arms and I felt a slight tingling at his words. I loved hearing his voice, too, although I would never admit it to him.

"So what *are* you wearing?" he asked.

"Nothing," I said.

"Nothing?"

I could hear the surprise in his voice. Of course, I had on a nightgown and robe, but if he wanted to have phone sex, I could play that game, too.

"What are *you* wearing?" I asked.

"Not a stitch," he answered.

I pictured him naked. The thought made me hot. I wondered if he was feeling the same thing. Suddenly, I wished I had agreed to meet him at his place. Sex with Don was better than anything I'd known before. And I'd rather have real sex than virtual.

"Don, I'm going to bed now. I wouldn't want to get you all worked up and then withdraw."

"Chicken."

"What did you say?" I asked. "Did you call me a chicken?"

He made a barnyard chicken call into the phone. I imagined him doing the strut around his living room.

Naked, of course.

* * *

I won't say that skinny woman clinging to Shane didn't shake my confidence. She did. And the other women who seemed to materialize in front of him took their place in line to push that confidence aside. They were all beautiful, young, and thin. But three drinks later and hours until the sun made an appearance wiped them from my memory. I didn't even remember Ella Francis existed. She'd disappeared from the crowd and hadn't been seen again.

Sometime during the night the furniture was moved and dancing broke out. Band members joined and an impromptu jam session ensued. Shane joined them for a while. Then he came to me, holding me and dancing with me several times. Unfortunately, he was often pulled away by the many women vying for his attention. I loved being in his arms, but I could see I had to share whether I liked it or not.

"Don't mind them," Jordan said next to me when I was watching Shane dance with another woman.

I glanced at him, but said nothing.

"Shane's always been like that, a magnet for the ladies. But he never takes advantage."

I looked at him then, both curious and surprised at the comment.

"I don't know why," he went on. "They throw themselves at him like dancing fairies. But you're the first woman he's ever brought with him. So you must be very special."

"We haven't—" I was cut off by someone calling Jordan to the phone. He smiled, apologized, and walked toward the cell phone being held in the air.

How could I be anyone special, I asked myself.

Shane and I had only met a few weeks ago. And he didn't know that I'd told him lies and was pretending to be someone I wasn't.

When the crowd thinned out, we found seats near the balcony and looked out on the night. Daybreak would come soon. Shane's arm was along the back of the chair and he held me close to him. We talked quietly for a while, then fell silent. It was a moment I'd want to remember forever. I was happy, yet there was something bothering me. I didn't want to bring it up. I wasn't sure the timing was right. Actually, I was sure the timing was wrong.

"Tired?" he asked. His head turned and he kissed my temple.

"I'm not used to such long days."

Shane stood up and pulled me with him. "Come on, I'll walk you to your room."

The sun was coming up when Shane and I reached my door. His room was across the hall. I slipped the electronic key in the lock. The soft click disengaged the mechanism. Pushing the door open, I took Shane's hand, pulling him inside behind me. I wasn't ready for the night to end even though the sun was already painting the sky.

"Are you sure?" he asked, after the door closed and locked.

"Very sure," I said, pushing aside pulsing questions that filled my head.

"I didn't bring you here for this," he said.

I kissed him lightly on the mouth. "I know," I replied. My voice held the emotion I felt and that the kiss intensified. It had only been a light touching of our lips, but the promise it held was enough to have me yearning for much more.

Boldly I pushed my hands under the sweater he wore. His skin was already damp. I lifted up on my toes and kissed him again. This time he joined me. Our mouths melded as if we were meant to be together. That out of the billions of souls on earth, the two of us had been put there by design. Destined for each other, destined to share in the one true purpose of life.

Shane found the zipper on my dress and pulled it down.

"I'm not thin," I told him. Ella Francis came to mind as his hands touched my bare back. "I have mounds and curves."

"And don't I know it," he breathed. "I'm planning to find each and every one of them."

He moved me back toward the bed. Slowly, piece by piece, we undressed each other, sharing kisses and finding areas of pleasure on each other. Shane made me feel special. He seemed to revel in my size, not tease me about it. I wasn't self-conscious with him. I was proud of the way he looked at me, his eyes dark with a hunger that made me think I was the only one in the world capable of satisfying it.

His hands were smooth as he caressed every inch of me. My body hummed with need and anticipation. I panted, unable to keep myself from the physical expression of the hunger I felt for our joining. I wanted him more than I thought possible.

Lying on the bed, I pulled him toward me. I wanted to be covered by him, joined with him. I wanted to feel his body inside mine with a strength so potent it wiped away any inhibitions I held. Shane must have felt the same. Grabbing his pants, he pulled out a condom and cracked the foil pouch. After protecting us, his knee spread my legs and he entered me.

A short sound of pleasure emitted from my throat. My body gained comfort with the invasion of his. He moved inside me, causing a profound joy to spread like fire as it rushed through me. I wrapped my legs around him as he dug into me. Harder and faster he stroked me. I could do nothing except breathe and match his pace.

The world seemed to recede at that moment. Nothing mattered except the pleasure I felt and how I could make him feel. My hands stroked his shoulders, my fingers raked over his skin. It was fire hot. Yet Shane's body pumped into mine, taking me time and again, until I thought I'd explode from spontaneous combustion. Yet I went on. Shane went on.

This was going to kill me, I thought, but I wanted it, wanted more and more and more. I wanted our connection, our lovemaking to go on forever. My body writhed beneath his, accepting his weight, accepting the pleasure code he knew and I was finding with each joining. My breath came in short gasps. Shane gathered my butt cheeks and held them, plunging deep into me, driving my physical enjoyment up several notches. If I thought I was going to die before, this was really going to kill me.

"Shane!" I shouted his name, unable to do anything else. I wanted to tell him how good I felt, how good he made me feel, but I was incapable of speech.

And then I felt it coming, the wave of sensation so powerful that the threat of explosion was imminent. The wave grew and grew, taking me up with it. I surrendered to it, allowing it to take me as far and high and it wanted. Finally it crested and for an eon I was weightless, suspended as pure energy, on some plane of pleasure that found every hill and valley of my body and stroked it into a fiery life. Sound had no existence in that place. It was completely quiet and open only to feelings.

Then it was over. We crashed back to earth, breathing heavily. Shane held me, hugged me close to him as if he was unwilling to end the moment. Both of us panted, sucking in air as if we'd been in a vacuum and just returned to an atmosphere.

"Damn," he said. His hands rubbed lovingly over my curves, making me feel warm and wanting him again. "Any longer and I'd be dead."

Chapter 16

The kitchen is the hub of most homes, and for the three of us, vacation made no difference. The smell of coffee wafted through the air. Frying bacon had my stomach juices churning. The mixture of aromas pulled me toward the kitchen and the opulent smell of a good breakfast. As I stepped off the last rung and took a step toward the hub of activity, I heard whispered voices. Lila and Jack were talking, but they weren't using normal inside voices. I strained to hear what they were saying, thinking it was probably about me, but the sound was too low.

Making enough noise to alert them of my presence, I walked into the kitchen. Going straight to the coffeepot, I poured a cup, adding cream and sugar.

"What's up?" I asked.

"I have an idea," Lila announced. "I think we should have a party."

Jack took a huge intake of air and held it for several seconds before exhaling. She looked up at me.

"That's a wonderful idea," she said. "We could invite a lot of those Howard men."

"Is that what you two were discussing before I walked in?"

Jack dropped her head, covering her surprise by drinking from the cup in front of her.

"Yes," Lila said, doing the opposite of Jack. The single word was strongly delivered. She lifted her chin, ready to take anything I had to confront them with.

I had nothing. I couldn't hear what they'd been discussing before I came in. My head was throbbing. Sleep had eluded me last night. I'd warned Don about getting excited, but the same was true of me. They wanted a party, and all I could think of was being in bed with him.

"We could invite some of the men we've met, too," Lila suggested, her voice lifting positively at the end.

My attention snapped back to her. "Does that include—"

She was nodding before I finished the comment. "Him, too. After all, Don's been nice to us. It would be rude to have a party and exclude him." She paused, giving me a stoic look. "And if there is nothing between you two, what difference does it make? But if there *is* something, then it's time you dealt with it."

She was right, of course. But her comment sounded like another challenge. Don had issued one challenge after another. And I felt like I'd failed all of them. I had no choice. It didn't matter if I agreed or refused Lila's suggestion. Neither answer was the right one.

"I do think having a party is a good idea. Meeting people in social settings gives us the chance to test them out, so to speak. We can determine if their personalities mesh with ours. I'm sure there are people looking for something to do after the sun sets. A party seems like the right venue."

A look passed between Lila and Jack that had me curious, but I didn't pursue a reason for it. I was sure they were setting me up. But I was clued into the game. And I was ready for it.

I hoped.

"So you're in?" Lila asked.

"Only so far. I don't want to invite Don."

"Why not?" Jack asked.

"He doesn't fit the profile. If this party is for us to observe the wealthy men on the island, we already know Don is not one of them."

"Ever think it's time you gave up on this plan?" Jack asked, her voice low and dragging as if she were whispering a secret that everyone knew.

The look I gave her could shut down the sun. "Have you forgotten that your entire life savings is tied up in this venture?"

"No, I have not," Jack challenged. After a moment she dropped her shoulders. "Amber, the plan doesn't seem to be working."

I looked from Jack to Lila. I knew Lila was seeing a guy who made furniture for a living and Jack was only just back from a weekend with a member of the band. Granted, he did know one superstar, but I still think he only wanted to get into Jack's panties. And by all accounts of her conversation upon returning, it had worked.

"Well, maybe what we need is a new plan."

* * *

The place was dressed for a party. Jack and Lila had outdone themselves, taking care of all the details. My contribution was a portion of the guest list. I was sure they had used Don as the other source. Sitting in front of the makeup mirror in my room, putting the final touches on my face, I could hear the caterers downstairs. They'd been there for an hour setting up tables, building pyramids of fruits and fresh vegetables, and God knew what else.

Standing up, I checked the hem of my dress. It was royal blue, sleeveless, backless, and stopped at the knee. The fabric had metallic silver threads running through it, causing the hem to swish when I walked. I loved the way it felt.

As I twisted around to leave the room, I got a glimpse of the driveway and immediately saw the logo of the St. Romaine on a van parked there. Anger flashed through me. I should have known there was something funky going on when Jack and Lila agreed to ride point on the party.

"All you have to do is provide a guest list." I imitated Jack's words. The tone of her voice should have been a warning. But it wasn't. I'd made myself clear that I did *not* want Don Randall invited. So what to my wondering eyes should appear but the black Adonis and his staff of uniformed caterers.

Leaving the window, I marched down the hall and into Jack's room.

"I didn't invite him," she said the moment I slammed her door shut. She stood in front of the bathroom mirror combing her hair.

"Not technically," I said. "You just made it possible for him to be here."

"I didn't."

"Then it had to be Lila. Or both of you in cahoots."

As if on cue Lila pushed the door open and came in. Jack came out of the bathroom and the two stood together as if each needed to be support for the other.

"It was me," Lila said. I could see she was planning to take all the blame, but Jack's surprised glance spoke the truth.

"I suppose there was no other caterer on the island except the St. Romaine?" I said.

"No," Lila said, shaking her head. "They were just the best." She looked peeved for a moment. "You said yourself, the food was good there. And we want to keep our guests happy. According to your plan, we're top of the line. What better way to reinforce that than to use the best available?"

"Now you want to use the plan," I said. "A week ago the plan wasn't working." I pointedly stared at Jack.

She took a step forward. "Amber, it's going to be fine. Don probably won't even be here."

"Wrong." I interrupted anything further she might want to say. "He's already downstairs."

"He's probably just checking things. You know how meticulous he is about details." Lila's voice was hesitant. She was making it up as she went along and I knew it.

I suddenly relaxed. "You know what?" I said. "It doesn't matter. I can ignore him." Sure, we were great in bed, I thought, but whenever we decided to talk, we ended up arguing and unlike fiction, our arguments did not turn me on. Except for our life in bed, two more incompatible people didn't exist on the planet. Tonight I would show Don Randall how little his presence meant to me.

"Come on, ladies." I started for the door. The

two of them parted, assuming I'd walk through them. And I would have. "We have guests coming."

I opened the door. The long hallway loomed in from of me. "I hope you're ready," I said, glancing over my shoulder. "There very likely will be a storm tonight."

Straightening my shoulders, I led the trio down the stairs. It was time to make sure everything was all right and to welcome our guests. Lila and Jack hung back when we entered the main room. Don stood in the center talking to one of the caterers. He was facing the doorway and I walked directly to him.

Magically, the caterer left as I came face-to-face with him. "Are you here as a guest or part of the staff?"

He flashed that disarming smile I'd come to know. My insides wanted to melt, but I forced them to freeze in place.

"Both," he said.

"May I see your invitation?"

I held my hand out. Invitations had been Lila's idea. She thought it made the party more elegant and gave it an exclusive feel. Not that there would be gate crashers on the Vineyard.

Don took his time. His hand went into his inside pocket and out came a black envelope. I recognized it immediately as identical to the ones we'd sent out. I even recognized Jack's handwriting. Behind me I heard her gasp, but I didn't turn to look at her.

Don pulled the invitation free of its sleeve and placed it in my hand.

"Thank you," I said, irritated that Jack had invited him. "Enjoy yourself." I turned to leave.

"Shall I save a dance for you? Maybe the last dance?"

He stopped my exit. Over my shoulder, I raked my eyes over him, then walked away.

The rooms filled immediately. Before I knew it there were people everywhere. Lila was smiling into the eyes of the man whose lap she'd been sitting on the night I'd spent with Don. Jack had made it her job to answer the door. I saw her go up on her toes and kiss one of the arriving guests. It was Shane Massey, the man she'd spent the weekend with.

So much for this party, unless it was for me to find a man. Obviously, the two of them had made their choices.

I didn't look for Don, but it seemed there was an invisible string that connected to us. I knew where he was by some form of personal radar.

"Amber!"

I turned as someone called my name rather loudly. Dr. Wilson Loring held a glass of champagne as he approached me.

"I've been looking for you."

I raised my eyebrows inquiring the reason.

"Let's dance," he said. Taking my arm without giving me time to agree or refuse, he led me toward the ballroom. Handing his glass to a passing waiter, he turned me into his arms. Surprisingly, the doctor was a good dancer and I found myself smiling and accepting a second dance with him. I hoped Don was looking, hoped he saw me having a good time. And hoped it was eating him alive. I didn't have to fake it. I *was* enjoying myself. And as my consumption of the expensive champagne we'd

ordered grew, so did my joy. I danced with everyone. The music got into my body, down to the
marrow of my bones, and I let it sing to me.

My arms were in the air and my hips were swaying from side to side. I sang to the music and partner after partner joined me on the floor. It seemed
like every man we invited came. But I wasn't count-
ing. I was too busy rubbing my body against whoever was with me.

My dress was drenched and my throat parched
after the notes to the last song ended. I headed for
the bar and something more to keep my high on.

"Pushing it a little hard, aren't you?"

I didn't have to look to know it was Don speaking. Even through the fog of my brain, I recognized his voice. And it still had the ability to get
inside me.

"I can handle it," I said.

"As you say."

He backed away. The bartender handed me a
champagne flute. With a smile, I accepted it and
drained it. Then asked for another. The man behind the bar said nothing. His expression didn't
change, but I knew he thought I was drinking too
much and too fast. I ignored him. Tonight I was
having fun.

Holding the second glass—or the ninth, I'd lost
count—I sashayed back to the dance floor. Instantly, a strong arm circled my waist and whirled
me around.

"Whee," I said, smiling as the room spun around
like a merry-go-round. A few drops of the liquid
spilled. I leaned with the glass to save the drink,
bringing it to my mouth and pouring it into the

waiting vessel. The arms around my waist kept me on my feet.

"Hey, Casey," I sang in a high-pitched voice when I raised my head and saw the man holding me. "When did you get here?"

"About an hour ago."

"Really?" I asked, opening my eyes wide. "Why didn't I see you?"

He took the glass from my hand. Why did people keep trying to take my drinks? They acted like I was drunk or something. I was just feeling good.

"This might be the reason." He indicated the wine. I reached for the glass. "Why don't we go outside and get you some air."

It was hot in here. I hadn't noticed it until he brought it up. "Air would be good. I didn't notice it before."

"Notice what?" he asked.

"You know what," I laughed. "Skin is remarkable." I looked at my bare arms. I pulled at the tight fit of skin, pinching it between two fingers. "It's sweltering in here. And the only thing holding me together, keeping me from melting and spilling out on the floor is my skin."

Casey turned me around. Directly in my line of sight stood Don. His gaze swept over me. It was as sobering as stepping in frigid water. Casey pushed me forward and I stumbled a step or two. Outside the night was clear, the stars bright and close. The moon looked like it had been stuck in the sky with kindergarten paste. It was huge and golden, hanging over the water, tumbling light on the shimmering surface. For a moment I was startled.

"You know," I said, thinking hard. "Tonight is a great night for a walk on the beach."

I reached down to take my shoes off. Dizziness rushed to my head and I swayed.

"I don't think so," Casey said, stalling my hands. "You need some black coffee and a bed to sleep off some of that champagne."

"Bed? I don't want to go to bed." My words came slow in my head and didn't seem to make sense. They sounded like a CD in a player that needed its batteries replaced. "Why don't we walk?"

He reached for my arm, but I stepped out of reach. "I'm going back to the party."

The look on his face told me he was getting frustrated. What did I care? I didn't ask him to come with me. And I had free will. I could go to the party if I wanted. After all, it was *my* party.

"I'll take care of her, Mr. Edwards."

Both of us turned to look at the man who'd spoken. It was Don Randall. What was he doing here? Shouldn't he be serving shrimp or something?

"Don," I said, frowning at him. Then I looked at Casey. "Let's go back to the party."

"She's a little tipsy," Casey said.

"Tipsy?" That was such a kind word. Kind! It was a stupid word. Who talks like that? He meant I was drunk. I was *not* drunk. I was feeling good. I put my hands up and started to dance again. I could hear the music from the inside.

"I've had this experience before," Don told Casey.

"Of course he has. He's the hotel manager. You know . . ." I paused with a shy smile. "I'll bet he has all kinds of stories he can tell you about—"

"Why don't we go find some coffee?" Don interrupted. The slight shake of his head toward the door was a signal I wasn't supposed to see. But I did.

"What are you two doing? Are you conspiring against me?" Conspiring didn't come out quite right, but I didn't try to correct it. "I'm going back to the party. I want to dance and there are guys in there who will dance with me."

"I'll call you tomorrow," Casey said. He walked through the door and into the party as if he needed to escape.

"You scared him away," I told Don.

"Let's walk." He took my arm and pushed me down the stairs.

I pull my arm free when we were on the ground. "I'm not going anywhere except back to the party." I moved to go behind him, but he stepped in front of me. I stumbled into his chest. His hand steadied me, then dropped to his sides.

"You're in no condition to go back in there."

"Says who?" I challenged, hands on hips, legs apart and the neck roll that every black woman on earth knows from birth.

"Says any of the men inside whom you want to fool into believing you're a rich bitch from Brooklyn."

"New York," I corrected. My high evaporated. Don had a point. Then it came to me. "What about them? They must be feeling as least as good as I am. In the morning, who will know how we acted?"

"You wanna take that chance?"

I thought about it a moment. I felt I was capable of returning without an incident, but then I supposed all drunks thought like that. "What do you suggest?" I asked.

"Take a deep breath. It'll help clear your head."

"Oh no," I contradicted. "I've seen that technique in too many movies. I take a deep breath and then pass out. I fall forward, you catch me and haul me over your shoulders like a sack of potatoes."

He laughed, a long, deep, belly laugh. "You can't believe what you see in the movies. They do it for the drama."

"Maybe, but I'm not doing it."

"All right, then at least take some time to walk."

After a moment, I nodded. Don reached for my hand, but I moved away from him.

"Don't even think you're going to get me back to your place. I'm not that drunk." At least not anymore, I added to myself.

Music played softly on the night air. Everyone was gone. Lila had disappeared with Clay. Amber bugged out early. I didn't see her leave, but she wasn't really in tune with this party. She was probably on the beach or somewhere with Don, whom she adamantly refused to see.

Shane and I sat holding hands on the back stairs. The moon was high and lighted the chairs and tables in the spacious backyard.

"Did you have a good time?" I asked, my head falling onto his shoulder. The two of us had hardly been separated since we returned to the Vineyard.

"I always have a good time with you."

I smiled and snuggled closer to him. Shane's arm moved to my waist, making me feel warm and safe. "You always know the right thing to say."

"They're not just words," he said.

His tone arrested my attention. I'd had a few drinks, too, and the buzz in my head had me floating on a soft plane. Part of it was due to the man with his arm around me. The other part was that echo in the back of my mind telling me everything I had could go away with the prick of a pin.

"Is that the truth?" I finally asked, leaning back to look into his face.

"Absolutely," he said without hesitation. His smile was sweet and disarming. For a moment I realized how often I'd looked into those eyes and forced back a nagging thought. After a moment his smile faded. "What?" he asked.

I pulled away, sitting up straight, my back against the porch balustrade. I reached over and took his hand again. Looking at it, I turned it over in mine and stroked his palm. His skin was warm, smooth and soft—musical. I could hear it without the notes I knew his hands could produce drifting through my head.

"What's on your mind, Jacynthia?"

I looked at him for a long moment. "It's hard to say," I began, hesitating and clearing my throat.

"Just say it." He leaned toward me, not moving his hand, but curling it in mine.

"We haven't known each other long."

He nodded.

"The summer will end soon."

"That's true," he acknowledged.

It was hard for me to broach this subject, but it had been bothering me since our first kiss. I needed to clear my head of the thoughts that concerned me. And Shane's one-line comments were becoming irritating.

"In the short time, since we met . . . I . . . I've become very fond of you."

Again he nodded.

"I mean, I think I'm falling for you."

He smiled. "Is that so bad?"

I nodded. The smile on his face turned to a frown.

"Why?"

"Because of Ella Francis."

"Ella—"

"I don't mean her in particular," I interrupted him. "I mean people like her. She's part of your industry. But so are the other women."

"What other women?"

"The ones who follow you, who follow celebrities, who crowd around you like they have a right to. The ones who want to meet you and bed you. The ones who will do anything to get to you."

"That's not how—"

I was already shaking my head before he finished his comment. "That's exactly how it is. I saw them at Jordan West's and I saw them at the concert. I see it in the news. Even the ones with the cleanest images succumb to the pressure of women throwing themselves at them."

"And you think that will be me? Indiscriminately picking some woman out of the crowd and taking her to my bed, condom already in hand?"

I said nothing, made no gesture to approve or deny his comment. I wanted him to say it wouldn't be him, but I knew the words would only mean something today. By morning, a week from now, a month from now, things would be different.

"I'm not like that, Jacynthia."

"I believe you." It was a lie. I was smarter than to think any man would turn down a gorgeous woman with practically nothing on, giving all the signals that she wanted to go to bed with him. And those women either followed celebrities or lived in the town where they were performing. The headliner wasn't always the person they sought. Members of the band were just as vulnerable. And with Shane looking like a screen idol, he was bound to be highly tested.

"But you don't trust me?" Shane asked.

"It's a little early to be talking trust. We really don't know each other very well."

"Are you trying to break up with me?"

"We haven't established a relationship, so we can't break up." My logic was flawless even though I felt we'd become a couple.

"You don't think what we've been doing is a relationship?" he questioned.

"Not in so many words," I said, struggling to keep my voice level.

"Well, let me correct that. I want you to be my woman."

Shane leaned forward and kissed me. It was quick and light, but long enough for me to get the point.

Oh God, I thought. This was not going the way I wanted it to. And I didn't know what way that was. My feelings confused me. I felt as if I wanted to go to the next step with Shane, but I was unsure what that was and more unsure if it could last for any amount of time after the summer ended.

I hadn't planned this conversation. However, the women I'd seen circling around Shane had been on my mind for days. Tonight it just came out, but him declaring he wanted us to be a couple hadn't been explored in my self-questioning or my fantasies.

"Jacynthia, I know all the things you're concerned about. I know we can't promise each other that nothing will happen. All we can do is take a chance—trust each other."

I searched his face for a long time, trying to find anything ungenuine about the way he looked at me. There was nothing. I wanted to believe him. I wanted to think that there was some assurance I could get. That if I crossed the line and totally opened my heart to this man, it wouldn't be broken by some future circumstance.

Shane broke into my thoughts. "I know what you're thinking."

"What?"

"That I can only speak for this moment. That sometime in the future, even if you are my woman, I will forget that and act in the moment."

I stared without commenting.

"I can't promise you anything about the future and some unknown woman or women. In my profession, you're right, women are always there and always looking for action. To this point I've been very selective." He paused, giving me a long look. I felt everything about me warm up. "I don't plan to change."

I nodded. It was all I could do. Shane was becoming very important to me, and I was at a loss for what to say or do.

"I have an idea," he said.

"What's that?"

"Why don't we take it one day at a time? Anytime you want to bail out." He put his hands up, palms out, as if surrendering to something. "I'll back away. No questions asked."

This wasn't what I wanted. I was falling for Shane. Falling hard, and I was afraid of hitting bottom, finding another Ella Francis and having my heart broken. Would it be better to get out now, before I'd reached the point of no return? Or should I cross the line and take the chance of future heartbreak?

"Jack, you can't read the future." Shane rarely called me Jack. His voice was soft, but there was a pleading quality to it. I read the underlying desperation in his words.

"I'll accept your plan," I said. "But only if it works both ways."

He stared at me. His eyes held an assurance that he knew his mind now and it would be the same in the future.

I wasn't as sure. I knew there was no way to guess, no way to read the future. "If for any reason, you want to walk away," I said, "there will be no questions on my part."

"Agreed," Shane said.

Chapter 17

The moon was full and high in the sky over the Atlantic Ocean. Clay and I danced on the sand. The breeze was cool and we both wore his dinner jacket. I had my arms inside the sleeves and he had his arms around me, holding and twirling me around while the surf played music. I hummed softly in his ear.

"Did you enjoy the party?" I asked Clay, speaking in a singsong contented voice.

"You were there," he replied. His arms tightened around me. "How could I do anything else?"

"It was fun."

"Yeah, Amber seemed to be having a great time," he said.

I wanted to laugh but kept my humor inside. Amber was a sight, but I thought I should support her.

"I shouldn't have let her drink that much. She usually sticks to juices and a single glass of wine."

"What was different tonight?"

"Don Randall has his eyes on her."

"Who's Don Randall?"

"The manager at the St. Romaine. They seem to

rub each other the wrong way, but secretly I think she's hiding behind feelings she doesn't want to acknowledge."

"Seems rather junior high schoolish to me."

"Maybe," I noted. "They'll work it out."

Ever since our first night on the Vineyard, Amber had been fighting her attraction to Don Randall. Jack and I could see she liked him, but he wasn't in the right tax bracket and Amber refused to be swayed from her plan of finding a rich man whose wealth she could share. Never mind that she and Don were right for each other.

I thought Orlando had left me overwrought and spoiled for another man, but it was obvious to Jack and me that Amber had been severely hurt by Emile. She put up roadblocks with this idea of marrying a rich man whether she loved him or not, and she refused to see past any of the dark walls she'd erected.

I could see it clearly, but dared not let her know. She had to work it out for herself.

"Yeah," Clay said. "So will we."

"So will we what?" I'd forgotten what we were talking about.

"We'll work things out, too."

Putting his hand under my chin, he lifted my face to his. His kiss was long and tender. Our feet stopped moving and we held each other, our bodies aligned, heads bobbing side to side as the kiss deepened and lengthened and our bodies went from solid to melding.

"The house is empty," I whispered, coming up for air.

"So is mine," he crooned against my lips. "My aunt

went to the mainland to visit a friend. She'll be back on Wednesday."

I smiled as the implication went through me. Heat poured over me and I no longer needed his coat for warmth.

Clay turned me around and we walked back to the house. The lights were on inside, but we didn't go in. I didn't want to be separated from him for a moment. We got in Clay's car and he drove to the Bluff. As soon as he turned the ignition off, he leaned over and kissed me.

"I feel like a teenager," I said. "Stealing into your mom's house after midnight. I'm sure one of your neighbors is looking out and ready to report that you had a woman here while she was out."

He kissed me again. "It'll backfire on them."

"Why?"

"My aunt thinks I need a woman. She's after me to find someone and settle down."

I stifled the hitch in my throat. As much as I wanted to, I wasn't going there. It implied marriage, and while I was falling for Clay, discussing marriage this early would surely have him running scared. If he'd ignored his aunt's comments and not been married up to now, he might have a commitment issue. Whatever it was, I wasn't going to discuss it.

"Let's go in," he said.

It was the first time I'd been in the house. The place was beautiful, but not my style. I preferred more traditional furniture. Clay's aunt obviously liked antiques. I couldn't see him living here.

"Did you make any of this furniture?" I asked.

He laughed. "Most of this is older than I am. My aunt loves antiques. She owned an antique shop before she retired. I think it was being in her shop that made me want to make furniture."

"You make this style?" I wasn't criticizing it. I'd learned that things could be different from what I wanted and still be in good taste. The antiques were lovely and didn't make me feel as if I'd stepped into the nineteenth century.

"Sometimes, but not often. Most of my clients want something more modern."

"Maybe I'll get to see some of it one day."

Clay walked toward me. Suddenly I was irrationally afraid. More excited than afraid. My heart was in trouble, and I was gun-shy about being hurt again. But Clay touched me. His hand came up and the back of his fingers caressed my cheek. It was a simple gesture, yet it forced away any doubts I had.

Still wearing his evening jacket, I reached up and put my arms around his neck. On tiptoe I kissed him. The world changed in that moment. It was both simple and monumental. A rush of strong emotion invaded me. I knew what I'd felt for Orlando was a drop in the ocean to how Clay made me feel. And after such a short time.

"I'll show you one now." His mouth spoke, but his eyes searched mine. After a moment he turned me and we walked to the steps that led up to his bedroom.

I stopped on the bottom stair. "Is this a line to get me upstairs?"

"It could be. But it's not."

Clay's arm went around my waist and my head rested against him. The fear that had accosted me earlier was a distant memory now.

In the upstairs hall, he led me to his bedroom. In the darkness, he took my face in his hands. I felt the roughness of his fingers as he rubbed them across my cheeks. He pushed the jacket from my arms. Silently it crumpled to the floor.

"It's the bed," he said.

My attention had been elsewhere. I hadn't noticed the bed, though I saw there was one in the room. Clay reached for a lamp and turned it on. I gasped. The headboard was massive, reaching almost to the ceiling. It had detailed scroll work and labyrinthine carvings. In the center were several waves, each one greater than the one before. I could almost see them moving, hear them crashing into each other.

"It's beautiful," I said, moving to touch it, to run my hands over the strong wood. "You carved this?" I turned to face Clay. He was standing near the lamp watching me. "I've never seen a bed like this before."

While the headboard was massive, there was no footboard. I didn't think Clay's six-foot-plus frame could fit into a bed with a footboard. He must have known that when he was building it.

"I've never made love in it," Clay said.

"Never?" I teased, unsure why the admission sent a jackknife of sensation through me. "Out of respect for your aunt?"

He shook his head. "Never found the right woman."

My stomach threatened to fall. What was he not saying? Did he really feel the same way about me that I felt about him? I watched him slowly approach me. My heart pumped so hard I was sure he could see it physically thumping through my dress.

"Until you," he whispered.

"This is too much." I was hot, melting hot. My body yearned for his. I wanted him to touch me. I wanted to feel his rough hands. I wanted them all over me, turning my body into one huge erogenous zone.

"No, it's not," he said, taking me in his arms. "It couldn't possibly be." He kissed me, slowly, tenderly, as if I were fragile. I'd never felt so precious in my life. Orlando used to tell me I was precious, but with Clay I felt it.

Clay's hands dug into my hair and pulled it loose. Then holding the crown of my head, he deepened the kiss. His tongue slipped between my lips and swept about my mouth. I loved the taste of him, the sweet wetness of him. A nectar mixed with wine and beach and moonlight.

My arms circled his waist. I felt the strength of his erection against me. Arousal sailed into my being like a battleship bearing down on a dinghy. The slam splintered my control and in seconds I was pulling his mouth to mine, devouring him, freeing him of clothes and touching his skin. He was warm and damp in places. My mouth kissed his cheek and neck before running over his chest and finding his nipples. Under the onslaught of my tongue, they pebbled to life.

I felt more than heard him groan. The sound was an aphrodisiac, egging me on. I found his belt and undid it. As I unzipped his pants and pushed them over his hips, my hand sought and found the essence of him. I ran my palms over taut skin, feeling the hard ridge of his penis. My throat went dry with anticipation. I wanted him inside me, wanted to feel the hardness of his body joined with mine.

Clay took my hands. "I can barely stand now," he said. "You keep doing that and I'll be on my knees."

"Maybe I want you on your knees," I teased.

"I work much better in a different position," he said. And proceeded to show me. With slow motions he removed the remainder of our clothes. By the time he finished I was sure I would melt from the sheer heat of anticipation.

His mouth worked the same magic as his hands, rendering me defenseless and in need of resuscitation. As I slumped in his arms, Clay lay me on the bed. He pulled a condom on and his body covered mine. Large hands took my naked bottom, lifting me to the perfect angle for him to drive into me. His first stroke was hard and deep. A pleasure bubble as strong as steel shattered inside me. I accepted the full invasion of his body.

His pacing was fast, as if he couldn't stop himself. Yet the pleasure I felt outweighed everything else. I wanted him, needed him. He seemed to complete me. Fill the void I hadn't known was there. My eyes closed as I arched my back, absorbing the rapture of the moment. I couldn't keep my eyes open. They alternated between being wide with consuming passion and closing in sexual delirium.

I'd never known anything could feel this good. That anyone could cause me to believe that I could fly without the aid of a metal fuselage and a pilot with years of training. Clay was my pilot and it was obvious he'd had years of training. Yet he needed no metal structure to soar into the heavens and take me with him.

I was light, weightless, floating on clouds, unbound by gravity, my body transformed into pure energy. Sensation took on a physical presence, combining with my cells and carrying me to heights even the boundless sky hadn't discovered. Clay's mouth found mine, remaking me into a body, one that writhed with his. His kiss was like a drug, his tongue plunged into my mouth as his body surged into me.

I cried his name as a tempo I thought beyond human endurance increased. Fire threatened our joining. Sparks of electricity snapped between us. Hot passion grew to screaming level.

Suddenly, Clay was holding me, clasping me tight to him. Together we reached a height neither had seen before. For an eternity he held me there, keeping me suspended in this new world until neither of us could keep the tenuous membrane in place. Together we descended back to earth. Our climax sucked all the air out of my body. I breathed heavily, hearing and feeling my heart beating in my head. My body sang with a choir of wonderment.

Unable to talk, I held on to Clay, communicating in silent surrender. Emotion welled up inside me like a huge roiling storm. My arms and legs went weak. Like a boneless body they slid over him. After several moments, Clay raised himself up on his elbow and looked at me. I smiled, unable to move. It took a while, but strength returned to my limbs and I ran my hand over his shoulder. He was damp and had a heady smell of sweat and sex. Leaning forward, I kissed his skin.

"I have something to say," Clay said.

I leaned back, resting my head on the pillow.

"I know many men have told you you're beautiful just to get to the place where I am now."

I tensed, not knowing where this was going. We'd just made love, perfect love. Was he about to spoil it?

"You are beautiful." He paused and I waited. "Not just here." He touched my face, then ran his hand over my body. I stifled a sigh of pleasure when his fingers touched my breasts. "You're beautiful inside, too."

I smiled, feeling my eyes mist. No one had said that to me since the fifth grade, when I was a gangly ten-year-old with not a hint of the breasts or curves that awaited me.

"I'm in love with you and I want you to marry me."

I choked, coughing and moving up into a sitting position at the same time.

"You're not serious?" I said. "You're only saying that because of what we just did."

He put his fingers to my lips to stop my speech.

"Yes," he said.

My heart sank.

"And no," he finished.

"What does that mean?"

Moving his hand, he said, "Yes, it is because of what we just did. And I want to do it again, every day of my life. And I want to do it with you. And no, that isn't the only reason."

I wasn't sure I could breathe. I hungered for his words.

"So, will you marry me?"

It was on my lips to say yes. To jump at the chance for happiness. I was sure I loved Clay. I was sure I could spend my life with him and be happy.

But I couldn't. It wasn't in the cards for us.

"What's wrong?"

"Clay," I started, unsure how to explain my life to him. Pushing the covers back, I found his shirt and pushed my arms through it. Not bothering to button it, I walked to the end of the bed and turned to look at him.

The bed looked as if we'd wrestled with the

sheets. It knew the secrets of what we'd had. What we'd done. Clay was right, we'd made perfect love. I put it out of my mind. I had to tell him the truth. If he wanted to marry me, he deserved to know that I wasn't the person he thought I was.

A stunned expression marred his features. I felt as if I'd somehow wounded him. I wanted to remove the hurt from his face, but I didn't know how. What I was about to tell him would only increase that hurt.

"I haven't been exactly honest with you."

"How?" He hadn't moved from his position.

"You think I've some rich society woman. I'm not."

"You're not?"

He sat up in bed, pulling a pillow behind his head and leaning on it.

I shook my head. "I'm a pharmaceutical rep from New York."

He starred at me for a long moment. Then he burst into laughter. It was a deep belly laugh and it went on long enough to make me angry.

"What's so funny?"

"I thought you were going to tell me you were already married."

"What?" I stammered.

He kept laughing. "So you're a pharmaceutical rep?"

I nodded.

"Why should I care? I don't mean that," he quickly corrected himself. "I mean, why should that make a difference?"

"Because . . ." I bit my lower lip.

"Go on," he prompted.

"Because we came here to find rich husbands."

He leaned forward. "All of you?"

I nodded. "But it's not working out that way. The moment I met you, I knew I wanted to spend time with you. I'm not really that interested in money. I'd love to have it, but I'll be happy with someone I love."

"Are you saying you love me?"

I nodded quickly. "I love you. But I understand if you want to withdraw your proposal. I tricked you."

"Can I take it that you won't be marrying me for my money?" he asked. I heard the teasing quality underlying his comment. It was my turn to laugh.

Clay got out of bed then. He came toward me. The atmosphere changed. The lightness of the moment fled like smoke under a strong wind. I followed his movement as he approached me. Holding my breath, I wondered what he was thinking. I couldn't blame him if he didn't want to see me again.

"Will you marry me, Lila Easton, pharmaceutical rep from New York?"

Opening my eyes, I groaned. My head pounded with a fury that felt like little people with hammers on the inside of my skull.

"Shit," I said.

The surroundings were all too familiar. And they were Don's. What was I doing here—and in his bed? I ran a hand through my hair. My head felt as big as the moon that had hung out over the ocean last night. And my mouth was as dry and thick as sand. I was thirsty. I felt like I could drink the entire Atlantic.

Moving my legs from the warmth of the coverlet to the floor and sitting up had me stifling a scream.

Pain zigzagged inside my head. The hammering had been replaced with a detonating bomb. I held it, trying to squeeze the pain back in place. Again I moaned. Or I made a sound. It was foreign to me, like that of a wounded animal, something on its way to death.

I raised my head thinking I might be able to stand when the glass sitting up on the nightstand materialized, a note propped up against it.

Drink this, it read. Who the hell did he think I was? Alice in Wonderland. I was no Alice, but I reached for the glass and picked it up. I could tell there was tomato juice in it, but I didn't know what else. I smelled it. It smelled like tomato juice. I believe somewhere I heard or maybe I saw it in some late-night black-and-white television movie that Bloody Marys were used for hangovers. Bloody Marys weren't my choice of drink. And now I could argue that champagne wasn't either, at least not in the quantities I'd consumed it.

I looked at the glass again. "Well, you can't make me feel any worse that I do now," I told the glass. I drank it, upended the glass, emptying it. It had a familiar flavor, but the aftertaste had me frowning. It didn't taste like it had alcohol in it. But there was something more than plain tomato juice swirling around in my body now. I lay back down and waited for the magic elixir to do its work.

Or to reduce me to the size of an inch.

Where was Don? What time was it? It hurt too much for me to turn my head and look at the clock, but the sun was high in the sky so it must be well after nine. I had no reference. It could be close to noon by now, but I hoped it wasn't lunchtime yet. My stomach growled at the thought of food. I was hungry, but my head was controlling everything and it wasn't moving from this pillow.

I closed my eyes. When I opened them again, the sun had moved. My head felt better and I turned to look at the time. It was 2:07. "Oh God," I moaned, pushing myself up in the bed until the returning pain stopped me. My gown lay on a chair near the bed. It didn't call for a bra, so I was wearing only my panties and stockings.

The bedroom door opened and I scrambled back in the bed, pulling the sheet up to my chin. Don came in pushing a cart.

"I figured you'd be up and hungry by now," he said.

"How did I get here?" I asked without showing any appreciation for the trouble he'd gone through.

"Don't you remember?"

Was that a sly smile on his face?

"Would I ask if I remembered?"

"Are you always this grumpy in the morning, pardon me, the afternoon?"

I ignored him. "Did I undress myself?"

"Would that matter?" He moved to open the cover on a plate of eggs and bacon. "I've seen you in all your brown and red glory."

My body went hot.

He came to the bed with the plate in his hand. I fit the sheet securely and accepted it. Food might make me feel better. "Thanks," I said.

He sat down on the bed, forcing me to move or his butt would be against my leg. It was warm and hard and I shifted away from it. It was that or drop the plate.

"I brought you some clothes, too," he said. He glanced across the room. I followed his gaze and saw my overnight bag sitting on the floor.

Gasping, I tried to speak.

"Jacynthia thought you might need these."

"Why?" I asked. I started eating the eggs and bacon. They were delicious and made my stomach and my head begin to feel better.

"You can't go home in that." He gestured toward my discarded gown.

I'd done it before, but thought this wasn't the time to bring that up.

Don leaned forward and took a piece of bacon. Biting into the crisp piece of meat, he never took his eyes off me. My nipples hardened and pushed against the sheet covering them. I hoped he didn't notice, but I'd come to understand that Don noticed everything. After a moment, he bent forward and kissed the skin just above the sheet.

"Don't do that," I said.

"Why?" he asked, bending forward to repeat the procedure. This time he pulled the sheet and pressed his mouth against the top mound of my breast. "Don't you like it?"

I did. I loved it. Heat washed over me and I wanted to relax and slide down into the mattress. But I said no. My voice wasn't very convincing. Don ignored me. He pushed the covers down an inch and repeated the kiss on the top of the other breast. His mouth felt so good. My eyelids swept down, but I opened them wide and slid up the bed. The sheet slid down and Don moved in, taking my breast into his mouth.

The pleasure that flashed through me was like an exploding light.

"I have a proposal for you," Don said.

"What kind of proposal?"

"Don't worry. It's not marriage."

"You were sure to get a no on that front."

"I'm aware of that." He continued kissing my breasts, driving me crazy and making it hard for me to concentrate on anything except how much I wanted him inside me.

"What's your proposal?" I asked, curious as to what he wanted.

"A date."

"Date? Haven't we already had this conversation?"

"We've agreed to a plan, but this date will be before that."

I grabbed his head before he could plant another kiss farther down my body, where he was gradually exposing more and more skin. "So you want two dates?"

"I want to do you a favor."

I laughed. "How is my going on a date with you doing me a favor?"

"It's a stress-reduction dinner."

"Stress reduction," I repeated. "I don't feel any stress." I knew he was teasing, and I had to steel my face to keep from smiling.

"Yes, you do. Otherwise you'd be sleeping in your own bed right now."

I refused to reply.

"So, why don't we call a truce for tonight. We can act as if we'd just met and I asked you to dinner."

The idea of spending time with Don without the animosity that accompanied our previous encounters was exciting.

"With me you won't have to pretend. We can have a leisurely evening together with no fighting, and no stress."

"I see. Where do you want to go for this leisurely meal?"

"Word has it that you never miss a Wynton Marsalis concert."

Jack again, I thought. Just how much had my *friend* told Don? But the thought of seeing Wynton Marsalis brought back my memory. I knew he was on the bill this summer, but since I'd come to the Vineyard my attention had been in a different direction.

"He's performing tonight. Would you like to go with me?"

I hesitated. He sat back. "No strings. Just two friends enjoying a concert together," he said.

I smiled, genuinely. "I'd like that."

"Good. I'll pick you up at six and we'll have dinner first."

He stood up. I was disappointed he didn't go back to nibbling my breasts. But after a while I thought of my own plan for tonight. Just two friends enjoying a concert and having a stress-free night.

Well, Don Randall, I'm not finished with surprises yet.

Chapter 18

There was no turning back now, I thought when I saw Amber come down the stairs. She was all in red. My eyes took a slow trip from her spike-heeled sandals to the clip she had in her hair. Tonight was supposed to be stress free. But I was overloading already. I had to force my thoughts away from her and me removing all that red before my hard-on lifted any farther.

"Hello, are you my date for the evening?" she asked. Her voice was deep and sexy, forcing me to concentrate on what she was saying.

"Yes, ma'am," I said. I was anything she wanted me to be.

"Where are we eating?"

I didn't answer immediately, since it took a while for my brain to remember how to talk. "At the Port."

"That's on the other side of the island."

"Have you been there?"

"Almost. We got there one night later than our reservation and couldn't be seated. We ate in the bar."

The Vineyard didn't have that many restaurants.

It wasn't plausible that I would find one Amber hadn't been to, considering the number of dates she'd been on. Yet I felt a little put off that she had been here with someone else.

"Well, tonight we eat in the dining room." I knew it was in bad taste, but I'd checked the reservations at the hotel to make sure that Amber's gentlemen callers were eating there. I didn't expect her to see anyone she'd met on the island, but just in case, I asked for a private table and I knew exactly where it was located.

"Shall we go?" she said. "We don't want to be late for the concert."

The waiter, whom I knew, seated us at the table I'd requested. We were shaded by a large open-woven screen that allowed privacy, but we could still see through it. The candlelight would keep us from being identified.

"You know, I don't know very much about you," I said after we'd placed our drink order.

"You mean the real me?"

"We have a truce," I said. "I wouldn't have put it that way, but yes, the real you."

"I can say the same about you."

I nodded. We'd been to bed together more than once. I knew every aspect of her body. I knew her secret, her reason for being on the Vineyard. But I didn't know if she had sisters or brothers, where she was born, what she really wanted out of life. Apart from the superficial scheme to find a rich husband, who was Amberlina Nash?

As to my bio, it was written, told to everyone on the island who asked. But it wasn't the real me. And while Amber might give me some insight into her life, I was bound to keep mine hidden.

"What would you like to know?" she asked, jarring me out of my thoughts.

"Parents?"

"Yes," she said and laughed.

The waiter brought our drinks, a virgin piña colada for Amber. Bourbon for me.

"My parents live in Florida."

"Were you born there?"

"I'm pure Brooklyn. They were born in Indiana. When they were in their forties, they tired of the pace of the city and decided to return to the place of their birth. I'd graduated from college and taken a job. I loved the city and decided to remain there. Two years after moving, however, my father got an offer from Disney and they moved to Florida. He works as an engineer." She laughed as if her father was in the room. "To hear him tell it, he makes the park run, keeps the rides safe, designs new ones. My mother is a fabric designer."

"And you write for a greeting card company."

She nodded. "The card company is in New Jersey. I go there several times a year for meetings, but mainly I work at home. With computers, teleconferencing, and the Internet, I can work anywhere in the world."

"Is that what you want to do with your life, write greeting cards?"

"It's a living. But I've thought of trying my hand at writing a novel."

"But . . ." I prompted.

"But it's hard to write a whole book. I start and then they go nowhere or I lose interest in the story."

"You were writing on the beach. Anything productive?"

"As a matter of fact," she smiled shyly, "it appears that something is coming together."

"You like it?"

"I do."

"Are you willing to tell me what it's about?"

She shifted in her seat as if she were getting comfortable. "It's about a woman who's trapped in a lifestyle she's trying to get out of, but her family and friends keep telling her she's doing the wrong thing."

"How does it end? Does she go her own way or succumb to the pressure?"

"Well, I haven't exactly worked all the details out yet, but I believe she's going to tell them this is her life and she'll live it her way."

"Bravo," I said. "Good for you."

"Me? It's not me."

"Isn't your life paralleling the character's?"

"No." She shook her head. "Linda is nothing like me."

"I thought writers always drew on personal experience in order to write characters."

"They do somewhat, but they can also take qualities from people they know or have met. After all, the author doesn't have to be a bitch to write a bitchy character."

"I see." Maybe she didn't see that the character Linda was her. I admired her for taking her future in her hands and deciding what it should be, but I was disappointed that she believed a rich husband was the answer to future happiness.

If I kept pursuing this conversation it would lead to an argument. So I decided to change the subject.

"What about sisters, brothers?"

"One of each."

"Married, single?"

"Both married and living in Florida."

"They're younger than you."

She nodded. "There's only a year between each of us, but both of them married right out of college."

"What happened to you? I can't believe you've had no offers."

"Why is that? You think the way I look makes men fall at my feet?" she teased.

Using myself as a model, that's exactly what I'd done. "I didn't mean it that way. You are beautiful, but you know that. You're also warm and giving and in my opinion you have a good heart."

"Why thank you, kind sir." She deflected the compliment with humor.

"I mean it," I told her.

"What about you, parents?"

"Yes," I answered, sitting back and giving her the same answer she'd given me.

"Where do they live?"

"They travel a lot, but their main address is Philadelphia, Pennsylvania."

"Is that where you were born?"

"I was born in France."

"Let me guess, Paris?"

"Bingo." She was close. "It wasn't exactly in Paris. We were staying in a small village outside of Paris."

"When did you leave?"

"Like you, right after college. I traveled a lot, seeing the world, doing dangerous things."

"Like what?"

"Racing cars, flying planes . . ."

"You can fly?" She looked suitably impressed.

"Well, what I was flying couldn't exactly be

called an airplane. It was held together by duct tape and hope."

"Sounds exciting." She leaned forward, cupping her chin in her hand. "What else did you do?"

"Once I joined a traveling circus."

"As what?"

"I wasn't the clown, if you were thinking that."

"I was," she admitted.

"I was a rigger."

"What does a rigger do?"

"Just what it sounds like. I put up the tent, checked all the lines, that sort of thing. Once I was a stand-in for the horseback rider."

"You mean the woman who wears a tutu and tights and does tricks on horseback?"

"Noooo," I said, elongating the word. "I mean the *guy* who wears tights and does tricks on horseback."

We both laughed. I felt relaxed. I loved talking to her like this. When we weren't at each other, weren't trying to convince each other, even silently, that what we were doing was all right, we actually liked each other.

"How long were you with the circus?" she asked, still laughing. She was probably trying to imagine me in tights, but she had no real idea how ridiculous I looked.

"About six months."

"What made you do such a thing?"

"Mainly to piss off my father."

"One of those phases?"

"He wanted me to come into the business and I wanted to—" I stopped, realizing my mistake. "Well, I wanted to do something else."

"What is the family business?"

The appearance of our waiter with dinner saved

me from having to answer that question. By the time his elaborate machinations in setting and presenting the plates were done, Amber was enthralled in her dinner.

"This looks wonderful," she said, taking a forkful of her prime rib. "Hmm," she said.

Mine was just as delicious. We finished the meal discussing the Vineyard and the concert. I dodged a bullet that time. I hadn't come this close to violating the agreement between me and my father since my first week on the Vineyard. Amber was astute and quick to pick up on a lie. If the waiter hadn't come at that moment, she'd have seen right through me. And I couldn't have her doing that just yet.

The concert hall's lights went down and an off-stage voice introduced Wynton Marsalis. Normally the bubbles in my blood would be for the smooth performer. Tonight I was jittery due to the man in the seat next to me. Don hadn't done anything special. It was a normal date, dinner and a concert. I'd been on many of them before. Yet I was having a much better time with Don than I'd had with any of the other men I'd been out with.

With him I could be real. He'd told me that. Tonight was proof. I wasn't on guard. I didn't have to watch what I said or pretend to be anything other than who I was.

I shifted in my seat. Don looked at me and I smiled. Then he took my hand and pulled it into his. It brought back my plan for tonight. He'd said there were no strings attached, but I had puppet-master in mind.

Marsalis's music should have taken me away. It

always had in the past, but tonight I could only concentrate on the feel of the hand in mine, the touch of Don's fingers, the softness of his skin and its contrast to mine. My hand wasn't just being held. The gesture was reassuring. I felt safe, protected, loved. Gently I squeezed his fingers. He glanced my way and I felt as shy as a thirteen-year-old experiencing her first crush.

The anticipation of wanting him overruled anything happening on the stage. I wanted to leave. I wanted to go to the beach, run naked in the surf and make love on the sand until the sun rose to turn our brown bodies golden.

Yet I sat there, cocooned in an aura of happiness, contentment, and longing. The concert ended and we joined the throngs of people exiting the concert hall. The night was perfect when we left, soft and velvety. Music drummed in my head and sang in my blood as Don's arm wrapped around me and we strolled toward the hotel.

"Are you okay with walking?" he asked. The concert was standing room only and it was a short distance from the hotel.

"I like to walk," I told him.

"What about your shoes?"

I looked down. My shoes were high-heeled and red. The hotel wasn't far and I was sure I wouldn't be pushing it to take the few steps to the entrance.

"I can handle it," I said. "We walked here and I was wearing the same shoes."

"And beautiful they are," he said. He looked into my eyes. I thought I'd dive into them. Even in the darkness the need was visible. "I can go and get the car and pick you up," he offered.

"I'm fine," I said.

"I love a woman who knows her limits," he said, humor evident in his voice. "You know when I first saw you, I named you Lady Legs."

"You did?"

"You were getting out of the limousine. One long leg came out of the car. On it was a red high-heeled shoe. I thought your legs must be nine miles long and I couldn't wait to see the rest of you."

"Did I live up to the anticipation?"

He put his arm around my waist. "Baby, did you."

At that point, I turned my body into his and wrapped my arms around his neck. In the middle of the street, I kissed him. His mouth immediately crushed mine. I sensed this was something he'd been wanting to do all night. I knew I'd wanted to do it since the first time I saw him. I turned totally into him, fitting my body into his. His arms hugged me so close air couldn't pass between us. Like teenagers in the height of hormonal conversion, we stood and kissed, our heads turning like a child's top from side to side as we positioned and repositioned our mouths.

"Do you know what I thought when I first saw you?" I asked when we'd separated from each other and resumed walking.

"What?" He directed me to the beach. Several yards away a bonfire was burning and we could hear the sound of laughter and music combined with the night sea and silver moon.

"You were standing a few yards from the house. Your hand was up shading your eyes and you were staring at me. Your gaze was so intense that for a moment I thought you could see into my mind."

"What were you thinking at that moment?"

I considered not telling him. "I wouldn't want you to get too big a head," I said.

"Ah, now I'm really intrigued. What did you think?"

"That you were a very attractive man."

He threw his head back and laughed. "When did you change your mind?"

"I haven't changed my mind," I said. My feet sank into the sand and I stopped walking. Grabbing hold of his arm, I reach down and removed my shoes. The wind blew gently against my arms. We walked away from the partygoers. Near a small curve in the land stood a sand dune.

Around the side of it lay a blanket. On it was a glass-covered dish containing fruit and cheese. Next to that stood an ice bucket, a bottle of champagne protruding from its depths.

I smiled when I saw the setup.

"When did you do this?" I asked, surprised and pleased that he'd prepared a place for us to spend time together.

"Earlier tonight," he said. "Let's sit down."

I dropped my shoes and took a seat. Don sat next to me. I looked at the wine. "Do you trust me with champagne after last night?"

"I have control of the bottle," he said. Opening the wine, he poured a portion into the wineglasses that accompanied the setup.

"What shall we toast?" I asked.

"Tomorrow," he said. Clinking our glasses, we drank.

"I have a gift for you," I said.

"You do." Don looked surprised, as if no one had ever given him anything. "What is it?"

Opening my small sequin-covered purse, I pulled

out a wrapped box. I extended my hand with the box balanced in the center of my palm. Don looked curious. The package was small, rectangular, a jewelry box, the type that men usually gave to women.

He pulled the ribbon and untied it. The paper came away and he dropped it on the blanket. I watched with anticipation. Every now and then Don looked at me, expecting a clue to what was inside the box. I smiled but gave nothing away.

Finally the unadorned red velvet box was free of its trappings.

"What in this?" he asked.

"One way to find out," I said, unable to keep the smile off my face.

Gingerly he lifted the top.

"It won't bite you," I said.

"It just that I never expected anything."

The top fully extended, he looked inside. "What is this?" he asked, lifting out the three six-inch lengths of gold string that lay on a bed of white velvet.

I took one and wrapped it around his index finger.

"Can't you tell when there are strings attached?"

"Does this mean what I think it means?"

"I don't know. My mind-reading skills aren't up to par."

"Are the strings saying you want to tie me up or tie me in knots?"

"Hmm." I smiled. "I hadn't thought of either, but the tie you up sounds like a winner."

"Then what?"

"Then I have my way with you."

"You don't need strings for that."

"What would I need?"

"It isn't what you need. It's what you don't need."

"What don't I need?" The air had turned fiery and we were whispering as if in the aloneness of the beach someone might hear us.

He slipped one strap down from my dress.

"This is the first thing you won't need." He kissed my shoulder. "And this is the second." The other strap fell to the side.

"How many are there?"

"I'm not sure, but I plan to count every one of them. In slow . . ." Kiss. "Exquisite . . ." Kiss. "Fine . . ." Kiss. "Detail."

I could hardly breathe. My heart pounded harder than the surf. The ocean lapped against the shore while my heart hammered as if raging against jutting rocks that stood in the way of an intended goal.

Don progressed with slow determination, his tongue laving my skin with fire that burned liquid and hot. Heat raged and cooled to a cold fire that seeped into my soul.

"You know this was not part of tonight's plan," Don said.

"It was part of my plan."

His head came up and he stared at me. I looked him directly in the eye, not wavering a bit.

"What else is in your plan?" he asked. His voice was deep and dark.

"Just wait. You'll find out everything you need to know."

"Sounds intriguing," he said.

"You have no idea."

Chapter 19

The moon was just as large tonight as it had been the night before. I lay against Don, his arms around my waist, as we watched it. The party down at the other end of the beach went quiet as many of the participants left for their temporary Vineyard residences.

"I feel like we're alone in the world," I said.

"I can be in a crowd and still feel alone with you," Don said.

I smiled. "Pretty words."

"I mean every one of them."

"You can be so charming when you want to," I said, snuggling closer to him. His arms closed around me. "You never see a moon this large in Brooklyn."

"It's here all the time. You should make a point of getting out of the city and looking at it."

"Fine," I agreed. "Once a month I'll come to Vineyard just to see the moon."

"Only the moon?" he teased.

"Well, I suppose," I shifted to look at him, "I suppose I'd have to take a room at a local hotel.

There's a very nice manager at the St. Romaine. Do you know him?"

"Very well," he said.

I liked the simple banter. I liked the freedom of being in his arms. The moon beamed over the water, shimmering a path that went from the Vineyard to the shores of Wales and the European continent. I felt as if I could jump on that beam and be conveyed all the way to a foreign land.

I was certainly acting foreign. I'd never been this happy. No one had ever made me feel the way Don did. I could be reckless, or loveable. I could be giddy or formal and he'd fall right into step with me.

"Listen," he said.

I cocked my head. "All I hear is the water."

"Right," he said. "The party must be over."

"And we're alone in our universe."

"Something like that."

"Did you arrange this, too?"

He shook his head. "My powers only extend inside the hotel. Outside its walls, I'm just a citizen."

"I could debate that," I said. I pulled myself up, getting closer to him, deliberately dragging my body against his.

"Is this a string?" he asked.

"One of many," I answered. Slipping a hand around his neck, I pulled his mouth to mine. He fell back onto the blanket. I went with him as he opened his legs and pulled me between them. I kept pulling myself over him until I was lying on his chest and kissing him deeply. Seduction was surprisingly easy, although I was quickly losing it. I wanted him as I had from that first moment when he stared at me under hooded eyes.

His arms went around me and he tried to push me onto the blanket, but this was my seduction and I was choreographing it.

It was impossible to keep from moving over him. I rotated my hips, evoking the desired response when I felt his erection rising.

"That feels good," Don said. His voice was lower than normal. I moved more, grinding my hips into his.

His hands went to my hair, threading through it as his mouth took mine in a kiss so strong it obliterated my thoughts. Moving his hands down, he unhooked the zipper of my dress and drew it down, exposing my skin to the night air. His hot hands went inside the fabric and caressed me.

I was already burning up. But something inside me pushed me. Forcing my mouth from his, I sat back, reaching for the buttons on his shirt. Quickly I undid them as he smoothed the dress from my shoulders and let it fall to my waist. The night air caressed my skin, a welcome coolness to the internal furnace that generated a red hotness. I was surprised Don's hands didn't melt where they touched me.

For long moments we stared at each other. The moonlight filtered over his chest where I'd undone his shirt and pulled it down his arms. Mesmerized by the sight of him, I couldn't drag my eyes away. He had an athletic body, strong arms, with cords that showed he worked out regularly. I remembered those arms holding me. I reached for him again. He removed my bra and cupped my breasts.

"You are so beautiful," he said. "All over beautiful."

Sensation ran through me. I couldn't speak. They may have been pretty words, but they were reaching places in me that hadn't been touched before.

With lightning speed we undressed each other and I was back in his arms. His body covered mine. His mouth covered mine. We rolled across the blanket in a tangle of arms and legs. Finally, I landed on top. I looked down at Don. My hair had fallen out of the carefully pinned-up style I'd taken time to arrange.

Don's hands washed over me, seemingly not able to find a spot to remain stationary. I loved him touching me. Lines of sensation, heated by the surfaces of his fingers, trailed over the indentation and curves of my skin. I straddled him and looked down into his face. Then I lowered my mouth and kissed him again. For the second time something inside me snapped loose. I couldn't get enough of him. I was hungry for him, desperate. I felt like an animal, wild and uncontrolled, unable and unwilling to stop.

Raising my hips I guided him into me, settling his penis deep inside. Pleasure shot through me like a drug. I moaned as raw rapture tunneled through me. My hips worked up and down, slow at first, then gaining an uncontrollable speed. My body took him in time after time. Instinct took over as I worked the rhythm of untold lifetimes.

Don's hands ran up my body to my breasts. His thumbs paused and brushed across taut nipples. I felt the sensation tighten inside me. My hips worked faster. I pumped onto him until I thought we'd burst into flame. Somewhere in the fog of my mind, I heard my name. Don was calling it over and over.

"I'm here," I whispered. "I'm here."

His arms tightened around me and in a moment we'd reversed positions, but the frenzy that drove us was ever present. Don pushed my legs around him and drove into me. I gasped at the added sensation that rocketed in all directions. Pinning my arms to the sand, he continued the rhythm I'd begun. I could hardly contain the sensations going through me or the feel of Don's body against mine. I moaned with pleasure-pain that seemed to pour from every part of me. In that moment I knew life had changed. Nothing would ever be the same again. I would never walk the same, never see the world in quite the same way as I had when the sun had risen this morning.

And then the rush began. I felt the rolling inside me, knew that soon the greatest pleasure in the world would push me up and over the edge. I staved it off, grunted with each stroke that drove a greater sensation through me. I wanted to keep the feeling going, wanted to continue this impossible pace. Even knowing I couldn't, I tried. Then on a high note, I called his name and the climax gripped me as the life-affirming dance reached its zenith.

Together we collapsed into each other's arms. Breathing hard, I tried to get myself under control. Don's hands traversed my naked back. I lay against him, forgetting to do anything except glow in the aftermath. His breath was as ragged as mine and his heartbeat as rapid.

We lay like that for a long time, neither of us speaking, just holding each other, letting the night surround us and staying connected in the most intimate way.

"That was a hellava string," Don said. "I can't wait to redeem the next two."

* * *

"You have sand in your hair," Don said hours later. He pushed his finger into it, combing through the strands.

"Among other places." I laughed. He looked a little embarrassed. I reached over and ran my hand down his face. He needed a shave, but at this time of night, or rather morning, it was perfectly understandable.

"We should be going," I said. "I haven't seen Jack or Lila in two days. I haven't even called them."

"They haven't called you either, so that must mean all is well."

Even though Don sounded as if he wanted to remain where he was, he pulled my dress strap up on my arm and shifted to a sitting position.

"Do you have to work today?" I asked as I lifted my sandals and we prepared to leave.

"Oh yes." His arms went around my waist and he pulled me into his lap. "And I am not looking forward to it."

"Why not?" I teased. "Is there something else you'd rather do?"

He consulted the lightening sky. "I can think of a thing or two."

"Me too," I said, stretching. "I'm going to sleep until I wake up."

"Rub it in," he said. "At least I get to shower before I have to begin duties. Wanna have one with me? It'll get all that sand off."

"And you on," I said.

The idea of going to bed with Don was appealing. I almost wimped out and let him take me back to the bungalow. We'd been on the beach all night, made love once, but I wanted more.

We reached the house and walked up on the porch. Don's car sat at the curb. His arm was around me as it had been for most of the night. Now we had to separate.

"Should I say good night or good morning?" I asked.

He turned to me, lowering his hands down to my fingers and holding them. "Why don't we hold it until tonight."

"What's happening tonight?"

He leaned forward and gently kissed me on the mouth. My arms came up and circled his neck. His body felt good next to mine. We hung together, supporting each other, until his mouth found mine. We kissed as lovers, hard and frantically. His hands skimmed over my back. Mine wove into his hair, over his shoulders and down his arms. Our mouths melded until we couldn't take a breath.

"See you tonight," Don said, taking a small step back.

"Tonight?"

"I thought we'd have dinner."

"Can't." I shook my head.

"Why not?"

I didn't want to tell him. It would spoil the wonderful time we'd had together. "I have something to do tonight."

"What?" he pressed.

I waited a long moment. "I have a date."

"You have a what?"

He dropped my hands and took a full step back.

"This can't come as a surprise to you. You were there when Casey said he'd call."

"Casey!" He nearly shouted the man's name. I checked to see if any of the neighbors were looking.

Someone was always watching the house, although the kiss a moment ago hadn't left me with any thoughts or cares about being seen.

"He's invited me to a concert."

Don started to say something, but stopped. He turned around and walked the entire length of the porch. I remained where I was.

"After the time we had tonight . . . after what we . . . after . . ." He couldn't seem to form a complete sentence. "You going to . . ." Again he stopped speaking. For a long moment he said nothing.

Crossing my arms, I looked at him. Anger grew inside me like a cancer. "Is that what this was about? What the date was designed to do? You thought if I went out with you that I would change my mind about finding a husband?"

"A rich husband," he corrected.

"That's good, Don. Really good. You got me. You had this whole thing planned, right down to the sex on the beach." He started to protest, but I stopped him. "Dinner, concert, the blanket, the champagne, even the cozy cove, which blocked out the world." I paced in circles, my anger growing. "What woman wouldn't be flattered, wouldn't think that she was the only person in the world. And all the while, you were just trying to change me. Well, don't kid yourself, Mr. Randall," I said flatly. "You're not that great a date." I was lying. He was everything I'd ever wanted in a man, but he didn't know that.

"So you're going ahead with this—venture?"

"Are you saying you want to be my husband?"

"No, I am not."

"Then we have no problem, do we, Mr. Randall?"

He calmly walked toward me. Coming to a stop directly in front of me, he smiled that charming smile. "None at all, Ms. Nash. Good-bye. I hope you enjoy your remaining time on the Vineyard."

He turned and left. I stood in place watching him. He walked directly to the car. I hoped he'd look back, but he opened the door and slid behind the wheel without so much as a glance in my direction.

Making a U-turn in the road, he was gone. I wanted to kick myself. I knew what it was like to feel like a heel. I'd had the best night of my life, been with a man who treated me like a queen, made love to me like an animal, and caressed me like a baby.

And I was letting him drive away.

After showering and shaving, I took a three-hour nap before starting the day. The weight of a long night bowed my shoulders. I'd hoped it would be a night I could look back on and smile while others wondered what the joke was. But that was not to be. It had started that way. Everything had gone according to plan, right up to the point when I walked up on the porch to say good night to Amber.

Then the moon fell out of the sky. After we'd spent such an idyllic time together, it meant nothing to her. How could she consider continuing to see other men when I was sure she enjoyed being with me? She was a woman on a mission and it damn sure got on my nerves. She was driving me crazy, but to her I was just another man on the Vineyard. Not the right man. Not anyone up to her standards. Not what she was looking for. Just someone to spend time with, have sex with when she wasn't pursuing her original goal. Just someone she could drive over the edge.

I was sure she enjoyed being with me. The problem was she didn't enjoy it enough to give up this crazy idea of finding a rich man to marry. I shook my head as I walked into the main door of the hotel.

"Oh no, you won't. I have a reservation for this hotel and I will not be sent somewhere else."

"Damn," I cursed under my breath. Why couldn't this be a calm day, I thought. I didn't need to have to deal with the disgruntled public today when I was tired and I really needed to kick something.

"May I help you?" I asked the rather loud man who was demanding something of the desk clerk. I glanced at the clerk, who looked relieved that I'd appeared.

"Who are you?" the man asked, his voice accusatory.

"Don Randall, manager." I offered my hand. He stared at it for a moment before shaking it.

"I have a reservation at this hotel. And this . . ." He paused to glance at the man behind the counter. "This man tells me you are full up. How can you be full up when I have a confirmation?" He shook a piece of white paper in his hand.

Obviously, he didn't travel much, I thought. It was normal for hotels to overbook rooms. In this case, the usual number of cancellations had not occurred and there was no space available. Several of our guests had decided to stay over an extra day. This was normal for a hotel. We couldn't tell them they had to leave when they were in possession of the room.

"I've tried to explain to Mr. Brooks that the rooms were not vacated."

"It's all right." I stopped him from speaking. Then turning back to Mr. Brooks, I said, "We have a couple of late checkouts, Mr. Brooks. If you would give us some time, we'll find you a room."

"I want a room now," he insisted.

"Please, be my guest in the restaurant while we get your room ready."

This brought an abrupt change to his attitude. I found that something free usually did that to irate guests, and food or drink was the best thing. It wasn't noon yet, and with his attitude alcohol would only enhance his irritable nature.

Offering to show him the way, I took him into the restaurant and gave instructions that his bill was to be put on my account. He smiled and offered me his hand as I left. Obviously he would order more food than he would if he were paying for it. But he was happy for the time being.

Going back to the desk, I spoke with the clerk. "Who do we have scheduled to check out today?"

The man punched in some keys and looked at the list that came up on the screen. Casey Edwards's name jumped out at me.

"Mr. Edwards is leaving." That would free up two rooms.

"He called a moment ago to say he was staying another week."

I clenched my teeth together. I wondered if his decision had anything to do with Amber.

"What about the Cooper party? They have six rooms."

"They decided to stay one more day and go on one of the excursions that hadn't been in the program they chose."

I scanned the list for another prospect. It was considered a good thing when a hotel was up to capacity. Usually that meant eighty-five to ninety percent. The St. Romaine was at a hundred percent.

"What about one of the bungalows? Could we put him there?" The bungalows were used by some VIPs and for staff emergencies. The buildings were appointed as well as the rooms, but they were in an out-of-the-way location.

"We booked most of those. The one that Mr. Romaine uses is free, but we never put anyone in there. And as luxurious as it is, I don't believe Mr. Brooks would want to be that far from the main building."

"I agree with you." Mr. Romaine was my father. He wasn't due to be on the Vineyard for a while. It was a last resort for anyone. I stood up straight, no longer looking at the computer screen. Casey Edwards's name continually stopped my eye, and that brought thoughts of Amber to mind. Maybe I should check Mr. Brooks's net worth. If it was high enough, I could put him in the house with Amber.

Straightening my shoulders and taking a deep breath, I dropped that thought. And picked up one that would solve the morning's problem.

"Mrs. Parker," I whispered and came around the counter to meet her. She smiled, holding her not-yet-a-year-old baby close to her breast. Mrs. Parker had mentioned the noise that kept her child awake during naptimes. In a matter of minutes, I'd given her the VIP room, and Mr. Brooks would take her room.

I felt as if I'd done my part as a host for the morning, but this was not to be the worst of the day. Problem after problem came up. Air conditioners didn't work, ice machines were out of order, reports of lost property had the staff searching.

I should have appreciated the problems since they kept my mind from going back to Amber and the anger I felt. What I needed was some exercise. But by the looks of things today, there would be no time to get in a game of tennis. Maybe I could sneak in a swim.

At 3:00 things seemed to calm down. I went toward the pool. Amber usually swam in the mornings. I knew she hadn't been there this morning. And I doubted she could come in the afternoon, especially if she had a date with Casey Edwards later tonight.

"Heavy date last night?" Jeff asked. I looked up at him. I was standing in the fitness room with no memory of walking through the doors.

"What did you say?"

"It's that bad?" he asked.

"I thought I'd go for a quick swim." I ignored his comment. Going to a small dressing room I often used, I began changing clothes.

"I'll bet it was that woman with the long legs and the perfect diving form." Jeff had moved closer to the room I was in. I could hear him clearly.

"Well, that's in the past. She'll be leaving the Vineyard soon."

"But not before you two enjoy a concert or two."

I stopped as if flash frozen. "What did you say?"

"You know they say the hearing is the first thing to go."

"I have no idea what you're talking about."

"Wynton Marsalis. Row eight, seats G and H. And you didn't come dragging in here until well after nine."

I stepped out of the room, wearing a hotel robe over my trunks. "You were there?"

"Several rows behind you, but I could have been on another planet for all you knew. You only had eyes for the woman on your arm."

I remembered the feel of Amber's waist, the way she moved, her long legs and the high-heeled sandals that emphasized her toned body. I thought about our lovemaking on the beach. I remembered her mouth on mine and how she completely lost herself in the throes of passion.

"She's here, you know."

"What?" I looked toward the pool. It was surprisingly empty.

"Not in there. She and her two friends are having massages."

Jeff gestured toward a closed door. It led down a long hall where there were private massage rooms.

"Who's she with?"

"Antoine, Mr. Hands."

Antoine was the best the St. Romaine had to offer. Women and men raved about his magic hands, how good he made them feel and could they take him home with them. I had thought of having a massage today. Thank God I'd opted for the pool. I didn't want to run into Amber. Not this soon.

"I'm going for a swim," I said. Going through the doors, I walked to the chair I usually used, dropped the terrycloth robe, and dove into the water. I swam, taking long strokes to move through the water. I concentrated on my breathing, on the distance from one end of the pool to the other. I counted the laps, forced myself not to look up at the diving boards and think of Amber standing there.

Exercise usually helped me. It got the kinks out of my system, relaxed me after the physicality of the act. Today I could only think of Amber being a few yards away, lying naked on a table covered only by a long towel. My mind could hear her moaning as Antoine worked on her muscles, removing any traces of stress and leaving her as relaxed and complete as the aftermath of sex.

"Shit," I said as pool water rushed into my mouth.

Chapter 20

The front door slammed. I jumped, turning in the same instant that I reached for a knife. Lila shouted from the front of the house.

"Anyone here?"

I came to the doorway of the kitchen, ready to defend against whatever or whomever she was running from.

"What's wrong?" I asked, panic in my voice.

She ran toward me, hugging me and turning me around in circles. I held the knife away from us.

"I'm getting married," she shouted, then looked at the ceiling and shouted again, "I'm getting married."

I was shocked. Here I was thinking she was angry with someone and slamming into the house, while she was so excited she couldn't contain her exuberance.

"Clay?" I asked, putting the knife on the counter.

"What were you doing with that?"

"Never mind." Explaining it sounded foolish now. "Who are you marrying?"

Lila stepped back. "Clay." Her voice dropped a level. "I know he's not what we expected to find

here, what we came here to look for, but I love him,
Amber. Please be happy for me?"

Lila was glowing. She looked happier than I'd
seen her in ages. I hugged her and stepped back. "I
am happy for you, Lila."

"But . . ."

It was there. I couldn't help but be concerned.
I'd come here with a plan, but I knew now that it
wasn't completely thought out. I assumed it was. In
the starkness of my Brooklyn living room, I'd
weighed all the angles. But there were things about
human nature that couldn't be quantified. I knew
that now.

I sat down at the table, pulling Lila with me.
"Clay seems like a wonderful man," I began.

"He is, Amber."

"Are you sure you love him?"

"Of course I am. I've never felt this way about anybody." After a moment she said it again. "*Anybody.*"

"Including Orlando Robinson?"

Lila smiled widely. It was the last thing I expected to see. "Amber, I thought I was in love with
Orlando. Even when we came here, I wanted to
call him, fall on my knees and beg him to get back
together. I was this close to dialing his number."
She put her thumb and forefinger an inch apart.
"Then I met Clay."

"And he changed that?"

She nodded. "Right from the beginning he understood what I was going through. He even offered
to help me through it." She was smiling again. In
fact, she didn't seem to be able to stop smiling. "I
was so angry with him. I practically threw him off
the porch. As an apology, he made me that doll's
chair with my name on it."

Understanding dawned.

"Since then we've done so much together. I didn't think I'd fall in love with him, or he with me, but I did."

"And he popped the question?"

"Last night." She nodded. "I told him the truth, Amber. I told him that I'm not rich but work as a rep. It meant nothing to him. He still wants to marry me."

I couldn't help being both happy and envious of Lila. She was so in love and so happy that she couldn't contain it.

"Lila, if he's what you want, then go for him."

"Do you mean it?" she asked. "Do you really mean it?"

"I mean it," I said. "I've never seen you happier."

"I am happy," Lila said. "I want everyone to be this happy. But, Amber, I want you to be happy, too."

"Me? I just said I was happy for you."

"For me," she repeated. "I want you to knock down that wall you erected around your heart."

I stared at her, unsure of what she meant.

"Since Emile broke your heart, you've avoided men."

"I have—"

Lila put her hand up to stop me from speaking. "You go out with them, but you don't let them inside the wall. Don—"

"Oh God, let's not talk about Don."

"You concocted this plan, and at the time I bought into it. After getting here it was fun. I liked the pretense, liked hiding behind another identity. It helped to be another person, someone who hadn't been hurt, who wasn't nursing a broken heart. But after a while I just wanted to be me."

"I'm not doing that," I said, but not really analyzing my words.

"Aren't you?"

Sitting in the audience with Casey was vastly different from the previous night when Don had occupied the seat next to me. Last night I couldn't concentrate on Wynton Marsalis. The electricity generated by Don's presence snapped like anticipation between us. Tonight I had no problem giving my full attention to Natalie Cole as she sang updated versions of her father's standards. All the electricity came from the stage.

Lila's words crept into my thoughts. Was I keeping everyone at bay? Did I develop this plan to find someone who could support me, but to whom I would have no emotional attachment? Was Emile still occupying my heart?

No!

I almost said it out loud. Emile was just a memory. I had loved part of him, but I understood with the whole of my heart that I didn't love him in the forever kind of way.

Natalie Cole's lyrics touched me, reminded me of how much I missed Don. He hadn't called all day and I didn't see him during my afternoon visit to the hotel for a long massage. Of course, I was glad he hadn't been around. The Vineyard was small and Don was known by everyone. Anywhere I went I was bound to run into him sooner or later. Right now I wanted it to be later.

Casey reached over and took my hand. I smiled at him, then turned back to the stage. I was aware of his hand holding mine, but there was nothing there, no electricity, no stirring in the pit of my stomach, no contraction between my legs.

Could I live with that?

I knew Casey was suppose to leave the Vineyard this morning. He'd changed his mind and added a week to his vacation. I was pretty sure I was the reason. He was what I was looking for—a man in his prime, with an ample bank account. I liked his son. Casey was attracted to me, maybe even falling in love with me.

So why wasn't I satisfied with that? Why wasn't I falling in love with him?

Don, I thought. Don had spoiled my plans almost from day one. But I was not going to let that happen. I squeezed Casey's hand a little harder and he looked at me with a smile. I settled back in the seat and watched the rest of the concert.

We left slowly with the crowd. There was no walking back to the car parked at my house. There was no stopping on the beach. We got into the car Casey had rented and drove the short distance in silence. He parked in the driveway and turned the engine off. For a long moment neither of us spoke.

"Did you enjoy the concert?" he finally asked.

"I love Natalie Cole, and the opening act was very funny." A young comedienne had come on in advance of the singer. The young woman poked fun at the some of the normal things in life, like the daily coffee run and the fact that there was an exercise challenge on the cover of women's magazines superimposed over a chocolate cake or some other sweet, fattening, artery-clogging dessert. I laughed thinking of the truths she told.

Casey turned to me. "What are you thinking?"

"I was remembering some of the jokes the come-dienne told."

He smiled as if he was remembering, too. "I've enjoyed being with you during this trip," he began. For some reason my stomach clenched. "Joel has enjoyed his diving lessons. He's glad we're not going home for another week."

"He's a wonderful child."

"I know. I feel so lucky to have him."

Another silenced ensured.

"You've been one reason that Joel has enjoyed himself. The diving is something he wouldn't have tried without seeing you do it."

"He only needed a little coaxing," I said.

"And you were there to do it."

I didn't know where this was going. Casey seemed a little nervous. And my shoulders were very tight.

"I've been thinking," Casey said. "I know we haven't known each other very long, but I feel that we're compatible."

Compatible, I thought. It wasn't the word I was looking for, not the word a woman wanted to hear. It should have been satisfying for me. After all, I wasn't really looking for love. Was I?

"You and Joel get along well. And Joel needs a woman's influence."

A woman's influence? He was about to propose. Suddenly I didn't want him to do that. I had come to the Vineyard looking for a husband, and I might be about to get my wish. But I wasn't sure I wanted this wish any longer. Let someone inside the wall, Lila had said.

"When we get back to our normal lives, I want to continue to see you. In fact, I want to see you as often as possible."

I said nothing. I didn't know what to say or how to let Casey know that my feelings didn't go any further than friendship.

"I thought I'd never love anyone except my wife. After she died, I thought my life was over, too, but then I met you."

I had to stop this, I told myself. I couldn't let him ask me to marry him. Even if it was my goal, I knew it wasn't right.

"I never thought I could feel so strongly about someone after so short a time, but I'm sure I love you. I want you to marry me."

Oh God, I thought. I'd won. This was why I'd come to the Vineyard, why I'd convinced Jack and Lila to spend their life savings on this elaborate hoax. But now, faced with the reality of it, seeing the brass ring within reach—or more likely a diamond large enough to skate on—I couldn't say yes.

"Casey," I said. "I know you miss your wife. I know that my affection for your son and the time we've spent together make us seem compatible. But we don't really know each other."

He didn't know me, didn't know that I was not who I pretended to be. I was a lie. I was an actor, playing a role to an audience that had no idea they were part of the play. I was a fraud.

"I think marrying would be a mistake."

"I don't. I'm sure about you."

I took his hand. "You only think you are. When you're back in your world, back to the routine of life, you'll see that this summer was a way to ward off loneliness and not real love."

I knew I was talking more about myself than I was to Casey. I was sure he wasn't in love with me. He thought I could fill the void his wife left in his son's

life and that we would make a good couple, but
we'd only have a shadow of a marriage. Eventually
that would become burdensome and we'd make
each other miserable.

"You don't feel the same way I do?" he asked.

I didn't answer. At least not in words. Slowly I
slipped my hand free.

The sound of voices woke me. Turning over, I
ignored them, even ignored the pangs of hunger
my stomach insisted on audibly playing like a tape
recorder. Sunlight poured through windows whose
shades hadn't been pulled down last night. Grabbing a robe, I wearily finger-combed my hair and
took the stairs with heavy footsteps.

"Excuse me, do you live here?" I asked, seeing Jack
for the first time in days.

"Not funny," she said flatly.

"Where have you been?"

Lila stood at the stove, stirring a pan of something that smelled delicious.

"Out with Shane would be my guess," I said, raising my eyebrows.

"As a matter of fact, I was," she confirmed.

"You should talk," Jack said. "Have we seen you
in the past couple of days? I suppose Don Randall
has been occupying your time." Just hearing his
name conjured both anger and passion within me.

I sat down and Lila slipped a plate in front of me.
Lila was no cook. I could only assume that Clay had
been giving her lessons. By the smell, he was doing
a good job. The meal was hers, I was sure of that,
but if the way I felt was on my face, she knew I
needed the food.

"So where have you been for two days and two nights?" I asked Jack. I poured myself a cup of coffee from the pot on the table and sipped. Looking over the edge of the cup, I waited for Jack to answer.

"Here," she said. "At least I was here last night."

"And the one before that?"

Lila joined us at the table. She hadn't said a word since I walked in the room.

Jack ignored my question. "I came in last night. I needed clean clothes. Lila was on her way out. And you," she paused and smiled, "were nowhere in sight."

"I had a date." Then I added, "With Casey."

I gave Jack a piercing look. She held it a moment. I relented. I didn't want to fight with Jack. To lighten the mood, I asked, "Has Lila told you her news?"

A look passed between the two them. I wasn't sure what it was. It was like they had a secret. I dug into the eggs on my plate and took a bite of the toast. I felt as if I hadn't eaten in years.

"She said you took it well."

Neither of them spoke for so long I stopped eating and looked at them.

"Has something happened?"

Jack looked up. "We got engaged," she said quietly, so quietly that I didn't think I'd heard her.

"Isn't that what we're talking about?" I glanced at Lila.

"*I* got engaged," Jack corrected.

"What did you say?"

"They got engaged," Lila said louder.

I looked from one to the other. "Both of you?" They both nodded.

A slow smile tickled the edges of my mouth, then broke out into a full grin. I forgot everything that had happened to me in the past two days. I jumped up and hugged Jack. "This is wonderful," I said. "At least one of us accomplished our goal." I hugged them again. "This calls for a celebration. We need some champagne."

"Amber," Lila said.

I barely heard her. I was thinking of wedding gowns, flowers, diamond rings.

"Amber," Jack called, but I didn't hear her either. "Amberlina," she shouted.

I stopped, froze in place at that strength in her voice.

"What is it?" I asked, my voice in a normal range.

"We didn't complete the plan."

I was confused for a long moment. Then it came to me. "Whom are you engaged to?"

"Shane," Jack said.

Both women extended their left hands. Small, but elegant diamond rings sparkled from their third fingers.

"Shane? Shane from the band and Clay the furniture maker."

"There's nothing wrong with what they do," Jack defended. "Shane won't be in the band forever. He's really good at what he does."

"And you expect he'll be at the top of the charts sometime within the next decade?"

"Maybe. Maybe not."

I look at Lila, but said nothing.

"Amber, I know we agreed to your plan, but life doesn't work by plan. You can't decide who to fall in love with just because their bank account promises you a cushy future. And is that really what you want?" She paused, giving me time to think about it even though neither of us expected me to answer. "My parents said the best times of their lives were the years they struggled to make it. They look back and laugh at the things they did together. It made their marriage stronger. One thing I've learned during this summer is that I want that kind of life more than I want a man I don't love just because he can afford me."

The three of us looked at each other. The only sound in the room was the low hum of the central air-conditioning.

"Amber, we want you to be happy for us."

"I am," I said, hugging her again and doing the same to Lila. "I'm sorry for my reaction. I haven't had the best two days. Lila lectured me on the merits or, rather, the pitfalls of our plan."

Jack smiled.

"You know I want nothing more than for you to be happy." I took their hands and squeezed them. My comment was genuine. I knew I would rather they be happy with husbands they loved than to be rich and miserable.

"When did this happen? Have you set dates yet? Tell me all the details."

I poured myself another cup of coffee and sat down ready to hear the happy details.

"Shane asked me last night. We were having dinner at the St. Romaine." Jack's face glowèd as she spoke. Her smile was wide and bright and she couldn't help twisting the ring on her finger. She looked like a little girl who'd received her coveted Christmas present. "During dessert, out comes this rolling cart with a crystal bowl on it. Inside the bowl is a velvet box. The waiter puts the bowl in front and me and leaves."

Jack took a swallow of her orange juice before continuing. "'What is this?' I asked Shane. 'I haven't ordered a dessert since we stepped on the Vineyard.'"

It showed, too. All the exercise and Jack's continuing to order salads instead of potatoes and rice was showing nicely on her body. She'd lost at least ten pounds since she'd come here.

"Shane tells me to open it and I find a diamond engagement ring lying on the white velvet liner. I swear all the air in my body was sucked out."

"I know exactly what you mean," Lila said. She sat across from Amber. "Shane and I were at his aunt's house when he asked me. I told him the truth of my coming to the Vineyard and he still wanted to marry me."

Tears gathered in my eyes. I had envied Lila yesterday when she told me about her engagement. Today both my friends had dreams and wishes they could hold on to. They'd found their mates. I wished I could join them, wished I had the same glowing feelings of love running through my veins.

I didn't. The love I had found on the Vineyard only made me miserable.

"There's something else," Lila said.

Both Jack and I looked at her. "Clay's aunt lives on the Vineyard. He wants her at his wedding."

"You mean come back next—"

Lila was already shaking her head. "He wants the wedding before we leave, before the summer ends."

"What?" Both Jack and I spoke at the same time. "That's only two weeks away." The summer had flown by, but I was really ready to leave the Vineyard now.

"We love it here and we won't be able to come

back for a while. The place is gorgeous. So we thought we'd marry here," Lila said.

"What about family and friends? Don't you want to plan a wedding, take time to get to know each other, pick out china patterns before the wedding?"

"Nope." She smiled. "We can have a reception when we get back. Clay is going to speak to the hotel today and see if we can have the ceremony in the garden."

"What about a dress? And our bank account is very low. We can't afford a reception at the hotel, not even for a few guests."

"I already have the dress. It was my grand-mother's. I called my mother this morning and she's FedExing it."

"It'll need alteration. And possible updating."

"They'll be minor. My sister was married in it two years ago. The two of us are about the same size."

I remembered the dress and the wedding. The woman who'd updated the gown had done wonders for it. Lila's sister was beautiful in it. Lila would look the same.

"I guess it seems everything is in place."

"Not yet. I have a hundred details to work out." She glanced at the clock. "So I'd better get started." Pushing her chair back, she got up.

"Anything I can do to help?" I asked.

Lila stopped the forward motion she'd begun. "I want you to be my bridesmaid. You, too, Jack, unless you and Shane want to make this a double wedding."

"Double wedding!" Jack's eyes grew as large as saucers. "That's a wonderful idea. Let me call Shane."

She jumped up and rushed for the phone in the other room.

"Hate to leave you alone, but I promised to meet Clay in an hour," Lila said.

"Go on," I said. "I'll clean the dishes."

There was a dishwasher, but I needed to do something physical. I filled the sink with soapy water and began washing the breakfast plates. Lila's comments about her parents came back to me. She made a lot of sense. Love meant more when two people worked for a common goal than it did if they just took the brass ring and lived the cushy life.

I'd struggled for years. I worked at a job that afforded me the ability to do it anywhere, but it was a dead-end position. In nine years I'd done nothing more than write jingles for greeting cards. I couldn't say those were the best years of my life, but then I didn't have anyone to share them with. Maybe if I had I'd have done more, pushed for more.

I thought Emile was the one, but now that I look back on that time, the two of us would never have made it. Emile might have known that. I didn't give him credit for it. My hurt had cut deep and I only thought of what I wanted, not what it would mean to us as a couple, as two people spending our lives together.

"You know, Amber." Lila stuck her head in the doorway, speaking as if the idea had only just occurred to her. "There's no reason you and Don can't join us."

"There is one little point," I said. "Don hasn't asked me to marry him."

"But if he did?" Lila asked.

I thought about the last time I'd seen Don, watching his back as he walked away from me.

"I don't think that's in the cards for us."

Who would think that two women could cause this much chaos? It's like a nor'easter blew through the house and deposited wedding debris in every room. The contents of at least one bookstore were lying about the house. Brides' magazines, cake decorating, flower arranging, hotel ballroom brochures were thrown about.

For the past week they had talked of nothing but weddings. I smiled and joined in when necessary, but it was downright depressing. I never told them Casey had asked me to marry him. Or that my relationship with Don—no, we had no relationship—whatever we had defined or not defined, was over.

Jack and Lila didn't appear to notice my sullenness at times. I tried to hide it. I couldn't help wishing I was one of them. That it was my wedding I was planning, poring over the details of. But each time the thought came to me, the man in the picture with me was Don.

I'd force the thought away, concentrate on either Lila's or Jack's needs, make myself think of what the two of them liked, what flowers they would want, what kind of music the band would play.

"I don't know what we're going to do. Maybe this is just not going to work," Lila was saying as she and Jack came in the room.

"What isn't going to work?" I asked.

The two woman pushed some of the debris away and plopped down on chairs.

"The wedding," Jack said.

"What happened?" Fear for my friends gripped me. "Have you called it off?"

"Called it off?" Jack looked confused.

"We can't find a place to have the reception," Lila explained. "We've been everywhere. With the music festival going on and the number of events already planned, there is no space for a reception."

"Do you think you can use your influence with Don and get us into the St. Romaine?" Jack asked hopefully.

I looked through the window into the huge backyard. I knew I couldn't approach Don. He probably didn't want to see me or even talk to me. Asking a favor this big would stretch any friendship.

And we were no longer friends.

"What about here?" I said, having an epiphany. Both women looked at each other and then at me. "It's perfect. You can have the ceremony in the backyard. We can have it dressed up with flowers and chairs. Then the reception can be both in and out of the house." I paused and looked about the littered room. "You have to admit, this is a gorgeous house."

"Do you think it would work?" Lila looked at Jack.

While I waited, they stood up and walked about the room as if they were only just seeing the house.

"I think it will," Lila said. "We're not the rich women anymore. We can have a wedding and reception in a house."

"It'll work," Jack agreed. "I think the ceremony should be inside. Imagine coming down that staircase." She pointed toward the wide stairway that curved at the bottom as if it knew it was going to deposit brides into the huge great room.

"You're right," Lila agreed. "This is great, Amber. I'm glad you thought of it. That's one huge problem off our hands. Now we need to get Jack a gown and have mine altered."

"Lila and I are going to take the ferry and go to Boston this afternoon. We'll stay overnight and hopefully find something tomorrow."

"I'll go with you."

"Amber, would you stay here and take care of some of the other details, like the cake, flowers, decorations? Time is at a premium and you're good at planning and organizing. With a place determined, we need a design of where to set things up, where to put flowers, and we need a caterer. Maybe Don can lend us a hand there."

There was no malice in Jack's voice. I was good at planning and organizing. I'd gotten us to this island, hadn't I? And I didn't relish the idea of being around blushing brides. Not in my state of unhappiness, but I felt Jack and Lila needed me. Or they should. I'd want them around if I was the one getting married. But Jack and Lila would also do whatever it was I needed done.

"What about my dress? I'm the only bridesmaid," I said. "I'll need something new to wear."

Again a look passed between Lila and Jack.

"What?" I said.

"We saw the perfect dress for you. It's in the gift shop at the St. Romaine."

I clamped my teeth down, tightening my jaws. Each time anyone mentioned the St. Romaine, my last night with Don and the way he'd created the perfect night jumped in my mind. Then I'd remember him walking away. I didn't want to go anywhere near the hotel.

"We asked the clerk to hold it for you. If you don't like it, no problem," Jack said.

"But I can't imagine you not liking it."

Jack and Lila knew me well. We'd grown up together. They knew my style as well as I did. Each year for my birthday or Christmas, I could count on loving the gifts they chose. If they said the dress was perfect, I had no doubt it was. The only problem was going to the St. Romaine.

And the possibility of me running into Don.

Chapter 21

What was that cliché, I asked myself as a giddy Jack and Lila waved good-bye from the ferry deck. If it wasn't for bad luck, I'd have no luck at all. The last time I'd come to the pier to see Jack off, I'd run into Don.

Apparently, today was no different.

My heart thudded against my chest when I saw him. He hadn't seen me yet. For that I was grateful, but instead of heading for the car and getting away from him, my legs and feet appeared to be rooted to the spot.

Don had a smile on his face, but he didn't look happy. It was amazing how two people knew when something was different about the other, no matter what the outer core showed. Don greeted an older man. He had silver hair and the appearance of a seasoned college professor. But his stature was that of command. I could easily see him in uniform directing some military operation.

Don shook hands with the man and they embraced briefly, in the man hug that was quick and affectionate. Then a beautiful woman ran into his arms and his entire demeanor changed. She had long dark hair that bounced as she ran. Her smile was wide, showing even teeth. She looked like a model, dressed in a pink sundress that clung to her curves. Her long legs ended in high-heeled shoes. I was thankful they weren't red.

The smile on Don's face was genuine and the hug was long. He kissed her on the cheek and pulled her arm through his as they turned toward the parking lot.

Envy, jealousy, longing swelled up in me as green as any giant in a field of peas. I wanted to run to him, snatch her arm free and let her know that Don was my man.

But he wasn't.

Don was a free agent. I had no right to assume that he was anything to me. I'd done everything I could to push him away. And now that he was gone, I missed him fiercely. I felt as if a hole had been left in my heart and only the man I now saw walking with someone he obviously loved could fill it.

Staying where I was, I watched them move toward the hotel's limousine. They talked easily. Don obviously knew these people well. He glanced from one to the other as they walked. His attention was for them and them alone. Never once did he glance in my direction.

When I felt it was safe enough, I returned to the car. I wondered who she was. What was she to Don?

"Amber."

I froze getting into the car. Hadn't I waited long enough? Sitting down in preparation for getting away, I turned and looked through the window. Casey Edwards stood there with Joel.

"Hi," Joel said, a bright smile and the remnants of ice cream on his face.

"Hi," I said. "What are you doing here?" I thought they'd left the Vineyard a week ago.

Casey looked a little embarrassed. "Joel and I stopped at that ice cream parlor over there. Then we looked at the ferry boats. And finally we saw you."

"I dropped Jack and Lila off. They're spending the day in Boston."

"I heard," he said. "Word has reached me that the two of them are getting married."

"Oh, 'tis true," I said.

Casey leaned into the car so his son couldn't hear what he had to say. "My offer is still open, Amber. If you change your mind it's a safe harbor."

I understood what Casey meant. He was a safe harbor. The demands he would make on my time would be low. I wasn't sure I wanted that. In fact, I knew I didn't. I wanted the fire, the heat and friction that had me exploding.

"I'll think about it," I said.

"Is that a promise?" His eyes narrowed.

I looked at Joel. "It's a promise."

"Why don't we have dinner tonight and discuss it? Seven o'clock?"

I nodded. "See you then."

Was I out of my mind? I asked myself that as I drove back to the house. Jack and Lila getting married was getting to me. I wanted to be married. It was why I was on the Vineyard. Casey was a good man. I loved his son. I could do worse. At lot worse. I thought of Emile and how disastrous that would have been.

Would being married to Casey be so bad? I'd have everything I wanted, everything this trip was about. It was within my grasp. All I had to do was say yes and I could go to Boston to find my own white dress to wear, too.

Dress! I hit the brakes, suddenly remembering I was supposed to go by the dress shop in the St. Romaine and look at the gown the two brides wanted me to wear. A car honked its horn behind me. I started up again, but didn't turn around. I had a better plan.

Inside the house, I called the dress shop and asked them to deliver the dress. After all, in their eyes I was still a rich woman. Rich women didn't have to go into shops unless they wanted to. The clerk was happy to send the dress over.

Twenty minutes later when the doorbell rang, I'd lined up a couple of florists and a bakery. I had appointments for tomorrow morning to see their work. I began to sketch the way the house and yard should look.

"You'll need to decide if you want this before I leave."

I was stunned to find Don Randall standing there with a dress bag in his hand. My legs nearly caved and my heart burst with an energy I hadn't known was possible.

"What are you doing here?" I asked.

"You ordered a dress to be delivered."

"I didn't expect you to be the delivery boy."

"There wasn't anyone else available. We usually don't get requests to have clothes delivered unless they're for one of the guests."

"I apologize for the inconvenience." I took the dress.

After the initial shock of finding him on my doorstep, I was glad to see him. As usual he wore a suit, his uniform of choice for the working day. The small tag that identified him as the St. Romaine's manager was missing, but for me it would be redundant. I could pick Don Randall out on a midtown Manhattan street during rush hour.

As I stood there looking at him, I knew seeing him after I took the final ferry ride back to reality would not be likely.

"I hear you're having a wedding here."

"Did Casey tell you?"

"Tell me what?"

I knew it was a mistake the moment the words came out of my mouth. I hoped Casey would wait until I gave him a second answer, but I never said it was a secret.

"Casey asked you to marry him?" Don asked, although it was more an accusation than a question.

I didn't know how to answer. Casey had asked me, but I'd refused. Yet this afternoon I had led him to believe I was thinking about it.

And I was thinking about it. Jack and Lila had found love. Casey was offering me the opportunity to get what I wanted. Why was I hesitating? Why was Don here acting like a protective father?

"Just a minute. Let me try the dress on and see if it needs returning." I went up the stairs, refusing to answer his question.

Jack and Lila were right. The dress was perfect. It was royal blue, a color that looked great on me. It had gentle folds that crisscrossed over the bodice and back. Spaghetti straps made of rhinestones looped over the shoulders and the skirt fell in straight folds to the floor.

I whirled around, smiling at the way I looked in the mirror, feeling the soft swirl of cloth about my legs.

I didn't want to take it off, but I knew Don was waiting for me downstairs. I looked at the price tag and gasped, but I'd suck it in and pay for it. This was my best friends' wedding. The dress was the least I could do.

But I might be living on peanut butter and jelly sandwiches for the rest of the year.

"I'll take the dress," I said, returning downstairs. Don was standing in the living room looking out of the big picture window at the ocean in the distance. He turned a second after I spoke. I wondered what he'd been thinking. "You can let the charge go through."

He nodded and started for the door. Something around my heart contracted and I didn't want him to leave.

"Don," I called as he approached the door. He stopped, but took a couple of seconds before turning back. "Can we talk?"

"Do we have anything to say?" he asked.

"We must."

"Why is that?" I asked.

"Because you're here. You could have had the dress sent over, but you brought it."

"I told you no one else was available."

"It wasn't an emergency, Don. The wedding isn't taking place today. The dress could have been sent tomorrow or even the next day. And you obviously have personal guests that you left to come here."

"Personal guests? How would you know that?"

"I was at the ferry this morning. I saw you greet them. She's very pretty."

"Thank you," was all he said. I'd hoped for an explanation of her relationship with him, but that was not forthcoming.

"So why did you really bring the dress?"

He looked at the floor then up at me. "I felt I needed to apologize."

"I'm not one of the hotel guests. You don't have to give me the customer service treatment."

He sighed. His eyes closed for a moment, then opened. At that moment he started toward me. I had an urge to run, move, do something, but like an indecisive idiot I stayed where I was.

One of Don's arms wrapped around my waist and pulled me into his body. With the other one, he raised my chin until I was looking at him.

"You are such a gorgeous bitch," he said. Then he kissed me, his mouth descending hard on mine. His hand moved from my chin to the crown of my head and held my mouth to his. I'd heard of and read about punishing kisses before, but if this is what that was supposed to be, it failed miserably.

I'd missed seeing Don, missed having him hold me, missed talking to him, seeing him on the beach in the mornings, and missed kissing him, snuggling up to him in bed.

I melted in his arms, sliding into the kiss as if we'd always been part of a couple, a pair, an us. His mouth softened against mine. The hard hands that kept me immobile encircled me in a caress. My arms went around his neck and I gave up any thought. I was happy where I was, content to remain there for as long as I could. His arms tightened and the kiss changed direction. His tongue invaded my mouth, sweeping around in a sensation that was both tickling and erotic.

My body tingled. I leaned into him, aligning my body to fit in all the places that aroused pleasure in me. I felt myself moan, the action involuntary. I was almost at the point of tearing Don's clothes off and taking him right on the foyer floor. But suddenly I was free. Cold air rushed in where heat had been turning me to liquid.

Don turned and was gone. The sound of the door closing echoed through the empty house. I sat down on the floor where I'd been standing, that hollow feeling growing larger inside me.

Weddings entailed a lot of details that needed attention. I'd promised Jack and Lila to take care of some of them. But I couldn't do it right now. I needed to get out of the house. I needed to find a place where there were no images of Don Randall. I'd promised Casey I'd have dinner with him at seven. There wasn't much time. But I was going to take it and get out of here.

The beach was my only option, but not our beach, not the one where I met Don, the one where we talked about ourselves, our dreams. I got in the car and headed for the other side of the island. There wasn't much that interested me, too many people having fun. Finally I found a place to pull over. It was on a hill, above the ocean. Sitting down in the sand with my pad and pencil, I could think of nothing to write except sympathy passages. I worked nonstop for an hour, refusing to allow myself to think about Don.

But there was Casey. I checked my watch and nearly jumped up. I was going to be late for our date. Rushing back to the house, I showered and dressed. When he rang the doorbell, I only needed to finish my hair and makeup.

"It's open," I called from upstairs. I watched him

come in. "I'll be down in just a minute." It actually took me ten minutes to get everything done. "Sorry," I said, entering the living room. Casey stood at the exact place Don had stood earlier this afternoon.

Casey turned. "It was worth the wait," he said, obviously appreciating my outfit. I wore red. Tonight I felt like it should be about me. I wanted to be noticed. I wanted every man in the room to know that I was there.

"I have a reservation. We should go." Casey checked his watch.

Grabbing a wrap, I slipped it over my shoulders and went through the door. Casey took my arm and guided me to the car. It wasn't until he was driving along the beach road that I realized he was heading for the St. Romaine.

"Where are we going?" I asked, fearing I already knew the answer, but needing it confirmed anyway.

"Often I tend to stay around the hotel, but tonight I hoped you wouldn't mind going a little farther."

I could have kissed him.

"I made a reservation at the Seaport. The concierge highly recommended it."

My elation slipped. If he'd spoken to the concierge, then undoubtedly Don knew where he was going and that more than likely I was the person he was going with. Shrugging off thoughts of Don, I turned my attention back to the man I was with.

It only took twenty minutes to reach the Seaport. As its name implied, it was a seafood restaurant. The motif was seashells and miniature ships everywhere. We were shown to an out-of-the-way table near the wall.

Dinner was a success. I laughed at Casey's jokes

and genuinely liked him. He was interesting, didn't talk about himself much. While he loved his son, Joel was not the primary topic of conversation. We spoke about art, books we read, places we'd seen or wanted to see, movies. When we got to our families, I steered away from the absolute truth. I remembered I was still playing a role and that Don was the only person who knew the truth about me.

There he was again, invading my thoughts. I was with Casey. I was having a wonderful time. I wouldn't let Don encroach upon that.

"I heard about your friends," Casey said when the coffee was served. "They're getting married."

I nodded. "The wedding is in a week."

"Is that enough time? When I got married, my wife took almost a year with the planning."

"Usually it does take that kind of time when you have to order gowns, order invitations, reserve the church and hall."

"I don't see why that would take more than a few weeks."

"There is a large demand for space, and of course there is the family argument."

We both laughed. "There is that," Casey said. "It came to a point when we almost eloped just to stop everyone from fighting."

"But the day turned out gloriously, right?"

"It was perfect. My mother cried. Her mother cried. I was never so happy."

"That's wonderful," I whispered. I wondered why he wanted to marry me. Obviously he was still in love with his wife.

"You might be thinking that I could never find that kind of love again."

"It did cross my mind."

"I don't expect to. I'd be content with only a fraction of it."

"So you believe there is only one true love for everyone?"

"Not exactly. I believe that love grows, that you can fall deeper in love with someone as time goes on."

"And you're willing to settle for that?"

"I don't look at it as settling. As I told you, I am in love with you."

I bit my tongue, but I still asked the question that was on my mind. "You believe that if you married me in time I would grow to have the kind of love you've experienced before?"

"I do," he said with the same reverence he would use for the marriage vow. "I haven't been looking for women. I resigned myself to being alone, rearing my son and taking what life gave me. But meeting you changed that for me."

"It did?"

"I can see you're very beautiful. You probably have male friends falling all over you. You may have other marriage proposals. But I do love you. And I can promise you that if you do marry me, there will be no one between us."

"Casey . . ." I started.

"You do feel a little bit of love for me, don't you?"

"Of course I do." He stopped me before I could say *but* . . .

"I know we could be good together. I can keep you in your current lifestyle, and in time you'd come to love me."

It sounded plausible. In fact, it sounded exactly like the life I intended to find when I embarked on this adventure.

"Will you marry me, Amber?"

I thought about it. It was as good as it would get. I'd have what I wanted and Don could go to hell.

"Yes," I said.

Casey got up then, a huge smile on his face. He pulled me out of the chair and kissed me. After a moment, my arms snaked around his neck and I joined him in the kiss.

"You did it!" Jack nearly jumped up and down when I told her I was engaged. "I am so glad."

"What about Don?" Lila asked. She couldn't have spoiled the moment more if she'd stepped off a cliff. I wanted them to be happy for me. I wanted them to embrace Casey, not ask about Don.

"Don has nothing to do with this," I said, my voice a little strained. Images of Don hugging the woman at the pier came to me. "Besides, I think he has other women on his mind." *And possibly in his bed*, I added silently. That thought almost made me gag. I covered it with a cough.

"What do you mean?"

"When you two left for Boston, I saw Don at the pier. He was quite intimate with a beautiful woman who got off the ferry. But let's not talk about Don. Show me the gown."

Thankfully the two of them got excited about what they'd bought. Quickly, they started to pull dresses, underwear, and shoes out of bags.

"Are we going to make this a triple wedding?" Jack asked, hope in her voice.

"I'm afraid not," I said. "Casey and I decided to wait until we were back on the mainland. We want to get to know each other a little better."

"Did you tell him?" Jack asked.

I shook my head.

"Shouldn't you base a relationship on honesty?"

"I suppose, but then we wouldn't be here."

"Good point," Lila said.

"Casey is leaving in the morning. He's stayed longer than he expected. I'm going to meet him and spend the day, but I've made a lot of arrangements. There's a list on the kitchen counter of the florists. The plans for the yard and the inside have been sketched out. I printed the pictures. The bakers included photos of cake designs. You choose the one you want. The minister had no problem with the change of venue. He'll be here at five."

I stopped, trying to remember the other details I was charged with.

"The dress you chose is fabulous."

"I knew you'd like it," Jack stated.

"Oh yes," I said. "You both have several messages by the phone in the kitchen. Apparently, word is out about the wedding and some of your friends are planning to come up for the nuptials. I'll see you around dinnertime, but don't count on me. Casey is taking me to dinner."

"Casey, Casey, Casey," Jack said. "Who would have thought it?"

With a wave, I ran out. I didn't want to stay around Jack. I knew she favored Don. But we didn't all get what we wanted in life.

Casey pulled to a stop in front of the house just as I reached the porch. Bounding down the stairs, I opened the car door and got inside.

"Hi, Joel," I said as I took my seat. He smiled widely as if he was glad to see me. "Are you ready for our picnic?"

"Yes, did you bring a swimming suit?"

"I have it on under my clothes."

"Dad says we can swim in the ocean again."

"That's right." During our last picnic, the three of us had gone to the ocean. We looked like a family. I wondered if Casey was trying to instill that in me by choosing to spend the day there.

"We have a pool in our backyard," Joel said. "But the beach is so much fun."

"It is," I agreed. Although I hated the grittiness of sand, I didn't want to spoil the child's happiness.

"Are we going to the same beach?" I asked Casey.

"Is that all right?"

"It's perfect." Farther away from the St. Romaine was fine with me.

For several minutes we drove without speaking. Joel settled in the backseat and looked at the sea on our left.

Casey broke the silence. "I hear the brides are back."

"I picked them up this morning. They are well into the planning."

"Is that the kind of wedding you want?"

"Every woman dreams of orange blossoms, white gowns, and a church full of family and friends. They're not doing that, at least not on a grand scale."

"I thought they would want all the trimmings."

It was an opening. Here was where I could tell Casey that I wasn't the heiress or the rich girl that I pretended to be. The limousine that brought us here was hired. It was taking all our savings to finance this summer. The words were on my tongue. Casey deserved to know. Jack had said trust was one of the essentials to a marriage. But somehow no words came. I didn't utter a sound about my status.

"Isn't that what you want?" Casey prompted.

"I thought I did." I looked out at the ocean. "For years I've dreamed of a huge wedding with twelve bridesmaids and all my family and friends in attendance." I looked back at him. "But now I think a small, intimate ceremony would be much better."

He nodded.

"What would you like?" I asked.

"Well, I've gone through the big wedding. I think a small ceremony would be best, but it *is* your first time. Are you sure you'd be satisfied?"

"I'm sure," I said. It seemed the right thing to do. Of course, Jack and Lila would be there. My parents would come up from Florida. The Disney park could survive a few days without my father. I could almost hear him saying those words. They'd been to visit me several times since moving away. Yet I hadn't called them with the news of my upcoming marriage.

Outside of Jack and Lila, I'd told no one.

Chapter 22

The table we were led to at the restaurant was on the opposite side of the room, far away from the one Amber and I had shared just over a week ago. I couldn't believe only a week had passed since I spent the evening here and subsequently, the rapturous night on the beach with Amber. I'd relived that night hundreds of times in my sleep and during daydreams that came upon me at the oddest and most inconvenient times. The absurdity of the night's outcome hung over me like a personal rain cloud.

Before my father arrived, Jeff had called me out on it during one of my morning rounds, asking if something in my life had changed. Apparently, there was something different about the way I'd been acting. And it was noticeable. I covered my behavior by telling him I was tired and had a lot on my mind. Both statements were true, but not for the reason Jeff thought. And he wasn't the only person who'd mentioned changes in me. I was going through hell and there wasn't a soul I could tell about it. The one person I wanted to talk to was off-limits.

Amber.

Not because she had set a limit. Because I had. When she said she was going out with Casey Edwards the very morning I was bringing her home, I felt as if the world was ending. After an earth-moving, soul-shattering experience, how she could throw me such a sucker punch was unbelievable.

Never had I met such an unreasonable woman.

"Do they still serve that crab imperial dish here?" my sister Tasha asked. "It was delicious the last time I was here." Tasha was the woman Amber had witnessed me hugging at the pier.

"They do," I told her. "And it's just as good as you remember it."

I knew it was. I'd eaten it the night I brought Amber here. I'd tried to convince my father and sister to eat somewhere else, but Tasha wanted to come here.

The place had Amber overtones everywhere. I remember how the light hit her face, how she smiled when we talked about things we'd done in our youth.

"I'll have the lobster Thermidore," my father ordered. He was very predictable. He always ordered the same thing or something similar. Not a risk taker when it came to food, he did risk quite a few major life changes, including taking over the hotel business when his own father died suddenly.

Raleigh St. Romaine took two ailing hotels and turned them into a first-rate chain. He'd taught his children to enjoy the finer things in life. He also taught us the value of money and to keep our heads out of the clouds.

I loved my father. Despite our previous relationship when I was rebelling against everything and living the fast, hard life, I respected his experience and his wisdom. I wanted him to be proud of me and to understand that I could do not just a good job, but a great one in the business.

He took a risk on me when he challenged me to take on the St. Romaine on the Vineyard. I knew he thought of me as a hothead, as the globetrotting, carefree man of my generation. He might not have understood my need to wander, my need to see the world and understand where I fit in it. But I thought, somewhere deep inside him, he envied me the freedom of choice, the courage to fly off into the unknown and find what was there. And in that prodigal experience, to find my way home. I wanted to change his opinion. Though I told myself, and even flung the words at him, that I didn't care what he thought, I knew I cared. I wanted him to approve of the man I'd become.

I ordered the crab cakes and handed the waiter my menu.

"Well, I'm impressed," my sister said, pushing her charger plate away and folding her arms along the white tablecloth. "Dad is, too, but he won't say it." She smiled at our father.

"I'll say it," Dad said. "When I'm ready." There was a lift to the corners of his mouth, but he was holding back a smile.

"Dad, you've looked at the books, seen the facility, observed the staff, even talked to the maids about Sheldon—"

"Don," I corrected her. "I don't want you to mistakenly call me that at the wrong time."

"Sorry, I'll remember. I think this incognito thing is silly, but that's you and Dad."

"The hotel is running smoothly. I am impressed," Dad said.

Emotion stretched my heart.

"You've proved it, Don." There was the slightest hesitation before he said my name. I'd been Sheldon most of my life. Early on they called me Shelly, but I put a stop to that in the second grade when a little girl named Shelley McGowan transferred into my class. All the kids teased me that I had a girl's name. Rebellious even then, I insisted everyone call me Sheldon. In college Sheldon had been shortened to Don. I could live with that. And then there was the line name my fraternity brothers gave me when I pledged, but I won't go into that. Until a year ago, when I became Don Randall, hotel manager, I'd been mainly known as Sheldon.

"I guess that means you get that hotel in France you're so keen on," Dad said.

I should have been happy. Living in France was my goal, something I wanted to do, and I'd agreed to turn the Vineyard property around in a year to get it. I'd loved living on the Continent, doing what I wanted. I loved the fast cars and the traffic, the small nightclubs and the pace of the people. I thought I could combine my days and nights if I had the hotel as income.

But I hadn't counted on Amber. I didn't want to be six thousand miles away from her. I wanted to be here or in New York with her.

I knew France would be the best thing for me. Distance had a way of changing perspective. When I knew she was inaccessible, it would be easier to forget her. Although I didn't think I could ever truly forget her. She'd ingrained her DNA into mine. Even surgery couldn't separate us now.

"I'm looking forward to it," I said, hoping my voice showed the right amount of enthusiasm.

"Are you sure?" Tasha asked.

"Of course. Why do you ask?"

"The reason," my father broke in, "is that I thought you might like to take over the Paris property."

The waiter brought our drinks and salads at the same time. I waited for him to leave, taking the time to plan what I was going to say.

As soon as he left, my father seized the moment to pitch the hotel in Paris. "The property in the French capital is in better financial condition," he said. "You won't have the problem of attracting guests. It's centrally located with a seasoned staff. The place is practically booked to capacity thanks to you. However, your workload will be much lighter even though the facility is larger."

It sounded like a sales pitch. Three months ago, I wouldn't have needed convincing. I'd have jumped at the chance to live and work in Paris. But three months ago Amber Nash's leg hadn't slid out of a limousine, and a week ago I knew I was in love with her.

The small hotel would give me a lot to do. It needed repair, marketing, and advertising plans to attract guests. I was good at that. Even though Martha's Vineyard attracted its own clientele, France also had an appeal. However, few people made the side trip to the Atlantic shore to visit the town of Les Pieux. I had plans to change that. With its strategic location to both London and Paris, the small seaport town was ideal for my purposes.

And despite my reluctance, I knew I needed distance between myself and Amber.

"Well, the option is still open," my father said. "You don't leave here for another month. If you change your mind, let me know. In the meantime, I take it you haven't notified the staff."

I shook my head.

"Anyone in particular you think could replace you?"

"Adrienne English. She's the assistant manager and fully capable."

"When are you going to let them know?" Tasha asked.

"I'll talk to Adrienne tomorrow. Then let the staff know on Monday. I'll give them a month's notice."

"Well." Tasha lifted her glass. "Congratulations!"

We raised our glasses and the three crystal flutes clinked musically before we drank. Through the curved glass I raised to my lips, I saw *her*.

"Damn," I cursed under my breath and shifted in my seat. There she was. And with Casey Edwards. Anger so fierce I had to dampen it by lifting and drinking a full glass of water. She was positively glowing. Her skin had changed to a golden brown and the white dress she wore set it off to perfection. She didn't see us, and I was thankful for that. Casey had his hand on her back as he guided her toward their table.

She should have been with me, I thought. But he was who she was looking for. A man with money. I had money, lots of it and a future that promised more, but she didn't know that.

"If that's what you really want," my father was saying when my attention came back to our table.

"I can't believe you want to give up Paris for that little hole in the wall," Tasha said. "Especially after the life you used to live."

"That's behind me now," I said. "I've grown out of the need to engage in daredevil sports and actions that could get me killed."

"That's a relief," my father commented. "I don't even think I want to know what your comment really means."

I knew he didn't. Sometimes I winced when I thought of racing fast cars and missing a pile-up against a wall by centimeters. Or the time I jumped from a plane and my parachute didn't open until I was in the kill zone. Yet that didn't stop me from trying things.

To see me now, I wonder if Amber ever thought that the calm hotel manager who solved the problem of overbooked rooms and rides to the ferry could guzzle wine all night and hang glide over the choppy waters off Costa Rica the next day with a hangover the size of the Atlantic Ocean?

What I was doing now was just as dangerous. The woman only a few yards away had me walking a tightrope. Below me was no net.

And it was about to get tighter.

"Excuse me," I said and stood up. I walked over to the table where Amber had her back to me. Her dress was low cut and I longed to run my hand down the smooth warmth of her skin, cover it with kisses and smell the unique scent that defined her and her alone.

"Don!" Casey said, standing up and shaking my hand. His smile was wide, as if he'd already drank a bottle of wine. As they had only sat down a moment ago, there hadn't been time for that.

"Amber," I acknowledged. She smiled, but lowered her eyes immediately.

"Join us." Casey offered me a chair.

"I have to return to my party. I only wanted to say hello."

"Thank you for dropping by," Amber said. It was the first comment she made and I could hear dismissal in her voice.

"Before you leave, let me tell you our good news."

"Casey . . ." Amber said as if to stop him.

"I want the world to know," Casey told her. "Amber has consented to be my wife."

The news shocked me. My heart stopped. I wished I hadn't joined them, since I was fighting to remain upright. Marriage was the last thing I expected to hear. My heart pumped as if it would burst. I looked at Amber. She stared at me, challenge in her eyes. This was why she came here. Why was I surprised? She'd been out with Casey more than any other guest. Her two friends were getting married. I knew from experience that marriage was contagious. And not just in women. Many of my friends had gotten engaged and married within short periods of previous weddings. Once one guy fell, the others were like dominos taking the leap to follow their hearts.

It hadn't happened to me, since I had no particular woman holding my heart at the time. But now I did. I was looking at her, the one woman who could have filled that space in my heart reserved for no other.

"Congratulations," I said, giving her a sardonic smile. I looked up at Casey and offered my hand. He took it. "You're the first couple to get engaged during my watch." I smiled, looked back at Amber. "I hope you'll be happy."

Then I turned and, without looking back, I returned to my father and sister.

"What was that all about?" Tasha said the moment I was in my chair. Both she and my father looked at me curiously.

"Guests at the hotel."

"Is that all?" Tasha asked. She glanced at the table where Amber and her new fiancé sat, then back at me. She'd gotten what she wanted. I felt like a fool.

I looked at my sister. "That's all," I said. But I was sure she didn't believe me.

Hell, even I didn't believe me.

Apparently my father didn't either. We returned to the hotel immediately after the meal. I'd wanted to get out of the restaurant the moment Amber came in; after learning of her engagement, nothing else seemed real. I went through the motions of eating. The food had no taste. I engaged in conversation but had no idea what we talked about. My eyes kept going to her table.

"I'll be in soon," I said when we stood at the path that forked toward the hotel and my bungalow. Since Mrs. Brooks and her baby were still in the owner's bungalow, Tasha and my father were staying in mine. The place only had two bedrooms. I'd moved into a single guest cottage. There was no room in the hotel anyway. All possible space was occupied. Something that pleased my father.

I usually made the rounds before turning in, checking to see that everything was all right and going over the details of the next day.

"She's very pretty," my father said after my sister announced she was going for a swim and started down the path to change clothes. Tasha reminded me a little of Amber. She loved to swim, too.

My relationship with my dad had improved in the last year. We hadn't been confidants since I was eight years old, but the regular meetings we'd had about the hotel had spilled over into father-son outings and long talks over good meals and bottles of fine wine. I felt like I was getting to know my father for the first time and he was getting to know me.

I looked around as if I expected to find Amber standing behind me.

"The woman in the restaurant. Is it serious?" he asked.

I didn't pretend that I didn't know what or who he meant. "Only on my side." I'd promised her I'd keep her secret, and even though she was now engaged to another man, I wouldn't tell my father that she thought my net worth too low for her purposes. I also wouldn't tell him that she drove me crazy in and out of bed. Or that the thought of her marrying another man made me angrier than I thought was possible without exploding. Especially since I was trying to hide it from the one person who'd been able to read my moods since birth.

"Does she know who you really are?"

I shook my head. "Telling her would have been a violation of our agreement."

"Well, I'd make an exception if necessary."

"Why is that?" I asked, wondering what he'd seen that I had not.

"I know you think I'm an old man, but I recognize a nose ring when I see one. And yours is apparent." He punctuated his statement by tapping his index finger against his own nose. "If you're really in love with her, and I can see you are, you'd better be the one to tell her who you are. You wouldn't want her to find out from some other source."

"Like who? No one here knows who I really am."

"You were quite the man about town just over a year ago. She might have thoughts about that."

"I told you the feelings are not mutual." *At least out of bed they're not,* I thought. If she found out I was Sheldon St Romaine, it would make a great deal of difference, and while I really wanted to tell her the truth, I didn't want her to look at me as just another bank account.

"It doesn't matter anyway," I said. "You saw the man she was with tonight."

My father nodded, apparently remembering Casey Edwards.

"She's engaged to him."

For several moments we stood staring at each other. My father appeared as stunned as I had been when Casey made the announcement.

"What do you plan to do about it?"

"Do?" Here was another question I had not expected. "Nothing. The lady has made her choice."

"Are you sure?"

"What does that mean?"

"It means that while you returned to your seat at our table, I could see the way she looked at you." He paused. "She didn't look at him the same way." Dad half smiled. Only the corners of his mouth rose. Without another word, he turned down the path and started for the bungalow, leaving me with a plate of confusing food for thought.

* * *

What had he thought? I asked myself that question for the hundredth time. When Casey kissed me good night, I was still thinking about Don. He and his party left the restaurant soon after we arrived. Relieved to see them go, I relaxed enough for Casey and I to finish our meal in relatively good spirits. Before that I'd been nervous and edgy, wound as tight as a new spring.

Casey and I took a walk along the beach and joined the continuously in-progress party. Dancing finally allowed me to stop thinking about Don for a while. The music was hot and fast and it obliterated everything else.

I'd been avoiding Don, hoping to get through the final weeks on the Vineyard without encountering him. But I'd learned this was a small island and it was hard to avoid anyone. All my free time had been spent with Casey and Joel. They were leaving this morning to return home. My non-free time had me running errands for Jack and Lila. When I'd agreed to Casey's proposal, I thought of calling Don. I wanted to tell him about my engagement first. Knowing I didn't owe him a preview announcement, I still felt he deserved the courtesy of hearing it from me. Casey took that away.

And now I wondered what he was thinking. I didn't go the beach and write or wait for Don to appear. I overslept and had to rush to the pier to see Casey and Joel off. I hugged Joel and kissed Casey. The kiss was chaste, evoking none of the fiery explosions that Don's mere touch could pull from me.

On my way back to the house, Don was still on my mind. I drove slowly through town, hoping I wouldn't see him along the street. After a moment,

I shook thoughts of him aside and parked the car near a shop I'd seen earlier.

Spending a few minutes inside didn't take my mind off him and I only bought a couple of books to take home. Leaving the store, I was lost in thought, which was why I didn't see Don and ran smack into him. His arms came out to steady me and keep us from falling to the ground.

I wiggled myself free even though his hands seemed to sear into my skin. "Excuse me," I said and attempted to walk around him. He stepped in front of me, blocking my escape. I had several bags in my hands as I'd just come out of a shop on the main street.

"I didn't get to fully congratulate you last night," Don said. "I see you've achieved your goal."

Shifting the bags to one hand, I removed my sunglasses and looked him squarely in the eye. Although I shook inside, my voice was calm and steady when I spoke. "I am not ashamed of what I've done. Casey is a good man. We'll be very happy together."

"But you're not in love with him." It was a statement, not a question.

"Your words, not mine," I replied.

"I see you didn't contradict me," Don said.

"What does it matter to you? I see you have a beautiful woman on your arm." I remembered the woman who'd kissed him at the ferry, and he'd been quite attentive to her last night. "It must be nice to be you, able to choose another woman with each turnover of hotel guests."

He nodded, also not contradicting me. "There are certain perks to the business."

Anger heated my face. I knew my newly acquired

suntan wouldn't cover the darkening of the blood that flowed there.

"So who is the lovely lady?" I couldn't help asking. I wanted to know who had replaced me.

"I'm sure you don't know her."

Understanding that this conversation had nowhere to go, I again tried to excuse myself. And again Don blocked my escape.

"I see Mr. Edwards and son left the Vineyard this morning. Is there to be no engagement party?"

"It'll happen later when we're back in the real world."

"You mean when you're back in that world where you can understand the full impact of a life without love?"

"You like to throw that word around, don't you?"

"People who are in love usually do. Casey used it freely last night. I haven't heard you use it once."

"Is that what it would take to have you move aside and let me pass? For me to tell you that I love Casey?"

His nod was nearly imperceptible. "I don't want mere words. I want the truth."

"And you deserve that? I suppose you think you are entitled to it?"

His face gave nothing away.

"You don't," I said. "I am not accountable to you or anyone else for my actions. But . . ." I stopped. "But I will answer your question. And I will speak the truth."

This time there was a reaction. Again it was so imperceptible that had I not been looking for it, I might not have seen it. Don's jaw tightened and I could tell he was holding his breath.

"I love Casey."

Don sighed, crossed his arms, and cocked his head. He looked at me until I felt uncomfortable. More uncomfortable than I already was, that is.

"Why don't we test that?"

"I'm in no mood for any tests." I pushed past him and took a step when his hand grabbed my arm and stopped me. He slapped a key in my hand.

I looked at it. "Oh no." I made a sound like a grunt and tried to hand it back.

"Midnight," he said.

"I won't be there."

"Liar," he whispered and disappeared down the street.

Chapter 23

This was not happening. I put a hand to my head and clenched my teeth. My jaws hurt from holding in the scream. Part of it burst out and I made a noise so rude people passing stared at me. I started moving. Momentarily disoriented, I couldn't think of where I had parked the car. I started and stopped twice, walking first one way, then back in the direction I'd come before I remembered.

Getting inside the heated vehicle, I threw the hotel key on the seat. If he thought I would even consider such a bald offer, he was mistaken. Not again. I was engaged now. And while I wasn't head over heels in love with Casey, I respected him.

Midnight!

The word rebounded in my head as I cursed Don. I wouldn't wait for midnight. I would return his damned key right now. He could find it when he got back to his bungalow. I wouldn't even leave a note. He could make what he wanted of it. I did not care.

Pulling out of the parking space, I headed for the hotel. It was the first time I'd freely gone there

since waking up in Don's bed the morning of our
date. As usual the place was a mecca of activity.
Finding a parking space took a while, giving me
more time to raise my anger quotient.

A car pulled out of a space and I whipped mine
into it with the speed of a NASCAR driver. Leaning
over, I grasped the hotel key from where it had
fallen on the seat. Slamming the door, I headed for
Don's bungalow. I jammed the key in the lock and
waited for the click that released the mechanism. It
didn't work. I tried it again, pulling it out and rein-
serting it. Finally I pulled it out and looked at it in
disbelief. He'd given me the wrong key.

As I stood there, baffled, the door opened and
she stood there, the woman from the ferry and the
restaurant. The woman Don had taken into his
arms and kissed. This was all I needed, a confronta-
tion with his new lover.

"Excuse me, I have the wrong room."

"Who are you looking for?" Her voice was soft
and sexy. She wore shorts and a ruffled blouse that
showed more skin than it covered. Not Don's type,
I thought.

"Don Randall."

"He's not here." She smiled.

"But this is his bungalow?" I asked the question
slowly.

"Yes," she said.

"And you are . . ." I left the question dangling.

"I'm his sister." She offered her hand. "Tasha St.
Romaine."

I took her hand in a tight grip, but my hand went
slack as her name registered. "St. Romaine?"

She nodded. "I'm sorry, I shouldn't have said
that."

"Why not?"

"Who are you?" she asked instead of answering my question.

"Just a guest," I lied. Then I remembered the my purpose for being there. "I came by to return this. Don dropped it and didn't notice."

I placed the electronic key in her hand and turned to leave.

"Who can I tell him returned it?"

I looked over my shoulder. "No one he'd know," I said.

I was angry before, but now I was burning mad. Don Randall! What a sham. He wasn't Don Randall. He was the owner's son. A hotel magnate, masquerading as a manager. Why? What game was he playing? And why did he lead me to believe he was a mere manager?

"Jack," I shouted, entering the house ten minutes later. I walked to the great room, which was full of wedding paraphernalia. Both Jack and Lila looked up, startled. "I need your help."

"What's happened?" Jack shouted back, following me as I went to the dining room table.

"I need you to look someone up for me. I need to know everything you can possibly find out about him."

"Who?" she asked. "Who's him?"

"Don Randall." I spoke his name as if it were laced with venom.

"Don? I thought you weren't interested in him."

"I'm not."

"Then why—"

I cut her off with a look that could freeze mud. "I want to know why he's been lying to me."

"Lying?" Lila said. "What's going on?"

"Jack, look him up."

I stood over her as she typed on the computer. We hadn't thought to research Don. He didn't fit the profile. There was no need to find anything about him. He was the hotel manager. Not on our radar. Not worth enough to be part of our plan.

I was burning mad.

A search screen came up with all versions of his name. Jack perused the listings. There were genealogy lists, marriage and death notices. Jack's fingers flew over the keys. She continued for several silent minutes, typing, looking at the data that filled the screen, discarding it, and typing again.

"There's nothing I can find on him."

"Is that strange?"

"Extremely," she said. "Everyone is out here somewhere. A Facebook account, a mention by a friend, a blog, something. Don is simply not here." She looked at me, perplexed.

"What about Tasha St. Romaine?"

Jack typed. The screen filled with notices of her. At the bottom additional pages were available.

"Click Images," I said. At the top of the search screen was a link that would bring up photos. The woman who'd answered Don's door came on the screen in a collage of one-inch photos. "That one." I pointed to a man and woman in the lower left corner. Jack clicked on it.

"That's Don," Lila said. "Who's the woman?"

"Tasha St. Romaine," I answered flatly. "She's his sister or cousin or some relative."

Jack and Lila looked dumbstruck. Both of them turned to stare at me.

"She's staying in his bungalow. I just met her."

Jack turned and started typing again. The screen

filled with links, mainly about the St. Romaine hotel chain. Jack quickly read through the data on the screen. She read much faster than I did and I didn't know what she was looking for.

"The owner of the chain is a man named Raleigh St. Romaine. He's got a daughter named Tasha. She's the CEO of the business. Raleigh is chairman of the board. He has a playboy son named Sheldon."

Jack typed in Sheldon St. Romaine and clicked on Images. Lila and I gasped as the screen was covered with photos of Don Randall.

I needed to escape. I needed to be alone. I needed to scream. Jack and Lila bombarded me with questions about where I was going and what I planned to do. I answered none of them. I needed some space. Grabbing my beach bag, I headed for the ocean.

"Can't we go with you?" Jack pleaded.

"I don't think you should be alone right now," Lila said.

I stopped at the door, realizing I was scaring them. "Don't worry," I said, trying to smile. "I'm not going to do anything crazy. I just need some time alone."

Unsure if that was a true statement, I didn't intend to go near Don or Tasha. I smiled reassuringly at Jack and Lila, hugged each of them, and walked across the street. I don't know why I turned toward the spot where I'd spent the night with Don, but I found myself there. I sank down in the sand, unable to go any farther, and I stared out at the water. I don't know how long I sat there. The sun set and night fell. The birds overhead stopped their cawing. The tide came in and water reached my feet. I kept asking myself the same questions. Was any of it real? Why had he goaded me? He hated the idea of me marrying for money. Yet all the while he was laughing at me. When I think that he even tried to find me a rich husband, I could scream. Did he tell them? Did they all have a good laugh at my expense?

I thought of Casey. Was he in on it, too? When I returned to Brooklyn would there be a phone call one day, an e-mail or a letter? *Dear Amber . . . It was all a joke.* I thought of Emile and his lies. Don had been no different.

Standing up, I wiped the sand from my legs and clothes. I'd mourned enough. Time to move on. The summer had not turned out the way I wanted it to. Casey would undoubtedly hear about me and he'd bow out of our arrangement. Jack and Lila would be off on their honeymoons and beginning their happy lives.

And me. I was a survivor, I told myself. I survived Emile. I would survive Don. If Casey backed out of our arrangement, I would survive him, too.

Now it was time for action. I'd return to the house and help my friends with their weddings and then I would go home.

It was time. Reality hit me squarely in the face.

The summer was over.

"You told her what?" I shouted at my sister. "I told you to be careful what you called me."

Tasha spread her hands. "I apologize, Sheldon. That's all I can do. I didn't tell her your name. I told her mine."

Tasha looked genuinely sorry, but I didn't care.

"And that I was your brother. How long do you think it will take for her to figure out who I am?"

She glanced at the floor, then back at me. "Why should that make a difference?" she pleaded. "You were going to tell the hotel staff on Monday. She's a guest. She's not likely to care who you are. Or is there something I don't know?"

She started to smile but stifled it when she saw that I was in no mood for games. This was serious. I was angrier at my sister than I had been since we were teenagers. I said nothing to Tasha. All I could do was turn and walk away, leaving her without an explanation.

Slamming the door to the bungalow, I headed for my car. I got behind the wheel and pushed the key into the ignition. The car roared to life with only a slight turn. With my hand on the gearshift, I stopped. I didn't owe Amber an explanation. I didn't owe anyone the truth. Yet I felt as if I did.

What was I going to say? This was exactly what my father had warned me about not twenty-four hours ago. What would Amber think of me now? I know we didn't have the best relationship, but I wanted to explain why I had to hide my identity. Now it must look like I deceived her. She'd been up front with me from the beginning. I had hidden my own secret.

And now, because of my sister, I needed to do some damage control. I only hoped Amber would listen to me.

Driving the short distance to the house she rented, everything looked normal. It was fully dark. The day had been busier than usual and I hadn't been back to the bungalow for hours. I didn't have to entertain my father or sister. I was sure Tasha had been on the phone or her computer all day, directing and managing the business even while wearing a bathing suit. My father liked the outdoors. At fifty-eight he still maintained the body of a thirty-year-old. It wouldn't be unusual to find him swimming or at one of the tennis courts, if not jogging along the beach. In that respect, I was sure I took after him.

I parked in front of the house, the same place I had been the day Amber stepped from the limousine. Lights blazed in the downstairs windows. Through the curtains I could see Jack and Lila along with the men they were now planning to marry.

Ringing the doorbell, I waited, looking over the porch to the water across the street. I turned when the door opened. Jack stood there.

"I don't think she wants to see you," Jack said before I could explain my reason for being there.

"Who is it?" Lila called and joined Jack at the door.

Her mouth formed an *O*, but no sound came out. Then the two men gathered behind the women. I felt like a display animal in a zoo as they all stared at me.

"Where is she?" I asked.

"She's wondering why you lied to her," Lila said, giving me a look that should have fried me on the spot.

"I want to talk to her."

Before Jack could refuse me, Amber's voice came from behind them. "It's all right, Jack." All eyes turned to look at her. Amber stood on the staircase halfway up. She walked down the remaining stairs to the landing. I could see by the stiffness in her body that she was holding her anger inside.

"I think you all should excuse us," she told Jack and Lila.

All eyes looked warily at me. "Are you sure?" Shane asked. He was tall and built like a surfer, all muscle and bone. And I could tell he was ready to protect her if the need rose.

"I'm sure," she told him.

"We'll be right in here," Lila said, ushering Clay away. Jack and Shane followed them, leaving Amber standing alone on the polished wood floor and me on the threshold.

"How about going for a walk," I suggested.

I stepped onto the porch and moved to the edge.

"This is as far as I go," she said, folding her arms in an unapproachable stance.

Walking back behind her, I reached in and closed the front door. The night was dark, devoid of a moon. The air was cool, an indication that the summer would soon be over.

"You met my sister," I began.

"You told me you had one. You forgot to tell me her name was St. Romaine or that you are not Don Randall."

"Let me explain."

She put up a hand to stop me. "You don't have to. You don't owe me an explanation. You owe me nothing."

"I know." I waited for a reaction, surprise, anger or anything. Her face was as closed as a locked door. "I'd like to tell you why I was using another name."

"Why?" She moved her arms, allowing them to hang at her sides. She looked relaxed, as if nothing about me mattered to her. I knew that couldn't be the truth. The nights in my bed told me as much, and the night on the beach was the crowning achievement. "We're nothing to each other. I'm engaged to someone else. I'll be leaving the Vineyard soon. When the weddings are over, I'm taking the ferry and going back to Brooklyn. You can drop me from your friendship list. We don't even need to exchange Christmas cards."

She moved then, preparing to return to the inside. I stepped in front of her.

"Haven't we done this dance before?"

"You're not in love with him," I said. "Why are you planning to marry someone you don't love?"

"I don't think that is any of your business. And we're not talking about me. You've already had your laugh on me. Now, please step aside."

I didn't move. I glanced through the window at her friends inside. They were looking through books and eating a large pizza. While they weren't staring through the windows, I knew they were cognizant of our presence.

"Look at them," I said. "They're in love. You can see it as if it were a palpable thing. Will anyone see that with you and Casey? In five years will the two of you hate each other and end up in divorce court? What effect will that have on his son?"

"That was low." Her voice was nearly a growl. She moved then. I didn't try to stop her. As she approached the door, I called her name. She stopped, her hand on the handle, but she didn't turn around.

"I never laughed at you."

Jack and Lila's wedding day was perfect. The sun was bright and high in the sky. The temperature was comfortable and the wind was calm. They looked gorgeous as they floated down the aisle to join hands and hearts with their husbands. Initially, they were going to have the ceremony in the house, but the guests who RSVP'd proved too many for even that large space.

When they took their vows, tears rolled down my cheeks. I don't know why. I was happy for them and I never cried; even at sad movies my eyes remained dry. But when Jack and Lila said "I do," the waterworks began.

I looked out on the crowd. Jack's mom was dabbing a handkerchief to her eyes and her father was blinking hard, trying to act as if the ceremony wasn't moving him to tears.

The wedding went off without a hitch, and as the brides and grooms were introduced for the first time as Mr. and Mrs., the house and yard were filled with people.

I stood off to the side, a member of the reception line. It seemed as if the entire village had turned out for the wedding. I shook hands and smiled, making the standard comments when someone was introduced or leaned over to hug me. But what I was thinking was that I was losing my best friends. They would remain my friends, but there would be differences. Their allegiances were to other people, to a commitment they'd vowed to maintain.

More of our friends than I thought came up for the ceremony. Well-wishers were everywhere. Don—or Sheldon—was not in attendance. Even though the caterers were from the St. Romaine, he was not there to supervise the staff. I had caught a watery glimpse of him on the fringe of the crowd during the nuptials. I guessed he'd left immediately after the ceremony.

I hadn't seen him in almost a week. Of course, I made a point to avoid wherever he might be and I'm sure he was doing the same. There was no reason for us to cross paths. We weren't lovers, and at this point we were no longer friends.

Casey and Joel came up the day before the wedding. They were leaving tomorrow. I was leaving with them. Jack and Lila were staying over a couple of nights, then going on their honeymoons. I wouldn't see them for another couple of weeks when they returned to prepare for their lives as man and wife.

Casey took my arm the moment the reception line completed its duties. Even though I was on his arm, and he kissed me at all the appropriate times, it wasn't the same. Don had read me correctly. I wasn't in love with Casey. I liked him, but I didn't love him. I was in love with Don—or Sheldon. I wasn't sure if I could get used to calling him Sheldon.

Then I remembered, I wouldn't have to. Tomorrow I was leaving the Vineyard. In time Don would only be a memory. My life was with the man on my arm.

"Hey, Dad, can I have some cheese?"

Casey nodded to his son, who ran off as if he was part of a relay team. Joel wasn't the standard sweets-eating child. He liked cheese and vegetables and ate them first. He also liked chocolate cake, so he wasn't totally unusual.

"What are you thinking?" Casey asked.

I hoped there was nothing on my face showing him what I was thinking. My mind was on what life would be like after I left the Vineyard. I smiled and looked over the yard. "Just that my friends are moving away from me. We'll all have different lives in just a matter of weeks."

He patted my hand. "It won't be a bad life."

I looked at him. "I know. It's just that everything is changing. I'll have to get used to it."

He kissed my cheek. "I'll be there to help you with the changes."

His words should have been comforting. I should have felt his strength, wanted him to be there to fill the gap left by my departing friends.

But I didn't. I felt alone and unsure of what was to come.

In the morning I told myself I was glad to be leaving, that I would not look back at the Vineyard as the ferry moved away. That I would not remember the times I'd had there, memories that would sustain me for life. I'd keep them safe in a small sector of my heart, pulling them out to touch and remember only in rare moments. Yet I stood at the railing watching the land recede.

It had been a memorable summer. Jack and Lila were still there, married and happily honeymooning. A single tear rolled down my cheek. Had I known that I would board this ferry at the end of the season with a ring on my finger and a pain in my heart, I'm not sure I would have come. But Lila and Jack wouldn't be insanely happy if not for my bright idea to find a rich husband.

I glanced at the door to the small restaurant where Casey and Joel had gone. The two came out as I looked. Joel ran over to me. I caught him as his small arms encircled me.

"Are you going home with us?" he asked.

I looked down at him and smiled. "Not this time. I have to go back to work."

He looked disappointed.

"But it will be soon," Casey said and Joel brightened.

"Did you have fun on the Vineyard?" I asked the child.

"Yeah, I wish we could stay there all the time."

So do I, I thought. With Don. But there was no Don. Don was an illusion, an apparition, a ghost I'd conjured up to act as a conscious to my scheme. The real man was Sheldon. Sheldon St. Romaine, playboy, race-car driver, bungee jumper, and the deliverer of electronic keys.

"Maybe we can come back another summer," Casey said, putting his arm around my waist. I leaned my head against his shoulder, as if I was remembering my days in the sun and regretting the fact that I had to leave.

All of that was true.

The hotel staff took the news in silence. For a long moment after I stopped speaking no one said anything.

"Nothing changes," I said. "The hotel will run as usual."

"You mean you're really *not* Don Randall?" Betty Miller, the head of housekeeping, asked. "You're Mr. St. Romaine's *son*?"

"And the man and woman in your bungalow are your father and sister?" This question came from one of the maids.

I nodded. "My father and sister have only good things to say about the running of the place. And he didn't send me here to spy on anyone. But if I had been, you all passed with flying colors. The jobs you do are exemplary."

A nervous laugh filtered through the group.

"Why did you come under an assumed name?" Frank, from security, stood near the door as if guarding the place against a terrorist attack.

"The reasons would take too long to explain. The short answer is, if I'd come as the owner's son, you'd all be uncomfortable around me, explaining yourselves each time I walked in the room. Some of you might have resented me." I scanned the crowd and saw a few heads bobbing. "I promised my father I could make a go of the hotel and I wanted to do that with your support."

"When are you leaving?" a reservationist asked.

"The plan is at the end of next month. But that depends on all of you." I paused, seeing the confused faces. "The place runs like a well-oiled machine. I could leave tomorrow confident that I was not leaving a void behind. But there are some personal things I need to clear up."

"Where are you going?"

"I'm taking over a small hotel in northern France. I hope to make it the place that people think of when the lights of Paris have dimmed. Or when they want a quiet place to relax."

Betty Miller spoke again. "Who's taking your place?"

I looked over at Adrienne, opening my arms in invitation. Adrienne stepped forward. A moment after she joined me in front of the group, applause broke out. When it died down, I said, "I'd like to thank you all for a wonderful year, for your friendship and dedication. And for being open to both accepting and suggesting new ideas. I know you'll all continue to be the best and no matter what anyone tells you." I stopped and pointed both fingers at the floor. "This is the best hotel in the chain. I know I'm leaving the place in good hands."

Strong applause accompanied the end of the speech. A few questions were directed toward Adrienne, and with many handshakes and hugs, the group returned to their duties.

I returned to my office, where Tasha and my father waited. Tasha turned from the window and my father stood up from a chair in front of my desk.

"How'd it go?" Tasha asked.

"Good. The place is going to be fine."

My father came forward and patted my shoulder. "I know how you feel. I felt the same way when I had to leave my first hotel."

I said nothing. Many people said they understood when they didn't. It was just something to say. Even though he was my father and I appreciated his sympathy, I didn't think he had any idea what was going through my mind.

"I'd become comfortable at the place," he went on. "I knew the procedure, knew the staff. We liked each other, worked well together. The place barely eked out enough money to keep the repairs paid for. Yet I loved it. I didn't want to go, but suddenly my father died and everything dropped on me. I had a wife and a small child." He looked from me to Tasha, who was younger than me. "And another on the way. If I wanted to give them a better life, make sure you two weren't scraping and barely making it the way my father had, I had to take a risk and get more people to come to the St. Romaine. I knew I could make it work."

I gave him a steady look. He knew I understood. The feelings were almost exactly the same. I didn't have a wife and child, but I'd thought of it, dreamed of it. I'd put Amber in that role. Lady Legs, tall, beautiful and commanding, like a queen. I'd proven I could turn the hotel around. But the woman of my choice was marrying someone else.

"You'll be fine," Dad said. "I'm very proud of you." Then he left the room. He was getting more emotional than I'd ever seen him. Anger was an emotion he understood and knew how to use. Love wasn't something he was comfortable with.

He loved me. I knew that. He loved everyone in his family. My mother was the only person he openly showed his softer side. With Tasha and me, it was usually tough love, but it had molded us, made us who we were.

"This hotel has been good for you, Sheldon," Tasha said, no longer needing to be careful about using my real name.

As usual we didn't stay angry with each other for long. All our lives we'd been each other's rock. I couldn't blame her for trying to remember a name she wasn't used to using. And she hadn't known how I felt about Amber. Or why I was so angry that she'd told her the truth.

"You're different, calmer, more in control," she said. "I'll be looking at the financials very closely once you get to Les Pieux." She said it with a smile. "I know you'll have people bypassing Paris to come to Les Pieux."

Tasha had positioned herself to take over the operation of the chain once Dad retired. She was smart and knew the business backward and forward.

Even though she was younger, I had no issues
with her running the empire.

"What about her?" Tasha asked.

I'd told her about Amber after I returned from
seeing her. Tasha quickly put two and two together
and understood that Amber showing up at the
bungalow with my key had more meaning than
just a guest finding a key. I admitted I was in love
with her.

"She's engaged to be married."

"Engaged is not married," Tasha said.

At that moment I knew there was more in my
sister's comment than her love for me or her wanting me to be happy.

She nodded, understanding. "I was in love with
a man and it didn't work out."

"I'm sorry, Tasha."

She held up her hand to stop me. "It was my fault.
I was stubborn and feeling it was my way only. I
wasn't willing to bend or to fight for what I wanted."
She took a step toward me. "But you've always been
different. You've always gone after whatever you
wanted. Don't let this be any different. Go get her,
Sheldon. If you love her and she loves you, then
she might just need to know that."

"You don't understand. She'd take me now because of the money."

"Money?"

"She found out I'm a St. Romaine. She came to
the Vineyard looking for a rich husband. She didn't
think I was in her league. But now things would be
different."

"She didn't find out until she came to the bungalow." Tasha spoke as if I should realize something.

"Yeah, so?"

"That was after we saw her in the restaurant."

I nodded, still not understanding where she was going.

"Sheldon, remember I told you I saw the way she looked at you?"

I nodded again.

"I've never seen a woman more in love. And she wasn't in love with the man at her table. But the more important item is she was in love with you *before* she found out about your money."

My sister was right. But could I be sure? She'd agreed to marry Casey. Would she do that if she was in love with me?

"Go to her, Sheldon. You've got nothing to lose."

I stood there looking at Tasha. Could she be right? Was Amber just waiting for me to force her to tell me she was as much in love with me as I was with her?

Suddenly, I was all action. Grabbing my sister, I kissed her on the cheek. "I love you," I said and bolted through the door.

I drove quickly through the crowded streets, impatient for people to hurry across the road or drive faster in front of me. Progress was steady, but slower than my thumping heart.

Nearly jumping out of the car when I got there, I sprang onto the porch, having little use for stairs. I was a man in love and I could fly if I wanted to. I'd convince Amber. I loved her and she loved me. I was the best man.

And she was going to know it.

Jack answered the door. She was laughing, but the smile on her face faded when she saw me.

"Where is she? I want to talk to her."

Jack said nothing for a moment. She swallowed hard.

"She's gone."

"Gone?" The word didn't register for a moment. I stared at Jack, waiting for her to explain, for her to take the word back and tell me the truth. A moment later my brain processed the word. Amber wasn't just away from the house. She was gone from the Vineyard, disappeared from my presence and my world. My heart sank like a ship hitting buried rocks.

"She left yesterday," Jack whispered, reverently, as if they were in a church.

"Where did she go?"

"She's going home." Jack hesitated and I knew what she was going to say. "With Casey and Joel."

The words drove a knife all the way to the hilt into my chest. I was too late. Amber had made her choice. Jack had said it all in one word.

Gone.

Chapter 24

The world should have returned to normal by now. It had been two weeks since I left the Vineyard, but it was just as upside down as it had been when I boarded that ferry in pursuit of an elusive dream. Casey called regularly. He'd brought a huge diamond ring with him when he returned to the Vineyard for Jack and Lila's wedding. I looked at my finger. The ring no longer adorned it. It was in my purse, in the velvet case he'd removed it from the night he placed it on my finger.

Several times Casey and Joel had called, inviting me to join them for the weekend. I pleaded work as my reason for staying away. It was a busy period, but I was a writer and none of the budgeting or meetings involved me. I could work from anywhere, yet I'd taken to going into the office just to turn the lie into truth.

I wasn't working today. I was on a plane, heading south. I was going to see Casey to return his ring. I knew I didn't love him, at least not the way a woman should love the man she married. I thought I could do it, but I discovered I wasn't that good an actress. I knew what real love was like. I knew the flames it could create, the need to be with one person. While I liked and respected Casey, he didn't love me that way either. We both deserved better. I was releasing him from our arrangement.

I was sorry for what I'd done. Sorry that Joel thought I would become a permanent fixture in his life. But it would be worse if we got married and then made each other miserable. Joel would surely know there was tension in the air and he didn't need that in his young life either.

The Atlanta airport was huge. After the plane, a subway took me to the terminal. Casey stood at the entrance to baggage claim. When he saw me, a big smile split his face. He immediately pulled me into his arms and kissed me. I had expected this and I wasn't surprised.

"I've missed you," he said.

I cringed when he released me. This was going to be harder than I thought. I didn't want to send him his ring back in the mail. I thought he deserved to see me in person. Now I wished I was someplace else.

"Can we go someplace and get something to drink?" I asked, my throat suddenly dry. And I needed to buy time. Even though I'd practiced what I was going to say in the bathroom mirror and on the plane, the actual execution proved harder than I thought.

"Of course," Casey said. "You must be hungry, too."

I wasn't hungry, but I was thirsty. Casey guided me to a seat in an airport bar. It was standard airport cramped space, but at this hour of the evening it was packed with people who had to fly, but needed to reinforce their constitution to get on a plane. I was there for the same reason. I needed to reinforce mine to say what I had to say.

I wanted a glass of wine or whiskey straight up, but I ordered a diet cola and took a long swig of it. Casey cradled a beer between both hands. For a while we sat looking everywhere but at each other.

"You've come to return the ring," Casey finally stated.

Surprise had me snapping my head up. "How did you know?" My voice was breathy and low.

"You were never very enthusiastic about it. And I could hear it in your voice when we were on the phone. And a moment ago, I said I missed you. The sentiment was not returned."

"I'm sorry, Casey," I reached into my purse and pulled out the case. "It's a beautiful ring." Sliding it across the table, I said, "The woman who wears this should love you unconditionally."

"I thought that was you."

I shook my head. "No, you didn't. Even though you told me you loved me, it's not like it was with your wife. And you deserve that, Casey."

I reached over and squeezed his hand. "I listened to your voice on the phone, too. You believe Joel needs a mother and you thought you could love me, that you should marry me."

He lowered his eyes, then looked up at me. "Joel had something to do with it. He likes you, but he wasn't the only one."

"Like isn't enough," I said. "There was a time when I thought it would be. I was even willing to marry you on that basis. But I know better now."

"A summer diversion?" Casey's eyes didn't show the amount of hurt that should be there if he really loved me. I felt better knowing that.

"You could say that," I said.

"But we're back to our real lives now."

"You don't seem all broken up about this either," I said. It was almost as if he'd been expecting it.

Casey waited a long time before speaking. He stared into space for a moment. I wondered if he was going to say something or if he wasn't going to reply at all.

"When I was about seventeen, I thought there was only one true love in the world. I was lucky. I found that when I was in graduate school. After my wife died, I never expected to feel that way again."

"But now you do?"

He nodded and took a drink from his glass.

"You don't feel like that for me?"

"I don't," he admitted. "That's not as bad as it sounds. My feelings for you are stronger than they've been for anyone else."

I smiled. I felt good that he found me a good second.

"You did teach me something this summer," Casey said. "I learned to live again. I didn't even realize I'd been hiding, afraid to take any chances. All my effort was channeled into helping Joel deal with his grief. But when I met you, I felt there was a life for me, too."

I smiled. Casey grasped my hand tighter, then released it.

"Casey, you're a wonderful man. I'm sure you'll find a woman who adores you."

"I wish the same for you. With a man, that is."

We laughed and it felt good. If he hadn't added the joke at the end, I knew something would show in my face to alert him to the fact that I'd already found my one true love. And I'd also lost him.

"Will Joel be all right?"

"I'm sure he will. You helped him, too. He's getting back to his old self. He's more active, returning to his activities. He even asked for diving lessons."

"Good," I said. I was glad to hear about Joel. I truly liked him and wanted the best for him.

"Well, I guess there isn't much more to say or do," I said.

"Aren't you going to stay?"

"I made my reservation to return tonight. I wasn't sure how this would go and if it went badly, neither of us would want to be around the other. If it went well, and it did, there's no need for me to be here."

"You have a point. At least let me take you to dinner at a decent restaurant. This is Atlanta. We have the best Southern food in the country." He opened his arms, proud of his city.

"I'd like that."

Geography didn't matter. Even the six thousand miles of ocean didn't keep Amber from invading my thoughts. I wondered what she was doing and if she and Casey had set a wedding date. For all I knew they could be married by now. The thought broke my concentration and I hammered my thumb instead of the baseboard I was tacking to the ballroom wall.

Dropping the hammer, I folded my thumb in my palm and held the pain in. The hotel in Les Pieux was worse than I'd thought. Everything needed repairing. My father had given me a large budget to do whatever the hotel needed to bring it up to the standard of a St. Romaine. A small army marched

in every morning and worked to bring the place
into a livable status. From there it was my goal to
make it a first-class facility.

I worked with the men in hopes of keeping
thoughts of Amber at bay. It worked during the day.
Most of the time. It was the nights that tortured me.
She'd invade my dreams or have me waking during
the night soaking wet and hungry for her.

"Mr. St. Romaine, your appointment is here."
Genevieve's voice broke into my thoughts. She addressed me in English, a language she wanted to
practice she'd told me during her own interview.

"I'll clean up and be right there. Please have her
wait in reception."

"She's already there."

Reception was the first room we'd renovated. It
needed to provide a calm and inviting place for
people who wanted to work in the hotel business.
So far I'd had no shortage of applicants. However,
most were unacceptable.

As was the woman sitting in reception waiting for
me. She was dressed like someone on her way to
the beach, not someone who could handle a group
of middle-aged women demanding straitlaced attention. She talked nonstop and I questioned if she
was really old enough to drive, let alone work.

As she left, I noticed her walking toward a car
in the small parking lot adjacent to the hotel. I
blinked twice as another woman slid out of the
driver's seat. Her back was to me, but her hair was
long and dark. My heart stopped, then jerked into
jackhammer action. As she turned, my adrenaline
levels dropped to zero. For a moment I thought it
was Amber. Her skin was the same cinnamon color,
but there the resemblance ended.

Time would heal the ache I felt for her. My father and sister had told me that. But in the two months since I last saw her, the wound was still fresh and new. And it had all started with a laugh. I turned away, almost laughing myself. My father had raised a cut-glass crystal goblet at dinner one night and challenged me to take over the St. Romaine on Martha's Vineyard without anyone knowing who I was. Without his name and implied influence, he challenged me to turn the property around.

I took the bet.

And I would never go undercover again. I was Sheldon St. Romaine. Not Don Randall. He was officially and forever dead. The persona had only ruined my life.

Jack was coming! I felt like I hadn't seen her in years, when in actuality it had only been a few weeks. Life was so different now. A few months ago, she, Lila, and I had started out on an adventure. True, it had come to fruition, sort of. But not like we thought and now, my two best friends were hundreds of miles away from me, beginning new lives, while I was back in Brooklyn.

Life had to change. I knew that. And I accepted it. I didn't want anything but the best for them. Of course, there was e-mail and the phone, but it wasn't like meeting in a local restaurant or pigging out in front of the television to talk about sex, men, and how they'd done us wrong.

We weren't going to a restaurant today. I'd splurged on lobster tails, one of Jack's favorite foods. The table was set and the salads crisp in the refrigerator. A bottle of wine cooled in an ice bucket. Jack wasn't driving, but she couldn't stay the night either. I wished she could. We never tired of talking, even though we'd known each other since our mothers pushed us in matching strollers.

As I added the wineglasses to the table, the doorbell rang. I tripped over my own feet and nearly fell getting to it. I swung the door open and screamed her name. Both of us threw our arms in the air and we hugged like long-lost friends.

"Come in," I said, pulling her through the door. "You look great." She did. Her skin glowed. And she must have been twenty pounds lighter. Her smile was wide and she'd had her hair braided in an elaborate style. "I like it," I said, walking all the way around her so I could see the full effect.

"When did you have this done?"

"A week ago. Several sisters from Vanderbilt created this in less than two hours." She put her hands up and touched her hair.

"It looks great. What were you doing at Vanderbilt?"

"I went there looking for a job, but I don't think I'm the academic type."

"I thought you were going to take some time off," I said. "Get used to living in the South. Find a church to attend and become a belle."

Jack laughed. "Me, a belle. That'll be the day."

"Well, come on and tell me what's happened. I feel like I haven't talked to anyone in years."

"Girl, I have a ton of things to tell you."

"Wonderful. I want to hear everything."

Jack dropped her jacket on the sofa and followed me to the kitchen. This was our sanctuary. We always ended up here. It was the heart of the house, a place where you could talk, eat, and enjoy. I'd redone some of it since my parents moved, refacing the cabinets and staining them a rich cherry. The appliances must have been World War II originals. I scrapped them for new versions. Then I ran out of money and had to live with what was left. I still had plans to do the rest, but for the time being, the status quo was serving me.

Jack stopped at the door. "Amber, you cooked." She sniffed the air. "It smells delicious."

"I can cook, you know."

"Yes, I know, but you rarely do it."

"I've turned over a new leaf. You and Lila have major changes in your life. It's time for me to think about what's happening in mine."

"You wanna talk about it?" Jack asked. I knew she meant talk about *him*, but I shook my head. There was really nothing to say that would change the situation. Better to get on with the things I could control. And Don Randall was not one of them. I couldn't call him Sheldon. I didn't know Sheldon. It was Don that secreted himself into my dreams.

"Sit down," I told Jack.

She took the seat she favored. I considered it hers since she always sat there. Getting the salads out, I sat one in front of Jack and the other one opposite her.

"I hear Lila is learning to cook," Jack said.

"Shane is her teacher."

We both laughed. "I wonder how much food gets burned."

"Shane is a good cook," I said. I remembered the delicious smells that came from the kitchen on the Vineyard the night I walked in on them.

"Yeah, but Lila can be a distraction."

We both laughed again. Mental pictures of Lila trying to fry or bake something with Shane right behind her in various states of undress entered my head. I knew that if Don was behind me, we'd never eat—never eat food, that is.

"So tell me," I began. "How was Barbardos?"

"Girl, I have never seen water so blue and trees so green. The place was fantastic, and the men . . ."

"Men?" I admonished. "Jack, you were on your honeymoon."

"I know that, but apparently the men in the islands didn't think it was a big deal. I had more propositions than I could count. Shane had to practically beat them away. But secretly," Jack leaned toward me, "I loved it. And to see Shane jealous, girl, that was priceless." Her hands went up in the air and waved a little.

Jack was happy. She was smiling and her conversation was exciting. I was so glad for her. She went on to tell me about the beautiful hotel room they stayed in, and about shopping on the island. She mentioned the huge swimming pool and how I would have loved it.

"To think," she said as I served the lobster. "I had barely been farther than the Brooklyn Bridge, and here in one year I've been to Martha's Vineyard, gotten married, and spent two glorious sex-filled weeks in an island kingdom."

"And don't forget you're moving out of the state."

Jack sat up straight as if she'd been propelled from behind. "You have got to come and see the house."

I relaxed. Her sudden movement scared me. I thought something was wrong.

"I thought Shane lived in an apartment," I said.

"It was a condo, and we're selling it. Luckily we already found a buyer and we close at the end of the month."

I noticed that already Jack referred to the two of them as *we*. Was it that easy to go from being single to being married? To think of yourself as a couple and no longer an individual?

I'd had boyfriends and male companions before. I thought I was going to marry Emile. Yet I can't say that I'd ever thought of any of them as connected to me so strongly that I only thought of us as a two-some. Not even with Don did I think of an *us*.

"What happens then?" I asked, mentally shaking thoughts of Don out of my head.

"Oh, Amber, you will love the house we found."

"That was fast," I said. "Are you pregnant, too?"

"No, I am not pregnant," Jack stated as if offended.

"Jack, it was a joke. You just seem to be moving faster than ever."

"Wasn't it you who's always telling me to make a decision and stop mulling over everything to death?"

"Not exactly in those words. And why do you pick now to start taking my advice?"

"Shane had a little to do with it."

Jack smiled, cutting the meat from her lobster tail.

"What?" I asked after a moment.

"I'm glad you're sitting down."

Jack had my full attention. She'd already said she wasn't pregnant. So what could it be?

"You know how you talked me into going to the Vineyard with you, saying that if I was lucky I could marry my life savings?"

I nodded. "And I remember how you cut your eyes at me as if I'd set you up."

"And of course you had," Jack said.

We both smiled at the memory. It was only a few months ago, and life was so different now.

"Well, I did."

I chewed my food, waiting for her to explain. She said nothing. After a moment I looked at her. An impish smile curved her lips.

"You did what?"

"I married him."

She wasn't making sense. "You married Shane."

"Yeah, my life savings."

I thought hard, but I wasn't getting whatever it was Jack was trying to say.

"I'm saying it worked, Amber. I found my young black millionaire on Martha's Vineyard."

A short beat passed before it sunk it. "Shane! Shane is a millionaire?"

"A few times over." Jack nodded. "It came as a complete surprise to me, but he makes good money in the band and he invests it wisely. Not like those Hollywood stars who lose theirs by allowing some untrustworthy firm to manage it. He manages it himself."

"Oh, Jack, I am so happy for you." I felt the tears misting in my eyes. "It couldn't have happened to a more deserving person."

"It could have happened to you," Jack said.

"Wait a minute." I stopped her. She was about to embark on the Don train and I wasn't going there. "Why were you looking for a job at Vanderbilt if Shane has that much money? You can travel with him until you actually do get pregnant."

I'd given her double openings. We could talk about her job search or we could talk about future children. I hoped she'd take one of them and forget Don.

"I need something to do. I'm not cut out for the country club crowd or the Bible thumpers. Shane says that if I want to work, he's all for it."

I was glad to hear that the two of them were on the same page. It was how I imagined marriage would be.

"That's enough about me. What have you been up to since I left?"

My life wasn't nearly as exciting as Jack's, at least not from what I had to say compared to her. A husband, a new house, moving to a new town, and being in love. I envied her. She'd accomplished everything we'd talked about.

"Amber, what about that book you started . . . last summer?"

I stared at my plate as if the meat didn't cut easily. Jack had hesitated. I knew she was going to mention the Vineyard. And thoughts of the Vineyard meant bringing up Don.

"I put it in a drawer, or rather it's buried in a computer file and not likely to see light for a while." If ever, I thought.

"Why? I thought you liked it."

"I did, but somewhere along the way I lost interest."

"Did you finish it?"

I shook my head. It didn't have an ending. Or it could have many endings. I couldn't decide if it was a comedy that would end with an absurd twist of conditions the way our lives had. I could make it a tragedy and kill off the hero, send him out to sea and let him drown. Or I could give the book the complete fantasy ending with a fictional happily ever after. As it was, it languished in my computer, hanging from a tree with no feet to reach the ground.

"What about your job?"

"You know I'm still there."

"But," Jack prompted.

"But what?"

"But you hate it."

"I don't hate it," I defended. "At least not totally. It pays the bills and I'm good at it. I get to work from home. What's not to like?"

"Do you still want to be writing greeting cards when you're fifty?"

"They'll all be totally electronic by then. The computer will write them. The computer will ask several questions and produce a menu of suggestions. The sender will select her own sentiment from a pull-down window." I was trying for lightness, but Jack's face didn't show the hint of a smile.

"I'm worried about you, Amber," she said after a moment.

"Why?"

"You don't seem like yourself. The sureness you always had has dimmed a little."

I started to say something, although I didn't know what. Jack stopped me with her next comment.

"When Emile left you were hurt, but determined to go on."

"That's how we ended up on Martha's Vineyard," I reminded Jack.

She ignored me. "Now that you and Don have split, you look a little lost. Like you don't know which way to turn."

"I know which way to turn," I told her, the

strength of my voice more sure than reality. "Don was just a summer diversion," I said, using Casey's term. "I guess my lost feeling is because of the changes that are going on with the three of us. We've been friends a long time. Now things are different, changing. For the better, of course."

"Not totally," Jack said.

"I know. But I won't be able to run over to your apartment and force you to do things you don't want to. I won't meet Lila for drinks in some trendy place in the Village. But this is the natural progression of living."

"Amber, you'll find someone. Just like you found Emile and Don."

"Well, let's hope they aren't exactly like Emile and Don." We both laughed. "But you're right. I know how to get back on the horse and go for another ride."

Jack knew how I felt about horses. I rode only once while we were on the Vineyard. The comment, however, brought another image to mind. I could see myself riding Don on the chair in his kitchen. I covered my reaction by drinking from my wineglass.

"So, when are you coming to see me?" Jack asked.

"I don't know. You and Shane need time to be alone. I'd feel like a third wheel."

"So, when are you coming to visit me?" Jack asked again.

"As soon as you get the boxes unpacked in your new house." I knew that could buy me some time. When Jack had packed up to move her things to storage before we left for the Vineyard, she still had boxes she had yet to unpack since she'd moved into that building nine years ago.

"Three weeks at the most," Jack said. "The truck with my things left this morning. Shane's already packed his condo. I'll give Lila a call and see if we can make it a reunion."

Chapter 25

I felt like a five-year-old, unable to muster an attention span longer than fifteen minutes. If it weren't for deadlines, I wouldn't know what day of the week it was. Having to send my work in every Tuesday and attend meetings on Friday kept me cognizant of the days. It was the nights that lingered minute by minute, sliding by at a pace so slow it seemed to move backward.

Fridays were the best days. They were the ones when I interacted with other people. At least I tried. Today was Friday, and I was on my way home from the in-person meeting in Manhattan.

Jack had gone back to Nashville and Lila had called to say she was back and looking forward to meeting us all at Jack's house. I was secretly looking forward to it, too. I wished I'd be able to tell them that I'd found someone new, but that wasn't the case. There was a man at the office who often looked at me with admiration in his eyes. I noticed that he managed to angle himself close to me at every meeting. I hadn't been interested in him before the summer, and he stirred nothing in me now.

At my door I stopped and pulled the mail from the box. There were the usual bills and advertisements, letters addressed to occupant. I sorted through the stack as I walked into the foyer and on to the kitchen where I dropped my purse and stepped out of my shoes. As I flipped the last envelope I stopped, as if I'd suddenly been flash frozen. I stared, holding my breath, feeling my heartbeat accelerate to the speed of a hummingbird's wings. The return address said the letter was from the St. Romaine on Martha's Vineyard. The handwriting was unfamiliar, but the envelope was addressed to me.

I looked at my name and address as if I'd never seen them before. My stomach, vaulting like a roller coaster, told me the letter was from Don. I both wanted it to be from him and was afraid it *was* from him. Why should anyone else at the St. Romaine send me a letter? I hadn't been a guest there. Don had extended hotel privileges to me, and I'd taken him up on them. Granted, things had spilled over, more like boiled over, but there was no reason I should receive mail.

With shaking hands, I pulled a letter opener from the kitchen desk and slit the top of the envelope. A single sheet of paper inside came free.

I read it. Then read it again. The note was from Don. I nearly dropped it when I saw what he wanted. The words on the cream-colored paper were enough to force me to sit down.

Due, it read. *One four-hour dance.*

"What," I said out loud. My voice was low, not loud enough to be heard by anyone, even if another person had been in the room with me. He couldn't possibly expect me to honor this promise.

The summer had already ended, and I was engaged when I left the Vineyard.

Looking down, I read it again. *As I completed my part of our verbal contract, I'll expect you to be ready at 8:00 PM Saturday to complete yours.*

There was no signature. I threw the paper on the counter. Why did he always have to goad me? Why couldn't he act like a normal spurned suitor and go away?

I'd refuse to go with him, except he was bound to show up on my doorstep and demand his due. I had promised, and he had introduced me to several rich men. Jack had checked them out and he'd been true to his word. But the summer was over. There was no End of the Summer Dance to attend.

Eight o'clock tomorrow, the note said. No address, no phone number, no way to reach him. He'd already left the St. Romaine on the Vineyard. At least that was the rumor. I would have picked up the phone and called, but I wouldn't know what to say. If he was there and answered the call, what then?

I knew it would be futile. Don was used to getting what he wanted and when it came to me, I couldn't refuse him, either. I'd promised him four hours. I should be able to survive that. "Should be," I stated aloud. I had done it in the past. This was just another test. One which I had to pass.

What was it going to be like to see him again, I wondered. I'd been like a person with multiple personalities since I read the invitation. One minute I was imagining him taking me in his arms and apologizing for all that had happened. The next I saw us fighting over everything, not able to stand being near each other.

I spent Saturday shopping, buying a dress, having my hair and nails done. I told myself I was doing it for me, that no matter how this evening turned out, I needed the fortitude that came with making myself look as good as possible. And I needed something to do with the nervous energy that seemed to have an endless pump going into me.

I was ready at 8:00 PM when the limousine pulled up in front of my door. Don got out and rang the doorbell. I opened the door and we stood facing each other. Two people who knew each other in the most intimate way said nothing. My mouth was dry and my heartbeat was loud and choking. All I could do was stare at him. Under the glare of the overhead light, I stared at the man I loved and didn't know what to say.

"What do I call you?" I finally asked.

"You made the date with Don Randall. Why don't you call me Don?"

I nodded. "Come in. I'll get my coat."

He stepped through the door and closed it. I backed away, then turned and went into the living room where the matching satin coat to my gown lay across the arm of the sofa. Both were black. I had nothing on that was red, not even lipstick or fingernail polish.

Don looked around. On the mantel were photos of my family. The room was neat and in order, the furniture comfortable and in soft feminine shades. I wondered what he was thinking. Did he approve or disapprove of my style? His eyes seemed to settle on a photo of Lila, Jack, and me. It had been taken the day we left for the Vineyard. We stood next to the limousine that would carry us to our adventure. I thought about how innocent we had been then.

how unenlightened we were of how that summer would affect our lives.

Picking up my coat, I opened it to slip my arms through the sleeves. Don was instantly behind me, taking the garment and holding it for me. Even though he stood a discreet distance behind me, I could feel his warmth. I wanted to step back into it, bury myself in his body, melt in the remembrance of things past and glory in things promised. But there was nothing to come. This was our final meeting. Once my four-hour obligation was over, Don would walk out of my life.

It didn't matter that I loved him. He'd never believe me if I told him. For three months, I'd extolled him with my wishes. He'd even been party to the scheme. Now that I knew the truth of his parentage, he'd never believe me if I told him I loved him for himself and not for the money he had.

I would keep my thoughts to myself. The night hadn't begun yet. I was sure it would be an ordeal, but I would get through it. Turning, I gave Don the smile I'd practiced in the mirror.

"Where are we going? I don't think there is an End of the Summer Dance in Brooklyn, and if there is, it's long over by now."

"I hear you're no longer engaged," he said instead of answering my question.

I dropped my head, flattening an errant sequin on my coat. "It wasn't going to work out." I looked up at Don. "You told me that. I finally understood it."

I saw no triumph in his eyes. Don didn't seem to be the same man. He hadn't said much, but the reserve he showed was unlike the man I'd known. Where was the commanding figure? Where was the underglow of laughter, as if he had a secret or a joke that no one else could tell? There was a coldness about him. Where was the hot sexual aura that surrounded him like an invisible presence?

I started for the door, still not knowing where we were going. Don followed me. I opened it and stepped onto the small stoop.

Don touched my hand, pulling me around. "Amber," he said and looked at me. Immediately, he released my hand. I watched his eyes cover my face detail by detail. Then he looked me up and down from hair to shoes. When his eyes came back to my face, he leaned in and kissed me on the mouth. His lips were soft and caressing. I couldn't move. I wanted to tilt into him, run my hands over his shirt and up to his shoulders. I wanted to melt against him and deepen the kiss. Yet I held myself still, feeling sensation skewer through me.

"Good night," he whispered as he moved back. Then he turned and took two steps.

"Don," I called, my voice hoarse.

He turned back.

"I'm releasing you," he said. "There is no dance. There was one, but it ended weeks ago."

I wondered if he really meant the dance or if the words had another meaning. Was he telling me there was no chance for us? That what we had died with the sun setting on our summer?

"Why did you come here?" I asked.

"To see you," he said. "And to thank you for honoring the promise."

He looked at me for a long time. I had the feeling he was cataloging me. "You should have worn red," he said. "It's your color."

He got into the back of the car and it sped away

I stood there stunned, watching the lights grow dimmer as the car moved farther and farther away.

I would never understand him, I thought. Why had he really come? I'd heard he went to France. Had he come all the way back here to stand on my doorstep for ten seconds and kiss me good-bye? Why did he force me to see him, when he knew what it would do to me?

Was that it?

Could this be another game he was playing?

Anger suddenly raged inside me. I expected him to come back and somehow between now and morning we'd repeat our attempt at spontaneous combustion.

But again, I was wrong.

Three hours was a lot of time to think. That's how long it had taken for the chauffeur to drive to Philly. I wished I'd been driving. It would have given me something to concentrate on instead of how good Amber looked in that black dress. Her coat matched it except for the splash of gold and purple sequins that ringed the collar, cuffs, and a three-inch stripe down the front.

Revenge! That's what I thought was on my mind when I'd sent Amber the note. Tasha tried to warn me it wouldn't work, but I knew better. The unpredictable happened. All the rehearsing I'd done before my bathroom mirror and in the car on the drive up, the words flew out of my head the moment I saw her.

Helping her into that coat, I knew then I wouldn't be able to pull it off. I wanted her right then and there. My plan was to take her to dinner and later dancing at the Rainbow Room. High above the city I could have one last moment with Amber Nash before I returned to France. But I knew I wouldn't be able to sit across from her making small talk and later holding her next to me without losing my mind. It was better to break it cleanly.

"Mr. St. Romaine."

It took me a moment to realize the driver had called my name. I looked up. He stood there waiting for me to exit the car. I'd been so tied up with my thoughts of Amber, I hadn't noticed we were back at my parents' house.

Getting out of the car, I thanked him and gave him the next day off. I was supposed to be in New York, not coming back until tomorrow. My father had offered me the car, so I wasn't imposing by giving him time to himself.

The house was dark when I got in. My parents turned in early and Tasha could be out with friends or upstairs checking the occupancy rate for the St. Romaine chain or watching stocks fluctuate.

For the second time that night, I was wrong. Tasha opened the door to the music room. She had two wineglasses in her hands.

"I heard the car," she said, offering me a glass.

Walking toward her, I took it. I needed a drink, probably something stronger than wine, but Tasha was looking after my emotional health, too.

She returned to the room. I followed her.

"Didn't go well, I take it?" she asked.

"Not at all," I said.

"How far did you go?"

"All the way to her door. The moment she opened it, I knew it wouldn't work."

"Sheldon, you didn't leave her standing there alone, did you?"

Not exactly. I'd kissed her good-bye, although I kept that information to myself.

"It doesn't much matter now," I said. "I'm leaving in a few days. She'll never have to see me again."

"And vice versa," Tasha said.

I stared at her. She leveled her gaze at me, not backing down. I'd seen this look before. It was the call-my-bluff look. She usually used it during negotiations. And it usually worked.

"Is that what you want?"

I didn't answer.

"I know it's not," she went on.

I was standing next to the large-screen television. The screen was black. Even though the room was full of electronic equipment and types of music from several decades, records, tapes, CDs, even an eight-track player that still worked, Tasha had been listening to none of it. A novel lay open and face-down on the sofa.

In a flash I thought of Amber's novel, the one she was writing on the beach when we used to meet in the early morning.

"Why don't you tell her how you feel, Sheldon?"

"She knows."

"She does?" Tasha was surprised.

"I told her when we were on the Vineyard." Tasha looked surprised, but before she could form the next question, I went on, "Before she discovered I was Sheldon St. Romaine."

"You're still the same man. It doesn't matter what your name is."

"It isn't my name that's the issue."

"It's your money," she stated. "I always thought that bet with Dad wasn't a good idea."

"The bet isn't the issue either," I told her.

"What is the issue?" Tasha sat down in the corner of the sofa. She curled her feet under her as if I was about to tell her some devastating news.

"I could never be sure."

"Sure that she loves you for you and not for the money you have?"

I nodded.

"Do you believe she loves you?"

I took a long moment thinking about the question. Amber had never said she loved me. But could the two of us be so right for each other, so in tune with each other's wants and needs and not love each other?

"She never said it," I finally answered. "But yes, I believe she loves me."

"And you're flying off to France without finding out for sure? Sheldon, this is so totally unlike you."

That was true, too. In the past two years plenty had changed in my life. Amber was only one of them, but she was a major one. "All I can say is that it was a defining summer."

The waters of the North Atlantic were gray and choppy. The land was dusty and sand colored, reminding me of the southwestern United States, while the streets were gray and old. Sunrises and sunsets were just as spectacular as they had been on the Vineyard. The town was quaint, with stone and brick row houses arching around roads in the order of the flow of land. Nothing was planned or arranged. It looked as if each one had been added on like an ever-expanding family.

I was beginning to love the town. And the hotel. It gave me a purpose, and I poured everything into it upon my return. I reconnected with friends I'd known just a couple of years earlier. While the architecture of the town might be the same as it had been a century ago, life had changed. Some of my old running buddies were no longer the riotous daredevils they had been in the past. Some had married. Others had been injured in various foolhardy exploits and were more cautious than in the past.

This was what my father had been trying to warn me against. I wasn't ready to listen then, but now I saw the evidence of what could be me. We got together for dinner and drinks, but in the end I realized that life would inevitably move on. I was no longer the same person I'd been, and neither were they.

I wondered about Amber. She was never far from my mind. Was she the same person she'd been last summer? What was she doing now? Had she found someone to replace Casey? Was she now Mrs. Rich, country club member?

I threw myself into the hotel. Both the life I thought I wanted and the one I left behind were denied me. The place needed repairs in many areas. We'd made major inroads and if all went according to plan, we'd have a grand re-opening in three months. People needed a reason to come there and stay in the St. Romaine. Like the Vineyard, we weren't the only choice for vacationers and tourists taking the trek up from Paris or across from England who wanted to find comfort and something to do. We weren't there yet.

But we would be. I'd give it everything I had. By the next year I expected the hotel to hold its own. It wouldn't make the renovation costs back for three years, but it wouldn't be an out-of-the-way place unheard of by tourists.

Two weeks later I sent a plan to my father and Tasha and presented it via satellite.

"It looks great, Sheldon. A little aggressive, but we saw what you did on the Vineyard. I say go ahead." Tasha was speaking.

"We'll have the funds transferred to your account in the morning," Dad said.

And so it began. In the next few weeks I kept myself so busy during the day I didn't have time to think of anything except renovations and future marketing efforts. My nights, however, were different. Lady Legs visited my subconscious on a regular basis.

And my dreams had me stumbling into a cold shower every morning.

"Jack, this is absolutely beautiful," I said as she showed Lila and me around her new home in Nashville.

"Who would have thought that I would ever leave Brooklyn. And for the South," Jack said. "But I love it here."

Jack was still glowing. Her love showed. Marriage had to agree with her. I stopped and mentally shook myself. Since returning to Brooklyn I classified most changes as before and after the Vineyard. It was supposed to be a change for all three of us. I can't say our goal wasn't accomplished. It was the unexpected changes that had altered my life. Jack and Lila got what they wanted.

"This is the master suite," Jack said proudly. She showed us a bedroom that was larger than her entire apartment near Prospect Park in Brooklyn. It had floor-to-ceiling windows that bathed the room in light. Jack liked color. The walls were a pearly blue, the bed coverings dark maroon with touches of pink. There was a fireplace and sitting area.

"Oooh," Lila said. "I like this." She sat down on the sofa and ran her hands over the silk fabric.

"Wait until you see the closet and the bathroom."

One led into the other. The bathroom was a dream, slate tile floor, river rock on the shower walls. A shower large enough for an entire family, with water jets coming from everywhere stood in its own alcove. The Jacuzzi bathtub was as large as a swimming pool and had jets in a hundred places.

"Are you sure this guy isn't rich?" I asked.

"Members of the band must make a lot more money than I thought they did," Lila said.

"We're comfortable," Jack said, but there was a smile that said more.

The yard was equally impressive. After the tour, we sat on the patio overlooking the huge pool and drank diet lemonade.

"So fill me in," Jack said. "What have you two been up to since the summer?"

Lila and I looked at each other and both hunched our shoulders. Lila started. "I quit my job in the city and moved to Washington, DC. I love it there. To think that the nation's capital was only four hours away and I never visited it. And now I live there."

Jack had a big smile on her face. I did, too, but mine had been painted on that morning.

"And I'm going back to school."

"What?" I said. Both Jack and I leaned forward in our seats.

"There are so many good schools in and around DC; I wandered over to Howard University during one of my 'getting to know the city' trips and decided to enroll."

"In what?" Jack asked.

"Teaching."

Jack's eyes grew larger. "Teaching what?"

"Math or science. I was a wiz in those subjects in high school and college," Lila said. "After touring Clay's factories and seeing a class of bright-eyed students taking in information like sponges, I knew I wanted to be one of the people helping them learn."

"Lila, I think that's wonderful," I said and hugged her. "But did you say Clay has factories? I thought he made furniture."

"He does, but that's a hobby. He has a chain of furniture stores and several factories that make the furniture."

Jack and I exchanged looks. "Several," we both said.

Lila laughed. "Yeah, isn't it funny that he turned out to be CEO of a huge corporation?"

She looked happy. They both did. "What does Clay think about this?" Jack asked.

Clay and Shane joined them. Both guys immediately went to their wives and kissed them as if they had only just arrived instead of being in another room. Sitting down next to them, they touched in some way, holding hands or draping an arm around the other's shoulders. It seemed so natural.

I wondered if they were conscious of it or if it was part of the marital ritual.

"I told them I enrolled at Howard University."

"Isn't that wonderful?" Clay asked. Shane looked confused and Clay explained. "Not only is she beautiful." He took a moment to kiss Lila's temple. "But she's smart, too, a combination I find irresistible."

"So, Amber, what about that guy you were seeing last summer? Wasn't it a blast to find out he was the son of one of the richest men in the country?"

Everything went still. I could see Lila and Jack turn to stone. Unfortunately, neither Clay nor Shane seemed to notice. Jack and Lila had been tiptoeing around me as if I were vintage glass. They were careful not to say Don's name as if even the vibration of air currents would cause me to shatter.

"The news was surprising," I said, committing to nothing, but inside my body was shaking. As much as I tried, I couldn't keep myself from reacting to the thought of Don Randall. I tried to think of him as Sheldon St. Romaine, but the man who was kind to me, who held me in his arms and made me feel like the world was my own private beach, was Don. And it was Don's face that superimposed itself on any devil horns and goatee I wanted to paint on Sheldon.

"I heard he was leaving the Vineyard," Shane said. "Where did he go?"

"I don't know," I said. "I haven't seen him since your wedding." It was a lie. I hadn't told Lila and Jack about Don's unfinished visit to complete the promise we'd made. I was still unclear about what had happened and what the reason for it was. I'd reviewed that night several times, wondering if Don had intended to go somewhere and decided against it when he saw me. Had he come to confirm my broken engagement? If so, why hadn't he done anything about it? The man was as much an enigma as he'd been when he pressed his room key in my hand the first night I'd met him.

"Was he there?" Lila asked. "I didn't see him."

"He stood at the back of the room during the ceremony. Then he left."

"Oh, honey," Shane said to Jack. "I forgot to tell you I made us a reservation for dinner at the Opryland. You'll love it there." Shane addressed me and Lila, going on as if he hadn't rocked my world. "It's a city unto itself. We'll need to go early so we can see the whole place."

The excitement in his voice showed pride in his city. It also focused attention away from me. But Shane wasn't doing it for that reason. He had no idea the torrent of feelings he'd unleashed in me with his comments about Sheldon St. Romaine.

I'd begun to separate them. They were two different men in my mind. I fell in love with Don Randall. Don had died when Sheldon took his place. My grief period was over. It was time to move on. My friends knew me to be resilient, to be able to work through the wounds that life dealt us.

But this wound was a major gash. It would take a little longer to get over.

"Clay, let me show you my studio," Shane said. Again with kisses to the women in their lives, the guys went off to the man cave.

"I'm sorry, Amber," Jack said the moment Shane and Clay were out of earshot.

"It's all right, Jack. You can't protect me from people talking about Don. To tell you the truth, it's not that much of an issue," I lied. I wasn't sure if they bought it, but Lila's next comment told me they didn't.

"Are you sure? You were pretty dramatic when you found out that he'd lied to you. For someone who says she doesn't care, you acted like you cared a lot."

"We're your best friends, Amber," Jack said. "We know when you hurt."

"I'm not hurt. Not much," I conceded. "I'll survive this."

"Do you want to? Do you really want to?"

"How do you really feel about him?" Lila asked. "We thought you'd fallen hard for him."

I had. Harder than I thought possible. I was prepared to marry a man I didn't love. Don saw through that. He opened my eyes to the fact that I would make three lives miserable.

"It doesn't matter what I feel," I said. "I don't know where he is. Shane said he left the Vineyard."

"We could check," Jack said, rising from her chair.

"No," I shouted. "I don't want to know."

Lila was on her feet, too. They went into the house, both glancing back at me with sly smiles on their faces.

I didn't follow. I didn't want to know. I really didn't. I even said I didn't.

But I did.

Chapter 26

The paper haunted me. It lay on the top of the chest in my bedroom. Jack had gone inside and somehow found where Don had gone. She didn't explain and I didn't ask. She came back and handed me a scrap of paper. It didn't matter that I told her I wasn't interested in Don, that I didn't want whatever was on the paper. Sheldon and I weren't compatible. He didn't believe in the same things I did. Jack didn't believe me. Tucking the paper in my purse, she said, "You can throw it away on the train."

Yet I'd brought that scrap of paper back to Brooklyn.

And now it haunted me. Who would ever think that something as small as a two-inch by two-inch square of paper could destroy all I thought I was? I pushed my hands through my hair and stared out the window into the cool night.

Les Pieux. I'd looked it up on Google Earth. It was in France, a small outcrop of land near the North Atlantic. For some reason I felt it was point-ing toward the Vineyard, toward our beach, the place where Don and I had made love. And where my world had changed. The place where I was sure I'd fallen in love with him.

Les Pieux. It was on the other side of the world. A small town that didn't see much other than a few straggling tourists. Why had Don chosen to go there?

And what was I going to do with the knowledge of his address and phone number?

I stared up at the moon. It seemed to be mocking me, asking me questions for which I had no answers. Balling my hand into a fist, I punched at it and turned around. I grabbed the scrap of paper from the dresser and picked up the phone.

It was answered on the second ring. "Jack, I need your help."

"Oh, no. There's that note in your voice. I'm married now. I can't be supporting you in your harebrained schemes anymore."

"Okay," I said.

For a moment there was silence. Then Jack said, "Amber, are you all right?" I heard Shane in the background. I also heard the concern in Jack's voice.

"I'm fine," I said resignedly.

"All right," Jack said. "What do you need my help with?" I knew her curiosity would get the better of her.

"I'm going to France."

I thought I understood what it meant to be tired, but now I know what the phrase *dead tired* really meant. Maybe I would sleep better tonight. Maybe my state of being would chase away the dreams.

The Les Pieux hotel was far different than the

Vineyard. There were no bungalows. There were
no secluded areas where foliage provided cover for
couples who wanted to be alone. The eight-story
building sat close to the road. I'd taken a suite on
the fifth floor. Usually, I walked up to the stairs, but
tonight, I stumbled into the small elevator, which I
planned to replace with a larger, more modern
one, and waited while the rickety equipment lifted
me to the fifth level.

The tradesmen told me it was unusual for the
boss to work alongside them. I told them the place
needed to be ready by spring, when the tourists
began to come. They shook their heads, not believing that tourists would venture this far from Paris,
and went back to work. That was one of the reasons, but it wasn't the only one. I needed the diversion. I'd worked with my hands before, but it was
often to be the mechanic for my own classic car.

When I was younger and money from home
hadn't poured in as regularly as I needed it, I'd
done much of the work myself. That included
minor repairs to the places I'd stayed. Some of them
weren't as well maintained as others. I never knew
that work would one day come to my rescue to keep
me sane.

The space of an ocean didn't keep Amber from
the front of my mind. I wondered if she'd found
someone else. She wasn't one to sit about and
mope. Amber would take life by the horns and move
on to the next phase. I pictured her in the white
dress and red shoes she'd arrived on the Vineyard
in. At night my dreams were of her wearing only
those shoes.

I headed straight for the shower and washed
myself under the slow drip of water, another project

on the repair list. It would have been better if I'd gutted the place and started from scratch. But the building had been there for three hundred years and local code would not let it be torn down. Even in this tiny town, there were preservation laws I would need to work within. The bones were good, however. The floors were strong and sturdy. The hotel had survived wind, weather, and war.

And working on it was helping me survive Amber.

At least I hoped the hard work was doing that. Grabbing a towel, I dried the water from my body and walked naked into the bedroom. I grabbed the edge of the huge comforter that was like a big flat pillow when I saw the white envelope lying in the middle of the bed.

Someone had been in the room. I looked around, wondering if someone was going to jump out from an unexpected location. The room was nothing like the bungalow on the Vineyard. It was just a small room with a shower. It had a sofa and a desk, set apart from the main room by a lattice-work étagère, making it a suite. There were only a few suites in the hotel, but they were small by U.S. standards.

I searched the corners of the room, the closet, and looked under the bed. Satisfied that I was alone, I picked the envelope up. My body went taut and weak at the same time. I sank down on the bed, unable to remain upright, as I stared at the printed words.

Don Randall.

I didn't recognize the handwriting. Who would know that name here? How had this have gotten here? I didn't remember seeing it when I came in, but then I hadn't paid much attention to the room.

My attention was on getting to the shower and washing off the sweat and fatigue of the day.

I turned the white envelope over and looked at the flap on the back. It was sealed. An unnatural feeling crawled over my skin. I didn't understand it and frowned, trying to give some significance to what it might mean. Gingerly, I slipped a finger under the flap and tore it open.

A key spilled out.

I jumped away from it as if a snake had been let loose. It fell to the bare wooden floor. I stared down at it. Electronic keys had not made it to this eighteenth-century structure. Of course, they would look totally out of place in a building this historic, but seeing it startled me.

Room 801 was the number on it. 801 was a suite. It hadn't been renovated, but it was clean. There were never many guests in the hotel. Due to the renovations, only a few rooms had been rented. I hadn't looked at the guest list. It had been a daily ritual of mine on the Vineyard, but here I had other concerns.

Reaching for the phone, I stopped before picking up the receiver, trying to think of what I would say to the switchboard operator. Then I lifted it. The operator came on almost immediately.

"Oui, monsieur?"

I recognized Janine's voice. "Janine, do we have a guest in room 801?" I spoke in English. My French wasn't that bad, but I didn't even think of trying it. My focus was totally on the key which I picked up and held in my hand.

"I will check, monsieur."

I waited. I began to feel the cold in the room. Getting a clean shirt, I pushed one arm into it, using the other hand to hold the ancient phone. Then switching hands, I pulled the shirt fully on. She was back before I could button it.

"Oui, monsieur. Mrs. Donald Randall from New York checked in this morning."

I started to say something, but changed my mind. *"Merci,"* I said and replaced the receiver.

It couldn't be. My mind refused to believe what it wanted to. Don Randall was a common name in America. It could be coincidence. But why was her key on my bed?

Unless . . .

I dropped the thought. Galvanized into action, I dressed and ran up the stairs. Coming out on the eighth floor, I went directly to room 801. There I hesitated. I had the key in my hand, but I was reluctant to use it. I knocked. There was no answer. Several moments later, I knocked again. Again, no response.

Looking at the key, I slipped it into the lock and turned it. The door swung inward. I saw no one in the small room that served as a living room. I crossed the threshold, stepping past the identical latticework étagère and into a room that was dimly lighted. The door closed behind me. I didn't turn to look at it. The vision in the doorway from the bedroom captured all my attention.

The first thing I saw was a long, brown leg coming around the door frame. The leg ended in a blood-red shoe. I thought all the air in my body had been pushed out. Looking up, I saw the white dress with a slit up the side and the promise of sensuality beyond sight.

"Amber," I uttered. My voice was so low, even I couldn't hear it.

She stepped fully into the room. "I'm not a dream," she said.

In a second, I'd moved across the floor and pulled Amber into my arms. I had to be sure she was real, sure this wasn't another dream, some false apparition coming to test me. She felt whole as I hugged her, solid against my chest. I buried my face in hers, sought her mouth as if I needed it to draw life.

Her touch was like fire, velvety soft and hot, with long red fingernails raking over my shoulders. I'd once compared her to a beautiful fire that drew its prey to the flame. I gladly followed that flame, mesmerized by the heat, yet drawn by its beauty and inevitable danger. I wasn't going to try to escape. I wanted her, as much as I wanted to continue breathing. I'd left her in Brooklyn, but I was never going to let her go again.

My hands ran all over her. I wanted to touch every inch of her body. I wanted to make sure she was here. That I hadn't lost my mind and brought her to life because I wanted her to be here.

As with the first time we kissed, the hunger took over. It was raw and fierce. I bent her backward, holding her to me while my tongue invaded her mouth, while I took in the sweetness of her, while I refamiliarized myself with her taste. Life had been hell without her.

And I wasn't going to go through hell any longer.

Even if this was a fantasy, if she would vanish in a moment, I would go with her. I would hold on to her for all I was worth.

I lifted my mouth, but not my grasp on her. "Amber," I said, needing to hear her voice.

"Yes," she replied, her voice breathy and full of sex.

"Are you here because you forgive me?"

She nodded. "I forgive you. And I love you."

I smiled. My heart soared at that moment. "Will you marry me?"

In the dim light I wasn't sure if I saw tears in her eyes, but they shone with something.

"I will," she said.

"Are you sure?" I asked, fear still gripping me. I wanted her more than I thought it was possible to want someone.

"I'm sure," she said.

"Good." I took her mouth again. For a long time neither of us did anything except enjoy each other. "Good," I said again when we came up for air. "Because I don't have a condom and I'm not leaving you to go get one."

I lifted those long legs and carried her to the bed. We undressed with the speed of teenagers, trying to get out of our clothes and hold on to each other at the same time.

I kissed her neck and made my way down her body. I felt her quiver under my hands. My body grew large and hard as I joined with her. I wanted her all at once, wanted to fill her body with mine, wanted to understand everything about her and what had brought her to me in the space of seconds.

"I love you," I said. "Don't ever leave me again."

"You just try and get rid of me."

Our mouths melded and there was no time for words. I wanted to be gentle, to savor the moment, to listen to her sounds as I brought her to climax, but time, distance, and abject need conspired against me. I took her hard and fast. Like animals in heat, we wrestled with each other. Our arms and legs tangled as we rolled across the sheets, each vying for domination, being both the aggressor and the prey.

Amber wrapped her long legs around me and pulled me into her. Like a slave, I went willingly. The room filled with animalistic sounds and the sweet undertone of sex while we took from each other, while we shared the most intimate ritual. I'd never felt so needy. My body, stone hard, dug into her and with each thrust she seemed to ask for more. And I gave and gave and gave.

I heard her scream as climax overcame her. A moment later I felt the rush inside me and on a final wave of sensation, strong enough to break away this piece of jutting earth, I collapsed, spent, sated, and in love.

My breathing was ragged. It had been a long flight. I was tired from anticipation and the stress of not knowing how Don would receive me. But I'd never felt so good in my life. I held on to Don, my arms and legs wrapped around him, denying any thought of flight. He hugged me just as tight. His hands smoothed over my body, down my legs, as if he was spreading hot lotion along my limbs. I reveled in the feel of them, hard and soft.

"I can't tell you how scared I was," I said when my heartbeat returned to normal.

"Scared? Why?" He kissed my shoulder.

"Scared you'd reject me."

I was scared, more than I'd been in the tenth grade when I wanted the cutest boy in my geometry class at school to ask me to go to the school dance.

This was infinitely more important. This was my life. I was sure of Don and unsure at the same time.

Suppose Jack and Lila were wrong when they convinced me to fly here and tell him how I felt? Suppose I was wrong? Don had come that last night to take me out, but rejected me at my door. Like a jilted bride, I felt bereft knowing he'd scorned me. And now I was putting my heart on the line, hoping that the gamble I was taking now would pay off.

Don stopped kissing my shoulders and stared at me. "Why would I reject you? I love you. You knew that. If anything, I was afraid you'd reject me. After all, I always knew your secret. You didn't know mine."

"No more secrets from now on," I said.

He raised a hand in the Boy Scout salute. "No more secrets."

"I have a question, though," I said. He shifted an inch, raising his hand and resting it under his head, waiting for me to go on. "That night, when you came to my house, to take me to the End of the Summer Dance."

He nodded.

"What happened? Why did you suddenly leave?"

"I didn't think I could handle it. I had so much confidence when I wrote the note. As the night grew near, I wanted to see you so much I could taste it. But when you opened the door and I saw you standing there, I knew it was hopeless. There was no way I could spend four hours with you and not want to take you to bed. Not tell you how much I loved you and beg you to marry me."

"Why didn't you?"

"You hated me."

"I never hated you. Not from that first moment in front of the house on the Vineyard. I was attracted to you. I think I even wanted you then. But that's not the real reason, is it?"

"No," he answered. "I wasn't sure you wanted *me*."

"You couldn't doubt that."

He grinned. "No, I didn't doubt that. It's the . . ."

"It's my idea of marrying a rich man."

"I thought once you found out who I was, the only reason you'd want to marry me had to do with my bank account."

"You don't have a bank account," I said. I lay next to him, my arm casually hung over his waist, my fingers playing on his back. "It's your father who has the account. You own a house on Martha's Vineyard, one in which I stayed, by the way, a few investments that keep you in clothes and cash, but nothing more."

He stared at me.

"You used to own a race car, but when you lost the last race, you also lost your sponsorship. This was one of the reasons you returned to the U.S. and took over the Vineyard hotel."

His eyebrows raised. "And how would you know this?"

"Jack," I paused. "She's a wiz at finding information." I smiled and kissed him.

"There's one thing I know," Don said. "Money or no money, I'm not letting you go again. We can get married right here, and I don't care who can attend the ceremony as long as there is one."

I kissed him again, this time longer and harder. "I can't wait," I said.

He frowned suddenly. "How did you get here?"

"On a plane."

He laughed. I did, too.

"I mean how did you get in my room?"

"I was never in your room."

"But the key?"

"Apparently Shane Massey has spent a lot of time in hotels and knows all the angles."

"Shane is here?"

"They all are, Shane, Jack, Lila, and Clay. They were either going to be my moral support or witnesses for the wedding."

"Witnesses," he said. "Definitely witnesses."